Malibu Betrayals

a Malibu Sights novel

MK Meredith

Entangled Publishing, LLC
2614 South Timberline Road
Suite 109
Fort Collins, CO 80525
Visit our website at www.entangledpublishing.com.

Select Contemporary is an imprint of Entangled Publishing, LLC.

Edited by Kate Brauning
Cover design by Kelley York
Cover art by iStock

Manufactured in the United States of America

First Edition July 2015

To my husband, Brian Meredith,
who, when I came home from work one day and said, "I
want to write romance," replied,
"Great. You've done everything else you've set your mind
to."
His unwavering faith in me, his love, and his own relentless
work ethic inspire every story I write.
He tells me, "I could never love you anymore than I do
today, until tomorrow…when I do."
And the butterflies never stop fluttering.

Chapter One

It was hard as hell to walk in heels with her toes crossed, but Samantha Dekker wasn't taking any chances. She'd keep them that way too, just like her fingers, until she sealed the deal. When Martin Gallagher called, she'd agreed to a meeting right away. Thank God for nepotism. Good luck hadn't been known to stick around her for very long, and she hoped that was about to change. After about a year out of the industry, not to mention the circus the tabloids had created with her face as the headliner, no one else would touch her with a ten foot pole.

Sam pushed open the door of the Chocolate Box Café, the cool air breaking the California heat. She adored this place for their decadent chocolate creations and to-die-for espressos. She narrowed her eyes at Martin's warm grin. What could he be up to?

"Sam, it's good to see you." He hugged her tight and for a brief second she sighed into the comfort of his fatherly embrace. He released her to pull a bar stool out from the small bistro table, but she reached it before he did.

"I've got it, thanks."

"You just can't let anyone help you, can you?" He moved a third stool around and sat to her left.

He was right; she was the worst when it came to asking for help and impossible when it came to accepting it, but this time she needed it.

She shrugged, then glanced at the empty stool across the table and then back to Martin with a raised brow. He cleared his throat and ran a finger under the collar of his Ralph Lauren dress shirt.

"Martin?" Curiosity edged her words.

"We'll get to that." He grinned in that wickedly sexy way of his that neither age nor marriage could diminish. Seconds later, he returned with her usual espresso and some frothy concoction of his own, and sat down. "You look good, kid, but still a mite too thin."

Sam forced a smile. Wasn't that ironic? It took losing her husband to achieve the thinness he'd demanded when he was alive, his voice still a mocking echo in her head. *Seconds, Sam? I thought you had more self-control than that.* "My appetite hasn't been the best, but I'm fine."

He nodded. "Good, good. Now, here's the script." He pulled out bound pages with a red cover. "Dive in and read this over. You'll see what's missing on your first pass. Don't second-guess yourself, just let your magic flow."

She took the manuscript from his hand and flipped through the pages, trying not to let him see her shake. How many times had her husband told her there were way more talented screenwriters out there than her? The old heavy weight of uncertainty returned to her gut, but she braced against it. She was running out of options. Her parents had floated her financially since his death, but more important than needing the money, she needed her career. She needed to find her way back—to herself. If she didn't, and soon, there'd be nothing of *her* left.

Pushing hair from her eyes, she glanced at Martin. The financial risk alone for a producer-director was daunting, but the risk to an artist's reputation—and their ego—was even greater. She'd fallen so far out of Hollywood that no one was willing to sign her name to a guest list, much less a contract, no one but him. He was as much a father figure as mentor to her, and she owed him. She wouldn't have made it through the year and a half since Ethan's death if not for the support of him and his wife.

"I don't want to color your perception, so I'm not going to share what I think this script is lacking. We'll begin shooting in a week, so you have some time." Martin pointed at the script. "One more thing." He took the script from her, put it on the table, then took her hand between his. He squared his shoulders and his glacier blue gaze pinned hers. Martin had the look of a Nordic Sean Connery—the kind of man women at any age still swooned over. Right now those striking good looks were shadowed by guilt. "There's something else I have to tell you."

Apprehension tightened her stomach, and she braced herself for the news. As long as she got her foot in somewhere, she'd be okay. "Are you naming someone else as the writer?"

He looked at her as if she'd gone mad. "Why the hell would I call you here and dangle the script in front of your nose just to tease you with it?"

She swallowed, her heartbeat easing in her chest. "Then what did you do?"

Martin huffed. "Why do women always accuse men of wrongdoing right off the bat?"

"Experience?"

"Got me there." He hesitated, then sighed. "Gage Cutler is playing the starring role, and he's the assistant director."

Embarrassment washed over her, stealing her breath.

"Gage?" Needing to bolt, she slapped her feet to the ground and shoved back from the table with such force her barstool crashed to the ground.

"She seems to be taking the news well."

Blood rushed to her head. She knew that voice, even if she shouldn't. She spun around.

Gage Cutler's broad shoulders flexed as he set the stool upright, his movements slow and careful, as if not to spook a wild animal. He watched her with guarded eyes—eyes that ever since the first night they'd met, she never could quite decide if they were blue or green.

Ignoring the tumble of her stomach, she focused on the increasing ache between her eyes. Him, of all people? Why was he here? She wanted to run, but the best she could do was wrench her gaze back to Martin's and pretend her guilt wasn't drowning her.

Martin got to his feet. "Sam, the past is behind us."

Pressing her lips together, she tried to swallow. Pulling Martin to the side, she whispered, "I blamed him, Martin. The things I said...oh my God. Why didn't you tell me he'd be here?"

Remembering that night always made her throat close up—how her husband had been so badly injured in the accident, how she thought it had been Gage's fault. That night she'd been robbed of her chance to leave. She'd finally come to her senses, finally found her strength. But how could she leave an injured man, even if he she hadn't made him happy in years? She was many things, but cruel was not one of them. In her anger, she'd blamed Gage. The things she'd said flooded her, burning her cheeks. She'd wanted to apologize no less than a million times, but in the end he was a celebrity. One for whom she didn't trust her feelings. If she'd learned anything, it was to stay as far away from them as possible.

"Sam," Martin began.

She thrust out a shaking hand to stop him, not once meeting Gage's eyes. "He's been dead for a year, and the paparazzi have just now finally left me alone."

Sam forced herself to take a deep breath. She should stay, apologize, and make amends, but her thoughts twisted in her head until she couldn't make sense of any of them. She grabbed her purse and backed toward the door, finally looking at both men.

Stumbling, she grabbed the door handle. Gage stood inches taller than Martin's six feet, with shoulders that appeared twice as broad. He took a step toward her, his brows furrowed, his blue-green eyes intense. She knew that face, that look, and she wanted nothing more than to step up and study it. But she couldn't. Not now and not ever.

For the second time in their history, she turned and walked away.

• • •

Sam yanked on the large cardboard box, but it didn't budge. Losing her footing, she fell back against the end table and smacked her elbow against the edge. Pain shot down her arm, and she held it, sucking air through her clenched teeth. The vase on top wobbled and then crashed to the floor, a resounding echo of her day.

She closed her eyes against the mess. Could her embarrassment be any greater? Wasn't her meeting with Martin enough? She pushed up away from the end table. So far, the day had been nothing but a horrible series of catastrophes. Her meeting with Martin had only been the beginning. Why hadn't he warned her? Playing out the events in her mind made her cheeks burn, so she shoved them away with ruthless determination.

She needed to feel productive, do something positive. It was time she took back the condo. She'd have moved out last year if it had been up to her, but after Ethan's death the condo had been paid in full by his life insurance. Selling in the current housing economy was impossible — at least for right now. She'd already lost so much, and she refused to lose more. Getting Ethan's belongings out of her home once and for all would do the trick.

It might have taken her a year — courage was a fickle mistress — but she'd finally thrown away Ethan's favorite painting. She hadn't sold it. She hadn't given it away. She'd thrown it in the trash — and damn it had felt good.

A photographer, no, *the* photographer, to the stars, Ethan had specialized in headshots for portfolios, PR, and any other media marketing where celebrities wanted to look their most beautiful. He'd considered himself a walking billboard for what he could promise. Blessed with the symmetry and coloring of a golden Greek god, he was his own brand, his own celebrity. And he'd made sure she knew it.

But after the car crash, the symmetry—the promise—disappeared, and he couldn't handle it. So he took his frustration out on her even more than before.

Acceptance was now her burden. Acceptance that she hadn't left when she should have. Acceptance that she was easy to leave. On a deep breath, Sam shook her head and grabbed a broom to clean up the broken vase. She needed to move ahead. One step at a time.

Sam grabbed an offending box and dove back in. Today, on what would have been their fourth anniversary, she was determined to finish this chapter and close the book.

She lost herself in separating film, equipment, and developed projects. Opening her third box, she leaned back on her heels and rubbed the back of her hand across her brow. With a sigh, she pulled out a shallow box and turned it over to look at the front. "The Teacher and the Student" was scrawled across the space in Ethan's bold handwriting. She stood, box in hand, and walked over to the kitchen island.

Opening the top, she set it on the counter, revealing the glossy eight by ten photos beneath. Her head tilted to the side as she flipped through the stack. Black and white photos of women ticked by like an old movie clip. Naked women. Naked women draped all over her husband.

Shock and disgust filled her mouth, bitter and sour. Tears stung her eyes, but pain—no, anger—blotted them out. She dropped the stack back into the box and sent it flying across the counter. It slid over the edge and slapped the floor, photos scattering everywhere. To think she'd been embarrassed that morning; this was complete humiliation.

"Son of a bitch!"

So much for packing his things being something positive.

Numb and dry-eyed, she rounded the counter and dropped to her knees. She grabbed the photos and shoved them back into the box. She should just trash all of it immediately.

But she wouldn't. She didn't want to forget. She didn't want to forget the pain caused by counting on someone else for her happiness or believing it was possible to find happy ever after in Hollywood. She'd known way back then not to date a celebrity or anyone even involved with Hollywood, but she'd broken her rule for Ethan, and look where that had gotten her.

Another reason to stay away from Gage Cutler.

An image of his face slid into her mind. Such a simple thing. A chance meeting, followed by a few hours of conversation. She should have never thought of him again, but that was the trick with simple—it seldom was. How often had she thought of him after the first night they'd met a couple years ago, especially during those lonely stretches of time when Ethan only showed up for breakfast and a change of clothes? Work, you know, but now she knew better. Disgusted, she slammed the lid onto the box and then slid it to the back of the cupboard over the refrigerator.

Resting her forehead against the cool stainless steel of the fridge, she wanted to laugh at how earnestly she'd maintained her distance from Gage. He had listened to her, and what's more, when he'd looked at her, he had really seen *her*, in a way her husband never had. He'd made her feel as if she mattered, and it had stirred something in her she'd never thought she'd feel again. Something she'd wanted so much it had scared her.

But she'd been a married woman, and that had meant everything to her. Even if she hadn't been married, she'd known better than to believe Gage had seen her as anything more than an evening of entertaining conversation. So she'd walked away from Gage to preserve her integrity, and had planned to walk away from Ethan to preserve herself.

Then, the car accident happened. The paparazzi had been chasing Gage, and Ethan's car had been crushed in the middle, leaving his face severely burned, disfigured.

A heavy weight settled in her chest, and she closed her eyes.

She'd blamed Gage for the wreck and made sure he and everyone else knew it. Grabbing onto his bad boy ways, she used the tabloids as judge and jury. Not one of her most shining moments. She grimaced. It hadn't been his fault, but she'd been too blinded by her own pain to see that then. Facing him again was mortifying. How the hell could Martin expect her to work with Gage after what she'd done?

In the end there was no question. She was the one who needed help gaining access back into the industry, and Martin opened the door.

She either stepped through it or waved goodbye to screenwriting forever.

• • •

Gage sped down the highway, trying to clear his head. What the hell had he been thinking, agreeing to Martin's announcement that Sam would be working the script? She'd told him clearly the night they'd met she couldn't have anything to do with him, and apparently the only thing that had changed was how strongly she meant it.

He gripped the steering wheel tighter. He couldn't blame her; she'd been through hell, but so had he. The industry still loved him, his fans adored him, but he wanted the respect of his colleagues, and that was a different monster all together.

Glancing down at the speedometer, he cursed and eased his foot off the gas. Now would be a good time to start earning it. He pulled through security and into his garage, and then made his way inside. The drive hadn't cleared his head as he'd hoped, and tension held on tight between his shoulder blades. Throwing his bag on the couch, he kicked off his shoes and made his way into his bedroom.

A locked-tight gated community and tight-ass security for his private beach blessed him with a view he could actually enjoy. The ocean was one of the few things that calmed him. He turned to open the sliding glass doors and slammed his toe on an end table. "Fuck! Shit!"

He dropped into the chair and checked his toe to find a torn nail and a welling of dark blood. Disgusted, he lowered his foot to the floor. Great end to a fucked-up day.

The sound of the waves crashing against the shore reached him, and he pulled in a breath. There was nothing better. Except maybe surfing. He was never more free than when tethered to a board.

He was similar to the waves he loved to watch and ride. His life would build momentum, crest, and then crash and scatter until it no longer resembled anything he recognized. Certainly nothing he intended, anyway. Sometimes the result would be terrifying, and nothing in the world would make him go back in, but then he'd remember what all his surfer buddies would say, "Eddie would go." That's all it took, that one phrase.

Seeing Sam had brought all of his memories crashing back. She still wore her dark hair long, and her large brown eyes appealed to him as they always had, making him want to trust her—against his better judgment. After she'd left the cafe, he and Martin had stood watching her. The silence had stretched until another patron walked through the doors and broke the uncomfortable spell. Martin had grabbed Gage's shoulder in an encouraging grip. "She'll come around."

Gage wasn't too sure. He was a reminder of everything she wanted to forget.

No matter what might have passed between them once upon a time, things were different now, and she'd walked away from him. Again.

He remembered her determined goodbye the night they'd met.

He remembered the overwhelming pressure in his chest as she'd turned on her heel and walked away, long brown waves flowing down her back.

No looking back.

Admiration and respect would have been the logical response to her fidelity. She'd had integrity, kept her promises, her vows, but he'd been unable to muster even the slightest hint of logic. Pain had taken over as he'd watched her leave.

Fuck me.

He'd tried reaching out to her after the accident, shocked when he'd found out the other car was Ethan's, but she'd refused him then, too. Blamed him.

Gage shook his head, and the same pressure squeezed his chest. The knowledge he'd be seeing her again, and soon, kicked his heart up to a steady beat. Anticipation? Fear—dread.

He walked out to the balcony, giving the table a wide berth. Leaning his forearms against the cool metal, he gripped his hands together.

He and Sam had shared a few stolen hours where nothing had existed but the two of them, connecting unlike anything he'd known. But that was two years ago.

He slammed his hand on the railing. The whole situation was total bullshit. There was nothing between them now, but a part of him wanted nothing as much as he wanted her to admit that something had passed between them then. Hell, he wanted them to find it again. He couldn't say he wanted her back, because he'd never really had her. But he'd never felt with any other woman what Sam had made him feel.

His eyes rested on his surfboard storage box. A few minutes out in the waves beckoned him, and he ducked back inside for his wetsuit. His shoulders relaxed, and a rush of adrenaline filled him.

Many things had changed in the past couple of years, and he was one of them. He wouldn't take off on a drinking binge, or speed in his car until he outpaced his problems. That was behind him—mostly.

He'd be a professional and give Martin his best film yet. It seemed like he could shit in a bucket and they'd still give him an Oscar, but that wasn't enough for him anymore. It was time to show Hollywood what he was really made of, and as far as Sam went, he'd win her over and show her what *they* could be made of.

People talked about second chances, and this was his.

Chapter Two

The following week, fueled with guilt and mortification, Sam walked onto the film set with hot coffee in hand. After everything Martin had already done for her, he was giving her a second chance to save her career. A calm washed over her, kind of like coming home. The area buzzed with controlled chaos, but as the production got underway, that control would be a longed-for memory. She smiled.

"No coffee for me?"

Sam stopped in her tracks. The warm baritone voice slid up her spine in a wave of goose bumps and knotted her stomach. Goose bumps were not what she needed right now; a huge black hole to jump into would do much better.

You're a professional, Sam. Yeah, a professional who spent an extra hour on her makeup and changed her clothes three times before finally leaving the house that morning. Of course, her nerves were due to her first day back on the job, not seeing Gage.

Pulling her bag higher on her shoulder, she switched her coffee from her right hand to her left. Where was the brave woman she used to be? Finding that woman was one of her new to-do's. Sam braced herself, then turned with her hand extended. She could pretend all day he didn't make her nervous as hell. "Good morning, Mr. Cutler."

Eyes lit with humor, Gage grasped her hand. She watched her fingers disappear within the warm heat of his strong grip. The sight of his muscular shoulders startled her, and she was at once aware of his warmth. Sam withdrew her hand, forcing herself to move slowly, though the urge to snatch her hand back and bolt raced through her limbs.

He raised his left brow, and she met his gaze head on, shoulders pulled back, and stretched to her full five feet, eight inches.

His lips quirked up on one side, a crooked smirk she was well acquainted with. "I'm surprised to see you."

She opened her mouth to throw back a quick retort, but her need to apologize filled her instead. "Look, I…"

Those blue-green eyes shimmered with something she couldn't name. Sam averted her gaze as if there was something of interest over his shoulder, shifting from one foot to the other. Looking at him directly was disconcerting, and his steady gaze knocked her off-kilter.

He was irresponsible and arrogant. A playboy with a toy box of Hollywood starlets. She'd known it way back then, and she knew it now. Nothing had changed.

Except everything had changed.

She glanced back at the larger-than-life actor for a brief moment. Formal, professional, that was how she'd handle this situation. "Well, good luck with the film. I need to go speak with Mr. Gallagher."

Gage pressed his wide mouth into a thin line and dipped his chin. "I'm glad you're here, Sam."

She tried not to think about why hearing her name from his lips raised the hairs on the back of her neck, but she couldn't ignore the sensation. "I need this chance. I'm here for me."

Sam paused. It wasn't like her to be so direct. At one time maybe, but she'd lost that woman somewhere along the way.

A warmth rushed through her chest. She was there for her, and Martin was helping her make that happen. Her life had been out of her control long enough. She couldn't say how terrified she was of messing up and not being taken seriously. That would be the quickest way to undermine her chances, but she felt the fear to the very end of each limb.

His features tightened with focus, and the muscles of his jaw twitched.

She wanted to smooth his brow, but squeezed her cup with both hands instead, popping the top off. "Oh!" Grabbing the plastic lid before it hit the ground, she stepped around him and made her way toward Martin. She couldn't escape fast enough.

"Damn, damn, damn." She wound her way around lighting, cords, boxes, and racks. *You are ridiculous, Samantha Anne Dekker.* Her throat thickened.

She shook her head and mumbled, "Doesn't matter."

"What doesn't matter?"

Startled, Sam slapped her hand to her chest. She stepped back, stumbling into one of the crew members, sending him reeling.

Martin grabbed her by the upper arm. "Whoa, slow down. You okay?"

Sam glanced about, mortified. Gage stood where she'd left him, watching, his hands hanging limp at his side, an unrecognizable expression on his face. Of course he caught her stumble. She shook her head, embarrassment warming her cheeks. *God, just kill me now.*

The camera guy made a much more graceful recovery and disappeared with a wave. She closed her eyes a moment and then turned back toward Martin. "You scared me."

His black brows lifted. "*You* scared me." He stacked a few boxes and then, relieving her of her bag and coffee, set them on top. He gestured toward a chair. "Have a seat. Now, what doesn't matter? Because if it has something to do with my script, every word matters."

Sam waved his words away. "No, no. Nothing with the script. Just talking to myself." She glanced around at the hustle and bustle of the film set. "You guys have made good progress."

Martin smoothed his hand over his bald head, then around to his chin, scratching through the white, groomed whiskers. He took in all the commotion.

She trapped him with a look. "I can't believe you're doing this for me."

"You took time off. Time you needed. A year and a half now, isn't it? Time to get back to work. Both Raquel and I understood how torn up you were."

Sam's gut twisted. "Martin, I'm just getting back on my feet, figuring out what to do next. I'm like a first draft of a manuscript. I need a little time to work out the edits. Are you sure you want to take this risk?"

"'In Hollywood, writers are considered only the first drafts of human beings.' Do you remember who said that?"

Sam dipped her head. "Frank Deford. You taught me everything I know."

"That's right, which is why I want you and no one else. Besides, I don't think all the edits in the world are going to help you, kiddo. Life's a rough draft. You just gotta live it. Starting now."

He settled his hand on top of hers and squeezed. "You're a writer, Sam, it's in your blood. You're too intelligent to waste such a gift." He tapped the script she'd pulled from her bag and set on her knees. "So, what do you think?"

Sam let the activities on set act as white noise as she flipped open the pages of the screenplay. She'd been studying it all week. Something impeded the sincerity of the scene. She couldn't put her finger on it, but she was close. She needed to get out and take a swim; that always opened her up, set her mind free. She'd found a great place on Pepperdine's campus where she loved to go. She really needed to get back into a routine. How long had it been?

"What do you think?"

Fidgeting with her pen, she tapped a section of the screenplay. "It's right here." She rolled her head from side to side. "I'm a bit rusty, but I'll find it."

Martin leaned close to take a look. With a sigh, he reached into his front pocket and slipped on his reading glasses.

Sam glanced at him and smiled. "Aw, don't you look scholarly." She stood, moving closer to the set, and Martin followed.

"Don't be a pain in my ass." He shook his head. "I agree

there's something wrong, but this scene? The dialogue's tight. The pacing perfect."

"Yes, but there's something—"

"Quiet on the set."

Sam edged in to get a better view.

Gage's character faced his mother for the first time about his diagnosis. The actor who played his mother expressed her emotions in a way that left Sam raw and unsettled.

Gage spoke. Sam leaned closer.

Her heart squeezed; the obvious regret he suffered ate at him more than the cancer ever could.

Sam's stomach tightened and she blew out a breath on a slow, steady count.

This is not real.

She snapped her fingers. "That's it."

"Cut!" The producer sent a searing glance toward Sam. She waved with a small shrug. "Sorry."

Scooting closer to Martin, she gestured toward Gage. "His feelings come across real and raw, which is perfect. But he's delivering them too soon."

Gage glanced over. "Too soon?" There was no mistaking the offense in his voice.

Sam smiled to herself. Actors. Spoiled little crybabies.

He strode toward them, and she immediately regretted saying a word.

She stood. "No, no, there's nothing wrong with your performance. You don't need me or anyone else to tell you how talented you are. But—"

He raised a brow, and if her palms weren't slick with sweat and her heart wasn't beating a mile a minute, she'd have wanted to chuckle.

"Your character left his mom for the big city, the fast pace and opportunity. You've portrayed him as a fast talker, slick and experienced, but with his mom, he's patient, calm. I simply think it's too soon." She took a breath. Big mistake. His cologne clouded her senses, and she swore the heat of his body radiated right through her. "What was I saying?"

Martin looked at her in question.

Oh my God, pull it together. "Oh, right. When people go home, they tend to revert to their former selves, but he hasn't been home long enough. I think you need to fight settling in too soon." She glanced from Martin to Gage to the producer. "Does that make sense?"

Gage nodded his head slowly. "Brilliant catch." He turned and walked back to his place on the set. "Let's run through this again."

The command for silence was delivered, Martin whispered in Sam's ear. "I agree. Brilliant."

Relief washed over her, and she repeated her new mantra over and over again in her head. *I can do this, I can do this.*

Her phone vibrated and she slipped outside to answer it, needing to shade her eyes with her hand. "Hello?"

"Oh, good. You're alive."

"Mom?" She lowered the phone from her ear and confirmed the incoming number. Shit. She should have checked first.

"Hey, Mom. I'm at work."

"Finally."

Sam smiled. "Tell me how you really feel."

"Are you coming to dinner Sunday? You've missed the last dozen, I swear."

Sam rubbed the sudden tension between her brows.

"Mom, it's just not a good time. I'll try soon."

"Sam."

She hated disappointing them. "I gotta go. Break's over. I love you. Dad, too."

"Sam—"

Sam disconnected the line, then dropped her phone in her pocket. They were always good to her. Supportive. Even when Ethan hadn't come to dinner with her for the umpteenth time because of work, they'd just nodded and smiled.

She walked to the edge of a rocky slope and looked out over the valley, a spotting of trees and cactus, large rocks, and a colorful burst of wildflowers. A *burst,* the only way she could describe the effect.

She was on a mission to take back her life, and she'd do it, too. But she was scared. She might not be good enough for a job like this. Ethan might have been right all along. For a second, she'd thought Gage might reject her idea and Martin might agree with him. It could have all been over just like that. "I'm an idiot."

"Now I *know* you're talking to me."

Sam whirled around. Off balance, she flailed her arms to keep from teetering down the slope.

Gage grabbed for her, pulling her onto even ground.

Unable to catch her footing, she landed against the hard planes of his well-built chest, and the impact emptied the air from her lungs. Her hands grabbed onto his unyielding biceps, the result of a personal trainer and dietician, no doubt. No wonder celebrities were so beautiful.

Pulling back, she put her hand out and pulled in a deep breath. "I'm sorry. Thank you. You scared me," she stammered.

He tried to steady her, but she took another step back.

Gage studied her, and she wanted to fidget under his gaze. "I didn't mean to, but I can't say I'm displeased with the outcome."

She stared at him.

"Your call was spot-on."

Her cheeks warmed. "Thanks, but the talent is yours."

His strong, capable hands played across his chest and rubbed. Mesmerized, Sam couldn't force her eyes back to his face. Her mouth suddenly dry, she tried to swallow. *What is wrong with me?* She moved to step around him.

He blocked her way. "Do you still hate me?"

Shocked, she stilled. "Hate you? I don't —"

"You won't even look at me."

Guilt tightened along her shoulder blades, and she turned around. "I don't hate you." She gripped her hands together at her waist. "Everything fell apart, and Ethan took his own life." But not until he made sure Sam suffered, too. She shoved the thoughts away. "I took it out on you, and then the paparazzi, the tabloids, they hounded me for almost a year."

Gage held her with an intense gaze. "I wanted to help. I tried to call but you shut me out."

She wished it could have been that easy, but she'd been so angry, and whether he'd been to blame or not, he was reckless; if it wasn't his driving, it was the women. Two women had actually come to blows in public, each thinking she was dating him exclusively. Everyone knew it. The news, the papers, never mind the tabloids, interviews from friends and family, every single one confirming his recklessness. His help would have only made things worse. As it was now, associating with him, even professionally, was going to make the paparazzi salivate.

"I couldn't take your help, especially after blaming you. And I can't risk any of that being stirred up again." She took a step back and shook her head.

He cut his hand through the air. "You think you were the only one hurt in this? You don't think I don't know what the news said? The papers? All lies. I was sober that night, heading home from Pepperdine's Smothers Theatre." His voice dropped. "Ethan and I were in two left turning lanes; I was on the right. When the light turned green, we both took the turn but he'd accelerated faster. The paparazzi sped out to cut me off, but must not have seen him. Their car hit his, broadside, and sandwiched him between them and a power line pole."

"Please." She pressed the heel of her palms to her eyes.

"I'm sorry, Sam. I have to. I know it's hard to hear, but imagine having it shoved in your face every day. The only place anyone heard the truth was the local news, but who listens to that anymore?" His hands fisted at his sides.

She stared. She'd been through so much, and it had been unbearable to have the man who'd brought her to her senses about her relationship be involved with the accident that kept her tied to it. She'd reacted so badly. "I'm so sorry for everything I'd said."

He held her gaze.

Shame urged her to look away, but she pulled in a breath and reached out her hand. "I am so sorry. The things I'd said are unforgivable, but—"

"I forgave you the moment you said them." He slid his

large fingers up the length of hers and gently gripped her palm.

She dropped her eyes to the ground.

He released her hand and then slid his warm fingers under her chin with gentle pressure, lifting her gaze.

Swallowing hard, she studied him.

The years had been good to him in many ways. He'd filled out, thicker, broader, his face more chiseled, his eyes more piercing. Age agreed with him, but also made his emotions that much more visible. His mouth, pressed into a thin line, only softened into a frown, the lines next to his eyes deepened as he narrowed his gaze. There was a reason Hollywood had kept him at the top, waiting for him to find his way back. He had an undeniable presence. One of the very reasons she'd made the decision she had back then.

He was probably the same bad boy Hollywood had always known, but she could admit when she'd been wrong. She'd hurt him the night they'd met by walking away. She'd hurt him after Ethan's accident by blaming him, and once again by avoiding him and his attempts to help her after Ethan committed suicide. Wow. She was on a roll.

"I'm sorry."

He stared at her, and his shoulders slowly lowered. He pulled in a breath with a brief nod. "You already apologized."

Relief that he really was accepting her apology was swift.

With a jerk of his chin, he asked, "What do you remember most about the night we met?"

"What do you mean?"

Cracking his neck, he pinned her with a direct look. "I've never forgotten you, forgotten that night. I shared things with you I've never told anyone else."

He couldn't be serious. The idea he'd ever pined for her was ridiculous.

Sam closed her eyes.

He'd thought of her, beyond the accident, even after she blamed him. She shouldn't feel a rush of warmth spread through her, but there it was. Was he serious, or was this simply Gage Cutler, an actor with an agenda? Though, she couldn't for the life of her imagine what that could be. She didn't have anything he'd want.

She opened her eyes to find Gage studying her. "I remember, too." She remembered for the first time in a very long time feeling relevant, listened to, noticed. She remembered realizing her marriage was over, that if anyone should be looking at her in such a way it should be her husband, not a stranger she'd just met.

She remembered deciding it was time to face the reality and move ahead, but it was shortly after meeting Gage that the accident had happened, and then she couldn't move at all.

And she'd been angry. At him, at Ethan, at herself. She'd imagined a life with a man who truly saw her, daydreams of being heard, but she couldn't do anything about it. Not then, and not now. "I don't know what you want from me here."

He shook his head. "I want you to admit we'd had something that night."

She put her hands out. "But why? What will that change? Do you want us to start where we left off? As far as Hollywood is concerned, you *were* the cause. How would that look?"

"Who gives a shit what they think?"

"I do. They were relentless after the accident and even more so after his suicide." She dropped her hands to her sides. "I can't go through that again. Whether I've thought of you or not. Whether we had a connection or not."

"But you admit we had a connection."

Her shoulders dropped. Why did he need to hear this so badly? "Yes."

"We could still have something." His jaw ticked as he watched her.

Seconds felt like minutes, and she couldn't help but fidget under his stare as her mind reeled to make sense of his words. Finally, he gave a nod, focusing on her with a smile, and then he stepped around her and went inside.

She was dumbfounded. How in the world was this sexy, powerful, A-list actor attracted to her? Her stomach tightened.

Well, they had something in common, because she'd never quit thinking of him, either.

Maybe it was simply a matter of getting him out of her system. A little fling, casual sex, the no strings attached kind of thing. All this time and emotion, worrying and wondering, made him so much bigger than he really was; she was sure of it. Wasn't she all about moving forward? Nothing serious, just enough to appease her long-brewing curiosity.

Short, sweet, and most of all, secret.

She just needed to figure out how to keep a secret like that in Malibu.

Maybe then she could get over her nerves and jumpiness around him once and for all. Nothing serious, because they had a movie to make, and the last thing she wanted were pseudo-reporters camping out at her doorstep again. In the end, nothing had really changed, since he was still in the spotlight of Hollywood.

It might not be fair to hold it against him, but that kind of attention disfigured everyone.

Chapter Three

Gage walked back to the house from his trailer the following afternoon, grumbling. If he had his choice, he'd kick back with a cold beer, but the cast and crew were having a lunch. One of those opportunities to get to know one another better. Which was something better accomplished during filming than any forced social hour, but the powers that be summoned him, and he'd promised himself he wouldn't be difficult.

Stepping though the door, he scanned the room and then slowed. Sam sat next to Martin in deep conversation, her hands gripped together in her lap.

Gage shoved his hands in his pockets.

Annoying as hell. Her silence when he'd mentioned they could still have something made sure he understood nothing could happen. Every fiber in his body tensed with the need to prove her wrong. They'd had something. Something he hadn't been able to forget. Fuck.

Making his way to the other side of the room, he looked for the seat farthest from where she sat with Martin. The last thing he needed was a long afternoon of awkward niceties, which would be worse than her silence. He busied himself chatting with a few of the crew and then looking through an old album collection used in the film. Some of Martin's inspiration was evident in the collection.

"She doesn't bite, you know."

Gage swung around to find Martin walking up behind him. A quick glance back across the table showed Sam busy, scrolling through her phone. "Yeah, well, she hasn't been mad at you for the last two years."

"There's no time like the present to start."

Gage dipped his chin in a nod. "Sure. The start of what exactly?"

"Hell if I know, boy, but you'll figure it out."

Martin had a look in his eye Gage couldn't place, but he let it go. His stomach rumbled, and the lunch couldn't be over soon enough—his beer was calling him.

Martin left him to go chat up the rest of the crew, and Gage continued to watch Sam. It was something, anyway, her admitting to a connection. She could have denied it. Doing so would have shut him down completely. He narrowed his eyes. There might be something more still between them, something she didn't want to or couldn't completely let go of.

He made his way around the table.

Sliding into the chair at her left, he took a casual sip from the water glass, using all his control not to laugh as she snapped her head around, eyes wide at the sight of him.

"Good evening, Sam."

"Hey." Her voice was a bit breathless, and her eyes darted everywhere around the room but his face.

He leaned back in the chair and settled his hands in his lap, calm and relaxed. At least that's what she'd see. She had no reason to know his heart pounded in his chest, or controlling his breathing took a lot of effort.

One of the biggest things he'd been learning was to quit looking back, and to move forward. There was no changing what had happened or hadn't happened between them, but he was very interested in seeing what could happen.

The crew filled in the rest of the seats and lunch turned into a low hum of conversation and clanking silverware. The crew got to know one another, the individual teams bolder with each other than they were with him or the leading lady. As a matter of fact, Gage's eyes settled a time or two on Martin's new assistant, Dani, finding her studying him so thoroughly she didn't seem to notice that he'd noticed until he'd wave. She'd tense in her seat and then returned the wave with a grimace, turning her attention back to her dinner. He understood how it was, because he felt the same way when he'd first started out, finding himself star-struck more than once.

Settling in to having Sam next to him, he devoured the food on his plate, very aware that she merely moved the food around hers. Why'd he find that so interesting?

"You've been keeping busy." Her soft voice raced shivers down his spine, and he gripped his napkin in his fist.

"How do you mean?"

"Your movies, what's it been? Two a year?"

He eyed her, not answering right away. So, she'd been paying attention. He swallowed his smug smile with another bite of food and then washed it down with water. "Give or take." Though, not every film was truly blockbuster status, they'd still made the list simply because he was in them. A few disappointments for him, but the best way to succeed was to fail, so he'd take the good with the bad and consider it all success. In this industry, his sordid past put butts in the seats, and that was all the studios cared about.

With a jerk of his chin, he nudged her. "So which ones have you seen?"

She grabbed her water glass and gulped back half of it. "All of them."

Barely able to hear her mumble over the din of the crowd, he leaned forward. He'd heard her, but not only did he want to make sure, he wanted to hear it again. "What was that?"

Her face flushed red to her hairline, and his gut tightened in response. She was embarrassed. He chuckled, a self-satisfied sound that would annoy her for sure. "All of them?"

"I work in the industry. Of course I watched all of them," she whispered.

He grinned. "Of course. The industry."

She stared at him. He'd give a year's salary to know what was going on in that beautiful head of hers. She had the darkest eyes. They unsettled him and made him want to trust her all at the same time. And that was nuts; he didn't trust anyone, especially women.

He'd made that mistake too many times already.

She tilted her head to the side and bit her lip, the flush in her face deepening. "I especially enjoyed *Dark Secrets.*"

Now that movie *had* been a blockbuster, many would say due to the writing, and others would argue it was the gratuitous nudity. He certainly wasn't shy, and he'd worked his ass off to be in the right kind of shape for that movie, but knowing Sam not only watched it, but enjoyed it, made him suddenly understand exhibitionism. He shifted in his seat and cleared his throat. "Is that right?"

She narrowed her eyes at him in challenge. "I'm a healthy adult female; I'm not the only one who's watched it more than once."

His voice lowered and took on a gravelly tone. "You watched it more than once?"

She straightened in her seat and finished off her water with a grin. "More than twice."

His body tightened everywhere. Was she flirting with him? "Well, then it seems you have me at a disadvantage." He leaned closer, holding her gaze. "And that doesn't seem quite fair." Images of her naked flashed in his mind, sending his tension from uncomfortable to torturous. Damn woman.

Tapping her finger against her lip, she bit the tip of it, giving him a thoughtful stare. "I'm okay with that."

He froze for a split second and then leaned back with a laugh. Well then, if she wasn't worried about playing fair, he wouldn't, either.

And he was right. Maybe they did still have something.

• • •

Sam braved the downpour that night and ran past the set trailers with her bag over her head, a not-so-great shield from the rain. They'd finished lunch and then filmed another sequence, working well into the evening.

What the hell had she been thinking, flirting with Gage?

She grinned, feeling alive for the first time in a long time. Playing with him and knowing she of all people affected him, sent a shot of adrenaline straight to her ego. She'd wanted to pretend they hadn't had a connection the first night they'd met, but they had, and it was still there. One she didn't quite know what to do with, but she couldn't deny the fact she wanted to find out. She held back a small squeal of nerves by biting her lip.

Rounding the last small building, her car in sight, she lowered her bag. Gage stepped away from the side, his wet hair slicked back, water dripping from his nose and chin. A black T-shirt was stretched across his wide chest and over his broad shoulders.

Her heart stopped.

"What's your game, Sam?"

Sam stammered. "It's raining."

He dipped his chin once. Wrapping his thick fingers around her upper arm, he steered her in a U-turn and up the steps of his trailer.

Sam threw her hands out at the door, like a damn cat avoiding a bath. "Wait a minute, what are you doing?"

"We need to talk." Without pause, he crowded her through the door and closed it.

Turning around, he leaned back against the door—her only escape. He ran his fingers through his sopping hair and then down his face, clearing his throat.

She jumped at the sound. Hadn't she just been flirting with him? Now she twittered about like some damn virginal sacrifice in a war lord's harem. And there was nothing sacrificial about being alone with Gage.

He laughed, and when his humor faded, he still held her

gaze.

The sound of his low, rumbling chuckle did weird things to her insides, topsy-turvy, inside-out kinds of things. He grabbed the hem of his shirt and pulled it over his head. *Sweet baby Jesus.* She looked everywhere but at him, but gave up and took in every inch of his taut, tanned skin. She never knew her peripheral vision was so keen. "What are you doing?"

"I didn't want you to get wet." He stepped toward her, hesitated, and then closed the distance between them. "I'm going to kiss you."

The husky promise pulled a squeak from her throat, and she slapped a hand over her mouth, heat rushing to her face.

Panic and something quite wonderful stole her breath. He stepped into her, hot unyielding skin pressed against her palms, and the smallest scattering of hair tickled the sensitive pads of her fingers. She swallowed against the lump in her throat.

The light in his eyes held hers and she froze, unable to move.

"There's something between us. Has been since the night we met."

Sam closed her eyes, but when he slid her hands around his neck, she snapped them open.

He stepped in, crowding her, gathering her body into his arms and up against his length. His chest rose and fell in rapid succession—in time with hers. Lips, full and wide, hovered over hers for a beat, and he whispered. "Admit it."

His warm breath wafted over her skin and goose bumps bloomed down her neck and chest. *God yes.* She was ready for a fling, for some fun with a gorgeous man who'd taken up way too much of her brain space. She didn't want to wait any longer, so she leaned in, stopping a hair's breadth from his lips and whispered, "Kiss me."

His quick grin and squeeze of her hips with his hands teased. He barely brushed his mouth over hers, leaving a tingle behind.

His heart thundered against her breasts, and the most delicious sensation rolled low in her belly. Finally.

Closing her eyes, she closed the distance between the heat of their wanting lips.

Gage brushed his lips against hers, absorbing her, pulling her tighter against him, releasing a rush of heat from her center through her limbs.

Something akin to breathing again washed over her.

She coiled her arms about his head and shifted higher in his embrace, kissing him back with all the pent-up *woman* she'd shoved down for so long. He moaned low in his throat, and a surge of power tightened her grip around his neck. Yes. This is what she wanted, what she needed.

Gage lifted her to the counter, and with a wide sweep of his hand, odds and ends crashed to the floor. The action, raw and hurried, called to a part of her she just realized existed. He wedged his hips between her knees, and she wrapped her legs about his waist, celebrating his lack of restraint.

"God, Sam, I've wanted to taste you forever," he whispered against her skin as he brushed his lips along her jaw and down her neck.

Her head fell back, and she kneaded his shoulders, lost as fingers of the most delicious fire licked up her spine and spread along her skull. She couldn't breathe, yet he was all the air she needed. She couldn't think, yet he filled her mind.

He found his way back to her mouth, his lips gliding in a whispered caress as his tongue slid against her own. She pressed into him, desperate to get closer, losing herself in the feeling of being desired.

Someone pounded on the door and they froze. "The rain's stopped. Five minutes until shooting, Mr. Cutler."

"Fuck."

Sam swallowed, wanting to giggle, but the effort would cost too much. "You aren't finished?"

He pulled back just enough for her to see his eyes narrow with an intensity she felt to her toes. "I'm not nearly finished."

She pulled in a shaky breath.

Stepping to the door, he leaned over and grabbed a dry shirt from the couch and then pulled it over his head. She stared at the striations of his muscles until he cleared his throat. She snapped her eyes back to his.

"We're not done yet, Sam." He opened the door and stepped out into the rain.

She stood where he'd left her, her heart pounding in her ears. She pressed her lips together and then opened her mouth, trying to form with her lips what her brain couldn't quite wrap itself around. *I want to do that again.*

She slid from the counter top, taken by surprise. She wanted the rush, the heat, the power. A smile stretched her mouth, and she dragged her lower lip through her teeth.

This connection to Gage might be just what she needed to move ahead after all.

Chapter Four

Gage pulled the lasagna from the oven and set it on the counter, taking a moment to enjoy the savory aroma. Sliding the French bread on to the middle rack, he smiled, then set the timer. Cooking was a recently discovered decompressor, and it turned out he was rather good at it. He only had a few minutes before his sister arrived, but he was just about ready. The distraction would be good. Shit, that was an understatement; the distraction was necessary. Ever since he'd kissed Sam earlier, the need to see her had grown ten-fold. The feel of her lips, her taste, stayed with him even in his goddamn dreams, and it had made for a restless night.

When she kissed him, she wasn't kissing him for a story she could tell her friends. She kissed him for her, and she'd lost herself in him just as he had in her. Leaving his trailer had been fucking torture, but the look of shock and loss on her face when he went acted as a salve.

Now he needed to figure out when he could kiss her

again.

The doorbell rang, and seconds later Belina walked into the kitchen with a grin.

She stretched out her arms and wrapped him in a tight embrace. "Hey, big brother."

He had friends and his dad, but no one got him like his sister did.

Anita, his housekeeper, leaned her head in. "Are you sure you don't need anything else, Mr. Cutler?" His housekeeper had been with him a half dozen years now. Hired from a controlled reference firm, she'd seen him in worse condition than anyone, but never once had a telltale sign of it shown up in the press. One of the few people he could trust. He'd keep her forever if she let him.

He looked from Bel back to Anita. "Thanks, Anita, but I think we've got it covered. Have a nice evening."

She dipped her head. "Yes, sir."

Bel poked him in the arm. "You lucked out with Anita."

He grinned with a nod. "She's awesome. You hungry?"

"You know me. Always."

Gage shook his head. Belina was tall, like Sam, but had the metabolism of an Olympic swimmer. He'd never seen anyone eat so much without putting on a pound. Women hated her for it, and most everyone else just tried to feed her. Him included.

Loading their plates with lasagna and French bread, he spoke over his shoulder. "Hey, make yourself useful. Pour some wine."

Bel stuck her tongue out at him.

He placed the food on the table and walked over to look out over the water lapping at the shore, and pulled the fresh ocean air into his lungs.

She joined him at the glass wall. "It's so calm."

Gage looked at her with a grin, then back to the ocean.

She turned and leaned against the side, facing his profile. "So, what's going on?"

"Nothing."

She grinned, a dimple deep in her left cheek. "Why do people always act like there isn't anything going on when, clearly, there is?" She raised her brows.

"Shit." Pushing away from the railing, he walked to the table and lowered into a chair. He gestured for her to join him.

That was the problem with people who "got" you. They saw too much, knew too much, and when that someone was a nosey, pesky little sister—shit. He sipped his wine, putting off her question.

Belina took her seat and picked up her fork. "You're always full of energy and excitement during the beginning of a new film." She flicked her hand at him. "This is not like you."

"What?" He shoveled a load of pasta into his mouth and spoke while he chewed. "You just got here."

"Yeah, and you aren't going on and on, telling me the direction your movie is taking, or which producers you're talking to about your next project."

He picked up his wine glass and took a long swallow, then set it back above his plate. With a grunt, he grabbed his napkin and wiped his mouth, then tossed it to his lap.

She threw her hands up. "So, who's the newest Cutler Queen?"

He winced at the horrible nickname given by the press

to the ladies he'd dated. Not one of them had their own identity, unless they were already considered "someone."

"Not seeing anyone."

"That's not like you, though I think it's good." His sister ducked her head as if dodging something.

"What's that supposed to mean?"

She waved away his words. "Come on. Don't act all hurt and sensitive. You date the worst options out there, women who would never commit in the first place or the kind you'd never want to commit to. So I just kind of wonder, what's the point?"

He waited.

Bel wrinkled her nose. "Besides that. Gaawd. The world knows your prowess, thanks to the tabloids."

It was true he hadn't been able to carry off any resemblance of a long-term relationship, but he couldn't help it if the women weren't interested in the long haul.

"And did you really get into a bar fight?"

"Tabloids exaggerate." He tossed back the rest of his wine and poured another glass.

Bel studied him and then leaned in. "They aren't all Mom, you know."

Gage needed the subject to change, yesterday. "Sam Dekker is working re-writes for the film."

"So, what's the problem? She any good?"

"We'd met before, both on business. All we did was talk, but there was something there, Bel, something I hadn't found before or since."

Her eyes widened and she leaned forward, giving his hand a squeeze.

"Turned out she was married. I knew the guy, a complete

tool. We went our separate ways, with her making it very clear I wasn't to contact her. She took her marriage vows seriously, and I can respect that, but it felt like I'd lost something significant." He grunted. "I can't explain it."

"Is she still married?"

Eyeing his sister, he said, "Samantha Dekker? Doesn't ring a bell?" The story had been all over the tabloids for months. The fact she didn't recognize Sam's name gave him hope for all mankind. Most people ate that shit up.

The tabloids were genius at sensationalizing the mundane. Every new magazine he saw his face splashed across made him more tired than the last. Tired of never being able to let go of past mistakes, tired of being disposable, tired of having his personal life be someone else's entertainment.

She blinked.

"Ethan Evans."

Belina lowered her hand, her movements cautious, as if not to spook a frightened child. "Ohhhhh." She studied him a moment, then took a small bite of her bread. "No problem, screenwriters usually do their job and then are off the set, right? It's not like she's there every day."

"I demanded that she be on set every day."

His sister's eyes widened, and she slapped her hand to her chest, leaning toward him. "Why? Why would you do that?"

He couldn't help but chuckle at her look of shock and the high-pitched tone of her voice. "Bel."

She shook her head. "No, seriously. Why would you?"

He drained his glass and reached out for the bottle.

Bel placed her hand over his, and he stilled, raising his brow at her.

"Slow down. I just got here."

After pulling the bottle out from under his sister's hand, he filled his glass and set it back onto the table by his plate. Tightness pulled in his chest, and he wanted to down the whole goddamn bottle just because he could.

She shifted in her seat and wiped her mouth with her napkin, watching him with worried blue eyes. "It broke my heart to see you so hurt after that accident, and the tabloids were so vicious."

"To her, too. I tried to reach out to her after the accident, and again after his suicide, but she refused. The first time with angry accusations and the second with silence."

"I can only imagine the pain she was going through. People handle grief in so many different ways." She shifted in her chair. "I admire the fact that she didn't let anything happen the first time you met. You weren't in any shape to understand it back then, but Gage, she wouldn't have been a woman worth pursuing if she hadn't. She did the right thing. I just—I'm worried after what happened with her husband, your involvement—"

He shoved back from the table.

She threw up her hands to stop his offended interruption. "Wait. I'm not saying you were responsible. God, no. I'm just saying it's complicated and messy."

Gage blew out a breath with a nod. Damn little sisters.

"But—"

"But what?" He scowled.

Her eyes softened. "But though I'm afraid you two have to overcome a lot—which really I'm not surprised, you tend to do that to yourself, kind of like a punishment—I say go for it."

He waved his hand. "Doesn't matter. She's not interested in anything serious."

Bel shrugged her shoulders. "Soooo…"

He shook his head. "Soooo…?"

Taking another bite of her lasagna, Bel chewed. Gage waited for her to answer and tapped his fingers on the table.

Finally, she swallowed. "Sounds perfect to me. I'd be more worried if she was willing to jump right in headfirst. Taking it slow and casual will give the two of you a chance to *really* get to know one another. People change, and are always changing, the healthy ones anyway. Don't rush it. In time, after seeing the real Gage Cutler, the one I know, Sam won't be able to walk away." Bel slapped the table. "Mark my words."

Gage stared at her. "Did you just Pepperdine me?" His reference to her professorship at the School of Psychology and Education at the University put a smile on her face.

"No, you aren't one of my students. I *sistered* you."

He settled back in his seat, his gut full. "Let's go for a walk."

Leading her down the steps to the beach, he spoke over his shoulder. "How's Dad?"

They walked along the sandy beach, skirting rocks the size of mounted movie cameras, with light conversation Gage only half listened to. Bel had given him a lot to think about. Maybe she was right. Time would be on his side. He and Sam had both been through a lot the past couple years. He knew he wanted to see her again, he wanted to explore the connection they'd had from the first night, and after that kiss, he actually believed he just might be able to.

A light sensation washed over his shoulders, one he

hadn't felt in a long time.

Hope.

. . .

The following day, Sam made her way through the film set in a dreamy haze of a post-kiss hang over. Every time she spotted Gage from across the room, her heartbeat spiked, and the little hairs on her body stood on end. She floated through the endless odds and ends of equipment and found a corner to work. Sitting down at a small table, she opened the manuscript to her marked page. She wasn't hiding so much as ensuring a quiet place to work while re-living Gage's kiss one more time without anyone noticing her ridiculous high. She closed her eyes with a smile.

"Sam."

With a shriek, Sam spun around and slapped her hand to her chest. "Shit! You scared me."

Gage threw his hands up as if to ward off an attack. "Whoa. You're way too tense." He reached for her shoulders. "I'd say a massage is in order."

Sam skirted away from him. His hands on her would be the opposite of relaxing.

Gage dropped his hands to his side with a lop-sided grin and then tucked them in his front pockets. "Chicken."

She ignored him and picked up her coffee to hold between them as a shield. Maybe he wouldn't notice her heart pounding in her chest.

Gage glanced at the cup in her hand, then back to her face. "Really?"

Those eyes of his always unsettled her, pulled her in—saw too much. Were they blue or green, damn it? "What? You have work to do, and I'm helping you stay on task." She threw him her cheekiest grin.

Gage closed the distance between them and then slowly slipped the cup from her fingers, which seemed to hold on to the damn thing like a lifeline. Leaning past her, he set it on the table, his cologne and his own personal heat filling her senses. She closed her eyes against the sensations blooming low in her stomach. Why did she always feel him? It wasn't fair, and possibly made her feel a little drunk.

He straightened in front of her and ran the pad of his thumb over her collarbone.

She snapped her eyes open.

Gage tilted his head to the side and raised a brow.

It was a good look, damn it. Sam shifted from one foot to the other, the light touch of his roaming fingers raising the tiny hairs on the back of her neck.

He spoke, his voice low, for her ears only, and she had to lean forward in order to hear him. "I want to kiss you again, Sam."

Only a hand's width separated her chest from his, and she wanted to close the distance and let the pressure of his body ease the need building inside. She could barely breathe.

Gage looked into her eyes and then trailed his fingers up the side of her neck, along her jaw to her lower lip.

He leaned forward, and she put her hand against his chest. His heat radiated through her palm.

"I think you were waiting for me. You found the most secluded corner in the house."

She took a quick look and couldn't argue. The area

she'd chosen to work existed behind boxes and shelves of equipment.

"I—"

The feel of his lips broke any logic or reason, and she sighed into the kiss. Sliding her palms against his skin to the back of his neck, her fingers delved deep into his thick dark hair and yanked him down until she could press against him. This was what it was to be kissed by a man who wanted her, instead of simply a sensation for her lips; she felt it through her whole body.

She lost herself in the increased tempo of her heart, warmth spread low between her legs, and she tried to get closer. It'd been so long, too long. His heat, his skin — his ability to see her like no one else. "I want you," she whispered.

She jerked back.

Gage sucked in a breath and pulled her back in, pressing a hard kiss to her mouth. "I'm not letting you take that back."

Her body flushed at the contact. She needed to do something about the fantasy she'd built up in her head about being with him, and get him out of her system. Reality would surely do the trick because dreams were always over-inflated expectations. Yes, that would work, and then she could get back to focusing one hundred percent on her writing. He was a distraction.

"Come to my place tonight."

Sam shook out her hands and turned for her coffee, keeping her eyes on him. As much as she needed to get him out of her system, she didn't want anyone finding out.

He moved with her, his eyes flashing with an intensity that scared her.

Her shaking hand knocked into the cup, making it tip

precariously. Startled, she lunged to keep it from falling completely over. Finally, with the cup wrapped in her sure grasp, she took a sip and at the same time put a hand out to stop him from moving in—which was becoming a ridiculous habit. "Stop. Go. You have work to do. We can't do this."

Gage frowned, and she wanted to ease his furrowed brow, but she clenched her hand into a fist. Touching him would be a very big mistake.

Sam recognized a thundercloud when she saw one and smiled. "Here, Gage. We can't do this here. I can't think, and we don't want anyone finding out. It's too hard."

He wiggled his brows at her with a decidedly wicked grin. "Hard is appropriate."

"Oh my God, go." Sam pushed him away, the heat of his arm making her want to pull him back to her instead so she could feel if the rest of him was just as hot. It would be. Damn him.

"Okay, okay, but later." Resisting slightly, he glanced back at her and held her gaze.

She refused to look away, but if she didn't get him to go soon, she wouldn't be responsible for her actions. The smooth curve of his lips, slightly parted, made promises she prayed to God they'd deliver, and her own tingled in anticipation. She swallowed. "Later," she agreed.

As he walked from her hiding spot, she shook her head and chuckled. Whew! That man could go from randy intensity to raunchy humor with the shutter speed of a high tech camera. She liked it. His playfulness, his intensity. He went after life, no sitting in the corner waiting for things to happen with that one. She admired him for it, but those same characteristics scared the hell out of her as well. They came with consequences. She was tired of paying for the actions of someone else, or for the association. The whole "guilty by" was tough to avoid in Hollywood.

But that kiss. Her toes still curled, and she grinned. That she could get all over. No one had to know, which would be better for Gage and her.

Pressing her hand to her lips, she grabbed her copy of the screenplay and went in search of Martin, a nervous excitement buzzing in her head. She was going home with Gage. Her brain had difficulty processing this new information, making hunting down Martin harder than she'd expected. The house they were using for filming was insidiously large, and she kept ending up where she'd started, which made her remember the damn kiss. But with Dani's help, she eventually located Martin pouring over the dailies.

"You're right," Sam said, watching Dani disappear into another room.

"Always."

Sam laughed and nudged his shoulder. "Yeah, right. No, about Dani, she is really indispensable. She works her tail off."

"Yes, she does. Now, let's talk." He pointed to the script.

They had a good discussion about Sam's concerns with a sequence in the script, though they had to circle around more than once.

Martin paused midsentence. "You okay?"

Instead of focusing on the words, she'd lost herself in the memory of warm lips and hot skin. "Of course," she lightly snorted and waved her hand at him.

Her cell buzzed. Reluctantly, she grabbed her phone. Martin waited as she flicked through the screens. It was a text from Mrs. Evans.

He did everything for you. All he wanted was a baby. Why were you so selfish?

She froze.

"Everything okay?"

She shoved her phone back into her pocket and forced her breathing to remain calm, an effort that cost her. "Of course." She smiled, though her stomach felt as if it were filled with rocks. She wished Ethan's family would leave her alone. If it wasn't his mother, it was his sister. The texts and phone calls had been a monthly occurrence since his death.

Blaming her, judging her.

I guess I know where he got it from.

But she could handle it. She needed to count on one person these days—Samantha Anne Dekker. She refused to burden her family with drama—especially about Ethan, since they never liked him in the first place—and she rejected the idea of telling Martin. Baseless, empty harassment, nothing more.

She forced her brain to cooperate and focus back on the task at hand. Most of her original concerns about the script were finally put to rest once she understood the vision, and another catch she made had Martin jumping up and hugging her. "That's my girl. You just saved us about a hundred thousand."

Sam couldn't help how proud she felt. Martin was like a second father to her—hell, to everyone in Malibu. It was thanks to him she'd become established in the business as fast as she had, and thanks to herself she'd lost so much ground. And now once again, he pulled her back in. Proving herself a good investment was necessary and filled her with deep pride. When it came to screenwriting, she was enough. Keeping the text to herself was best. There was no way she'd risk screwing up this opportunity with drama.

Pulling her shoulders back, she left Martin and headed back to her desk. If she could find it again, that was. She rounded a stack of storage bins and found Gage tucked off to the side in a director's chair, pouring over the script. She took a deep breath and studied him closer, letting the warmth and excitement infuse her. She'd never seen him look so light, so…free. Something in his expression pulled at her. She wanted to feel that light and free someday.

Well, today was as good a day as any to work on that. *Come on, Sam, buck up.* It was time to work on that life she wanted so badly.

He lifted his gaze, and the beginnings of a smile curved his lips, his eyes a bit unfocused, but as she got closer they narrowed in on her with pinpoint precision. He slowly lowered the script to his lap and leaned back in his chair. "You look pleased with yourself."

She glanced around and then placed her hands on his denim-covered knees, delighted when his muscles tightened under her grip. All morning she'd had trouble focusing, almost embarrassing herself during her conversation with Martin. It was only fair if Gage suffered from the same affliction, wasn't it?

She slid her hands just a bit higher as she stood just between his knees. His heat radiated through his jeans, warming her palms, and her fingers twitched against his rock hard thighs.

He looked at her hands, then up at her face with a raised brow. "What are you up to?"

She bit her lip and then licked them, leaning close. She could see the individual crystal flecks in his eyes and each hair of stubble along his jaw.

His nostrils flared just before she brushed her lips along his in a feather light caress. Her heart took off, and every nerve ending in her body went on high alert.

Strong arms gripped her wrists, keeping her where she was. She grinned against his mouth and whispered, "Does this help you concentrate?"

He tried to deepen the kiss, but she pulled back just enough to keep it light, teasing, and received a low growl.

"Hell no," he said.

His immediate response satisfied her newfound high, the feeling of being desired like a hit of some rare, exotic drug.

"Good."

Chapter Five

Light and easy, light…and…easy. Sam laughed at herself as she repeated the phrase to herself as the crew wrapped up for the night and headed home. She couldn't tell if the nerves turning her stomach were completely excitement or a little fear as well. In a very short time she'd be alone with Gage, touching him, being touched by him. Her stomach tightened.

She hadn't been intimate with anyone in years, and the last few times she had been weren't worth remembering. In fact, they'd been humiliating and awful. When she'd first been with Ethan things had been good—he was a perfectionist after all—but as soon as they were married everything had changed. Once he achieved the status he'd wanted with a wife, she was merely a means to an end, a tool to be used. Never again.

Martin walked up and placed a hand on her shoulder. "You and Gage seem to be getting along well."

Careful to keep a neutral expression on her face, Sam

shrugged. "Yeah, we are. Thank you again for this, Martin." She winced. "I never got to apologize for my reaction at The Chocolate Box."

Martin studied her, a spark of something in his eye. "My pleasure, and no apology necessary. I should have warned you, but I was afraid you wouldn't show." He gently shook her shoulder.

"You're probably right." She laughed. Sometimes she was her own worst enemy.

"Heading out?"

"I am. Just need to grab a few things first. I want to write tonight, work out some of the kinks from not working for a while. Have anything I might like?"

His hand disappeared into his bag and appeared with a script. "Check this out. Take as long as you like."

That was what she loved so much about him; he trusted her and believed in her enough to hand over one of his scripts.

She held the pages to her chest. "Thank you."

With a wave, he disappeared through the door.

Gage said goodbye to a few fellow actors and approached Sam in long, easy strides, setting off sparks of excitement up her spine. What would it be like with him? More of the heat they'd already shared for sure, and the fact left her breathless and overwhelmed. She tensed as he closed the distance, her fingers rising a bit. To pull him in or keep him at arm's length, she wasn't sure, and giggled at her silliness.

"Ms. Dekker." He spoke in a formal tone as if he was all about business—and not the horizontal kind.

"Yes, Mr. Cutler?"

With only a couple people trailing behind, he lowered

his voice to barely a whisper. "I like how that sounds."

Heat flushed her neck and face. *Pull yourself together, Dekker.* She glanced over his shoulder as the last crew member slipped through the door.

"Ready? You can follow me in your car."

Her eyes opened wide. His words sounded so casual but were laced with so much more. She wanted him more than she'd wanted anything or anyone in a long time. Pure, un-adulterated, physical, base-need wanting. Hell yeah, she was ready to go. "Let's go then."

Gage stepped toward her, a possessive look in his eye. "Really?"

She almost laughed at the hopeful disbelief in his tone, but nodded instead. If her goal was to keep this light and casual, to get him out of her system, the best thing to do was to treat it that way. If they waited for the perfect time, it put too much importance on the sex.

"This is going to be the longest damn ride of my life."

Sam grinned as she watched Gage take off to his car. A few minutes later, she pulled out of the driveway. She changed her mind no less than fifty times on the way, questioning how she of all people was going home with Gage Cutler.

Her heart hammering in her chest, she followed him through three levels of the tightest security she'd ever seen. She could have used this set-up when she'd been married to Ethan.

Finally, they pulled into his oversized garage and the door lowered, closing them into an oasis of privacy.

He was at her door, opening it and grabbing her hand before she had turned her engine off. Laughing, she put a hand to her stomach and followed him through the garage. He fumbled with his keys, and then swore, pushing Sam against the door and kissing her.

She loved his taste and the feel of his hard body against hers. Sam played with the hem of his shirt. Pulling in a breath, she slid her fingertips under the hem, refusing to be a passive bystander. He sucked in his stomach at her touch. "Wait, wait, let me get this."

Sam's stomach twisted in knots. She stilled, watching him slip the key into the lock. His hand shook, and he wiped it on his jeans with a chuckle.

What if she sucked? She almost laughed but couldn't get anything past the lump in her throat. Her best defense had always been "fake it till you make it," and she needed to tap into that right now.

He wrapped his arm around her waist and hauled her up against him. She squealed against his mouth, and they pushed through the door, practically falling through the entrance.

Once inside, he locked the door, tossed his keys to his foyer table, and turned toward her. She sobered a bit, slowly backing away down the hall. He followed and her heart took up a heavy rhythm. The gleam in his gaze stopped her, held her immobile. She stood in the middle of his living room. She wanted him to catch her, to take her. Make her forget her fears, her worries—release the hold he seemed to have on her.

Light and easy and fun.

In two strides, Gage had her in his arms. Lifting her, he encouraged her legs to wrap around his waist. He dragged his lips against hers, catching her lower lip between his teeth with subtle pressure, then sliding his tongue in to taste her, his hands in her hair, holding her head hostage. The heat of his torso radiated through her slacks and intensified the fever building between her legs.

He walked through the door into his bedroom. Without letting her go, he flicked on his fireplace and, stepping over to the sliding glass doors, pushed a button that shut the enclosed window blinds with an almost imperceptible whisk. Then with a growl, he stalked back to the bed and followed her body down with his.

"You have no idea how I've wanted you." He groaned next to her ear, rough, desperate, his breath sending shivers down her spine. Or maybe it was his words. She didn't know. Couldn't think. Didn't care.

His hands explored everywhere. Gripping and dragging along every contour with focused intensity as if afraid at any moment she'd make him stop—as if. He caressed along her jaw, then pressed her breasts together, burying his face in her soft mounds, then down her body to her waist. He grabbed the hem of her shirt, hesitating a moment, holding her gaze, and then pushed it up, baring her stomach. This was it. She'd be bare before him, nothing shielding her, nothing to hide behind. A moment of complete terror swept through her and she tensed, her body ready to bolt even if her head couldn't keep up.

"Easy," he whispered.

Easy…that's right. Light and easy. This is for you, Sam. The thought steadied her, but once they did this, there was no going back; this moment, now, was the point of no return.

Looking into the desperate heat of his eyes, she saw all of her pent-up desire and need mirrored there. She wasn't in this alone. It was time to start trusting herself.

Decision made, she lifted to help get her top up and over her head.

He released a gust of breath and a low groan that told her more about his desires than any words would have. Without pause, her bra followed; he paused and stared at her. "Goddamn, you're beautiful."

The wet heat of his mouth around one nipple, then the other shocked her right out of herself and into the present as she arched up, pressing closer.

Wanting to feel him, taste him, she yanked his shirt over his head, then pulled him down to feel the hard planes of his chest against her breasts. "Oh. My. God."

"We haven't even started, and there is no way I'm rushing something I've waited so long for." He slid down the bed, taking her slacks and panties from her waist. He returned, towering over her, his eyes glinting from the firelight—they looked almost clear the way they glowed. She stretched her arms over her head, streamlining her tall form to show its best angle, enticing him to hurry.

His gaze intensified as he unbuckled his belt, the muscles clenching in his jaw.

How many beautiful bodies had shared this bed? And how long ago—a week, yesterday? Not now, not tonight. They didn't matter. She focused once more on the intensity of his gaze. Besides, a look like that promised no other woman was in his head or bed but her.

He unbuckled his belt before pushing his pants and boxer briefs to the ground, never looking away. The length of him jutting out, long and hard and thick. Her mouth watered.

She sat up and reached for him, but he caught her hands,

pushed them above her head, and pressed her back onto the bed. She would have lain on a bed of nails. Wanting nothing more but to touch him, taste him, feel him inside of her—finally. She might not have ever said the words aloud, but she'd wanted to since the night they'd met.

His long, heavy form covered her with a delicious weight. His clever hands finding her everywhere, the mound of her breasts, the dip of her collarbone, the long length from under her shoulder to her hip. A firestorm of want and need rushed through her. She spread her legs and wrapped them around him, tightening her grip and rubbing against his length.

"Now." She all but whimpered and didn't care. She couldn't wait. She'd already waited too long.

"No."

He took her mouth again and then trailed his tongue down her neck and over one breast to her nipple. Her body screamed for speed. But he wouldn't be hurried, and his hands massaged with a gentle, almost feather-light touch. She wanted him to grab, to demand. She pushed against his hands to increase the pressure—to relieve the intensity. She'd lose her mind.

He wouldn't let her.

His tongue continued down the center dip of her abdomen, the firelight dancing with the shadows on his shoulders. Each muscle bunched under the effort to hold himself up. She yanked him closer.

It was like trying to move granite. Strong arms slid under her knees and opened them wide. Then his hot, wet mouth found her and licked at her center, his tongue circling around and around. Her world went black, pressure pushing her higher, her lungs struggled to pull in air, and then she exploded in a bright light, her hips arcing, pushing against his mouth as wave after wave of pleasure sliced through her. She fisted the bed covers, trying to fight against the building pressure.

She needed him with her.

He laved at her once, twice, lingering wherever she responded most intensely. "Almost. God, you taste so good."

His words turned her on and the pressure continued, a tight fist, low in her core that tried to flow hot and fast. Each lap of his tongue carried her higher again.

How could this be possible? Light and easy. Light and easy. Desperate to touch him, to take him with her, she pulled at him to slide up her body and reached down around her thighs to find him, cupping his balls with a gentle pressure.

He reared up, and holding her head between his hands, demanded she meet his gaze. "Look at me." His voice was ragged.

She resisted. "Now, Gage."

"Look at me." His voice dragged along her nerves with its desperation. Did this mean something to him? Could it? No. He was Gage Cutler, movie star. He—

"Sam."

She couldn't hold back any longer. Her eyes locked onto his, and every fiber of her being became more sensitive than before.

He released her to make quick work of a condom, never breaking eye contact. Sliding one hand back under her head and the other at her waist, he hesitated one second more and then plunged into her, holding her gaze as she went.

She closed her eyes against the intensity, her core squeezing him, pulse after pulse.

"Open your eyes. I want you to see *me*." His command was hoarse.

It took great effort to lift her lids. But when they locked eyes, her light and easy mantra abandoned her to the reality of his heavy and hard body, and he drove forward again. This time when she cried out, he followed only seconds behind, eyes locked with hers.

He thrust into her, increasing tempo, and she pulled him in harder, deeper, her heels pressing against his ass. Her center twisted into white-hot pleasure, until with one endless stroke, she flew over the edge, his name on her lips. "Gage." Her body convulsed around him again and again.

She'd never experienced anything like it before.

He followed right along with her, a long groan from deep in his throat.

Her body pulsed from her center to the ends of her fingers and toes as he continued to hold her gaze. Ripple after endless ripple.

She thought she might have died. But one thing she knew.

Green. His eyes were definitely green.

Chapter Six

Blue, his eyes were blue.

Gage leaned over Sam, smoothing hair from her damp forehead. "You're beautiful."

Muscles, liquid from too much heat, refused to cooperate, and she lay paralyzed. She stared into his eyes, always drawn toward them. His words were sweet, but she wanted to giggle, because she was so not beautiful. Very few were truly beautiful if they lived in a fifty-mile radius of L.A.

Besides, beauty had been Ethan's business, and he'd explained why she'd never make the cut. Her features weren't quite symmetrical, the tip of her nose too perky—a bit too cute. Brown eyes would never be as desirable as blue or green, and looking into Gage's, she might just have to agree. He was delicious.

"That is just post-coital blindness." She smiled and lifted her head to press her lips against his. Her belly tightened. How was it possible to want him again so soon, so badly? A rush of giddy energy washed over her.

"Light and easy" was back as her book of life.

Gage rolled onto his back and took her with him until she lay on top of his chest. "I just gave you a compliment. It's mine to give. Just say thank you."

"Thank you."

"Wow, that was convincing." He pushed her brown waves back over her shoulder and ran his fingertips along the top of her shoulder and down her arm.

She studied him, his thick brows over serious eyes, rugged features, a wide—and might she say, talented—mouth. Men had an easier time of it. Rough, imperfect features lent a certain amount of danger, all alpha male, outdoorsy, and capable; that worked for her as "pretty" men never could. Looking at him threatened to become a favorite pasttime. She'd never get any work done with him around.

His warmth penetrated deep, and she snuggled into him, a definite perk to sex. Resting her chin on her hands, she looked down at him. "I want to do that again."

His grin stretched ear to ear, and he cupped her ass in his large hands. "That is the second best thing I've ever heard."

She raised her brows and, trying not to get distracted by the length of him growing against her stomach, asked, "What's the first?"

"Hearing my name on your lips when you come."

Her cheeks burned at his words. In one swift move, he had her underneath him once again, and she laughed. He nuzzled the side of her neck and then took her earlobe between his teeth. Goose bumps ran the length of that arm, making her shiver. "So you liked it?"

He yanked his head up and looked at her, incredulous.

"Liked it?" Supporting his weight on one arm, he cupped her face with his other hand. "*Liked it* hardly expresses what just happened."

The heat of his breath caressed her lips before his mouth did, and she greedily took as much of him as she could. She slid her tongue along the slick heat of his, stirring all the nerves along her skin once again.

He broke from the kiss, tracing an invisible line from her lips, over her jaw, down her neck, and across her collarbone as he explained, "I like a good massage. I like a great cup of coffee. *That* was—well, that was something I've never experienced before."

Any doubt left over from Ethan's verbal slaps slipped away with each word Gage uttered. He continued trailing his finger over the swell of her breast and around her nipple until he reached the hard-nubbed center. She arched and sucked in a breath.

One time wasn't going to be enough. She'd hoped a great bout of sex would get him out of her system, but she'd been very, very wrong. Her body continued to play back every caress, every tug, and wanted it all again and more. A casual fling would be perfect. It was all either of them had time for, and since she'd never get serious again with a celebrity, there'd be no confusion.

Light, easy, and the hottest sex she'd ever known.

She licked her lips. "Me neither." Running her fingers into the hair at the nape of his neck, she gave a gentle pull and then scraped her nails carefully up and over the crown of his head, eliciting a small shiver. "It's never been that way for me. I haven't been with anyone in a long time."

He brushed the palm of his hand back and forth over

her nipple and then palmed her breast with a soft flex of his fingers. "Well, you were fantastic. I can only imagine what you could do with a little practice."

Her jaw dropped open, and she tugged his hair, none too gently this time.

He laughed but pinned her with a direct look. "So what are you saying, Sam?" He adjusted his position and lodged himself firmly between her thighs, bracing his weight on his arms.

Struggling to keep her brain on task, she pulled in short rapid breaths. "I'm saying I want to do this again sometime. You know. Have fun, nothing serious."

He dropped his chin to his chest, but she could see the pull of his lips into a grin. She pinched him on the arm and tugged him back to her so she could kiss him. "Don't laugh at me."

Kissing the end of her nose, his eyes bright, he said, "I am so not laughing at you."

"I could use a little fun. Writing and working on the movie during the day, and then you and I could blow off a little steam during down time."

He stared at her a moment, holding her gaze in that way he did where she couldn't look away. She bit her lower lip. Had she said something wrong? It had been a long time since she'd done anything like this.

"You're writing? I mean, besides script work."

It took her a second to catch up, but relief and his question warmed her, and she smiled. "Yes. I took some time off after, well, you know. And there was so much press and drama, no one wanted to be bothered with me on set. No one but Martin. Anyway, I've been wanting to sharpen my skills.

If I'm back in Hollywood, I want to be the best, not just take advantage of an opportunity. I want to take back what was mine." She heard the wavering in her voice end on a smile.

Pressing one more kiss to her mouth, he pushed up from the bed. "Then that is exactly what you'll do." He swung his legs over the side. "Come on, as much as I want to do all of that all over again, we have an early morning."

A contented sigh escaped her while she watched him dress. She could watch that rerun all day long. He had such strength, not just in the way he moved, or the bulk of his body, but in his very being. Surviving in Hollywood demanded it, no doubt, and he was a survivor where sometimes she worried she was only trying to be.

She narrowed her eyes and pushed up from the pillows. That might have been her yesterday, but today she was moving forward.

• • •

Gage leaned back in his chair and sipped his espresso as he and his sister waited for their dad. He gave his practiced façade of calm and detached, but in reality he was giving himself a high five and a Buddy Christ wink. He'd known he and Sam would be amazing together, but the reality of it was something else altogether. It left him feeling like he could go bench press with Schwarzenegger or keep pace with Olympian gold medalist, Bolt. He'd gotten her to open up for now, and he wanted to celebrate, but the work was just beginning.

Staring off over the sea of unfamiliar faces, he watched his dad, otherwise known as DC or Dean Cutler on Pepperdine Campus, make his way to the table. Heads were on a swivel along the way, and Gage only hoped to have that much charisma in twenty years. He leaned back with a self-satisfied grin, lacing his fingers on top of his stomach. To Sam, apparently he did.

The tight squeeze in his gut brought back memories of sinking into her body and the addicting flavor of her lips. He hoped she felt something for him, too, something strong, because now that he'd had a taste of her there was no going back. Having her open up to him only strengthened his desire. And he was a man used to fighting for what he wanted—and getting it.

Cutler Senior took his seat and a sip of his mimosa, turning to Gage. "So, what's been going on?"

The owner of the place had played football with his dad back in the day. He always saved a back corner table partially shielded with a half wall and hanging ferns, giving the family regular solitude in a world that thrived on intruding.

A sense of well-being filled him as it always did when he was with these two. They'd been a tight-knit trio ever since Cecilia Lombardi decided Hollywood was more important than her two children and devoted husband.

He'd been eight years old and his sister younger still. Gage never could get the idea out of his head that they'd just not been good enough, and his mother's continued denial on the red carpet of any familial relation to him drove the notion home.

"I've been thinking long and hard about this, and spending time with Martin, studying."

His dad nodded. "And."

"I want to take a dive into directing."

Bel laughed. "Well, it isn't like you to tip-toe."

He grinned.

"This is huge. What about acting?" his dad asked.

Gage pulled in a breath. "I love acting. It saved me, and now I want more. I want the creativity, the chance to turn my vision into reality. I'll still act, but I see myself slowly exchanging one for the other."

"You've always been so creative. I think this is the perfect way to dig deeper, to really see one of your visions through to fruition. You know how I feel about dipping your fingers into more than one pot. Your sister and I are behind you one hundred percent. Just tell us what you need, and keep us posted."

"I will. I'm really excited about this. More than I have been in a long time. It is a change I need, and it's a chance for me to really show what I'm made of."

Bel shook her head. "What are you talking about? You're one of the hottest actors in Hollywood."

Gage flattened his hands on the table, focusing on spreading his fingers as wide as he could while he talked. "For right now, but that won't last forever, and it doesn't mean anything. Not really. I can be in a movie that's total crap and it still sells. That doesn't say anything about my talent or worth, only the current trends and celebrity crushes. Right now I'm it, but when I'm not, what do I have left?" Flexing his fingers, he dropped his hands to his thighs. "I want respect for my talent and vision, not just fame because I've got a certain look."

"Then if it's what you want, it's what you'll do. I get it," she said.

"There's more. I got offered a chance to co-direct and star in a new project. It has amazing potential."

"That sounds like good news. Why the serious face?" Bel raised her brows.

He sighed. "Cecilia is part of the cast."

Both his dad and sister leaned back in their chairs. His dad was the first to speak. "Does she have a major role?"

"No, a small one. But you know how she is." Gage darted his gaze to his dad's. "Sorry."

Bel reached her hand out and touched the top of Gage's hand. "Does Sam factor into this?"

DC raised a hand. "Who's Sam?"

"One of his friends," she said, making air quotes around the word "friends."

Gage sighed. "She doesn't actually, not this specifically, but since you brought her up, loud mouth, things on set are fine. She's a talented writer."

His sister's eyes narrowed in that analytical way of hers, and a huge smile lit her eyes. "I'm glad it's all working out. You know we're excited about *any* plans you make."

Remembering last night, he shifted in his seat. He wasn't saying another word, besides they wouldn't want to know what was on his mind right then. And as far as Cecilia was concerned, he wanted to keep her as far away from Sam as possible. There wasn't anything to discuss, and the little there was he needed to keep a big fucking secret.

Gage covered the bill and a few minutes later herded them out under the back covered patio and into the bright California sun where they said their goodbyes. He and Bel stood a moment just in the shadows of the awning, chatting. "Hey, there's a young woman over there trying not to be noticed by you. A fan?"

He glanced over and saw Dani, Martin's assistant, turn

three shades of red at being caught. He invited her over with a wave.

"Hey, Mr. Cutler."

"Gage, and this is my sister, Belina."

Dani shook Bel's extended hand and ducked her head. Her mass of hair, tucked up under a messenger hat, escaped in wispy tendrils, and her fitted top matched her dark-washed skinny jeans. She had a rockin' figure, which for some would be even more enticing due to her shy demeanor, but she seemed very young. On set, she was efficient, always on hand to help out, worked hard, and never seemed to tire.

"Are you headed to the set?" he asked.

Dani nodded. "Yeah, but my car decided to go on strike. Could you tell Mr. Gallagher I'll be there soon? I called him, but hearing from you will confirm my story."

"No problem. But why don't I take you, and we'll figure out your car situation later?"

"Really? No, I couldn't. Are you sure? That isn't necessary. I don't want to bother you."

Bel laughed. "Are you kidding? Driving a pretty woman around is never a bother to Gage Cutler. One of the reasons people find him so charming."

He narrowed his eyes. "Nice." He turned toward Dani. "Never mind her, she's a brat. Come on, let's get to work."

Before he could step away, Bel leaned up and kissed his cheek, her blond hair fluttering in the breeze. "Look, I know you don't want to talk about it right now, but do me a favor and be careful with Sam, with your expectations. Protect your heart, okay? Love ya, big brother."

Gage smiled in return. His sister worried, and he got that. But he wasn't worried. There were certain things he wanted in his life, new directions he wanted to take, and Sam was one of them.

He hadn't gotten where he was by taking "no" for an answer.

. . .

Sam tried to focus on her work, but her eyes kept drifting to Gage. It had been a couple days since they'd been together, but the sight of him still turned her inside out. They'd planned on meeting for coffee out at his place, but plans had to be cancelled. Gage's work was demanding, and he was often given very short notice, whether for last-minute meetings or interviews.

She enjoyed watching him. Every move he made, his expressions and gestures, seemed different now. Stronger and sexier. Like she knew something no one else did, a special heated secret. Giving in, she pushed away from her desk and stepped closer, watching from around the corner of a shelf full of equipment. Ever since they'd talked about the dialogue earlier on, he'd nailed his character. With every "Action!" she'd found her mind drifting away from the screenplay in front of her and getting lost in the drama on the set — and memories of his performance between the sheets.

She blew out an excited breath. *Pull it together, Dekker.* Going back to her desk, she stopped short and then sat down, leaning on her elbows to take a closer look. Spread across the top was a magazine opened to a section sporting pictures of Gage — and another woman.

A heavy weight settled in her gut as visions of Ethan's eight-by-ten glossies crowded her mind. There, in full color,

Gage walked along the beach with a lithe blonde, laughing at some private joke, and another picture showcased them in a tight embrace.

No. No. This was not happening. She slapped her hand on the magazine and bunched it in her fist. This was why she had her no celebrity rule.

Being one of his groupies in a revolving door of willing warm bodies would never work for her. Besides, it was dangerous. She only slept with one man at a time. She deserved the same consideration.

Why did he push so hard for them to be together if he was seeing someone else? He knew her better than this. She tripped on that thought and slowed down. Smoothing the magazine out, she studied the front again.

Her emotions, raw and exposed, softened as she looked at the joy on his face. Whoever the woman was, she made him happy. Sam rubbed the back of her neck.

When the crew stopped for a quick break, she walked up to Gage. "Can we talk?"

He raised a brow but put his hand to the small of her back and guided her through the crowded space and out the door.

In the privacy of his trailer, Sam slid the magazine in front of Gage. "I know it's nothing; I mean, I don't know."

"What the hell?" He flipped through the magazine. "Shit, my sister's going to be mortified." Glancing up at her he said, "Where'd you get this?"

She blinked in mute relief.

"Sam."

"That's your sister?"

With a nod, he pushed a box in front of her, with a

hesitant smile. "Here, I got you something."

"You didn't have to do that." Tilting her head, she glanced at him and then slowly lifted the lid. There inside was a decadent peanut butter truffle from The Chocolate Box—perks of being a celebrity with a whole crew at his fingertips, she was sure. But the thought was just the same, and her heart took a little stumble. Biting into the chocolate, she didn't care, and she didn't have to fake the look of pleasure on her face, either. She always felt this way with him. "Delicious. Peanut butter's my favorite. Thank you."

"I remember."

She looked at him. He'd remembered from the night they'd met, the night he'd made her see everything she hadn't been getting from her marriage. It mattered. She couldn't put a finger on exactly why, but he'd listened to her then and listened to her now. And it mattered. Old insecurities released their grip one finger at a time with each word he'd spoken.

She bit into her chocolate again.

As far as the magazine went, he'd been on a walk with his sister, and the paparazzi jumped on the photo op. Any time spent with Gage came with the risk of paparazzi, rumors, and gaudy headlines. What she didn't know was how it made its way to her table. She watched as Gage pushed it from him, and she cursed the damn paparazzi.

The gossip they'd spread about Ethan and her marriage before the accident had made her look like a fool, and now that she knew there'd been some truth behind it, she *was* a fool. What had come after his death had been even worse.

The pictures with his sister reinforced Sam's reasons why she'd never be serious with a celebrity, but it also reminded her that she and Gage needed to keep their fun a secret if they didn't want their pictures plastered everywhere as well. The tabloids were cruel and unusual punishment.

"Her name is Belina, which she hates, but it means Goddess, so of course our mother had to have it." Gage looked at the picture on the pages of the magazine.

Goddess? Of course? Sam didn't know anything about his mother to understand that comment. Nothing beyond the rumors that floated about connecting him to Cecilia Lombardi, but no one really believed that nasty tale. Besides, the woman was adamant about the fact she didn't even know Gage, and he was nothing if not consistent when it came to commenting on rumors.

He didn't.

"My dad and I call her Bel."

Sam smiled and looked down at the photo. They were obviously siblings and close ones at that. It explained the freedom she'd seen on his face. Their coloring alone—and not to mention their body language—practically screamed brother and sister. At least it did now that she knew they were. She shook her head. "She's very pretty. I'm sorry, but I had to ask."

Dang it, don't apologize, Sam. You are allowed to ask questions.

He picked up her hand, staring at the two together, and then pressed his lips against her knuckles. Heat seeped in and snaked up her arm. He lingered there and she let him.

"I'm not going to see anyone else while we're seeing each other, Sam."

"It's not like I have any right to ask, but—"

Pressing his lips into a thin line, he looked away and

then back to her eyes. "You're right, but I can offer it."

Her phone buzzed, and she peeked at it, distracted by the honest intensity in his eyes.

What in the hell is wrong with you?! We want what's ours.

Her hands went numb, hurt pounding in her chest, and she pulled in a breath to try and ease the discomfort. It didn't work. Tapping the screen, she closed the text and slid her phone into her pocket.

"What's wrong? Something happen?"

The concern tugged at her. It wasn't a common experience for her, from a man. Uncharted territory. She wished she'd met Gage years ago. She'd have written a different story for herself then, but then again he'd still be a celebrity.

Sam shook her head and forced a smile on her lips. Standing, she said, "No, no. Everything's fine. We need to get back to the set."

He nodded as he pushed up from his seat. "Fine, let's finish this first." He held out a morsel oozing with creamy peanut butter. She pushed the text and the magazine out of her mind, and held his eyes as she wrapped her lips around the sweet, sucking on his finger as he slid it from her mouth. His eyes dilated, and she grinned. Without warning, he snaked his arms around her waist and pulled her in tight. "You should really share."

As he moved his lips over hers, she closed her eyes with a sigh. She could get used to sharing if this was how it was done. Sliding her tongue against his, tension raced deep to her center, forming a tight ball of need. She pressed into him, closer, and ran her fingers up over his shoulders and into his hair, loving his groan as she tugged with a gentle grip.

She'd have to stay on her toes. A physical relationship with Gage promised to be fun, and she counted on moving forward. But the man saw too much, already knew too much—and that could be dangerous.

Maybe the new her liked a little danger. That would teach her to think light and easy would actually be easy.

Chapter Seven

The crew broke for the day with the plan to reconvene later that evening to shoot a night sequence. Sam and Gage had decided on working late and had dinner called to the set. She gazed out the front window, lost in thoughts of him as the landscape changed with the lowering sun in shadows of shifting colors and textures.

Neither mentioned the tabloid, to Sam's relief, but it still left an itch behind her shoulder blades. Being with Gage, even in a no strings, no commitment kind of way, wasn't wise. She glanced at Gage through lowered lashes as he approached. But damn if she could help herself. He gave her something she needed—to be desired and to desire. It was heady, and she wanted more.

"That was really sweet of you today, the way you helped Dani out."

He shot her a brief look, then focused his attention back to the script in his hand. "It's what anyone would have done."

"No, it's not. Especially not a celebrity. I'm just saying. It was sweet."

He grunted, a sound more noncommittal than saying nothing at all. The sun's light, shining through the large picture window, washed through the profile of his eyes, and they glowed. His rugged features and a day's growth on his jaw made her fingers itch to explore every angle. She wanted him, was drawn to him. A giddy excitement bubbled in her stomach, withering her appetite for food and wetting her appetite for a different kind of consumption altogether.

Gage dropped to a chair at the table and crooked his finger at her.

The small thrumming in her heart increased as she approached him. "What?"

He took her hand and pulled her toward him, between his legs. Lifting the hem of her top, he leaned forward and ran his tongue along her skin just above her waistband, sending waves of goose bumps along her skin. She sucked in her breath.

"I've been waiting forever to get my hands on you again."

She closed her eyes and then snapped them open as she fell to his lap. He gripped her head in his hands as he kissed her, and she wrapped her arms around his neck to get closer. The thrumming in her heart turned to full-on crescendo. She smiled against his mouth. "I don't know if I'll ever get used to that."

He laughed. "That's a good thing."

"Like I said earlier, you're sweet, but you need to be careful. One of these times you might help out the wrong person. What if Dani had been a crazy Gage Cutler fan? God knows there are plenty of those running around."

Gage grimaced. "Please."

When Gage didn't answer, she looked up to find him staring at her with those eyes of his, more green than blue at the moment.

She pressed a kiss to his mouth again. "I'm serious. Everyone wants a piece of Hollywood's bad boy." Sam wanted to yank back her words and shove them right back into her mouth.

Holding her gaze, he dragged his thumb over her lower lip. "Are you jealous?"

She tensed. "What? No." The indignation in her voice was not helping her cause at all. She could see his ego growing with every word. Shit.

"I haven't been a bad boy for a long time. I've changed. Started changing years ago. Hollywood's just slow on catching up. The dating, the drinking, reckless driving. I haven't had a traffic violation in over two years. I drink socially, but I try not to use it when shit's tough."

She nodded, warming that he'd share with her. He was changing, but the kind of change he talked about took time and constant effort. Being a celebrity made it ten times more difficult, because Hollywood didn't like to say goodbye to its bad boys.

Sliding his hands to her ass, he squeezed, and in a low, rough voice said, "You have no reason to be jealous. Besides, the one who needs to be careful is you. I'm hungry, and I feel like I haven't eaten for days."

A knock at the door promised dinner and a way out of her screw-up. Jumping up from his lap, she laughed, then skirted around the film equipment to the front of the house. Thanking the security guard, she took the bags and made quick time of getting back to the dining room. As she slid into her seat, she studied Gage's face and parceled out dinner.

"Tell me more about your feelings toward these crazy Cutler fans."

Ignoring him, she looked him over from across the table, and purposely biting her lower lip, pushed her silverware around and then lined each piece up in straight lines once more. "Do you know your eyes are sometimes green and sometimes blue?"

He cocked a brow. "Really? You want to talk about my eyes?"

That showed what he knew; his eyes really were alluring. She raised her brows.

Gage stared at her a moment and grinned, taking a long swallow from his glass. "Fine, last I checked my eyes were blue."

Adrenaline emboldened her as she held his gaze. "Not when you're coming; then they're green."

Gage choked.

Sam's heart lurched and her face flushed a few thousand degrees hotter. Flirting with him was its own kind of high, and she wanted more.

A bark of laughter broke from his lips, and he tried to muffle it with his napkin, knowing security wasn't too far off. Gage leaned in. "To be honest, I've never seen my eyes when I—"

Sam threw her hand up. "No, God, don't say it again." She squirmed in her seat as heat flushed her skin. She wasn't sure if it was from her embarrassment or his gaze.

He slid those damned eyes up and down her body, at

least what was visible above the table, and took bite of his scallops, chewing while he teased, "Are you kidding? I can totally get on board with this change in topic."

"I'm not changing the topic." Her face warmed.

He cocked his brow again. "I want to hear more about the color of my eyes, and *anything* to do with 'coming.'"

Well, she did start it. Sam snatched a piece of ice from her glass and sucked the end of it. Then, with slow purposeful movements, she ran the cube over her jaw and down the side of her neck. If they were going to keep this fun and playful, she needed to do her part. Besides, pushing the envelope was more fun than she'd ever imagined. She might just need to try it more often. Her voice low, forcing him to lean closer, she said, "Your eyes are blue when you're calm, in control. But when you get hot, when your body tightens with wanting, they glow a light cyan. As you get closer—you know what I mean by closer."

Gage all but lay across the table, paying rapt attention to her every word. He nodded with the slightest of movement.

"When your skin slides against my skin, my breasts pressed against your chest, your body so tight, so hot that it can't handle even, one…more…stroke. Bam!" She slapped the table.

Gage jumped, and she laughed. He grabbed his napkin to wipe his brow and downed the rest of his water in one long swallow.

"Green."

"What?" Gage asked. She tried not to enjoy herself too much, but he deserved it. If he wasn't going to let her off the hook, she'd put him on one.

"Green; then your eyes are green. A bright, luminescent

green. Your eyes are so light it seems like I can see through them." She looked at him with an innocent smile and then took a bite of her salad.

Gage held her gaze while she chewed. He watched her mouth, and she felt his gaze all the way to her toes, and that darned shiver returned. Without warning, he grabbed the bag and tossed in his utensils and napkin. "We need this packed up to go. Now."

"What?"

Gage continued to sweep his eyes over all of her secret places. "You're going to show me."

Gage placed the rest of the food into the to-go bag and stood.

She put her hand out to stop him. "You can't be serious." Actually, this was exactly what she wanted. "On second thought…"

He remained silent and offered her his hand, palm up. She took it with a giggle, and he pulled her to her feet. "Go, I'll meet you," he said.

Sam made her way to her car, smiling as she watched Gage's car lights disappear in the distance. Stepping through the driveway gate, she listened to the crickets chirp and looked over all the color the early evening painted on the canyon. Turning toward her car, she froze and stared in horror as Ethan Evans' mother lifted her chin a notch higher. Dread spread throughout her limbs, heaviest at her heart, as she gripped her keys tighter in her hand. She couldn't imagine how the woman found the set, much less knew Sam worked on it.

Gage's car approached and pulled to a stop behind Mrs. Evans', and he got out.

He jerked his chin toward the woman. "I saw the car and then remembered there shouldn't be anyone here besides security."

"*This* is how you honor my son's death? Cavorting with the man responsible? I knew you had no class, Samantha, but this takes you to a low *I* didn't even see. Ethan was an artist." Ethan's mother waved her hand as if in disgust at Gage. "This *man* is nothing more than a common man-whore."

Sam sucked in a breath and took a step toward the woman. "How dare you? Gage isn't responsible, and you know it."

Ethan's mother continued, relentless. "On second thought, you two do deserve each other."

Gage moved in front of Sam, his hands fisted at his sides. She reached out to stop him, but he resisted her efforts. Once he stood nose to nose with the woman, he towered over her, breathing hard through clenched teeth. "Now I see where your misogynistic bully of a son got his manners. Stay away from Samantha."

Mrs. Evan's jaw dropped open, and her eyes narrowed into slits. "Or what?"

He stepped forward, and she almost fell trying to get away from him.

Sam swept past the woman, grabbed her things from her own car, and then marched back to Gage's, nodding at him to get in. They slammed the doors closed against her accusations, and Sam trembled, her chest both tight and heavy—and something else.

"I'm so sorry you had to see that. I'm sorry she said—"

"You aren't responsible. You stood up for me, and I'll always do the same for you. I watch out for my friends, Sam."

She shot him a look, his words warming her heart. The last thing she wanted was anyone else hurting him the way she had. "But you shouldn't have to. That woman can turn a white dove into a creature of the night with her foul breath alone."

He chuckled and then shot her a hard look. "I'll call my lawyer, and he'll see to it that any comments from the Evanses will be silenced."

He was sweet to try, but Sam knew the power of gossip. It played a part in pushing Ethan to take his own life. Lucky for her and Gage, Mrs. Evans had no photos to go along with any of her dosed poison. In tabloids, words were water, but photos were wine.

Once the woman's headlights disappeared from sight, Gage asked, "Why were things so bad with Ethan? Is it why his family is treating you like this?"

Settling deeper into the seat, Sam pulled at a string on her slacks. "He'd been the perfect boyfriend, painted a beautiful picture of our future together. Then once we were married it all changed. He was never home, but he also didn't want me going out alone. Always so jealous. He hated that I had a career and that I was good at it. I finally realized he married me as a way to enhance a status that only he saw. Like being married to someone in the industry increased his chances of success, kind of like a politician. Show the happy couple, happy family. Now I know it was a means to gain the trust of young starlets." She grimaced. "Turns my stomach."

Gage sighed. "And his family?"

"He was their golden boy; he could do no wrong. I never measured up in their eyes, and they agreed I should be home waiting on him instead of carving out my own career. He'd wanted me to get pregnant, but by that time I knew ours wasn't a family to bring a child into. Now that he's gone, they've never forgiven me."

Leaning forward, Gage brushed his lips across her brow. "You're more than a prop, Sam."

Sam grabbed his shoulders and pressed her mouth to his. He understood. She didn't know how, but the man got her. She'd never been able to put her pain in words before, but he saw it right away. She'd been nothing more than a means to an end with Ethan. She wasn't sure which was worse, feeling worthless or being seen as worthless.

But not now, not anymore, and not ever again.

Pulling back, she grabbed his hand, feeling lighter than she had in years. "Let's go. I have something to show you."

• • •

They rode in silence until Gage pulled into his garage. He grabbed their dinner, walked around the car, and opened the door for Sam. Anger and concern rolled in his gut. The nerve of that woman. How could the two women closest to Ethan Evans not have seen what a dick he was? He shook his head.

Sam stepped out with a questioning look.

"We still have to eat. And since my *preferred* menu is no longer on the table, this will have to do."

His humor pulled her lips into a smile, as he'd hoped. A wave of protectiveness washed over him, whether he had the right to feel it or not, and he reached for her hand. "Come on."

She slid her hand into his.

He couldn't believe how much she'd dealt with over the past year. Most people wouldn't have handled it with her grace or courage. Shit, she still lived in the home where she'd found her husband dead.

It was really no wonder any kind of relationship with celebrities terrified her. Hollywood hadn't exactly been gentle and wouldn't be in the future, either. Living in the spotlight wasn't for sissies. That was for damn sure.

They stepped onto the sun-warmed California beach sand behind his house and made their way down to the water's edge. He spread a light blanket out on the ground.

Sam raised her brows. "Aren't we prepared."

He winked. "You'd have been disappointed if I wasn't. I don't want to tarnish the bad boy reputation you still think I have." He tipped his chin, back in the direction they'd just come. "I keep it in my trunk with a few other odds and ends."

"Of course. By the way, you've earned the reputation. I haven't given you anything."

"How about just an inch?"

She laughed. "Okay, okay. I'm just teasing."

They kicked off their shoes and sank to the blanket. Gage emptied the bag, placing their meal in the center. "How long has that been going on?"

She met his eyes, then looked at the waves rolling in and ending in a frothy layer of bubbles at their toes. "Since we said, 'I do.' His mother couldn't stand me or the fact he'd married a writer when he was surrounded by beautiful Hollywood actresses."

"And here I thought she didn't like actors."

"Not for me, no, but for her son. I'm sorry about that. You didn't deserve her wrath. That *was* for me."

"Really? Because if I remember the tabloids correctly"—he curled his fingers into quotation marks—"Playboy hot rod Gage Cutler killed photo journalist superstar Ethan Evans."

She swallowed with a wince, then quickly took another bite.

He didn't need a confirmation of his sins. "Is that why you stayed away from me after he died?"

Sam hesitated, her troubled brown eyes wavering. "Yes. I was wrong. I'm sorry, Gage."

The pain in his chest spread to his gut, and the few bites he'd taken sat like a stone in his stomach. Wiping his hands with a napkin, he nodded once, then looked on down the beach.

He gritted his teeth. His career, his misdeeds, would always haunt him. They would always lead judge and jury to condemn. It didn't matter what changes he'd made or would make. His mistakes were a brick wall, ten feet thick, and no one was willing to open a door and let him walk through, much less leave it behind. But Hollywood was a funny monster. He'd still get the best movies, still received the highest awards. The industry loved a screwed-up super star, but what he wanted was for them to love *him*.

Continuing down this particular road could only hurt him more. He tried to swallow. "Why didn't you tell me?"

Sam paused. "Tell you what?"

"The Evanses."

"Why would I bother you with that?" She shrugged.

"So I could help."

"Aww, Gage. I couldn't expect that from you. You aren't my boyfriend, and we aren't dating." She put her hand out.

"I'm not being mean. I'm just clarifying where we are. It wouldn't be fair of me to ask you to fix my problems. "

Irritation burned his throat like sour whiskey. "That's fine, but we are friends."

She grinned. "We are friends. But don't worry, I can handle it. They're my problem. Besides, it's just words. Harmless."

"Words are not harmless."

Something passed over Sam's face, but she shuttered the emotion and continued eating.

Gage lay back on the blanket with his hands behind his head and sighed. He loved the ocean, the fresh air, and the sounds of the crashing waves. With his eyes closed and the setting sun warm on his skin, he could disappear into his senses. No disappointments, no one to disappoint. No reason to want or be wanted.

He glanced at her. She was right. They weren't dating, but that was simply semantics. He'd help her anyway he could. He cared, goddamn it. "How'd you get into screenwriting?"

"It's in my blood. We've a distant relative, Thomas Dekker, from back in the late 1500s who was a theater writer." Preening, she said with a wink, "You could say I was born for it." Laughing, she lay down on her side. "Seriously, though, I've always told stories, written them down. I was a movie addict growing up. My mom would bribe me with them to get good grades and do my chores. It worked. After college, my dad introduced me to Martin, and that was it. He taught me so much."

Gage nodded. "As he does. I don't know what I'd do without him myself." Martin was a mentor to so many in Malibu. Gage understood Sam's reverence for the man, because he shared it too.

Rolling to face him, she lay with her head propped up on one hand, and slid her other down his forearm until she found his hand on his abdomen.

Turning his over, he laced his fingers through hers. Their entwined hands raised and lowered with his breath. Exactly what he craved. A connection that rode the tides of life without letting go.

The heat of her hand remained on his for less than a second before she drew away and sat up, as if remembering something. The loss of warmth first chilled him, but then he saw it as a challenge. He gripped his hands together to keep from reaching out to her—for now.

But there was no way in hell he'd ride this wave out alone. She might not see it yet, but she was coming with him.

Chapter Eight

The evening sequence flowed seamlessly. The timing, the pacing, and the performance of the actors, a director's dream. Gage acted with an unexpected edginess that worked perfectly for the scene they'd been after.

Sam glanced at the screenplay. With no reason for her to hang around the rest of the day, no more polishing necessary, no more dialogue to doctor, she stood. Why was she still there? She didn't want to touch the answer to that question. If the rest of the manuscript proved this brilliant, she'd seriously question their decision to have her on set. *You know why Gage wants you here and why you want to stay*.

Sam squared her shoulders. Maybe she did, but she was there for another reason as well. Dialogue and pacing killed many manuscripts. Having a master saved a lot of money in the long run. She was that master.

She was necessary, and it felt damned good.

Screen timing could make or break a sequence, and she

had a knack for figuring out just the right combinations of dialogue and subtext. Her extra work had been paying off, too. She pulled in a breath with a nod.

The crew called for a break, and she went in search of Martin. No matter how many excuses she gave for hanging around, none of them held a kernel of the real truth, and frankly, there was no reason for her to stay any longer tonight. As she skirted in and out of all the different mountains of equipment, she stopped to watch Gage chatting with the crew.

She smiled. The man was a magnet. Everyone smiled, completely engaged with him. Dani stared in rapt attention, taking a few pics with her phone and then leaning in to hear better, next to a camera man who did the same. Sam couldn't blame her.

"He's something, isn't he?"

Without thinking, Sam breathed, "He is." *Shit!* She spun around. "I mean —"

Martin put his hand up to stop her. "Don't make me call you a liar. I will." The man still radiated his presence, as she imagined he had in his prime. He stepped up beside her and watched as she had. "It's time."

She didn't want to ask. "Time?" Not wanting to give him the chance to expound, she rushed on, "time for me to go home? Good, that's what I thought, too. As a matter of fact, I was just coming to find you to say good night. I —"

"Nice try." He turned toward her, and placing his hand at her lower back, maneuvered her over toward two director's chairs. "Sit."

She complied with sagging shoulders. *Fuhhhh!*

"When are you going to move on? I see you spending

time with Gage." He put his hand up when she opened her mouth to argue. "I swear, if you deny it, I will call you out in front of every person here."

"I'm not denying anything." She laughed. "We're friends. I think he's an incredible actor."

He studied her a moment and then moved on to her great relief. "I talked to your father yesterday."

Okay, she wasn't relieved at all. "You what?" An ache formed between her brows. Now that had her attention. She was very close with her parents and two siblings. So close she hadn't wanted to burden them with her pathetic drama—any of it. Instead, she'd just cried off from family dinners with the excuse of being too busy with the film. *Damn. I bet Dad called.*

"You haven't been home, and you haven't been going out. You can't count working with Gage. Hell, you dance around the poor man like he'd shock you if you got too close."

Sam puffed up her chest and sputtered. Little did Martin know it was simply a symptom of wanting to jump Gage's bones, and she wanted to keep it that way. "I do not—this is silly. You can all quit worrying about me. Between you, Raquel, and my parents, I swear. I admire Gage, his work. It still amazes me that I can create a story, but the true art is bringing it to life. He does that."

"Well, that's something, then. I always knew you had good taste."

Martin and her father had been close friends for years. It was lovely, but at times felt as though she had two dads. "I should, you made sure it was similar to yours." She paused. "You know, I'm actually doing really well. I may not share every moment of my life. But I've been doing things. Important things. I'm writing, I've decided to get out to the water regularly, slowly making changes in the condo." She rubbed his shoulder. "Quit worrying."

The intensity of his eyes lightened, the deep creases at the corners softening. "Can't help it."

"You don't need—"

The old man growled. Actually growled.

Sam sat back in her chair and chuckled. "Look, I'm fine. Tell my dad I'm fine. Better yet, I'll go tell him myself this weekend. I just—"

He stood. He bent and kissed Sam on the top of her head. "I'm glad you're okay. Keep at it. You never know, maybe you and Gage."

She shook her head and smiled. "Don't start. You know my rule."

He put his hands up. "Okay, okay, just throwing out ideas." Clearing his voice, he called the crew back to work.

Sam stepped away, out into the cool night air, and called her dad. She hadn't meant for them to worry. For Pete's sake, she called every Sunday, but apparently that hadn't been good enough. He'd called Martin! Geesh. She felt twelve years old again.

Her dad's voice answered strong and steady on the line—just like him.

Minutes ticked by and Sam enjoyed every one. They talked longer than she'd expected. Some of the crew had trickled out and off the set when her mom's voice eventually carried across the line. "Honey, say you'll come to dinner Sunday."

A noise behind her made her turn around, and she

found Gage walking up to her with his hands shoved into his front pockets. An idea took shape. A brilliant one, if she did say so herself. "Mom."

"Don't 'mom' me. I already know you'll have time. Your father spoke with Martin—"

She made a silly face at Gage. "Mom, can I bring a friend?" Her mother had been a huge fan since he'd started out, and Sam was going to have great fun exposing him to her mother the fan-girl. The silence on the other end worried her. "Mom?"

"A friend?"

"Yeah, Gage Cutler. We've been working a lot together, and I know you're a huge—"

"Gage Cutler? In my house?" Her mother's scream carried over the line and straight to Gage's ego.

Sam rolled her eyes as he puffed out his chest. It was all very simple. She'd bring Gage home for dinner, and her family, including Martin, would get off her back. No more, no less.

"Bring me to what?" He smiled down at her with those damn intriguing eyes.

Turning slightly, she said into the phone. "Mom, I gotta go."

She tucked her phone into the pocket of her slacks, turning back to face him. "So, yeah. That was my mom. I have to go to dinner Sunday."

"And."

She tucked her shirt more firmly inside her waistband and then smoothed down the front. "I was wondering if you'd come with me?" She put her hand up, rushing on. "We wouldn't have to stay long. I know you're busy—"

He took an immediate step toward her and then tucked his arms behind his back. "Sam, I'd love to." His eyes shone bright, and he sported a grin that could compete against any she'd seen in his many photo ops. The air rushed right out of her lungs.

The man was so much, all the time. His genuine acceptance of going to her family's home made her want to climb him like a flag pole to stake her claim and run in the opposite direction all at the same time.

Before he totally lost his head, she warned. "No funny business. We're friends, but I don't need my mom making too much of this. If we aren't careful, she'll have an officiant scheduled before dinner's over."

He overplayed a feigned look of disappointment, slapping his hand over his chest. "You don't trust me? What did I ever do to you?"

She eyed him. "Plenty, and I liked it, but my parents never need to know."

He gathered her up against him. "I like when you talk dirty to me."

Slapping him on the arm, she pulled away with a laugh. "Oh my God. Whatever." She put some distance between them. It was the only way she could think. "This will give my family something to ease their worry. They've had a rough time of it this past year. I don't want them to worry anymore."

He turned toward her. "Look, you don't want anyone to know we're kind of seeing each other. I get it. But don't you think when it comes to your family, the best thing you can do is let them see you moving forward? Then they'll all lay off."

But if her parents saw her making friends, working—not

hiding—it would go a long way toward giving them some peace. Ethan's suicide hadn't only been hard for her.

He had a point, but there needed to be rules. She put her hand out. "Before you agree…"

Mischief danced in his eyes. "I already did." He couldn't help but smile; he was so damned pleased with himself.

"There need to be rules."

That sobered him up a bit. "Like?"

"We are not dating. We're friends, coworkers." She ticked each item off on her fingers. "There will be no insinuations, no innuendos, no cleverly colored phrases indicating we've been together."

His brow furrowed. "Sam, this is your dad we're talking about. The last thing I want to do is put the idea of me sleeping with his daughter in his head."

She grinned. "Good point. Okay."

"Yeah?" A grin spread ear to ear across his face.

"We can drive together, but we'll pull directly into my parents' garage and close the door. My mom won't tell anyone; she won't want to do anything to keep you from coming."

He wiggled his brows.

"You think you're so clever." She rolled her eyes.

Gage laughed, and with his hands on her shoulders, steered her back into the house. "Yes, I do."

Once inside and back in her secluded corner, he turned her around to face him and walked her back against a work-table with slow, purposeful steps. "I'm going to meet your parents."

"It doesn't mean anything."

"I know, but I'm going to enjoy watching you squirm."

Well, the joke was on him. Her family never shut up. He'd be exhausted by the night's end and beg to never go back. She stuck her tongue out at him, but pressed her lips against his to shut him up instead. His hands closed around her hips, pulling her closer to him, and she reveled in the fact he couldn't get enough of her, either. She mumbled against his lips, teasing. "Don't make me change my mind."

The cold metal of a table against her back caught her attention. The voices of the crew mingling outside before heading home could be heard through the closed door. She slanted him a look. "What are you doing?"

Gage crowded her. "You still have to show me." He ducked his head and breathed in against her neck, then dragged his lips past her pulse and up to her lips. Bending her back over the top of the table, all she could do was hold on or lose her footing.

Her stomach exploded into a fury of tiny flutters, and she spoke against his mouth. "Wait."

He pulled back slightly, but his lips still tickled hers with each word he uttered in precise bullets. "I. Don't. Want. To."

"Take me home, to my home."

His tongue, sliding down the side of her neck, sent goose bumps erupting along her skin. He stilled. "You want me to take you to your house?"

She knew what he was thinking. The home she'd shared with Ethan. But she was taking it back, making it hers. Having him in it—and she meant *having* him—would do the trick. "Yes, we need to go wash the filth of our encounter with Margaret Evans off of our skin."

He hesitated. She didn't blame him if he'd changed his mind about their situation. He had something to lose, too. "I don't know. If anyone sees us — "

"I live in a condo full of retirees who are in bed by seven at night. I rarely, if ever, see anyone. We'll be careful." A warm sensation spread through her core when he pressed his body tight against hers. His heat, the pounding of his heart, could be felt through the layers of fabric that separated them.

He growled low in his throat. "Come on."

She was taking control of her own life, damn it. Living, feeling, and experiencing pleasure in her home, her space, on her terms.

They made it back to her place in record time, slamming the door closed with a well-aimed shove of Sam's foot. She shoved at his jacket, but he held her too close to make any head way, and he pulled at her shirt, but she was too engrossed in loosening the belt and buttons of his jeans.

She growled, a playful but frustrated sound, and stilled his hands. "Me first."

Pushing his jacket off of his shoulders, she let him work on dropping it to the floor as she unleashed his belt and whipped it out with a resounding ziiiiip. Grabbing the front of his jeans, she struggled with his zipper, her hands shaking. Finally, she shoved the denim over his hips, dragging his briefs down with them, and he was left standing in her kitchen in his full naked glory. Her mouth went dry, opposite the forecast of her panties, and she slid her hands over his chest and then down the ridges of his hard abs. "Sweet Jesus, you are too much."

She swallowed as he removed her top and bra and then pulled her up against his chest. The heat of him was waking her body like a cold splash of water. She was tired of hiding. It was time to take charge of not only her life, but her pleasure, too. She all but dragged him to her shower. Turning the knob for the water warm, she slid up his body.

Never in her whole relationship with Ethan would she ever have touched him quite like this, taking control, making demands. She couldn't have pinned his arms back like she was with Gage. She couldn't have groaned her pleasure like she did with Gage to let him know how much she wanted him. Ethan would have told her to stop embarrassing herself, where Gage encouraged her to do more, say more, and feel so much more.

Gage picked her up, and she wrapped her thighs around his waist. He stepped into the shower, their tongues skimming along one another, slick and sweet. The hot water ran along their skin in rivulets, and Sam lowered her legs until she stood in front of him, his length trapped between her thighs and pressed against her core. She pulled back just a bit, then pushed forward, shuddering at the feel of him sliding against her.

He pressed his mouth to hers and pulled her close. There was such give and take, it heightened every sensation—almost too much to bear.

Every hard angle and muscled mound of his body called to her, and she kissed him back.

His hands caressed her everywhere, the caps of her shoulders, the length of her arms, along the dip of her spine, and over the round curves of her ass. "Sam."

"I'm showing you." She pushed him down to the shower bench. He pressed his lips into her lower stomach and rubbed his slick fingers between her legs. Pleasure struck fast and sharp, making her knees tremble. She threw her head back and pressed against his hand. Twisting at her waist, she wiped the fogged up door, revealing the mirror over the sink through the vertical slices of glass that ran floor to ceiling. A perfect view of their naked forms enticed them to watch, from only a few feet away in the narrow but long bathroom. Voyeurs and exhibitionists all at the same time.

"God." His voice strained, Gage maneuvered her, pulling her back to straddle his legs, her back to his chest. The heat, the steam, his slippery skin. The feel of his wet lips gliding along her ass. Low in her belly, a white-hot knot of need pulsed heavy and insistent. She wanted nothing more than Gage, right now, her way, this moment. And he wanted her to have him. The knowledge was addicting.

Grabbing his thighs for support, she lowered her hot, throbbing body onto him and watched as he disappeared into her. The sensation of his slick heat stroking her insides, along with the image of their naked bodies in the mirror, pulled a moan from her throat.

Sam splashed the door with water, clearing the steam. "Look, Gage, look at your eyes."

Gage glanced up over her shoulder and his grip tightened at her waist. Her hair hung over her shoulders in dark wet strands around her breasts, his length disappearing into her. But his eyes. They glowed a bright green in contrast with the dark color of her own. Their gazes locked.

She didn't feel shame or embarrassment, but instead raw hunger and urgent need.

Sensation sliced through her body, stealing her breath, building, pushing. He flexed his body beneath her. Pulling out. Pushing in. She reached to a corner shelf and grabbed her mini vibrator. As he moved, she swirled the small device against herself, free, open. This was her, all her, and never again would she hide what she wanted. With Gage she didn't have to.

He never blinked. His eyes grew more intense as he watched, his efforts only increasing. Sam, too, couldn't tear her gaze from the seductive image in the mirror. Their breaths came out in short gasps. Heat rising. Intensity sharpening, stretching.

Sam swiped at the glass door again. His eyes on her filled her with a power she'd never known before. The gentle vibration built in heat and burst into a white light of ecstasy. She bucked back against him.

Wave after wave shot from her core outward, and she buckled forward. Gage held her with his hands on her breasts, forcing her down his shaft with increasing speed.

He pulled her back until she met his gaze once again in the mirror, and she braced her hands against the shower glass wall. Deep rolling throbs radiated from her center with each thrust. Moving one hand to his hard thigh and the other over his hand at her breast, she gave up all control of remaining upright. He flexed and pulled, demanding a deeper entry with each stroke until his head dipped and his lips pressed into her shoulder. His body tight. Both of them straining forward. He never let her falter.

Another wave of pleasure exploded from where their heated flesh joined, and she matched him moan for moan on his last thrust.

Her body limp and pulsing in small echoes, she followed Gage down to the bench and slid her legs out long in front of them, dropping her head back. Gage rained kisses along her neck, up her cheek, and turning her head, captured her lips. The shower continued to spray around them, water sluicing down their limbs.

Sam pressed her lips to his jaw. "Now, I feel clean."

Gage laughed. On a sigh that could only be of exhaustion, or exhilaration—probably both—he all but melted back against the shower wall.

Sam smiled, and pulling his arms around her chest, gave a tight squeeze, the resulting ebb and flow still drumming through her body in light pulses of heat.

Pressing her fingers to her lips, she stared at him through the glass like she was seeing him for the first time. He gave her so much more than he received. In all her time with Ethan, he'd never given her a fraction of what Gage showered upon her, as if he was the one being given a gift.

She bit her lip to keep it from trembling. The idea that she'd simply get him out of her system revealed itself—or rather her—to be ridiculous. It was a shame that foresight wasn't as clear as hindsight because then it may have saved her from her great plans.

She should have known better.

Plans only make you take the first step. They rarely lead you to your destination.

Chapter Nine

Gage and Sam walked onto the film set with the rest of the crew the following morning, calm and collected as if they'd never even entertained the thought of sleeping together. They'd finished their shower the night before and then devoured her cupboard of pastries—a rebellious addition to the kitchen after Ethan had died—talking late into the night. Not until after one last round did they fall into a deep slumber. Well, at least Gage had.

Sam had worried well into the early morning. Conversations deep into the night did not go along with light and easy. She needed to rein them both back in. It was okay if Gage couldn't, or didn't want to; she could and knew she had to. But right now she felt too good to do anything about it. Too warm, too happy—too whole.

They made their way around the line of trailers nearly running into Dani as she hurried around the corner of one.

She pulled up short with a quick look over her shoulder.

"Oh, hi guys." She gave them an absent-minded wave of her fingers and then continued past them at a brisk pace without looking back.

"She's always running from place to place. I'm tired just watching her." Sam shook her head with a chuckle as they made their way inside.

Martin looked up from his table and sent a wink her way. Heat rushed to her temples, and she double-checked to make sure there was appropriate distance between her and Gage. She felt torn in two; on one side she was having an illicit, exciting affair, and on the other she remembered how good it was to share a little of herself last night. She'd opened up to him a little more with each minute. About her family, about Ethan. Gage hadn't been able to understand Ethan's perception of Samantha Dekker. To Gage's way of thinking, there was only one. Only one that had any basis in reality, anyway. His. She appreciated it but couldn't help the pinch that settled between her shoulder blades.

They wound their way back to her worktable when Dani stuck her head around the corner, smiling, and a bit breathless.

Sam smiled with a shake of her head. "Wow, Dani, you are working double time today."

She shrugged and stepped around the shelving. "Busy, busy. Sorry, Mr. Cutler," Dani said, stepping close to Gage.

A little too close as far as Sam was concerned, but before she could finish the thought, Dani turned to her, placing a hand on her arm. "Mr. Gallagher has a few scenes he wants Ms. Dekker to work on right away."

Gage smiled. "See ya later." It came across cool—friendly and dismissing—but Sam had special privilege that allowed her to interpret the smile with a whole different heat.

A high-pitched laugh turned his lips from lava to ice. He froze and then straightened, any good humor a fleeting memory, his face a mask of cement.

Sam reached out to him. "What is it?"

He clenched his hands at his sides but pasted a smile to his face, the effort obvious. With a shake of his head, he waved them on. "Nothing, go. You've got work. I'll catch up with you later."

Sam followed along with Dani but watched Gage over her shoulder. She couldn't help but cut her eyes toward the woman laughing like a crow and then back to Gage. He visibly winced.

Looked like there might be a new cast member. Everyone knew of her feud with Gage, but the woman in question was B-list at best. No one paid attention to her antics—he shouldn't, either.

Cecilia Lombardi caught their glances from the corner of her eye. She turned her head toward Gage and then lifted her nose in the air with a dismissive turn of her head. Sam stopped in her tracks, digging her nails into her palms.

Dani tapped on her arm. "Sorry to rush you, but Martin's waiting." Sam swore Dani smiled, not in a friendly "come along" fashion, but more of a secret amusement kind of way.

She shook herself. For Pete's sake the girl's been nothing but helpful.

Sam nodded, but cut one last narrowed look at Cecilia Lombardi. Sam followed Dani through the maze of cameras, lighting, and cords, barely listening to the assistant ramble on about her excitement for Hollywood. Concern for Gage muddled her focus. She craned her neck to see if he was okay, only to find him still standing in one spot, staring across the room. What was going on?

Shaking her head, she turned her focus to Martin. He grabbed the screenplay. "I want you to take a look at a few scenes that are coming up. I don't see them working with Gage."

He marked the pages and handed her the copy. "I'll need it by the end of the week. Shooting the scenes starts the week after. I want you to take a close look to make sure we have it just right by then."

Sam took the bound papers. "I'll work on it. No problem." She flipped through the pages until she came to the places he'd marked and scanned over the troubling scenes. She choked. "Martin!"

He shook his head with one quick movement. "I don't want to hear it. You'll know what isn't right."

"This is a sex scene."

"An important sex scene. This is the last time his character will feel a woman in his arms, and he knows it. And you know Gage."

Sam shook her head in denial. "I don't know him that well."

Martin stilled her with a hard stare. "You're a woman."

She tilted her head. "Thanks?"

He waved away her sarcasm. "I need another perspective. I want to make sure it's right."

She tapped the screenplay on her thigh. Irritation, or was it embarrassment, settled on her shoulders. She strained to see through all of the equipment to the other side of the set. "So, what's going on over there? Lombardi's hardly worth worrying about."

Martin cleared his throat and pushed up from his seat. "I've got work to do. Take it up with Gage." Then he spoke, sotto voce, as he ambled down the stairs, "God knows I have to."

. . .

Gage turned his back on his mother and made his way as far to the other side of the set as he could possibly go. An ache radiated along his jaw. He forced himself to relax, unclench his teeth, and take a few deep breaths. It amazed him how, at thirty-eight, the sight of the woman smacked him back into his childhood.

It had taken days before Belina had quit crying. She'd refused to be alone. Terrified either he or their father would disappear next. Gage had a persistent shadow from that point on. Though there had been times he'd wanted to strangle her, he wouldn't change a thing. He didn't know many people fortunate enough to have a relationship like he did with his family.

Gage grabbed his copy of the screenplay and flipped through it. He tried to study his lines for the first sequence of the day, but his mind wouldn't cooperate. Images of the last time he'd run into Cecilia crowded to the forefront, blurring the words on the page.

During a premier of one of his movies, they'd bumped into one another on the red carpet. The reporters pounced like hungry hyenas, and the camera flashes were blinding.

Cecilia outright ignored him any time their paths crossed. Rumors had circulated about their relationship, but she firmly denied any association, and he refused to respond at all.

That night, she never even made direct eye contact with him, and they'd been standing within two feet of one another, at *his* premier no less.

The opportunity to capture the two of them at the same time in a photo was too much for any of the paparazzi to resist. His mother loved to feed the frenzy. She'd ranted about the treatment, even deflected questions by saying he'd been a "wanna-be" trying to steal her limelight.

Like he'd need to.

Though that fact didn't ease any of his pain.

How much had he drunk that night? Gage shook his head and licked his lips, suddenly thirsty. It wasn't even ten in the morning yet. But that was before; he was different now. Having to remind himself of the fact annoyed him even more.

Martin Gallagher rounded a corner and stopped in his tracks. His hands were clasped in front of him, and he had a determined set to his jaw.

Gage narrowed his eyes.

Martin threw his hands up. "Now, boy, I know what you're going to say."

"Really?" Gage tossed the screenplay onto the work surface and faced the director. "If you know what I'm going to say, then what is that woman doing here in the first place?" He worked hard to keep his voice from rising. The last thing he wanted was an audience, or for his mother to hear him and start spouting off in histrionics. Each of the scenes she'd caused so far only worsened and strengthened the rumors. The last he'd heard, they were lovers. He'd been sick to his stomach.

Martin sighed and walked toward him. "I know. She's dating the producer. From what I understand, she dropped by to say hello and hoped for the opening in the cast."

Gage gritted his teeth. "I'd heard. I just hoped you'd say no."

"Gage, be reasonable. Don't let her—"

"No. If she's in, I'm out." His heart pounded in his chest as tension tightened down on his shoulders like a vice. He was all bluff and bluster, but seeing her was like getting smacked in the face with a baseball bat. The bright light from an opened door beckoned to him. The set felt like a dungeon, and he needed to escape. He made his way toward the fresh air, pulling a slow breath in and forcing it out.

"Gage. Where are you going?"

"I'll be back for first call." He waved his hand just above his shoulder without looking back.

Cecilia Lombardi might be in bed with the producer, but those were dirty, dirty sheets, and he'd tear the house down around them trying to find a way not to have to shoot a film with her.

Gage tried to shove his mother out of his head as he worked through the long hours. The whole last sequence had been a debacle. He'd been too tense and it showed, which affected his leading lady. The producer, pissed because he'd have to face a lonely bed after having to send his girlfriend home, took it out on Gage—which, though not fun, was well worth the aggression. And Martin terrified the crew, since the sequence resulted in such, well, shit.

The vicious cycle didn't end until the beyond-frustrated director threw his hands up in defeat and called an end to the day.

Gage wanted no part of that and steered clear of Martin. He collected his things and made a beeline to his car. He pulled open the door and tossed his belongings to the passenger's seat.

"Were you really going to leave without seeing me?"

The voice spoken so softly behind him took him back to the night they'd first met in the bar. He dropped his chin to his chest. He wasn't sure if he had the energy to fight his past or fight for his future at the moment.

Sam laid a hand on the center of his back.

"I'm tired. Besides, someone might see you."

Her hand left his back. "Can I come with you?"

"I don't even know where I'm going."

"Let's go to my place. We'll be careful."

The heaviness in his chest fought with the desire to have her close. He nodded once, then walked around the car, and checking over both shoulders, opened the passenger side door.

Sam picked up the items he'd tossed there and got in, settling his things on her lap.

Gage closed the door and walked back around to his side. He had to figure out what to do with her. She didn't want help but wanted to give it, and she didn't want to be taken care of but needed to be, didn't want to be seen, but got in the car with him.

Well, part of that wasn't exactly true. She could technically take care of herself. But if she wasn't pushed out of her comfort zone, she'd never leave it, and there were too many wonderful things about her when she did. He'd been watching her bloom little by little.

He settled in the car, the events over the past weeks rolling through his mind as he drove. His breathing calmed as he pictured Sam's light-hearted smile and steamy glances. He tensed in his seat, the tightness in his chest shifting.

He glanced at her profile, then focused his gaze back to the road ahead. She'd curled up in the corner, her arms wrapped around his bag, staring off into the distance, a slight upward tilt to her lips. A comfortable warmth filled his chest, and he settled more deeply into his seat. It was nice having someone to ride along with, sharing space, enjoying the silence with no need to talk. Comfortable, comforting.

Apparently he wasn't the kind of guy women held on to. Oh, many wanted a piece of him. Many wanted to benefit from whichever of his talents drew them near, but he caught onto their games with the first glance. They were never interested in the work, the mundane of making something that would last.

He sighed.

Sam reached out and laid her hand on his thigh, the heat of her touch immediate, his body's reaction more so, and he quelled the urge to shift in his seat again. He wanted to laugh at the ridiculousness of it all, but he felt too raw.

"Are you going to tell me what happened back there?" she asked quietly.

Gage's first instinct was to say nothing, his second was to say, "nothing," but she wouldn't buy any of it. Besides, he couldn't stand it when she did that to him. "Cecilia and I don't exactly mesh well."

"I'm familiar with her antics. She makes no sense. Why get so freaked out over rumors? Besides, an easy 'no' would answer the question. I don't get all the drama or why she's so vicious. Unless, you insulted her or something in the past?"

Gage cut his eyes to her. She still had no idea, and he didn't feel like telling her, either.

"No, no, of course not. Sorry." Sam shifted in her seat and studied him, biting her lip.

Gage blew out a breath and pulled into Sam's parking lot. He turned off the engine and then gathered his things from her lap. They walked toward the condo entrance, the evening air cool and humid against his skin, soothing him.

Sam remained quiet during the elevator ride up to her place. They pushed through her front door, and peace filled him when she closed it and locked out the rest of the world. He walked through the kitchen and living room to the windows, dropping his bag on the ground at his feet.

She watched him and then poured them both a drink. He took the scotch and let the deep bite roll around his tongue before the burn warmed his throat. "Wow, that's smooth. My dad would love this."

She shrugged. "I learned a thing or two from Ethan. Only the best." She raised her glass in a toast, her fake chuckle telling him more than her words.

He pressed his lips together with a nod.

Sam stepped up next to him and watched the waves wash up on the shore. "You're close to your dad and sister. I'm glad you have them."

Gage dipped his chin and glanced at her. "Very. Our dad made us his focus. He was there every night to help us with our homework and tuck us in at bedtime. He never missed a game or recital."

She smiled and ran her hand down his arm. "That's wonderful. So…" She paused, and he wished she wouldn't ask.

"What happened today?" No such luck.

Gage drained his glass. "Like I said, we don't get along."

Sam set her glass on the closest table, stepped before him, and looped her arms around his neck. Wariness shone in her eyes, and she hesitated, but instead of pulling back, she inched up on her tiptoes and rested against his chest. He'd never tire of the feel of her soft body against his. The scotch on her breath and glistening on her parted lips was an invitation he'd never be able to resist or forget.

"I know what you need," she whispered, just before brushing her mouth against his. She tasted of everything sweet and savory in his life. He wanted to ring Ethan's neck for making her doubt herself.

Sam pressed closer, and her heart drummed insistently against his chest. Tightening his grip, he angled his head, diving deep, and taking her with him. She moaned and increased the pressure of her fingers gliding along his hairline, sending all the blood in his body straight to his groin. He slid his tongue along her lips, and she opened for him, sliding her tongue against his. She rubbed his back, caressed his shoulders, and then snaked her hands once again back into his hair. Her touch reached everywhere, much deeper than she'd ever intended, he was sure. She accepted him in ways he'd never known he craved. Against impossible barriers, she knew more about him than anyone outside of his sister and dad, and asked for nothing to keep the knowledge safe, secret.

Gage walked her back toward the long sofa, unfastening her pants along the way. Removing her shirt, her bra. He knew she was distracting him, using sex to ease his pain, and the sweetness of it all made him even more urgent to get his hands on her. To feel her softness. Now.

As soon as his palms filled with the weight of her breasts, relief and possession raced through him. He had to find a way to prove to her they could work, Hollywood be damned.

He broke from the kiss just long enough to tug his shirt over his head. Then he took her mouth with a groan. Following her down to the couch, he wrestled with his pants and kicked them off his legs before settling between her thighs.

"Now, Gage. Don't wait." Sam's breathy demand pulsed straight through his dick. If it were possible to double in size, his would have in that moment, his pleasure so intense it hovered on the edge of pain. He kissed her mouth, then her neck, her breasts, laving one nipple with his tongue before moving on to the other, all the while torturing them both by pushing just the head of himself into her and then pulling back out. She fisted her hands in the sofa pillows.

He didn't need to be told again. Enveloping Sam in his arms to anchor his weight, he flexed his hips, giving them both what they craved. A distraction, a break from the weight of simply living day to day bore down on them. Grabbing at his ass to pull him deeper, harder, she arched her hips up hard against his pelvis, and lost herself, taking him with her.

A growl tore from his throat, the tight, unbearable pressure at the root of him exploding.

Gage held on, shocked by the intensity. No doubt, by the way her body sprawled boneless beneath him, she'd felt it, too. She'd come with him tonight mind and body, but what he needed to do was make her stay.

He cared about her, could see a glimpse of the life they could have together. He'd been with other women before, he'd never deny it, but no one who accepted him the way Sam did. No one who made him feel like he didn't have to keep secrets, or hide behind a shield of security and trusted friends and family. No one who didn't leave him feeling used. He rolled to his side on the sofa, tucking her in close.

Her damn rule remained his biggest hurdle. He needed to find a way to get her to make an exception for him. To prove to her that when he was the celebrity, it would be an asset, not a death sentence.

Chapter Ten

Gage followed the curves west on Malibu Canyon Highway, staring through the windshield and wishing he were on the waves with his board and Sam, instead of in the car. He was looking forward to meeting her parents, but damn it was a beautiful day to enjoy the surf.

"Can you slow down? If I have to go, I'd like to get there alive."

Gage cut his eyes at her. She had a white-knuckled grip on the door armrest. "Sam, I'm only going five miles over the speed limit."

She opened her eyes wide. "There's a specific speed limit for a reason."

He eased off the gas pedal, wondering what was really bothering her. "Are you looking forward to seeing your mom?"

Sam turned in her seat to face him better. "I am. She's amazing."

"But?"

"But, they're nosey and bossy, and have been worried about me, which makes all of those other qualities increase by the nth degree."

Gage picked up her hand and placed it on his thigh, enjoying the heat of her hand through his slacks. It made him feel connected, whether she was aware of it or not. "That's their job. What else would you have them do? What would you do if it had been your sister who'd gone through what you have the past few years?"

Glancing at her and then shifting his gaze back down the road, he could feel her eyes roaming his face.

"You see a lot more than I'm used to from a man."

He pulled one corner of his lip up. "What are you calling me, a woman?"

She squeezed his thigh. "No way, you're not that perfect."

His jaw dropped, and he grabbed her hand when she tried to remove it. Pulling it to his mouth, he nipped the sensitive skin on the underside of her wrist, grinning as she squealed.

"Okay, okay. You're the most perfect *man* I know."

With a wink thrown in her direction, he pressed her hand against his crotch and immediately grew as her warmth seeped through his jeans. But instead of yanking her hand away in shock, she flexed her fingers and rubbed her hand up and then back down. He went from teasing to teased in a fraction of a second, and he was hard as fuck to prove it. He loved this side of her, when she let her walls down and had fun.

Grabbing her hand back into his, he laughed. "Whoa. We'll never get to dinner if you keep that up."

Sam crossed her arms over her chest and stuck out her lower lip, which only made him want to suck on it. Pulling his thoughts back under control, he asked, "Why'd you stay with Ethan for so long?"

She remained quiet for a minute, and he thought she might not answer. Tapping her finger lightly against the passenger window, she said, "I was going to leave the day of the accident. Then I couldn't, and then his death came not long after."

"Suicide."

She pulled in a breath. "Suicide. Since then, my family, and just about everyone else I know, won't stop telling me what an asshole he was. It's embarrassing. Not because I don't agree, but because I do. I can only take so much of what a fool I was being shoved in my face. That's why I haven't been to my parents' in a while. I thought it was easier to just stay away so we didn't argue — "

"Why?"

Sam turned toward him. "What?"

"Why? Why did you argue?"

She ran her hands back through her long brown hair and arranged it about her shoulders. His fingers itched to slide through the silky softness.

"Look, it's taken me time to discover, or rather accept, how Ethan really was. Nobody likes to fail. I portrayed a happy, functional marriage, and not one of my friends or family questioned me, no one ever told me otherwise. Even when I'd decided to leave him."

Gage watched her.

"I'd decided to leave, but like I said, the accident. After he'd died, everyone took great pleasure in letting me know just how much of a douche he was. On top of the aggressive persistence with the paparazzi, it hurt. And it was humiliating."

With her chin resting in her hand, she leaned against the door and stared out the front window. "If nobody liked him, why didn't they tell me when he was alive? Why didn't they encourage me when I'd decided to leave? I felt like, no, *feel* like a fool when I think about it."

Gage nodded. He understood. People in his life helped shape him into the person he'd become. Some he'd like to thank, and others he could have done without. Second-guessing himself, his true talent, the kind of man he was, had become a daily habit. A habit he was determined to break. It wasn't easy. "Because they love you."

She snorted.

"Seriously. They didn't want to hurt you. You wouldn't have believed them or admitted it anyway, so what would have been the use?"

She sent him a disbelieving look.

"Think about it. How often do people kill the messenger?"

"And now?" She dropped her hand to her lap and straightened in her seat.

"Now, everyone who loves you wants you to move on, and I think they believe it would be easier for you to do if you realized you really haven't lost anything. When it comes to your relationship with Ethan, you still have you. Which is all you really had all along."

"Wow, I sound pathetic."

"No, you sound loyal, strong, and determined." Gage ran his hand along her arm to her shoulder and gave a light squeeze. "There's nothing for you to feel humiliated about."

Sam breathed deep and cracked her neck. "Yeah."

Gage tilted his head, glanced at her, then back to the road. "What?"

A quick shake of her head ended the conversation, and she grabbed his free hand. "No, you're right."

"Sam, did he ever hit you?"

She scoffed. "That would mean he'd have to touch me. No, his was more of a very specific kind of verbal lashing. Consistent and mean, but said in a way that sounded as if he was trying to help. About my weight, my talent, my looks."

He gripped the steering wheel wishing it were Ethan's neck. The fucking bastard never deserved her. "I'm sorry that he did that to you."

She dipped her chin. "I'm sorry I let him." Leaning into his side, she dropped her head to his shoulder and laced her arm through his. "You are really good at taking care of people, Gage."

He pressed a kiss to the top of her head. In one moment she dismissed their relationship as nothing more than a casual fling—which stung like a son-of-a-bitch—and the next she declared he very capably took care of her. The contrast, the bouncing back and forth, made him hopeless *and* gave him hope. He couldn't help but read into every word, every action. It was exhausting.

Gage peeked down at her. Her pert nose and softly squared chin, her deep brown eyes—he'd lost himself in them more than once. Her hair, he loved to bury his face in the silky mass and breathe her in. She left the scent of spicy citrus everywhere, on his clothes, his pillow. How many times had he dreamed of her with that scent floating about his head?

"We're here." He grabbed a trucker hat and sunglasses from the back seat and put them on. They pulled into the driveway of her parents' home in a gated community, Malibu Canyon, and straight into the garage. "Looks like a fun place."

Sam nodded as she got out of the car and hit the button to lower the garage door. "Yeah, they moved here a few years after my sister moved out. They wanted to downsize but still have a lot of activities for…" Color rose in her cheeks.

Gage dropped the hat and glasses to the passenger seat and got out of the car. "What?"

"Grandkids."

With a grin pulling at the corners of his mouth, Gage walked around to the passenger side and leaned against the front. He wanted at least two, but he wasn't about to share that tidbit with her. She'd bolt before he finished the sentence, so instead he shoved his hands into his pockets.

The garage door reversed its descent, grating its way back open, and he stepped back.

"Sam, darling!" A woman with one too many injections of Botox dipped under the door with her miniature Shar-Pei. "Oh, honey, it's been far too long." She spared Sam the briefest glance before stepping up to him and tapping his chest with each word. "And you are even better in person."

Gage tilted his head, and with a step back, stuck his arm out to its full length, making the woman take it while staying at least two feet away. "Gage Cutler, and you are?"

"Oh, I know who you are. Everyone knows who you are." She licked her lower lip at him, something he loved when Sam did it, but on this woman it was all he could do not to laugh. Changing tactics, she stepped back and swung her arm around Sam's shoulders. "Hasn't Sam told you? I'm practically her aunt, since me and her mom are positively inseparable."

Sam shook her head. "I don't—"

The woman grabbed Sam's cheeks between boney fingers and thumb, squishing Sam's lips forward into a pucker. "You've been gone far too long. I keep telling your mother to get you here for dinner, and look—"

She whispered toward Gage, "Dee always takes my advice."

Dropping her hand from Sam, she sauntered back to Gage. "Now for you, my handsome young man. After dinner, why don't I show you around the neighborhood—"

Sam stepped between them, shoving the woman gently aside, and grabbed Gage by the arm. Talking over her shoulder, she led Gage to the door into the house. "So sorry, we've got to go. Dinner's ready, and you know how Mom hates to serve a cold meal."

"Samantha!" The woman tripped over her dog, which let out a yelp.

The door swung open, and Mrs. Dekker held Gage at arm's length with a grin. "Gage Cutler."

With a look directed at Sam's mom, Mr. Dekker made quick work of getting the nosey neighbor out of the garage.

Sam scolded in a hard whisper. "Mom."

But Gage leaned in and placed a kiss on her cheek, then handed her a bottle of wine and chocolates. "Thank you for including me, Mrs. Dekker."

She made a swoon face with her hand at her brow, winning him over in a heartbeat, and waved his words away. "Please, Gage Cutler in my home? You're always welcome, and call me Dee. All the kids' friends do."

At thirty-eight, being referred to as a kid made him chuckle, and he nodded. "Okay, Dee." Sam was the spitting image of her mother but had her father's dark, fathomless eyes. A warmth spread through his chest.

Addison Dekker, Sam's sister, reminded him of his own. Blond hair like Mr. Dekker but the sparkling blues of her mother. She bounded up to him and pulled him in tight. "Oh, the dreams I've had about you."

Sam's jaw dropped. "Addison!" She turned to her mother. "Mom?"

Dee laughed and wrapped her arm around Mr. Dekker's waist. "What? Who hasn't?"

Gage laughed. He held Addison in to his side, enjoying Sam's sputter.

A tall man, no mistaking him as Dekker Senior's son—a twenty-year-younger duplicate—walked in to join them. "What'd I miss?"

Sam rolled her eyes. "You don't want to know." She extended her hand. "Luca, Gage Cutler. Gage, my brother."

Addison released Gage to give her brother a hug. "Mom and I were just saying Sam had the perfect opportunity to spice up her sex life."

"Oh my God. Dad." Sam shot her father a look, appealing for some assistance.

Mr. Dekker shrugged. "Sorry, honey, but I can't complain. After your mother watched *In Her Lover's Arms*, she couldn't get enough of me."

"We're just friends, colleagues." Sam nudged her sister's shoulder.

He'd normally be a bit uncomfortable with the attention,

but this banter wasn't for him. This was some sort of hazing for Sam. Besides, he was with Mr. Dekker on this one; the idea Sam couldn't get enough of him was more than he could hope for, and it was a fool's wish. He rubbed his chest.

Gage tried to hide his laugh behind his hand, but a chuckle slipped out.

Sam's father laughed. "I like this one. He's going to fit in just fine."

"So who's the big mouth, huh? One of you told Crazy Kat from next door that Gage would be here. She practically assaulted him in the garage." Sam's poor attempt to change the subject pulled more laughter from each of the Dekker clan—all except Dee, who looked around everywhere but back at Sam.

"I wouldn't call it assault—"

Sam pinned him with a look. "She was all over you." And then she abruptly stopped, eyes wide, and busied herself with something on her mother's foyer table.

Gage did everything he could do to keep the satisfaction of that little encounter from showing too much.

Sam was jealous. He could smell it, and it was glorious. He'd have to thank Dee later for her big mouth, as Sam put it.

It only further solidified his belief Sam had feelings for him. She wasn't the type of woman to be with someone she didn't. Rubbing his hands together, he grinned. This was going to be fun.

The crew filed into the open space of the kitchen and dining area. Both rooms opened up to the living room and a large outdoor living area that overlooked a resort-style pool, surrounded by lush tropical flowers and palm trees.

He could see his children jumping into the water and hear their screams of delight. He turned away. His fucking heart refused to listen to what his mind thought it knew, only making him more determined.

"Gage? Did you hear me? Which one?"

He swung back from the window, pulling in a breath, to find Sam holding up a bottle of red wine and a bottle of white wine. She tapped her foot. He grinned. She was so annoyed right now, which was so fun to focus on. Gage walked up to her and took both bottles from her hands, then handed them to her brother, Luca. "Red, please." Then he winked at Sam, taking advantage of the fact the rest of her family had their backs to them, distracted with food preparations.

She rolled her eyes and looked away, with a half grin.

"Quit pretending you're mad at me. Your sister's right about your sex life," he whispered in her ear.

The corner of her mouth quirked. "I'm not pretending."

He wanted to drop a kiss to her mouth but held himself back. It sucked, but he'd just make up for it later. "Liar."

Addison called out from the other side of the breakfast bar. "Sam, when you're done with your new friend, I'll take him. A good shower will take care of that sloppy-seconds issue."

"Addison Dekker." Her dad grimaced. "Too far."

Sam stepped in front of Gage, separating him from her sister's lascivious grin. "Addi, no matter how funny you think you are, Dad will never want to hear you say the words, 'sloppy seconds.' Ever."

Mr. Dekker groaned, and Dee put her hands over his ears and kissed his cheeks.

Gage grinned. He'd been doing a lot of that since they'd

shown up. He liked this feeling. His dad and sister would, too. Wouldn't that be perfect?

"Save your lusty little ideas for your books." Sam walked into the kitchen and wrapped her arm around her mother. "Addison is a Corporate America survivor turned romance writer. We're really proud."

"Wow, that's great. Anything I might have seen?"

Addi dove into the new subject, her gaze shifting from one parent to the next. "Not yet. But you will."

He was missing something, but he wasn't sure what.

Dee moved next to her youngest and smoothed her long blond hair. "She's finished her second novel and is now working on her third. Both finished manuscripts are off to editors and agents. We're very proud of her. If we could only get her to move back home and let us take care of her until she gets a contract."

Addison leaned into her mother's hand. "Thanks, Mom, but I can take care of myself. Besides, I love Aunt Addi's bungalow."

"But, honey—"

Luca barged into the conversation. "You can't even make your own bed, much less take care of a house on your own. Poor Aunt Addi's place is going to fall apart."

Sam's sister narrowed her eyes and grabbed the wine Luca was about to sip. "If I'm so helpless, go pour another glass."

Gage watched, fascinated. The independent streak with the two sisters was a study in psychology. Sam's was from not being taken care of enough, where her sister's appeared to stem from being taken care of too much.

He imagined her parents had wondered where that little

girl went once she'd married Ethan. As dinner progressed, however, they never said a word. Not a mention of his name, the incident, or anything related to it. Apparently, Sam's strategy had worked. Her family avoided talking about Ethan or sharing their opinions of him for fear of driving her away again. He didn't think they saw her absence as a means to protect herself, but rather a stubborn declaration that her life was her life.

He wondered if Sam saw that.

Gage smiled at Addi. "My sister gets annoyed with me, too."

Luca piped up. "Sister? What does she do?"

Gage eyed the man for a moment. A big brother habit. "She's a professor at Pepperdine. Education and psychology."

Luca thought for a moment. "Pepperdine? I attended Pepperdine." Silent once more, he stared at Gage. "Cutler, no way. You're not related to DC are you? Dean Cutler?"

Gage took a bite of his tortellini and nodded. "Yep, he's my dad."

"No shit?" Luca shook his head.

"What, honey?" Dee placed her hand over her son's.

Luca shook his head. "Dean Cutler was one of my professors. Not only that, he's responsible for getting me my job. Without his recommendation, I wouldn't have made it. Too competitive. He gave me the edge I needed. Had the connections." Sam's brother grinned ear to ear. "Oh, Mom, you'll like DC."

"As long as it benefits me like Gage's movies do." Mr. Dekker waggled his eyebrows and ogled his wife, tickling her side. Dee slapped his hand away with a chuckle.

Sam threw her hands out. "Oh my God, Dad."

Her mother spoke up. "Honey, when you brings friends like Gage along, what do you expect?"

"You all to behave," Sam said, her voice strained.

Gage threw his arm around Sam, with a teasing shake. "I'll take the misbehavin' any day."

"Like I said, he'll fit in just fine," Mr. Dekker said.

Gage winked at Sam and then tilted his head toward her dad. "I hear you're good friends with Martin Gallagher. He and my dad just started meeting for scotch tastings now and again. You'd probably enjoy yourself."

Sam's father grunted, interest in his eyes. "Ya don't say? I'll call Martin."

Sam whispered under her breath, "That's all I need."

Gage patted her hand under the table, and she stuck her tongue out at him, her lips quivering up at the corner, unable to resist the humor in it all.

Family could be terrifying, but when they truly loved one of their own, failure didn't exist, loneliness never stood a chance, and hiding wasn't an option. He could be that for Sam; he would be.

Turning his head from side to side, he cracked his neck.

He'd made his decision a long time ago. Now he just needed to be patient and put each piece into action. He'd be damned if he'd ever let her walk away. She simply needed to see how well they could work.

And he was just the man to show her.

Chapter Eleven

Sam opened her eyes, heavy from a deep night's sleep. The weight of Gage's arm thrown across her stomach was warm and comforting. She felt so good she was compelled to squirm—just a bit—to see if it was real.

She turned her head toward Gage. His lashes lay dark against his skin, his expression relaxed. Worry-free. Contentment pulled a sigh from her. She liked to see him this way. Unguarded. Sleeping. In her bed. Her eyes widened and she slid out from under his warm embrace.

No, no, no. Gage in my bed is not something I need to get used to. If he only he wasn't so damn good at being in it.

Scooting to the edge of the bed, she raked her gaze over him. His shoulders extended beyond the width of the king pillow, a bronzed mass of muscles. The spray of dark hair that shadowed his chest beckoned her fingers to run through the texture of springy softness over smooth flesh. A much different physique than Ethan's slight, toned frame.

Ethan was not the man she'd led herself to believe he was. He'd been ill, and the illness wasn't anything she could ever wrap her head around. She hadn't wanted to fail, so denial had become her best friend, but it was time to allow for her mistake and admit that Ethan had been no man.

Not like Gage.

She shot up.

Chilled, Sam grabbed her robe and slid her arms into the softness. She belted it, tight and secure like a shield, as she walked out to the kitchen. No more thinking. Coffee.

She rummaged around the kitchen and set up a tray of coffee, bacon, and fresh strawberries. Tray in hand, she opened her balcony doors, inviting the morning breeze into her home. She turned back to the living room and placed the tray on the coffee table separating two sofas and then settled onto one. Her beach didn't boast the security Gage's did. Only a few yards of sand left nowhere for paparazzi to hide, but they'd tried.

After Ethan's accident and the barrage of tabloid hype, they'd hounded the two of them day and night. Taking pictures of their windows and speculating on making love to a monster, hounding her at premiers and accusing her for Ethan not being at her side. A few even tried to scale her back patio to get pictures of his disfigured face, but fortunately, mirrored windows let them see out but no one to see in. Ethan had become so obsessed with what they'd reported about his face, he'd refused to take any clients.

The onslaught never really ended, and then when he committed suicide, it had increased intensity ten-fold. Murder in Malibu had been a hot topic they salivated over. She couldn't even go to the grocery store or pick up coffee down at the Country Mart without camera flashes blinding her and accusations hurled in her face.

She blinked away the memories, and her appreciation of the empty beach chased the coldness away, the waves greeting her with a gentle melodic rhythm. Sam pulled in a breath, and leaning back, sipped her coffee and then sighed.

She'd had fun yesterday. Her family adored Gage as she knew they would, and if it were possible she liked him even more after how sweet he was with her mother and sister. She about died at their teasing, but Gage soaked it up and gave some back. What was she going to do with him? And wasn't that the problem?

Switching gears, she tried to analyze her reaction to the neighbor in the garage, but she didn't want to think about what had really gone through her head when the woman touched him. She can't remember ever really wanting to run anyone over before, but in that moment, she'd have done it. Twice.

"Can I join you?" Gage sunk onto the sofa that paralleled hers and reached for the cup of coffee that awaited him. He took a swallow and raised his mug before looking at her. "Thank you. What a nice way to wake up, though I can think of one better." He winked.

Heat rose to her cheeks. Seriously, after last night how could he even suggest it? If a marathon for lovemaking existed, they'd have swept the gold. She abhorred the thought that hanging out with her family had been some kind of foreplay, but barely touching him all night, watching what she said, had driven her mad. She couldn't wait to get him back to her place.

She glanced at him from beneath her lashes as the

corners of her lips turned up. And that was another thing. He always said thank you. Any time she did something for him, they were the first words passing his lips. It was all so new to her.

"Come over here." Gage spread his legs, covered in a light-weight pair of sweats, and patted the cushion between his thighs.

Golden light and shadows alternated across his broad chest as she moved toward him. She loved how low his sweats hung from his hips. The skin just above the band begged to be tasted. *Geesh. I'm no better than he is.*

She closed her patio doors and pushed the button to open the top panels near the ceiling and then snuggled back against his firm frame. He shifted until she rested at an angle that allowed her to still enjoy her coffee.

He slid a bright red strawberry against her lower lip, and she opened her mouth. She bit half, and as she chewed, he popped the other in his own mouth. Next came a piece of bacon, and they continued to share the food until nothing remained on the tray, save an empty plate.

"This is my new favorite breakfast."

Sam could feel the rumble of his voice against her back. He pulled her against him tighter still and rested his chin on her shoulder next to her ear. "Beautiful, isn't it?" His gaze focused on the blue undulating horizon.

"It is one reason I never moved." A few moments of quiet passed. "They really liked you. Thank you for going with me."

He pulled her back tighter to his chest. "I really liked them. Your sister is hilarious, and your mom? I can see where you get your spurts of feisty from."

She pinched his arm playfully.

"They're so happy. Always laughing, it's awesome to be around couples like that."

She nodded, thinking of how much fun she and Gage always had. The bottom of her coffee mug in sight, she set it on the table beside them and then wrapped Gage's arms about her waist. God, he felt good, which was not good at all, but she snuggled in anyway.

Her feelings for him had all the markers for something more serious, much deeper than a fling. She tensed and then turned her head just enough to see his face. He rested with his eyes closed, a look of contentment on his relaxed face. She closed her eyes briefly and then stared back out at the tossing waves. Confusing herself was one thing, but confusing him wasn't fair at all.

• • •

Sam stood on the film set, heat rushing to her hairline. "What?"

"He doesn't think you hit the mark." Martin Gallagher shook his head, confusion furrowing his brows. "I have to agree."

A bitter taste filled her mouth. She didn't hit the mark? They wanted organic; she gave them organic. They wanted a true intimate expression of the character, and she gave it to them, using the best of what Gage had to offer.

"*Gage* said that? He really isn't accepting my work?"

"It's not so much not accepting as it is needing you to fix it. "

She'd delivered some of her best work yet, the sex scene

Martin had asked for specifically, so how the hell was there anything to fix? "But I did."

Gage walked up and Martin gave a sigh that Sam could only imagine was relief. Coward.

It wasn't that she couldn't take criticism, but her work was spot-on to the needs of the scenes. How could she have been so wrong? When she'd turned her work in, she'd been positive they were going to love it.

She spun on him, the screenplay held out in her hand. Her voice low and not a little bewildered, she grated, "Are you serious? This is damn good work." Ethan's voice mocked her with echoes from the past. *Come on, Sam, there are plenty of writers out there more experienced than you. I wouldn't hang your hat on this career, honey.*

Gage put his hands up. "Hey, wait a second." Surprise lit his eyes.

"Wait a second? Gage, this is some of my best writing yet." Her stomach twisted.

The man she'd she thought she knew so well cocked a patronizing brow. "Your best? Really?"

She nailed Martin with a look, who for the first time in her experience looked lost, and back at Gage, who stared down at the script in his hand like it was the plague.

She took it from his hand. "Let me see that."

She flipped the pages open to one of the changes she felt held the most impact. "Look at this." Her finger slid down the page until it stilled about halfway. She glanced down at the page and then made a face and jerked back. "What the hell? These aren't my changes."

Martin's head shot up. "What?"

Sam pressed her lips together and shook her head.

"These are *not* my changes."

Gage put his hand out, a half smile of concern lifting the corner of his mouth. "Sam."

She rolled her eyes and dug into her bag. She pulled out her script and shoved it toward the two men. "Take it."

Broad shoulder to broad shoulder, the two men bent their heads and read from her screenplay. Low grumbles and grunts joined the hum of the working cast and crew on the set. Martin pointed to a spot on the page and Gage nodded. Gage counter-pointed, and her mentor dipped his chin.

Gage looked up. "This *is* brilliant."

The tension fled Sam's gut, leaving her dizzy. Her shoulders relaxed and she nodded. "*That* is my work."

Martin tapped the other screenplay, his brows raised. "Then what is *this*?"

Sam stared at the offending object and then flipped through to the area she'd worked on, and recoiled in a combination of humor and horror. "*This* is awful. Why would you think it was my work?"

Her mentor looked at Gage and then back at Sam. He rubbed his hand up and over his sparsely covered dome. "That's why we were so confused, girl!" His voice was harsh and tinged with embarrassment. "I asked for the intimate scene, and this is what we got back. Why would we think it wasn't yours?"

Sam paced, smacking the script in her hand. Her pulse raced. She wanted to be sick. She spun to face the men. "Who would do this?"

Anger raced through her like it had a deadline. She didn't know which was worse, someone screwing with her writing, or her immense relief that Gage believed her. His opinion shouldn't matter. She knew the quality of her work.

"More to the point, why?" Gage stepped in front of her and settled his hands on her shoulders, his thumbs pushing into her tense muscles.

Sam let him work the knots out of her shoulders. Anyone would need comforting in a situation like this, but the truth was he comforted her better than anyone else could. Closing her eyes, she counted backward from ten. Her shoulders slumped, Sam lifted her lids to look at Gage. Tears stung and she blinked to hold them at bay. "*This* is why I hate Hollywood."

Martin stepped forward. "Sam, don't be ridiculous."

She slowly raised her hand to stop the older man and then directed her focus back to Gage. He stood very still, his eyes blank. If it weren't for the rhythmical clenching in his jaw, she wouldn't have been sure he'd heard her. But he had. Good. That was good. She needed a little distance, a little space. So much had changed from a few weeks ago, and she needed to breathe and catch up.

Sam ticked her evidence off on her fingers in weary acceptance. "The magazine on my desk and now my work?" she whispered. "My work?"

Sam bit her lip, tossing the script onto the work surface behind Martin. "I need to get out of here."

Gage stepped forward, his eyes filled with concern. "Sam."

Martin shot her a disappointed look. "Let her go."

Sadness drummed through her in slow, steady beats. She turned from the two men, crossed the set, and escaped through the opened front door.

Stress tightened against her skull like a vice. Gage wasn't at fault, nor would she ever expect him to approve anything but the best of her work. The simple truth, the truth she knew all along, still remained. Being with Gage made her a target.

She'd suffered in front of that firing squad enough already.

Sam made her way to her condo, changed into her suit, and raced out her patio to the beach in record time. Dropping her bag on the sand at the base of the deck stairs, she toed off her flip-flops. The midday sun had warmed the tiny grains, and she sunk her toes in with a sigh. She'd been wanting to get back into the water. There was nothing a swim in the ocean couldn't wash away.

Sam edged her way to the water, stepping around stones and driftwood. When the surf washed up and lapped at her ankles, she stopped and sucked in a big breath, blinking back tears. The problem wasn't Gage; it was Hollywood, but the two went hand in hand, and that wasn't about to change. Temptation was everywhere, with every job, every movie, and every film promotion. She'd never be able to handle it if he cheated, to have a second man cheat on her, so why put herself in a situation that would risk it? Divorce rates among celebrities ran close to eighty percent. She wasn't one, but that didn't increase her chances by much. She couldn't have another failed marriage, especially one she could see failing all too clearly.

She pulled another breath of salty ocean air into her lungs. Gulls called to one another overhead, and the waves buffeted against the rocky beach in a soothing cadence. She relaxed her shoulders and rolled her head from one side to the other. She slipped into the water to her waist, then stretched her arms long, taking one solid stroke at a time parallel to the shore.

Panic. Dread. Both feelings had swamped Sam when they'd told her the script work hadn't been good enough. Flashes of Ethan's condescending face had taunted her. *"Why are you still trying so hard, Sam? It's pathetic. I just don't want to see you get hurt. Stay home. We can finally have a baby."* When Sam refused to quit working, he shook his head in disgust. *"It would be one thing if you were any good."*

How had she not seen it before? She swam faster. Stroke, stroke, stroke, and breathe. Again.

She could see, now, Ethan's attack on her abilities stemmed from his own insecurities. He couldn't stomach a successful wife. The idea she could earn good money, possibly better money than he could, chipped at his own self-worth.

The kick of it was, when you heard something long enough it began to stick. She'd just begun to build her professional esteem back up when Martin and Gage had delivered the news this morning.

She put too much stock in Gage's opinion of her abilities. It stunk of the same old game with Ethan. She hated herself for such weakness. The two men were nothing alike. It certainly wasn't fair to Gage.

Her husband was dead, which did not make him a martyr or a good person. She needed to knock it off. The fact it was so difficult to do so gnawed at her. What kept her tied to a man who never loved her in the first place?

She wasn't responsible for his death.

She wasn't.

But she couldn't help but wonder if he'd known she'd been ready to leave.

Swimming between a rock and a pier, she picked up her pace, racing against her thoughts. She wished it were a race she could win.

After a few more laps, she dragged herself from the water and lowered to the edge, a towel slung about her shoulders, knees drawn up, arms wrapped tight, the point of her chin rested on her kneecap as she scanned the horizon.

"How long are you planning to hide?" Gage asked as he lowered next to her. Warmth radiated from him and spread through her, and she sighed.

She should have been surprised to see him, but she wasn't. It was as though he had a second sense where she was concerned.

She looked up and down the shore, thankful to find it empty. "You shouldn't be out here. Martin's going to kill you."

"Please, they have plenty to do before I get back. If I were there right now, I'd be sitting in my trailer. You didn't answer my question."

"I wasn't hiding. I was swimming. How'd you know I'd be here?" She peeked at him.

"It's your favorite thinking spot."

She dipped her chin in confirmation. "Yes, but how did you know that?"

Gage shook his head, glanced out over the blue waters, and then back to hold her gaze. "Don't you get it yet?"

Her chest tightened. She didn't want to get it; she was afraid to look too close. He terrified her, his intensity, his openness. The guaranteed pain when they parted ways.

She'd poured all of herself into her relationship with Ethan until only a shell of her former self remained. Crawling back out of that hell had been difficult. *Was* difficult.

Gage stared out at the ocean. Sam stared at Gage. In profile, the sun shone through the light of his eyes, and she couldn't look away from the hard line of his jaw. She knew frustration burned at him, hurt him, but she couldn't help that.

He turned his head and locked eyes with her. Something passed over his face she couldn't quite place.

"I'm a descendant of an English playwright, Thomas Dekker," Sam said, her voice just loud enough to hear over the crashing waves.

"I know. You told me."

He understood without trying. A phenomenon that should comfort her. She dipped her chin. "It's in my blood."

Gage leaned back on his arms, his shirt pulled tight over his well-muscled chest. He nodded. "I get that. Martin gets that."

"But I don't always get it." She faltered, unable to find the words to explain. Sam gathered her hair and twisted it into a knot at the back of her neck. "What I mean is writing is personal. Every word I put out there is a part of me. And writing in Hollywood? Hell, it's excruciating. I've worked hard to prove myself. So, this morning—"

Gage shot her a look. "You don't think I get that? Writing's a lot like acting that way. There's no tougher way to put yourself out there than being in front of a camera."

"You're right. Of course you'd get it. But you have a family that has supported you, built you up."

"And you don't?" he snapped, his voice sharp.

Sam could feel the tension radiating from him. So much for him being understanding. She had the strongest urge to go inside and leave his ass on the beach. "Are you trying to fight with me?"

He pushed forward and sat with his hands slung over his pulled-up knees. "I'm trying to push you out of your victim role, Sam. You've been there so long, I don't think you know how to get out. I've met your family. You have all the support you could ever want and more."

"Look, Mr. 'I've got the answers to everything,' yes. My family supported me. But I was married and my husband didn't." She stood and paced in front of him. Then planting her feet to face him, she swung her arms out wide. "I don't know one time that the man didn't tell me I was chasing a dream I had no business chasing."

"And you believed him?"

Frustration made her want to scream. He was such a blockhead. "No! Yes! Why can't you understand?" she yelled. She straightened and lowered her arms, wrapping them around her waist.

"It's over."

She blinked and shook her head. Exhaustion weighed her down and exasperation clogged her throat. "What?"

Gage rose to his feet and approached her. She pulled away from his grasp, but he grabbed hold and held her steady. "You are not a victim anymore. You were, no question, and I could kill the man for it, but you're not anymore. Sometimes, though, you still act like one. I want you to see you're a survivor."

She pulled away.

He didn't try to touch her again. "Look, I know you're afraid; this business is terrifying, I get it. You have an amazing talent, but it won't matter if you don't believe it. Believe it,

Sam, because then you win. I'm not saying it's easy. But you are strong. Stronger than you give yourself credit for."

A dull ache throbbed behind her eyes. She was so tired. Tired of her doubt, of fighting to find herself, dealing with the masses of Tinsel Town, and now harassment. Why was she fighting? She *was* strong.

She'd been so afraid of failing for so long, she didn't remember how it felt not to be. It was about time she learned. Squaring her shoulders, Sam lifted her chin. Whoever was screwing with her would have to try harder.

She walked back and stood in front of Gage. Staring into the endless depths of his eyes, she whispered, "I'm sorry." Before he could answer, she went up on tiptoes, leaned into him, and pressed a kiss to his mouth.

Gage lowered to the sand, and she sat next to him, digging her toes into the sand. "So, how *did* you know this was my thinking spot?" Sam resisted him when he tried to tuck her into his side. She yearned to sink into the steady, strong beat of his heart, but that wasn't her place.

He blew out a breath, flexing his fingers. "Don't you remember?" He dipped his head to look into her face. "The night we met."

They'd shared so much. Heads bent close, whispering a secret for a secret, their tumblers littering the bar counter with nothing but melted ice and cherry stems. She'd gotten so lost in his unwavering gaze that by the time she looked around, they'd been the only people left, save for the bartender. It had changed her that night—being listened to, being heard. She'd opened up more to Gage than she did to her own family.

It had been the first time in a long time she'd felt as if

she mattered.

He'd remembered.

The ocean sounds broke through her memories, and Gage still tried to hold her by the water's edge. Wasn't that just like him?

She stepped out of his arms. He was getting too close, crossing over their line of light and easy. Finding a way to reestablish what they had as a fling was necessary for the good of both of them. And she needed to be the one to do it.

If he wasn't going to be more careful not to get hurt, she'd have to.

Someone needed to save Gage from himself.

Chapter Twelve

Sam and Gage pulled into the driveway of the set and parked the car. With a quick glance outside, he turned toward her and snaked his hand behind her head. He held her gaze for a heartbeat and then kissed her, a gentle touch, unhurried, just the lightest caress of his lips against hers. He slid the tips of his fingers down her cheek and then dropped his hand to hers, lacing his fingers between her own.

Her breath hitched and a warmth washed over her chest. Pressing her lips firmly against his, she pulled back and quirked her brow. "You sure do know how to help a girl cheer up."

He studied her a moment, and then as if resigned to whatever conclusions he'd come to, leaned back and looked out the front window. "Go on in. Martin should be ready for us by now, and he may need to go over your actual script changes with you. I'm going to go talk to security."

Guilt settled on top of her shoulders. She didn't mean

to hurt him, but she needed to hold him at a safe distance. Maybe distance, actual, physical distance was what she needed to keep her head straight.

Sam got out and closed the door. Film sets buzzed with activity. So many people, and any one of them could be responsible for screwing with her. The persistent and annoying question of the year was why.

She listed off everyone she knew well and those she'd just met, and couldn't come up with a single reason for any of them to put such energy into her.

Getting her to leave the film or something to do with Gage were the only solid motivations she could come up with.

Well, they'd have to work a lot harder. She wasn't going anywhere. Though she had no illusions about a future with Gage, she'd be damned if someone would have a say in her writing. Her fear wouldn't go away all at once, but half the battle was knowing what she fought against, and now that she knew, she'd fight to win.

Pulling her shoulders back, she pasted a smile to her face.

Show time.

"Hey, Martin." She forced a bounce in her step as she waved to her mentor. With a breezy smile, she lowered into the chair next to the older man. "How's the script look? Ready to go?"

Martin looked up with worry. "You're okay?"

Sam stretched her smile wider. "Absolutely." Under her breath she added, "I'm really pissed, but I'll be damned if I'm going to let whoever's doing this know it."

"Good, good." He blew out a breath.

She stared at him. "What's wrong?"

Furrowing his brow, he slipped a piece of paper in her hand. "We need to be more careful. I don't want you to worry. We're going to take care of this."

"What?" She turned the paper over in her hand, unfolding it until it lay flat on her thigh.

"It was left on your desk."

Keep swimming alone. You'll only make my job easier.

Cold fear slithered up her spine. "When did you find this?" she whispered.

"Just a few minutes ago. I already informed security, and I'll talk to Gage."

Her mind couldn't process the idea someone had watched her swimming, had been waiting for her. Her shoulders tightened down in a vice. Had they seen Gage? Fuck. Her eyes smarted behind tears, and she blinked them back.

"We need to call the police." Martin pulled out his phone.

Sam placed her hand over his. "The last thing you need is this to go to the press during one of your films, and with Gage and me both working on the set? It'll be an Ethan Evans nightmare all over again. I can't take that, and I don't want it for you." She sat back. "There has to be another way."

He slid his phone into his pocket and balanced the screenplay on his lap. "I understand—"

"I just can't, Martin."

He put his hands up. "I've spoken with security. I want someone with you at all times."

Gage walked up, a determined look in his eye. "My thoughts exactly."

She looked between the two men and shook her head.

"No."

"Don't argue. I've already arranged it," Martin said.

"Absolutely not." Sam spoke low through gritted teeth. "I will not have some stranger tracking me. Besides, that will only give satisfaction to whoever is pulling these little pathetic pranks."

Gage drew his brows together. "*Pathetic little pranks?* Are you serious? Someone is threatening you."

Sam waved his words away. "Fine, hire more security on set, but have you seen yourself lately? You're more than capable of taking care of me."

An intense light lit Gage's eyes, and Martin grinned. Sam realized too late what she'd implied. She opened her mouth to clarify.

"Then it's settled. Gage, can she stay with you until we get a handle on this?"

Sam snapped her mouth shut and then tried a logical approach. "That is not necessary. Besides, there's no way he can do that with his schedule."

"Actually, I can. I've been working with Martin on directing while working on the film to break into an opportunity that came up. The next project won't need me for a few weeks. Besides my training and coming to the set, I've been lying low, waiting for the right time to announce my shift into directing."

That's right; he wanted to direct. She hadn't realized how serious he was about it, thinking it was more of something he was just playing at, trying out. *Light and easy, remember?* He'd had no reason to discuss it with her.

The director stood and shared a passing glance with Gage before Sam gathered the rest of her thoughts. "Not only is it necessary, it's mandatory. Unless you'd rather I call your father?"

The hilarity of the situation choked her. "Are you kidding me? You'd call my father? I'm not twelve."

Martin placed his hand on her cheek. "No, but you are just as stubborn as when you were. To be honest, I'd feel better if you did tell your parents. Stay with them. Let them take care of you. Your father would be welcome to come to the set with you. I'd love to get Frank on set…We'll get him a pass—"

Abject horror turned her stomach. Her father on set? Oh, hell no. "What kind of options are those? He'd be here with my brother in a second, and then I'd have *no* peace."

Martin actually looked disappointed.

"If you want my dad on set, invite him to a film I'm not working on, besides—"

"Then what solution do you have, Sam? You won't let me call the police. You can't stay alone. I'm scared for you, and I don't like the feeling one bit. If anything ever happened to you, Frank would—"

"Okay, okay." She threw her hands up to get him to slow down the guilt trip. There was no way she'd put her sister in any danger, and her brother was already a no, since he'd run to their dad before she'd finished explaining. Staying with Raquel and Martin would be exhausting. They loved her too much to keep their noses out of her business, and besides, last she heard their youngest, Liam, was staying with them, something about work in his condo. Damn it.

It would be fine. She could stay with Gage. It would only be a few hours of the day, since they burned candles at both ends working anyway. She could maintain her distance, keep everything light and fun.

"We'll hire additional security to watch you on the set and with errands, so you won't need Gage twenty-four seven."

She watched the older man walk away, then swung around to face Gage. "You have to agree this is ridiculous."

Gage faced her with his arms crossed at his chest. "It's a sound idea, and honestly, I feel better having you with me than someone else."

She threw her hands in the air. "You men are all the same."

"Stay close." He pointed to a chair next to the producer and waited for her to nod before joining the crew.

"That's the exact opposite of what I need to do," Sam whispered, as she sunk into the chair. She grabbed her screenplay and pretended to look through the notes Martin left for her. But she couldn't see anything but trouble. Her hands went numb, and she felt light headed. She'd needed distance from Gage to slow things down, and now she was moving in with him. A small kernel of doubt seeped into her well-laid plans for distance, and her chest squeezed in panic.

That evening, Sam dropped her bag on the floor near the pantry wall, grumbling. "I still think this is over the top."

"Just think of it as a slumber party. Two friends hanging out. Besides, Anita is a spectacular cook."

Sam rolled her eyes. "I am not having your house cleaner cook for me."

"She gets paid to do it," Gage said, twisting his lips in offense, but the emotion didn't quite reach his eyes.

Sam waved away his posturing and picked up her bag. "Can you show me to the guest room?"

Gages stilled. "Guest room?"

She stepped toward him, willing him to understand. "You know this is still just a fling, right?"

He pressed his lips together with a nod. "A fling, yeah, I know. You mean the thing where we're sleeping together but nothing else."

She looked down at her feet and then back to him on a shaky, indrawn breath. "I know we've been getting closer, and you have to know how much I appreciate your friendship."

He flinched, and her heart cried out to give him what he wanted, but that would only destroy them both in the end, and she couldn't let that happen. *Because* he meant so much. She reached for him and then let her hand drop back to her side. She couldn't stand the irony of trying to comfort him from the pain she'd caused. Forcing herself to finish, she blinked rapidly. "But it has to be physical only. I can't afford to do that kind of damage to myself again. Or to you." She ended on a whisper, hoping he'd heard her, not sure she could say the words a second time.

Gage scrubbed his face with his hands and sighed.

Sam changed her bag from one hand to the other, tilting her head. "I'm going to be staying here with you, and we see each other on set almost every day. On top of that, you've spent time with my family. This is really cozy for two people who aren't actually building a relationship. I just want to make sure we keep things in perspective. I'm trying to be smart here, trying to make sure we don't get hurt."

He palmed their two sets of keys that had been sitting together on the counter, lost in thought. Finally, he tossed one set of keys to her and placed the other in a bowl at the end of the counter. "Of course you are." Watching her for what seemed like an eternity, he finally gave in and reached out for her hand. He gathered her in, his heat, his scent, enveloping her at once, and he hovered his lips over hers.

"What are you doing?"

"Keeping it physical."

Sam closed her eyes. It wasn't as if she could see anyway, the feel of his mouth on hers was blinding.

This was going to be harder than she thought.

Chapter Thirteen

Sam weaved her way back to her desk, feeling relaxed for the first time in the past few days. She and Gage had both been swamped with work, with his time spent on the phone handling strings of interviews and meetings with his agent while she'd been tentatively looking into a few future projects and continuing with rewrites on the film. She had a stack of manuscripts that needed a read through, too, but couldn't seem to find the time. She didn't know how couples did it when every day seemed like it was on fast forward.

A swim at her favorite place off the coast on Pepperdine Campus under the ever watchful eye of security helped put things into perspective, gain a little levity. Pulling in a breath, she tossed her bag onto the table and then stopped short. Her bag knocked over a stack of tabloid magazines. *What the hell?*

Sam tilted her head to the side and then recoiled in shock. A cover showing photos of Ethan's suicide in the foreground and the accident in the background with Gage standing by, unkempt and with wild eyes, lay on top. The headline CUTLER ACCIDENT STARTED ETHAN EVANS' SUICIDAL SPIRAL screamed at her. She placed a hand over her trembling lips, trying to swallow past the lump in her throat. Her stomach twisted as she pushed the top magazine off of the pile with her pencil, only to reveal another of Ethan's disfigured face.

Cover after cover revealed the horror show she and Ethan had lived. More headlines taunted her, ETHAN EVANS: SUICIDE OR KILLER WIFE? and ETHAN EVANS: PLAYBOY AT THE MANSION. Every one reminding her of the pain they went through and mocking her with the truth of Ethan's actions that had been right in front of her eyes the whole time.

She stared at the picture of Gage and Ethan next to each other, and an overwhelming sense of dread weighed heavy in her stomach. Tension gripped her shoulder blades, and she craned her neck trying to find any clue around the area she worked. The hairs stood on the back of her neck as she stared at the stack of memories she wanted to forget.

Trying to muffle a cry, Sam grabbed the magazines and her bag. She rushed past security and straight to her car.

The security guard called out, "Ms. Dekker, let me drive you."

"No." She needed to be alone, no questions, no advice. Without further explanation she ducked into her car and drove the winding roads through vision blurred by tears, security following close behind. Her mind spiraled in dark memories as she made a pit stop at her condo and then made fast work of the traffic, finally pulling into the first set of security passes, leading to Gage's home. That's what she wanted right now, the knowledge that no one could get to her.

Once inside, she hauled two bags from her condo into the guest room and dumped them on the ground. Pulling herself together, she informed Anita that she could go for the day and tried to ignore the security guard who set up post in the kitchen. Once she heard the blessed door close and silence followed, she opened a cabernet and then drank it right from the bottle.

A few sips and a few steps brought her back to the bags she'd brought, and she tipped them over with her foot. Tabloids spilled out in a gross waterfall of lies and manipulation, forming a collage of tragedy. She sank to her knees, taking a swig, and picked up the first one. Headlines about how she'd never work in Hollywood again mocked her with misquotes, creating a climate within the screenwriting community she hadn't been able to weather. How other screenwriters, her friends, would have ever believed what was printed in those stories stunned her, but they had, or at least they thought everyone else did. And that was worse. So they kept their distance, closed their doors. Her chest hurt as the memories tumbled over each other again and again.

Their actions gave credence to all of Ethan's little digs. *You really don't believe you matter to any of them, do you, Sam? Come on, you're a screenwriter. Disposable. Remember that.* His words a not too subtle reminder of where she stood with him as well but delivered with a large dose of saccharine—which everyone knew tasted sweet but left you poisoned. He'd been right, though. People didn't like drama and pulled away from those surrounded by it. But it wasn't really her as much as wanting to protect their own agendas. Guilty by association was a strong allegation in Hollywood.

Sam tossed the magazine aside and picked up another. She flipped the tabloid over to the back and then looked at the front again, giving it a high salute with her wine before tipping the bottle back for another drink. After Ethan died, the harassment didn't stop, but increased in the media's insatiable thirst for dirt. They just knew she'd been doing something unsavory all along, but when they couldn't find anything, they'd made it up. Snapping pictures from behind bushes and jumping out at her from behind cars. Anyone would look suspicious with their hands thrown up in front of their face.

Headlines like ETHAN EVANS' BLACK WIDOW splashed the front page, making it look like she'd planned the whole sticky web and would make it her mission to do so again. She threw the magazine down and took another long swallow, trying to keep her tears from surfacing. She'd given Ethan too many already.

The thing was, he'd hidden who he truly was and had made sure he was loved, and she was nothing more than an afterthought. Afterthoughts had a strange way of becoming the main target once the bull's eye had been hit.

Their marriage and his death had been a tragic situation turned lurid by society's lust for blood and blame. Coping? Healing? She'd been barely breathing.

• • •

Gage walked into his kitchen and dropped his bag on the table, relieved to find security on post. When he'd seen Sam's car, the first thing he thought was that his stubborn woman had snuck off alone.

He took the guard's hand in a firm shake. "Thanks, man. I've got it from here."

It had been a good day off from the set. He took Sam's need for distance seriously—just not necessarily with the same outcome in mind—and took advantage of the extra time to help down at the university theater, a perfect fit for an afternoon off from the set. He'd been involving himself more and more with the theater students as a guest speaker time and again. His dad had approached him with the idea, and he'd warmed to it right away.

Acting had saved him, given him purpose, an amount of freedom reality couldn't achieve. If he could help encourage and inspire a kid like he'd been, help them find direction, an outlet, then he'd jump through the security hoops to do it.

The university kids, full of passion and possibilities, reminded him why he pursued acting so long ago. He enjoyed every conversation, rehearsal, and theory discussion. The students weren't yet jaded by the reality of Hollywood.

Gee Gee, the department head, and an old friend, had shared her plans for the next stage performance, and a few of the scheduled events in the next coming months. He'd love to attend, but only if he could sneak in without pulling attention from the event itself, which wasn't likely, so she promised him a recorded viewing.

Gee Gee was an exotic creature, a combination of Louise Brooks and Cleopatra, who loved nothing more than the theater—except her husband, Ian. He and the couple had become fast friends, and he owed them a lot. Sam would love them.

He toed off his shoes, pulled off his socks, and dropped them inside. The cool tiled floor felt good on his feet as he walked to the refrigerator. He opened it and stared at the overflowing shelves inside.

He grabbed the milk and took a chug from the carton. He'd wanted to share more of his help with the theater kids with Sam. She'd love the interaction and with her writing she could add a lot to his visits, but that didn't mesh with her "fling" approach to their relationship. For now. The last drop of milk hit his tongue, and he crushed the carton in his hand and then tossed it into the trash.

He needed to show Sam being with him didn't have to be a repeat of her life with Ethan. The paparazzi laid off unless he gave them a reason not to, or the times he purposefully went out very publicly to boost his visibility, but some of it, much of it, could be controlled. If he could just show her.

Fuck, he hated feeling desperate. He was a goddamn man, a Hollywood movie star. Insecurities and yearnings were for the damn characters he played, not him. He shook his head.

He liked a challenge. He dropped his feet to the ground and leaned forward onto his knees. Rubbing his face with his hands, he thought of what he'd need to do in order for her to give them a chance. The paparazzi and the lifestyle were two of his biggest obstacles, and he couldn't blame her. Good decisions in Hollywood seemed as hard to come by as winning an Oscar, but at least he was changing his part of that every day.

A small cry grabbed his attention, and he made his way to the guest room. With a small knock, he pushed the door open to find Sam sitting cross legged on the ground surrounded by tabloids, used tissues, and an empty bottle of wine. Taking the sight of her in, he rubbed his chest. "What happened?"

The magazines were ghastly. What had he just been thinking about control? By the looks of this mess, Ethan had handed it all over. It didn't look like the man had even tried. Maybe he thought staying on the front page was better than disappearing completely. And of course, he hadn't given a damn about Sam.

Gage shoved the magazines aside and lowered to the floor, pulling her into his arms. She resisted at first, looking at him in surprise. Tears streaked her face, and her eyes held a world of horrors in their depths. Pressing his lips to the top of her head, he tucked her in tight and just held her until she settled with a sigh.

On a hiccup, she wiped her nose with a tissue and pulled slightly away. "I'm sorry," she whispered.

He shook his head. "Don't be. Why do you have all of these?"

She tucked her head into his chest. "Ethan had started the collection. They'd tortured him, but in a weird way he seemed to like even this kind of attention. After he died, I kept them to remind myself not to make the same mistakes again. I picked them up from my place today after I received a stack as a little gift at the set."

"Oh, babe." He didn't try to say anything else. There were no words. She needed to finish purging whatever emotions she had before he could expect her to move past the ugliness of it all.

"I'm here for you. I hate you've had to go through any of this, and being so grossly reminded is cruel. We'll find out who's doing this. I promise."

She nodded. "It's a good reminder."

He lifted her face with a light touch to her chin. "No. This isn't anything you need to be reminded about. This could have been stopped, Sam. It didn't need to happen."

He didn't need for her to say the words to know she was thinking about her reasons for not getting serious with celebrities, and he wanted to argue immediately and aggressively about how wrong she was. But now was not the time. She needed someone to be gentle with her, someone to simply care. Leaning back against the bed, he pulled her more snuggly between his thighs, with one leg up to support her back and the side of her face against his chest. He brushed his fingers through her hair.

Figuring out exactly what he needed to do to guarantee damage control from the tabloids moving forward would be key. He needed to show her the paparazzi wouldn't poison their relationship like it did with her marriage. They'd limit their public appearances, tighten security, and he could work with his PR team to have statements on the ready.

Gage sighed. Ethan had done a number on her. He wished he could raise the man from the dead just to punch him in his pretty face. But in the end, it didn't matter. Gage was here, and he wasn't going anywhere.

She pulled in a shaky breath and smiled at him. "I'm sorry."

He shook his head.

Sliding one finger over his lip, she smiled when he stilled and rewarded him by continuing to caress his lips and his jaw with light strokes as she spoke. "I found the magazines, and they hit so hard I didn't think much before ending up here. Going through them all again was kind of like flushing out all the old dirt. I'm okay, really I am. I just needed to do this, so I could really be finished. Which is a big change from a year ago. I used to throw each new magazine on top of the growing pile and close the storage door against them. Knowing they were there and what they said only festered, but now I'm done. Whoever left the stack for me actually did me a favor. It was one of those things I really needed to deal with but kept avoiding."

She held his gaze. "Thank you for being here for me, for not trying to rush me or fix it. For letting me do this on my own time."

He nodded, she'd never know what doing nothing had cost him, but he'd do it again.

"I don't know what to say to you when you hold me, how to thank you."

"You don't have to say anything. I'm just doing my job."

She peered at him from the corner of her eyes in confusion. "I'm a job?"

"You're my friend. And it's my job to be there for you, to support you. Anyone would have done the same."

A watery laugh escaped from between her lips. "No, they wouldn't."

"Then they aren't really your friend."

She rested back against him and closed her eyes.

He settled in for the long haul, giving her all the time she needed.

Eyeing his board on the back deck through the bedroom window, he longed for the surf. How long had it been since he'd been out on the waves? One of the main reasons he'd paid the exorbitant prices of his gated beach was so he could surf whenever he wanted—needed.

This was one of those times. If he was going to convince

her, he needed a well-strategized plan and nothing could get his brain in the right frame of focus as a good round with the waves. There was something about battling with Mother Nature that opened his brain to all possibilities and rejected limitations—nothing like sweating it out with one woman to figure out exactly how to win over the one you really wanted.

He grinned. Every woman in the universe would banish him for analogies like that.

All in good time. He needed to take things one step at a time with Sam, show her how well they worked together on and off the set, prove to her that the horrors she faced because of Ethan's fame weren't necessary, so when the thought of leaving entered her mind she wouldn't be able to stand it.

Because he couldn't.

• • •

The white stucco walls, round turrets, and reaching archways made Sam feel as if she stepped through a doorway straight into Italy. "I love coming here. It's like arriving in a fairytale."

Raquel pulled Sam into her embrace with a smile. "Come in, come in."

Sam followed her through the large open living space, with a spectacular view of an infinity pool through wall-to-wall glass doors, to the spacious kitchen. Raquel and Martin had been *the* power couple of Malibu and goods friends for as long as she could remember.

The elegant woman smoothed her hair into place as she studied Sam. "It is so good to see you. I've missed you so much."

Sam blew out a breath. "I've missed you, too."

"I've always been here for you." Raquel pulled her in for a hug.

Sam sighed, squeezing her friend in return. "I know. I wasn't a good friend there for a while. I'm sorry."

Holding her at arm's length, Raquel smiled. "Pish. You didn't need to be a good friend, but I wanted to."

Dressed in a flowing silk tunic of white and deep purple, Raquel glided through the main room to the doors that led to her backyard paradise. "Join me? It's beautiful out."

Sam followed, thankful for her slew of wonderful friends, Gage included, and settled into a cushioned lounge under a deep brown pergola draped in sheer white organza. He'd held her, just sat there and held her. It was almost too much, like she didn't know what to do with such kindness. No demands for her to feel better, no rush. She'd never experienced anyone like him before, and though they couldn't be serious, she wasn't about to do anything to hurt the relationship they did have. If she could help it.

Looking around the backyard, she smiled. "God, this is heaven."

"I love it out here." Raquel sipped her drink and eyed her over the rim of her glass.

Sam pulled back her shoulders. "I need to talk to you about something. Ask you really, but you have to swear you won't say anything to anyone. Especially Martin, he'd never be able to keep his mouth shut." She threw up a hand as her mouth dropped open. "No offense."

Raquel waved her words away like she was swatting at gnats. "Please, I have a long list of things I don't tell that man for that exact reason."

"So Gage Cutler." Her voice trailed off as Raquel's smile grew broader. "Quit looking at me like that."

Raquel feigned an air of boredom. "Like what, dear?"

"Like you just won some sort of victory." Sam set the glass on the table. She couldn't imagine what was going on in her friend's head.

Raquel sat straighter in her seat and tried—unsuccessfully—to contain her smile. "Of course not, darling."

Raquel loved her and wanted to see her happy, but Sam had to figure out how herself, not have it orchestrated by someone else. She cleared her throat and rushed the words out. "Gage and I have been seeing each other, having a fling of sorts. Nothing serious, you know my rule." God, it felt so good to tell someone, to hear the words aloud.

Raquel nodded calmly, sipping from her glass.

Sam could swear the woman was ready to burst, but she remained silent. Maybe Sam only imagined it, since she herself had so much going on inside. She straightened in her seat. "You know how it would look with the accident. I can admit now that Ethan and I were broken, but if Gage and I got serious, it would look like we'd been in bed together from the beginning. The tabloids would devour a story like that."

Raquel's eyes sparkled with enthusiasm. "You are so much stronger than you think, really. Darling, the tabloids are a symptom of celebrity, not the prognosis. You can't make your decisions based on whether or not you'll end up on the front page again. Besides, a man like Gage has a lot he can do to remedy that."

Sam sighed. He was very good at taking care of her, like nothing she'd ever known before, but—there was always a "but." "He's still a celebrity, under the microscope. The life-style. I already made that mistake once. As much as I care for him, I don't want that for me or my family. I don't want Hollywood in my relationship, not just the tabloids, though they are the worst of all, but the community, the fake friend-ships and plastic associations. Gage will always be a part of it."

"Do me a favor."

Sam nodded, the yearning in her heart reaching for any silver lining.

"You are enjoying your time with him. Right?"

"Yes, he's wonderful, but—"

"Just give yourself this time. Darling, life is so short, even when it feels like an eternity. Please. Enjoy the friendship."

"I don't want to hurt him any more than I have."

"Of course you don't. And he is so very pitifully vulner-able, isn't he?" Raquel raised a brow.

Sam shook her head and chuckled. "I know, I know."

"You've come a long way since last year."

"I'm fighting to get my life back." Sam looked out across the pool to the ocean view beyond. The warm sun relaxed her, or maybe it was simply being with Raquel. Sam wasn't sure, but for the first time, she wanted to talk about Ethan's suicide. "There must have been something I could have done, Raquel. Gotten him help or talked to his fam-ily." Her voice, barely above a whisper, wavered. Leaning back, she wrapped her arms about her waist while images of Ethan's stiff, lifeless body flashed in jarring succession. Echoes of accusations and resentments followed the ghastly visual memories, and she breathed slowly against the tight-ness in her chest.

Raquel paused, then with purposeful, smooth, movements slid to the edge of her lounge and pinned Sam with a look. "Darling, look at me."

Sam lifted her gaze. "Maybe Ethan's family is right. He'd wanted a baby; I'd said no. I think he knew I was going to leave—"

"No." Her friend raised her hand, palm out. "I'm sorry, but listen to me carefully." The compelling rush of the large stone waterfall was the only sound. "Whether he knew or not, you were not responsible. He was a sick man, fighting demons you and I cannot comprehend." Her eyes pleaded with Sam.

She opened her mouth to argue. Guilt tightened her throat, and she struggled to swallow past it.

Raquel tilted her head in that regal way of hers, asking for silence. "Years ago, when Martin and I had just been starting out, he'd put our savings into a project. Success would mean riches—failure, rags. It failed. Our savings gone. Our credit shot. No hope of owning a home. The idea of procuring a backer for any future projects impossible—so Martin concluded." She placed her hand on Sam's knee. "Darling, I came home to find my strong, virile husband passed out on our bed, an empty bottle of sleeping pills on the floor. I was devastated and pissed."

Sam grasped Raquel's hand. Her stomach twisted with grief for her friend, for herself.

Raquel straightened and stretched. "I blamed myself."

"Oh, Raquel. Why? You had to see it wasn't your fault."

Raquel leveled a look at Sam with startling green eyes. "You're right. It wasn't. Martin needed help, but he tried to duck out on our life, thinking I'd be better off without him."

She finished her water and held Sam's gaze. "I wouldn't let him. He needed help, and I hadn't seen it. That, I did feel guilty about. But we got help, together. Now, we're stronger for it."

No one should have to face that kind of fear. A fear that never really healed, no matter how much time passed. "That explains why you watch him like a hawk."

"I know my dear husband isn't in the danger he'd been in before, but I won't take any chances, that's for certain."

Leaning back against the lounge, Sam focused on the rushing spray of the waterfall. "I appreciate you sharing this with me. I can only imagine what you must have gone through. But my situation is different."

"How?"

Raquel hadn't held Martin back, they were a team, and she supported his plans for career, coordinated galas, set up meetings. But Sam had held Ethan's hope in her hands and had no intention of giving it to him. She couldn't give it to him. Deep down, she knew she'd made the right decision—for her. Now, it was something she'd have to live with.

A future with Gage would only add to her selfishness. She placed a hand over her stomach. Wouldn't it? Gage was just stepping in to a whole new chapter of his career, and a public relationship with her would bring the whole mess with Ethan back up and might ruin his chances at directing or landing other major roles.

Besides, even if she could admit she cared more than she should, he wouldn't want to put up with her issues.

If Gage ever had the chance for a happily-ever-after, especially under Hollywood's microscope, he needed someone with better odds.

Chapter Fourteen

After saying goodbye to Raquel, Sam headed home. She weaved in and out of traffic until she sat by Gage's security gate and then in his driveway. On a sigh, she pushed open her door and took the path that led to his front door. What was she going to do with this inexplicable pull he had on her? She'd admit, even if just to herself, he was more than a fling. She didn't want to think too much on what that actually meant besides pain, especially since being with her would tie him back to Ethan's death and damage everything he was trying so hard to repair. She'd just shove it away for now. Maybe take Raquel's advice and enjoy the friendship.

Gage appeared without a word as she stepped through the door and he pulled her into his arms. "You're exactly who I wanted to see."

She resisted the warmth of his arms and then gave in and hugged him back. She wouldn't have too many more chances, and this was her favorite place to be. In time their problems would fester into something ugly, just as they had with Ethan.

It felt like eons ago now, but when she and Ethan had first started out, all fresh-faced and new in the industry, they'd been a team, at least she thought they had been. Could she have been so wrong? As Ethan's career had taken off, and his influence offered him endless opportunities, he'd slowly changed, and she became a status rather than an actual person. She hadn't noticed at first because she hadn't wanted to, but the truth had become too much to ignore. Meeting Gage that night had forced her to face her marriage — at least until the accident.

With a grin, he took her hand, his palm callused and warm, sending shivers up her arm, reminding her of the feel of that combination against her skin.

Gage pulled her into the living room. The fireplace glowed, and shadows and light flickered against the walls. "I've been worried about you. How are you doing?"

Sam laughed, a low tight sound. Her heart pounded in her chest and her fingers tingled. "I'm okay, if you don't count my complete mortification of yesterday. I'm sorry I reacted that way."

Wrapping his arms around her, he hugged her again. "I hated seeing you so hurt."

She buried her face in his neck and breathed him in. "I know. You knew exactly what I needed. I'm sorry you had to see that, but I'm glad you were there. But I'm okay now. I went to see Raquel," she added with a giggle. "And she says, 'Hello, Darling.'"

He raised a brow and flashed a smile. "That's the Mother of Malibu all right."

Sam met his gaze. "Yes, she is." She blew out a breath, laughing.

Gage took her hand again and pulled her down onto his lap as he sunk into a deep, cushioned armchair. He tucked her hair behind her ears and ran his fingers along her cheek, over the sensitive spot at the joint of her jaw, down her neck to her collarbone.

Sam shivered and grabbed his roaming fingers. "I told her about us."

"Really?" The smooth tone of his voice skimmed down her spine, following the path of his fingertips, and she shivered.

"I needed someone to talk to, ya know? A girlfriend. She isn't going to say anything to Martin."

"Yeah, right." He laughed. Her mouth shot open again, and he covered it with her hand. "You haven't kissed me yet."

Her shoulders relaxed, and as soon as he moved his hand, she pressed her mouth to his with enthusiasm. Pouring all of her emotions into the kiss, her hands roamed over his face and his shoulders, just to make sure he was real.

Breaking from the kiss, he kissed each corner of her mouth and then her nose, regardless of her protest. "What did you guys talk about?"

She lost herself in his steady gaze, in the blue-green of his eyes, in his interest. "You and Ethan being celebrities and what that means."

Gage slid her from his lap to the chair and stood, and she immediately missed his warmth.

What had she said?

He put his hands behind his head and stretched. Pacing back and forth in front of the fireplace, he muttered under his breath. He stopped, opened his mouth to speak, then closed it and continued to pace.

He lifted his hand and then dropped it to his side, and perched on the arm chair of the seat next to hers. He pressed his lips together and then sighed. "I'm trying really hard not to be offended. Regardless of what you think, I'm not in the habit of putting those I care about in jeopardy."

Sam's heart picked up its beat. She knew he cared for her. She spent most of her time worried he wouldn't and worried he would.

"But to compare me with your asshole husband?" He shot her a look, both intense and wounded. "If you care for me, even a little, don't ever do that again."

Understanding dawned. Sam widened her eyes. "Oh, Gage, no. That's not what I meant. I told her about our fling, about how wonderful you are, and then I talked to her a little bit about Ethan's suicide. Raquel really helped me."

He pushed his fingers back through his hair. "I thought with the whole celebrity thing—"

She stood and then stepped up behind him and wrapped her arms about his waist, so warm and solid beneath her touch. She rubbed her cheek against the strong muscles of his back. His scent enveloped her, and she closed her eyes. "I'm sorry about not being able to move in a more serious direction. I know I hurt you the other day, and I hate myself for it."

Silence followed, but he dropped his hands on top of hers and squeezed. "I'll accept your apology on one condition."

"On one condition?" she asked with a laugh.

His hand shot out and grabbed her wrist before she could get away. Pulling her to him, he waggled his brow.

"Let's burn the magazines."

Her heart expanded beyond the point of pain and into something else altogether. With a watery-eyed nod, she said, "Yes."

Dipping down to look her in the eye, he checked in again. "Yeah?"

She nodded. It was time to burn the rest of her garbage.

There was no better way to see into her future than by clearing the path that led the way.

Sam got out of her car, looking around her familiar condo garage. They'd burned the magazines, watching them go up in flames the colors of the rainbow. It had been more cathartic than she'd ever imagined, and having Gage there standing beside her had been empowering. Not because she needed a man to move ahead, but because this man, this friend, wanted to support her move toward setting herself free.

Afterward, they'd snuggled on the couch, and Gage had fallen asleep during a movie, but she was too revved up. She took advantage to run to her house and grab the clothes she meant to get earlier. Nothing had happened in a while, and she needed some space, some distance. He'd be pissed if he woke up before she got back, so she needed to make this quick. Pulling her bag higher onto her shoulder, she headed toward the elevators.

The sound of someone clearing a throat startled Sam, and she whirled around. Her hand on her chest, she pulled in a breath and willed her heart to slow down. Ethan's younger sister leaned against the wall wearing pretension and bitch like a trench coat. Great.

"Oh, Brigette. You scared me."

The young woman smirked, then corrected Sam. "*Brigitte*." She pronounced her name with a French flair Sam found amusing. Brigitte had tucked her hair into a French twist with practiced perfection. Her pink lips were lined and filled in with a matte lipstick, her tweed suit wrinkle-free. She pulled on her driving gloves at the wrist with a bored look. "You should be more careful, Sam. We'd hate to hear that you got hurt because you're unaware of your surroundings."

Sam tilted her head to the side as the young woman circled her with slow, steady steps. The Evans family bred predators; how had she not seen that? Adopting her own bored look, Sam glanced at her phone. "What could I possibly help you with, *Brigitte*?"

"We want the rest of Ethan's work."

"I gave you what I think he'd like for you to have already."

A violent shake of her head sent a few pieces of the woman's coiffed style free. "No. We want his work. He'd have never trusted you to decide what he would choose for us. You have no right." Her voice shook with rage as she paced, then swung around. "You were never enough for him. He had nothing left after the accident, and he killed himself."

She stepped in front of Sam and placed her hands on her hips, visibly forcing some self-control. "I want them now." She turned toward the elevators. "I'll go with you, even if it means setting foot in an apartment you've soiled with your whoring ways."

Sam's jaw fell open before she could stop it. *Whoring ways?*

The smug look that settled onto Brigitte's face was the last straw. Sam reached her limit, sick and tired of their bullying. Were they that desperate for Ethan's photographs? She'd done them a favor, though they didn't see it that way. Handing over his work would only expose them to his dark, dishonest side. She couldn't imagine the ever-proper Mother Evans would want detailed photographs of her golden child in various degrees of nakedness, fornicating with his models.

Sam shook her head. When she'd first found the photos she thought perhaps they were innocent, that she'd overreacted—until she reached the photos on the bottom.

Her palms were slick with perspiration and the air hung thick and heavy. She forced herself to paste a pleasant, if a tad patronizing, smile upon her face.

"You disgust me. I can't imagine what my brother ever saw in you. I'm waiting for his things."

"You'll be waiting a long time."

Brigitte stomped her foot. "Bring me his photographs."

Sam pushed the button on the elevator, then turned back and looked at the ignorant woman.

Brigitte smoothed her hands down her skirt and pulled on her gloves once again, a determined look narrowing her eyes. "Now."

"No." The elevator doors opened and Sam stepped through.

Brigitte, red faced and hands fisted at her sides, stared at Sam as the doors closed.

Sam collapsed back against the corner of the elevator, using the handrail to stay upright. She pulled in deep breaths until her heart returned to its somewhat normal rhythm.

She couldn't let them find out what he'd really been like.

Regardless that his family seemed to relish *their* cruelty, she didn't and never would, which gave her some peace, but more important was the absolute humiliation the photos produced. If she did anything with them, she'd destroy them.

Even though she'd been part of the Evans family, she'd never been an Evans.

Sam dropped her head back with a sigh, thankful for small favors. She placed a call to her brother, Luca. At the very least, he'd be able to give her an idea of any legal action she might need to take. She'd prefer to keep it as quiet as possible, but she didn't want to be stupid, either.

About thirty minutes later, Sam placed a cup of steaming coffee in front of her brother at her kitchen table. "Black, strong with no fuss, just the way you like it." She ruffled his hair. "Thanks for coming over."

Luca ducked his head away from her and then took a tentative sip. "You always make the best coffee, second to Addison." He winked and then set the cup down, wrapping his hands around it. "This is serious, Sam. I can file a restraining order."

"Isn't there anything else we can do?"

He brushed a hand back through his dark blond hair. "Look, with her threat and what's been going on at your work—"

"How do you know about that?" Sam lowered into a chair opposite her brother. *Damn it.*

"Gage, and before you get all up in arms, it should have been you. Why didn't you tell me?"

"I didn't want you guys to worry. As it is, I've agreed to twenty-four hour supervision. Besides, it's work."

"First off." He made a point of looking about the room.

"I don't see anybody here."

Sam winced. Gage was going to take this personally. No more privacy for her in the near future. "That's my fault. Gage fell asleep, and I thought I could grab my things and get back before he woke up."

Luca shook his head, looking at her as if she couldn't be trusted to cross the street alone. "Not surprised. Second, anyone could be harassing you at work; it doesn't have to be one of the crew. There are ways people can gain access."

"I'll be careful."

Luca sipped his coffee and ran the bottom of his knuckle around the rim of the cup. "What I don't get is why you haven't just told them what an ass he was."

Sam's heart lurched. For a split second she thought he knew about Ethan's indiscretions. Ha! Indiscretions—that was a stretch. But she'd kept the discovery to herself on purpose. She wasn't just hurt by what he'd done, she burned with humiliation. A humiliation she'd rather not broadcast.

Sam shook her head. "They'd never believe me. You know how they are. Ugh. I don't want to talk about them anymore." Appreciation for her brother warmed her heart. She walked around the table and kissed his cheek. "I'll be careful, and if anything happens, I'll let you know. But please, don't tell Mom and Dad. The last thing I need is them showing up on set."

The front door slammed. "Don't worry, she's not leaving my sight again."

Sam whirled around at the sound of Gage's voice. He glanced at her and then away, but she went up to him and wrapped her arms around his middle anyway. "How'd you know I was here?"

Luca shoved the chair next to him out with his foot so Gage could take a seat. "I called him."

"Luca," she gritted out. "That is why I called *you*. So he wouldn't be bothered."

Gage held her so tight she thought she might pass out, and then set her aside. "Don't you ever do that again. Do you know how worried I was when I woke up to Luca's call and you nowhere in sight?" Gage sauntered across the kitchen and dumped his bag on the floor next to the counter and then dropped into the chair next to Luca. "I'm sorry. Won't happen again."

Luca grunted. "Like she gave you a choice. Don't think we all don't know how stubborn she is."

Sam rolled her eyes. "Luca, you are not helping."

Gage looked down at his hands, spreading his fingers wide, and then rested his forearms on the table. "What I can't figure out is why Ethan's family is so bent on making her life hell. What's in it for them? What's the point? If she's such a drag on their family pedigree, you'd think they'd want to sweep her under the rug."

"Exactly. Doesn't make sense." Luca glanced at Sam.

She shot a look from her brother to Gage, who apparently wasn't even looking at her right now, and back. She'd lost sleep wondering the same thing. What was the point?

"I want her to apply for a restraining order but she won't. Stubborn, shit." Luca snorted in disgust.

"If they do anything else, we'll file. Okay?" She crossed her arms. "I'm not trying to be difficult, but I don't want to make this into something bigger than it is, either."

"Don't worry, I'm still not letting her out of my sight."

Luca dipped his head in acknowledgement. "Thanks.

She thinks she's invincible."

Sam threw her hands up in the air. "Enough. No more talk about the Evanses or the stupid pranks on set. I'll be careful and keep someone with me, no exceptions. Okay?" She was touched that they took her safety so seriously, she did too, but they spoke about her as if she purposefully placed herself within the Evans' clutches. Something she'd never do again.

Both men gave a nod of confirmation, lips pressed into a thin line, jaws set, and then they settled into talking industry. Luca wanted to work for a specific studio and Gage had a few contacts. Sam wondered how men did it, shifting from tense to chill with such ease. She still hummed on a sharp edge, but looking at Gage, she wasn't sure it was only due to Brigitte's little visit, damn stubborn man. He thought all her reasons for not being together were excuses, but they weren't, they were precautions for her and him.

She looked Gage over, his intense concentration, eyes neither blue nor green but somehow both. His broad shoulders filled the space, as did his solid, long legs stretched out before him. Solid, that was the word for him right now. Dependable. Strong.

And it terrified her. Getting used to him being there for her would only lower her defenses and set her up for a harder fall in the end. She hugged her arms around herself instead of wrapping them around him like she wanted to do, instead of letting him fix everything, protect her, and take care of her. She was falling for him too hard and too fast, and wanted to dig her heels in just to gain her breath, to gain back some control.

But she had to give him credit where credit was due, and

found herself relating to him on a dangerously deep level because of it. He'd changed from the man he was two years ago, was changing, and he had no intention of stopping.

And neither did she. Lifting her chin, she straightened her spine. Her life was exactly that, hers, and she finally felt as though she was taking it back. She'd focus on tomorrow instead of next week or next month. Having a plan with the restraining order was a solid step to gaining some control.

She continued to watch him, curious about how the sight of him had such a visceral effect, like a warm vibration deep in her chest. She dug her nails into her palms.

Her grip on light and easy was slipping.

Chapter Fifteen

A few days later, the director called the main cast members to the set, and Gage brushed past her, as if on accident, his hand gliding along her backside. She jumped and then busied herself smoothing the front of her shirt, hoping no one noticed. On set he was always polite and courteous, but made sure he knew where she was every second of the day. It was disconcerting and made her want to get him back to his place so she could see his wicked grin, wanting him to be everything but polite. She waved her hand in front of her face.

Sam stared after him, her head pounding. The past few days had consisted of hard work and hot sex. She couldn't complain. But she wanted to. Falling into bed at night with a work-worn brain and Gage-warmed muscles lulled her into a false sense of contentment. False because it wouldn't last. Couldn't last. The end would come. But forever wasn't what she'd asked for. How'd the saying go?

He delivered on exactly what she wanted, a fling—light and easy.

For now, she needed to enjoy every moment. Then someday, armed with the knowledge of what made her happy, she'd meet a man and fall in love. A man like Gage, but capable of sustaining the long haul with her and her past. A man whose reputation and career wouldn't be damaged by her baggage.

The thought didn't comfort her.

Finding a seat with a good view of the action without getting in the way, she settled in to work. Mesmerized by Gage's talent, Sam lost herself in his character, in the story. A particularly heart-wrenching sequence wrapped up, and she sighed.

"It's just a movie, you know."

She twisted in her seat to find Martin standing behind the chair next to her, holding onto the back with both hands. "Hey. It's really something. I think you have a winner here."

His eyes twinkled and he nodded. Clapping his hands once in obvious glee, he made his way around the chair and plopped into it. "I know it. Believe me, I love to see you cry."

Sam rolled her eyes. "Thanks."

"Don't get me wrong, but for you to get emotionally involved in *this* setting"—he waved his hand to encompass the chaos of the set—"with all of the equipment and side noise, well, that says something about this movie. Something big."

She grinned.

Bushy black brows narrowed, and he leaned toward the screenplay on her lap. "Working?"

She followed his gaze and picked up the script. "Just tweaking."

"Good, good."

He didn't ask to see her changes. The knowledge he trusted her was another bump up in her self-confidence. She wasn't going anywhere. She loved her work.

Glancing around the set, she studied each member, each face. Who wouldn't want her here?

Martin tapped her knee. "Okay, I better get to work before the other director gets pissed." He stood to leave. "Sam."

She looked up into his serious face.

"I remember the young screenwriter you were back in the beginning. You worked your ass off to be the best, wouldn't take no for an answer. You built relationships, proved yourself time and again; it's good to see that woman back in the game."

Sam nodded, her throat tight. "I just hope everyone else will feel the same."

"Doesn't matter, they'll be the fools in the end."

Writing was as much a part of her as breathing. She loved it, and the idea that she'd considered walking away or was being pushed away because of Ethan made her stomach hurt.

What had happened?

A boy, a desire to be loved, false promises.

But that was then; this was now. She pulled in a deep breath and smiled.

The producer approached with a friendly, determined, set to his mouth. Sam nodded in greeting.

"Sam." The quiet but intense man nodded in return. He handed her a business card. "This is for you. Cecilia wants to discuss business over lunch."

Immediate warning bells went off in Sam's head. "No, I don't think that's possible."

His prominent brows furrowed. "I have conceded to Gage's wishes that she remain off the set—not without my own personal consequences, mind you. This is the least you can do."

"The least *I* can do?" She laughed. "I'm here because of Martin; I don't have to do anything." An idea took shape, curiosity driven. "But I'll think about it."

"Think about it. You've returned to writing from a year of mourning. You could use a few strong allies in your pocket." He pushed the card into her hand.

After he left, she turned the card over. A sexy red-lipped pout covered the front of the card with Cecilia Lombardi's information. She wrinkled her nose. On the back of the card, etched in pink ink, the time and place. *John's Garden, Malibu Country Mart, Thursday 1 p.m.*

Apprehension filled her gut. *Talk to Gage.* She shoved down the warning. She'd tried that, but it was one conversation he'd been tight-lipped about. He didn't like the woman, and she really didn't want to go, but business was business.

She stared at the card. What could the woman possibly want from her? Sam shook her head. It was with tentative steps that she was walking back into Hollywood. She at least needed to find out what the woman had to say.

Her security shadow would keep Cecilia in line, though Sam couldn't really credit the woman with more brainpower than it took to dress herself in the morning.

But she was done taking chances.

Even with Gage? She pushed up from the chair.

Sam meandered through the piles of equipment, which

promised to topple with one careless touch, until she reached her favorite work place.

As she stepped up to the table, she slowed. Tilting her head to the side, she attempted to make sense of the tangle of material sitting on top of her screenplay. A pair of men's boxer briefs. A small scrap of paper drifted to the floor. Sam picked it up, then slid onto her stool.

Annoyance tightened the muscles between her shoulder blades as she read the scribbled writing. *His favorite pair. I thought he'd want them back.* The words were accessorized by an oily kiss print from red lip gloss.

"Seriously?" She dropped her head back and her hand to her lap.

Gage rounded a shelf containing boxes of film. "What's up?"

Sam held up the boxer briefs. His eyes widened. "Hey, those are mine."

She knew he had nothing to do with their appearance. But fatigue challenged her patience. Wasn't this the exact thing she worried about? The pranks, Ethan's sister, Cecilia, and now this—it was too much. Exhaustion pulled on her like an anchor.

She tossed them to him. Needing fresh air, she passed by Gage, and with a discreet squeeze of his fingers, she slipped him the note.

She didn't blame him, but every day came with reminders as to why they shouldn't be together. This was just one example of how Gage being Gage Cutler would intrude upon her life. Maybe they could keep the press in line and find a way to keep the tabloids in check, but that still left all the people.

. . .

Gage stepped onto the front porch. He'd wanted to follow Sam immediately, but speaking with security had been the priority. He spotted his stubborn woman sleeping on an outdoor sofa. He shook his head.

Security planned to scour the area, search all trailers, and review all entries onto the premises. He rubbed the back of his neck. Talk about bad timing. He paced a short area of the porch and then pulled up to the wooden railing, slamming his hand on it. This stupid shit was pushing Sam further and further away. It was one thing if she was his, he'd ask it of her then because it'd be worth it and they'd be in it together, but all this trouble for a fling was ridiculous. The issues at work and the tabloids. He didn't even want a fling, never wanted it, and his plan didn't seem to be working. They either needed to get serious, or he needed to let her go.

He looked out over the yard, a cold dread heavy in his chest. Maybe that was the point—maybe it was time to stop trying.

"Fuck." He pushed his hands back through his hair. His jaw ached from clenching it too tight for too long. Too much.

He lowered beside her without jarring her position. Within seconds she turned toward him and snuggled into his side. He clenched his fists. It was the same old cliché, but why couldn't she turn to him when she was awake?

The briefs were just like the ones he owned, but the specific pair left for Sam were not his. What he wanted to know was who the hell placed them there and how the hell they knew what he wore.

Gage picked up her hand. "Hey, Sam. Time to wake up."

She jerked and pushed forward to sit on the edge of the cushion. Her body swayed, and Gage placed an arm around her shoulders to steady her before she toppled to the concrete. "Whoa."

She licked her lips and pushed her long brown strands from her face. Blinking several times, she focused on him with a smile. "Hey, how long have I been asleep?"

"Not sure. No more than forty-five minutes. Which reminds me." He twisted to face her straight on. "What about 'be careful' don't you get?"

She frowned. "What are you talking about?"

Gage pushed up from the sofa and stepped toward the front edge of the porch. "There's some sicko doing their damnedest to make your life hell, yet you fall asleep out in the open with no one around."

"Exactly, no one was around. Besides." She jerked her thumb over her shoulder. "He's never more than ten feet away, even when I pee." Her eyes rolled, and he had to stifle a snort at her annoyance.

Gage leaned forward to see around the corner of the porch to find security scanning the yard. The man locked eyes and gave him a smooth nod.

He narrowed his eyes at Sam. "Don't be an ass."

Gage gripped the front porch post until his knuckles turned white. He'd wanted to grip her shoulders and give her a good shake when he'd seen her sleeping, damn stubborn pain-in-the-ass woman. But she'd been exhausted and needed space. He gave it to her, but only as long as he could keep an eye on her while she took it.

Her association with him made her life harder. He

clenched his fists. He wanted to prove to her life with him under Hollywood's microscope wouldn't be easy, but it could be done if there was a reason, like if they were going to quit messing around and get serious about one another. He wanted to punch something.

He forced a breath through his lips and dropped his head side to side, cracking his neck. "I'm just worried about you."

Sam glanced about, avoiding his gaze. "I know."

Turning, he leaned back against the post and hooked his thumbs through the loops of his pants. Birds chirped above the soft rustle of the leaves, a slight wind blew just enough to be heard, but not enough to disrupt the quiet solitude free of voices. The perfect setting, really. Because even with Sam standing before him—he stood alone. "Could it be one of the Evanses?"

The question seemed to spook her. "I can't imagine what they'd gain, and besides, we haven't seen them around here."

"Doesn't matter, they're a wealthy family. Finding some-one to do their dirty work is simply a matter of the right motivation."

She stepped up beside him and wrapped her arm about his waist. "This is all so frustrating. You and I are supposed to be having fun. Light and easy, remember? But instead, we're dealing with stupid threats and petty harassment. I'm so tired of it all."

The tension in his shoulders eased a fraction, but still kept a tight hold. *She* was tired? So was he, tired of the threat of losing her, tired of not being enough to make her stay, tired of wanting someone who might not want him back.

After they figured out who was harassing her, it would

be best if he took his leave. The idea had merit, but left him with a gaping hole.

Light and easy? Fuck.

None of this was easy, but letting her go promised to be the toughest challenge of his life.

Chapter Sixteen

Sam dragged herself into the deli to meet Cecilia Lombardi, her protective shadow following her in and settling near the door. Bone-tired from a restless sleep, and an even more restless morning, all she wanted waited for her back at her condo: solitude and her bed. Gage had been distant and polite, distracted with security and trying to figure out who was behind all the pranks. She missed his carefree affection, him swinging his arm around her shoulders or pulling her in for a kiss. She'd find herself reaching out to him, only to find him casually stepping away, studying each and every crew member on the set.

After they'd finished filming yesterday, he'd driven her home and then locked himself in his room. She'd made dinner, drank wine, channel surfed, all in hopes he'd emerge from his hermitage. In the end, she concluded her own banishment and went to bed. Rising before her alarm—and why not? She never really did sleep—she'd shuffled around the kitchen making coffee and toast.

Gage had joined her, silent and brooding, besides a non-committal grunt in greeting and a kiss on the cheek. More silence followed in the car on their way to the film set. By the time they parked, she'd wanted to scream.

He got out of the car and sent her a salute. "I need to speak with security."

She'd stood staring at the door he'd disappeared through for at least five minutes, her ire building. She didn't think he was trying to be rude, but it felt it all the same.

The morning slogged on like a film with no plot. Finally, when lunch time approached, she'd slipped out with no issues. She'd assured Martin she'd be escorted throughout her meal and then be back on set in an hour.

Now as she stood scanning the patrons, guilt crept in and took a strong hold of her shoulder blades, making her wonder if she should have told Gage. Too late to worry about that now.

She rolled the tension from her shoulders and approached Cecilia.

The woman wore cheap like a second skin. Her bright red nails skimmed down a leopard print dress that belonged on a twenty-year-old in a club at midnight, not a fifty-something in a deli at noon. Sam pasted a casual smile on her face and pulled out the chair opposite of the B-list wannabe starlet.

Cecilia added more blood red lipstick to her already overdone lips. With a practiced fluidity, she dropped the tube back into her clutch. "I did say one p.m."

The woman's attitude set her on edge, and she answered without thinking. "Yes, well, it's close enough."

Cecilia narrowed her eyes.

Not in the mood, Sam snapped, "What do you want, Ms. Lombardi?"

"Oh, come now. Friends call me Cecilia."

"We're not friends."

"We could become the best of friends."

Sam sipped the ice water left for her and prayed for patience. "Why would we become best friends?"

Cecilia leaned close on her elbows, her fingers loosely entwined, and made a show of looking past Sam to the guard by the door. "You've been through a lot, Samantha, haven't you?"

Sam stiffened. What was this woman getting at? She answered with caution. "Sure, but many people have."

Over-processed curls slid over Cecilia's shoulder, and she flipped them back with a dramatic flair. "Look, you and I could be a good team. I've been looking around, Sam. There are those who think Hollywood is just too much for you. As for me, well, I'm dating a very powerful man."

Sam choked on her water. Powerful man? Yeah, so powerful that one threat of leaving from Gage and he barred the woman warming his bed from the set.

Cecilia scowled. "My lover has many connections. If I were you, I wouldn't turn my nose up so fast. With those in Hollywood who demand you for their scripts and those who don't want to disappoint my talented boyfriend, ours is a match made in heaven. You simply require my participation in the cast, and I will require your participation in the writing. We'll have access to twice as much work as going solo."

Sam's stomach turned. Even without whatever conflict Gage had with this woman, Cecilia was not a presence Sam could tolerate long—and she'd reached her limit. Pulling her shoulders back, she shook her head. "No, thank you, I prefer to go solo."

Cecilia slammed her manicured hand on the table.

Her eyes widened. She pulled in a breath through flared nostrils and peeked from side to side as if to assess the damage. In a low voice she gritted out her words. "Solo? Is that what you call it? Aligning yourself to the likes of Martin Gallagher and Gage Cutler? By the way, I'd be careful of him if I were you. Why you'd even consider being seen with the man is beyond me. He's tried to tie himself to every successful tail in Hollywood in order to rise in his career." She sniffed, leaned back, and tipped up her chin. Looking down her nose at Sam, she continued, "Even mine."

Sam's gut tightened, and she clenched her fists under the table. *Relax. Count to ten.* The chatter of the deli broke through the drumming in Sam's head. She loosened her fingers and shook out her hands. Resting her palms on the tabletop, she leaned forward and kept her voice low. "Gage Cutler is a talented actor who has risen on his own merit, but you know that. The idea his success has anything to do with you is laughable." She made a sound somewhere between a laugh and a cough. "What really happened between the two of you?"

Cecilia stared at Sam. Her skin turned a bright shade of red, quite close to matching her lips and nails. She stared at Sam, rigid and unmoving until the slight trembling in her hands gave her away. Sam had yet to see someone work so hard to maintain control.

On one hand she pitied Cecilia. She was aging fast, and Hollywood was leaving her behind as if she never existed. Her strategy of sleeping her way to the top did nothing more than lower her street value.

With a shake in her voice, Cecilia shot back. "No more laughable than the fact that you're working with the man who killed your husband. Or have you been since the beginning? Maybe your plan all along? I bet your mama's proud."

Sam shot up, her chair slamming to the ground in a loud clap. Pure rage squeezed her chest, making it impossible to breathe. The guard approached her table, but she raised a hand to stop him. A sick dread filled her stomach.

Cecilia tilted her head to the side. Glee glittered in her eyes, providing an almost youthful glow to her skin. "Smile, Samantha, people are watching."

She tipped her chin to the poisonous woman, and with as graceful a move as possible retrieved her fallen chair. She'd never receive any useful information from the narcissistic woman, so why had she thought she could?

"Until next time, Miss Dekker?" The woman grinned like a Cheshire.

Sam broadened her smile. "There will never be a next time, Ms. Lombardi."

The woman's satisfied smile thinned to a tight straight line and she shot Sam a cold look. "You *need* me."

"No, I only need *me*," she said. With that, Sam turned on her heel, and on shaky legs, made her way back to her car.

Guilt of all shades washed over her. She should never have gone to the lunch; she should never have started something with Gage. He deserved a woman free of baggage, and their pasts were too entwined in negativity.

But one thought pierced her to the core. She never should have married Ethan. Why had she? Had she used *him*? He'd accused her of exactly that toward the end. Maybe he'd been right. Was she no better than Cecilia Lombardi?

Sam shook her head. No, he'd been different in the beginning. He'd made promises, describing a beautiful picture of love, family, and a future full of glamour and excitement. She'd been hooked from the first line, but it didn't last through the first act.

It had been a relationship doomed to fail from the beginning, but she hadn't wanted to see it.

She refused to make the same mistake twice.

Later that evening, Sam stepped out of the shower and wrapped a towel around herself. She'd been using Gage's bathroom, since she wasn't comfortable making extra work for Anita, and some nights she didn't make it back to the guest room like she should have. Tension increased in the back of her head. She'd never had sex with someone who was too busy to even talk to her before. Maybe she was just being insecure, making it all into more than it was. But she felt his distance, when, with everything going on, she craved his closeness. She grabbed her toothbrush and then frowned. Both toothbrushes usually rested bristles up in a small cup, but Gage's brush now lay on the counter on the opposite side of the sink. A thrumming joined the tension in her head, and gripping her towel tighter, she marched out to the living room, toothbrushes in hand. "What's this all about?"

Gage glanced up at her from a script and then returned to his reading. "What?"

She clenched her teeth together. "Seriously? Are you seriously going to play these little games?"

"What games? I've been working my ass off to try and help figure out who's behind all the nonsense on set, not to mention film a movie." He slapped his manuscript to the couch and glared at her. "And who's playing games, Sam? I'm only trying to respect what you asked for. You said no relationship. Last I looked, people who aren't in relationships don't keep their toothbrushes in the same cup."

"Oh, you can have sex with me, you just won't put your toothbrush next to mine?"

He twisted his lips and sent her a look.

She squeezed the brushes tight in her hand. "This is so stupid."

"Are we seriously arguing about where I keep my toothbrush?"

"This isn't about the toothbrushes." Heat flushed Sam's cheeks.

Staring at her, Gage pushed up from the sofa. He walked up to her and took the toothbrushes, then threw them to the couch. His jaw twitched. "What? What do you want, Sam? Are we together, or are we not? We have sex, we sleep in the same bed, but I can't help you. I can't worry about you, I can't *do* any of the things a man does for the woman he cares for, and now you're mad because I moved my toothbrush?"

Tears formed in her eyes, and her vision blurred. "You know why."

Gage turned away and then swung back to face her, his voice grating with emotion. "Don't you get it? I want a relationship, Sam. Something real. I know it's scary, I know we'll have to work at it, but I also know it will be worth it."

Joy and sorrow collided, burying her under their weight. He wanted *her*, something serious with *her*. This larger than life man who helped her become a better version of herself, but she couldn't risk a relationship she knew would fail again. She wouldn't do that to herself or to him. "I can't give you what you want."

He closed his eyes and pulled her to his chest. The warmth of his chest radiated through her body, and her throat constricted. Where she could never end up was the exact place she wanted to be.

He looked down at her, his gaze intense. Opening his mouth to speak, he hesitated, and then tried again. "Why?"

She dropped her chin. "You know why." Oh, how she wanted to. More than anything in a long time, the desire to build a life with him pulled at her with an urgency so sweet it hurt. Her heart twisted, the pain tearing through her chest. Admitting to caring about him was one thing, but knowing he really cared about her, wanted more, made a terrible knot in her stomach, leaving her to long for what could have been. She hated hurting him, hated the pain in his eyes, but she feared him hating her more. And in the end, that is what would happen. She'd already seen the ending to this particular movie.

He bent his knees just enough to bring him to eye level, holding on to her waist. "It doesn't have to be as bad as you think. Yes, there'll be pictures, silly articles, but that's it. You can deal with that, Sam. I know you can. Let me show you." He held her gaze. "You care for me, so show me you trust me, too." With a smile stretched by both hope and fear, he lowered his head, and his lips barely brushed over hers. Once. Twice.

The sensation ran through her nerves straight to her toes.

"It'll never work, Gage," she whispered against his mouth, her heart splitting in two.

He froze and stepped back. Her fingers flexed to pull him back and fill the cold left behind, but she dropped them to her sides.

He opened his mouth to speak, but she shook her head. "It won't, and we both know it. You are a celebrity above and beyond anything Ethan aspired to. But even for his level of celebrity, the press intruded so far they pushed him to suicide, and I can't let them hound me like that again. I won't. Not to mention, they would jump all over our relationship without hesitation. You've worked so hard repairing your reputation. Do you really think you wouldn't resent me if our relationship screwed that up for you? There's no way you wouldn't, and I couldn't blame you. I couldn't stand for you to hate me." Her chest ached, and she struggled to swallow past the lump in her throat, but she lifted her head and pulled her shoulders back.

Gage sliced his hand through the air. "Excuses, they're all excuses, Sam. It doesn't have to be that way."

She picked up a sofa pillow, held it to her chest, and whispered, "Excuses? Everything I'm afraid of happening keeps happening. Those aren't excuses. They're facts."

"And you've survived every one."

She stared at him. Her heart full of feelings she couldn't do anything with. Arguing with him about their future was useless. She pulled in a breath and whispered, "I'm trying to figure out if it can work. But I don't see how. I need more time. Can you give me that?"

He dropped his chin to his chest and closed his eyes. "You don't know what you ask, Sam."

"Don't I? I know it won't be easy, but it's better for us in the end."

"*You* think it's better."

"Yes, I do."

He studied her. "For the record, I don't think time is the issue. But fine."

She stared back, each second feeling like a minute, wondering why it was the painful things in life rather than the pleasurable things that dragged on for eternity.

• • •

The next day, Sam walked through the familiar chaos of the set with two cups of coffee in search of Gage. They'd formed a tentative truce.

Thank God, she didn't think she could handle his disappointment any more than she could his silent treatment.

Gage stood chatting with other cast members, dynamic, captivating. It was no wonder they all hung on his every word. He turned to greet Sam and spotted the coffee. Deep appreciation shone from his eyes.

She ducked behind the shelves to her workplace. As suspected, he rounded the corner in less than two seconds. She giggled.

He took the offered cup and tipped back a mouthful. "Oh, you have no idea. Thank you."

She watched him and her lips trembled. She'd never met someone so thankful for such little things.

Gage gave her a half smile. "I'm sorry about the other—"

"Me, too."

He snaked a hand around the back of her neck and

pulled her close.

She leaned into his embrace and closed her eyes.

"Tonight we need to—" His body tightened next to her. The warmth in his eyes frosted over. "What's this?"

Sam leaned forward to take a look at the magazine he'd picked up from her table. A photograph of her and Cecilia Lombardi splashed across the front cover. Both women leaning forward, as if conspiring, smiling. In bold letters the words, LOMBARDI IN BED WITH DEKKER, HOLLYWOOD'S LATEST LOVE STORY all but screamed from the page.

Gage took a step back.

She stood before him, dread settling in her stomach. "Gage."

Betrayal turned his face to stone. "Do you really think so little of me?" He stood and towered over her.

She crossed her arms. "Listen to me. I know how this photo looks, but it's not what you think. It was business."

"It doesn't matter."

She winced as the set quieted with his unexpected outburst.

Sam held Gage's eyes. She had to make him understand. "Gage."

"I forbid you to ever meet with that woman again. For anything."

The words rang in her ears, and she tensed.

Sam shook her head. "Don't."

Gage stepped forward, brow raised. His jaw clenched and his eyes glowed cyan. "Don't? Don't? Are you fucking kidding me? Cecilia Lombardi, of all people? I don't care if she holds the fate of your career in her hands. There is never a reason for you to meet with that woman." He paced the room. "I didn't deserve this, Sam. You, of all people, know how I feel about her."

"But I don't." Her chest rose and fell, fighting for breath, trying to make sense of it all. "And I want to. The producer asked me to go, and networking is part of this business. I needed to see what she had to say." She rushed on. "It was useless, but I had to know."

Gage didn't pause, didn't stop, just walked from the room. She wanted to run after him, to make him understand, but at this point chasing him would cause more of a scene.

Panic turned in her stomach. What had she done? When would she ever listen to her instinct? She should have never gone. The last thing she'd ever wanted to do was hurt him again. The coffee churned in her stomach. Her head spun and she sat down.

Lombardi could rot in hell, but at the rate Sam was moving, she'd get there first.

• • •

Gage flopped down onto the bed in his trailer, Metallica blaring from his stereo. He hoped the music would drown out his thoughts, but so far, the heavy guitar sets only made him feel worse. His mother and Sam? He squeezed his eyes shut.

Gage rolled to his side. The cozy warmth of his trailer failed to soothe as it normally did. The dark wood, muted grays, and bold black, offset by shots of white, jarred him like a rip in a film reel. He closed his eyes against the space.

What had Sam been thinking? Seeing the woman he cared for *laughing* with his sorry excuse of a mother made him sick. His stomach churned and he wanted to vomit. Still might.

Maybe he was wrong about Sam. The woman who snagged his heart years ago with her soulful eyes and sweet, determined ways might have changed into a stranger.

Suicide changed the people left behind.

A knock on his trailer door persisted, even after he ignored it.

"Mr. Cutler."

He recognized Dani's muffled voice. "Mr. Cutler, I'm not leaving."

The knocking continued, and he slammed his pillow over his head. The knock changed to a pound, rattling the walls and his bed. *Goddamn it.*

Growling, he charged from the bed and yanked open the door. "I will have your ass thrown from the set if you don't go away."

The young assistant, efficient as ever with her hair tucked under her messenger cap, smiled in return. Her bright, sunny ways did nothing but annoy Gage at the moment. "What do you want?"

She walked up the steps and breezed past him inside his trailer. Caught off guard, Gage stepped back. He left the door open and leaned back against the jam, his arms crossed at his chest. "Talk. You have two minutes before I throw you out of here."

Dani reached her hand toward him, a business card dangling between her fingers.

He stared. "You're down to one minute."

She rolled her eyes. "Oh, for Pete's sake, take it."

Gage raised an eyebrow, but she stood her ground.

He snatched the card from her hand and flipped it over. "So?"

Dani sighed. "Mr. Cutler, the producer gave it to her. Look at the back." She gestured with her hand.

Gage rotated his wrist and read the back of the card.

"Ms. Dekker really had no choice. She's trying to rebuild her name in an industry unforgiving when it comes to anyone but actors." She waved her hand up and down in front of his form. "You all can get away with murder."

His eyes shot wide. "Sorry?"

Clearing her throat, she continued. "The public loves a story of redemption, but for writers?" She shook her head. "Come on." Dani walked to the door.

Gage stepped aside.

"Besides, I saw her yesterday afternoon, and she was fuming. A fan of Cecilia Lombardi she is not." Dani hopped down the trailer stairs.

Gage called out, "Thanks, Dani." The tension in his shoulders released its tight grip just an inch. Maybe he'd been wrong.

"I didn't want *you* giving up on Sam." She gave him a jaunty salute and disappeared into the herd of crew members and equipment. A few curious gazes made eye contact, then darted back to whatever occupied their efforts.

God save him from any more rumors. Gage sighed, stepped back, and pushed his door closed. He needed a few minutes to calm the barrage of emotions before looking for Sam. The look of shock and confusion that crossed her face when he shoved the magazine under her nose supported Dani's claims. In the moment, however, it was a look he couldn't—no, wouldn't—accept. The idea she'd have anything to do with his mother was too much.

He wanted to believe she met Cecilia without any deceit, and that she'd dreaded the meeting with his mother, only to leave with a bitter taste in her mouth. *That* was the Sam he recognized.

Maybe it was time to tell Sam who Cecilia really was. He rubbed the back of his neck. Admitting the woman was his mother to Sam made his stomach turn, but if he wanted her to do the hard things for him, he needed to do them for her. She always complained about her baggage, but she didn't understand he was already accustomed to carrying a heavy load.

Chapter Seventeen

Gage found Sam bent over the screenplay with Martin, their heads together, whispering. He placed his hand on her work space above her manuscript. "We need to talk."

She looked up, surprised to see him.

He grabbed the screenplay and handed it to Martin. Rounding the table, he grabbed her hand. "I have something to say, and I need you to listen." He was acting all alpha gorilla, but he couldn't help himself.

Martin held his hands up, and looked at Gage as if he'd lost his mind. "Is that really how you treat a lady?" He shook his head. "Besides, you two can't go anywhere, shooting's about to start."

Gage released Sam's hand, but only to guide her by the shoulders. "It can wait." He continued to push her toward the front door, though she dug in her heels.

"Come on," the director shouted with a resounding smack of paper against his knees.

Gage stepped through the door behind Sam and called out over his shoulder. "Five minutes."

Once outside on the front porch, she pulled away from him and swung around. "You can't do that. This is my job."

He cocked an eyebrow. "Would you have listened?"

"Like you did for me this morning?" she shot back, her hands on her hips.

"Exactly." He stood at the porch railing, and she joined him.

He needed a second, the truth of it all constricting his chest and stealing his air. Blowing out the little breath he did find, he stepped next to Sam and studied her profile. Dark eyes looked straight ahead out over the landscape, lush lips pressed together in a firm line under a pert nose. He reached out and pushed the silk of her long brown hair back over her shoulder.

"There's something you need to know about Cecilia Lombardi."

Sam turned toward him. She leaned her hip against the railing and crossed her arms. He figured she wasn't quite over their earlier confrontation, but at least she was willing to listen. She listened like no one he'd ever met, all in and fully engaged; he never saw her eyes glaze over or her focus wander off. And what was more? She wasn't even aware she did it.

He spoke low. "This isn't something very many people know, and I'd like to keep it that way. My dad and sister have been through enough. And, frankly, the facts just don't matter anymore."

A knot twisted in his gut and he focused on a dark boulder about halfway across the property. "I told you about my mother walking out on us."

Sam sighed. "Not fair, Gage. I want to be mad at you."

A half smirk broke the firm line of his lips. "But you remember?" He glanced in her direction and then back across the yard.

"Yes."

"Cecilia Lombardi is my mother." A heaviness settled in his gut as silence settled over the yard.

"Gage."

"She denies it, vehemently. Denied it from the start. I figured my best bet was to keep my mouth shut and hope the rumors would go away."

"That must hurt."

A raw, rough laugh escaped from his throat. "Seems to be the way of things for me."

Sam's mouth dropped open. "That's not fair."

He rubbed the back of his neck, looking down at the floor, then back to her. "No, it's not."

She watched him, but she didn't deny it, didn't protest the fact.

His shoulders sagged. "As far as Cecilia goes, it shouldn't hurt. She's not worth it." He turned toward her.

She stepped in close and pulled his head down until their lips met, and he sighed into the kiss. She spoke against his lips. "The loss is all hers. You wouldn't be the same man had she stayed."

He ran a hand through his hair. "Seeing the two of you together, I overreacted. I'm sorry."

Sam studied him, her eyes wide, and she smiled. "I knew there was a reason I didn't like the woman. She wanted me to join forces with her. I told her no, and she wasn't happy."

She tilted her head to the side. "There's one thing I don't understand."

"What's that?"

"I'd think she'd want to claim you to help her career."

He shook his head. "You can't understand crazy. She always blamed us for her dreams *not* coming true, so there's no way in hell she'd allow the association to make sure her dreams *do* come true. You know the saying, 'cut off your nose to spite your face'? That's her."

Sam frowned. "That's so sad." She bit her lip and wrapped her arms around his neck. "I'm so sorry I went. Had I known, I'd have never gone. You have to see that." Running her fingers through his hair, the light touch sending shivers down the back of his neck, she lifted on tiptoe and kissed the corners of his mouth. "I care about you, more than I should. I really wish things could be different."

Gage swung his arm around her shoulder and led her back inside. There was nothing more to say today. He'd simply have to find a way to change her mind. Time to get back to work, on the film and on keeping Sam.

•••

Later that evening, Sam sunk into the couch next to Gage, wishing the tension between them would go away. She glanced at him from beneath her lashes. He stared at the TV, but she doubted he was paying any attention. Turning toward him, she plucked at the fringe of the blanket lying in a heap between them. "Thank you for telling me about your mom." She'd been thinking about him ever since he'd shared, hating what the woman had done to him. Gage had given her something Ethan never had—respect. He talked to her, apologized. He'd been selfless with part of his life he didn't share with anyone. It all warmed her.

He turned to her and warm lips caressed her temple and then trailed down her cheek, feather-light, to the corner of her mouth. She lifted her lips to his. One brush, and then two, a million wouldn't be enough.

Lifting onto her knees, Sam straddled his lap and poured herself into the kiss. She angled her head, sliding her tongue along his, and then pulling back, bit his lower lip with a gentle tug. She'd loved how he felt, how he tasted, the way he slept with his arms crossed above his head, and the lingering scent of his cologne after he got ready in the morning. Her throat burned, and she swallowed. Everything was so different with him. She stilled.

"What's wrong?"

Looking down at him, she brushed her fingertips over each brow and down the bridge of his nose. Nothing was wrong with him, and that was just it. She was terrified, but the fact remained that everything was different with him, better, bolder, more beautiful. Just maybe—

He kissed her once more and then held her from him. "Do something for me."

She wiggled her brows. "What do you have in mind?"

He palmed her ass and squeezed until she giggled. "There's been a lot going on, and my dad and Bel have heard a lot about you."

A soft, sweet unfurling in her chest made her inhale with a slight catch in her breath. He wanted her to meet his sister and dad. A warm flush of gratitude stretched her lips into a smile she had no power to stop.

"Look, I know we can't be more than what we are now, but that doesn't mean we need to hide from the people we love. I'll make it clear we're friends, but I think after all this time, they deserve to meet you."

Sam rolled the pros and cons around in her head as she watched the intensity in his face. He'd done something really difficult for her and had a strong relationship with his family. Lumping him in with the average celebrity no longer seemed fair. With every want and need at his fingertips, he tried to curb his once-reckless behavior.

The hopeful look in his eye was her undoing, and her resolve crumpled with each heartbeat. Besides, she really wanted to meet them. To see him in his element, with the people he loved and who loved him. She nodded.

Gage grinned against her mouth. "Thank you."

She'd do anything for him. He'd never believe it, but it was true.

He might be the one celebrity who could actually handle that kind of power.

. . .

The next day, after being released early from the set, Gage and Sam warmed in the sun on his front patio. He pulled her close. "Why are you so nervous?"

His voice startled her, and Sam shook out her hands. The muscles in her shoulders were so tight her fingers were almost numb. "How about they're the people you love, and they're going to hate me if I hurt you?"

Squeezing her close, he chuckled. "They don't bite." He leaned close and nibbled her earlobe.

She laughed and pushed him away. "I hope not like that, at least. This is a big deal. They're important to you." Sam wrapped her arms around him, wishing he could understand everything she felt just by her touch alone. "I know how much they mean to you, how much you mean to them. And after the stupid tabloid, I owe them the courtesy, if nothing else, but I'm worried about their expectations. And I really, really want to meet them."

"Their expectation will be that they're well-fed and entertained. I think we have that covered." He brushed his lips over hers, eliciting a small shiver that reached her toes. "And I'm so glad you want to meet them."

She *was* happy. She only wished it were under much simpler circumstances. Circumstances where she and his sister could get pedicures and gossip about the latest hot actors just so Sam could tease Gage about it afterward, or DC could meet her dad for game of golf and then meet Martin for drinks. Normal, everyday things, lovely things.

"Did you hear me?" Gage's words broke through the voices in her head.

"What?"

"There they are." He pointed to a tall elegant man with an athletic build, and a petite woman around her own age with a chic style, blond hair, and Gage's eyes.

Sam blew out a breath; her heart sped. She gave a nod. "Your family's beautiful. I can see where you get your good looks."

Gage raised an eyebrow and pulled her back to his side. "Oh, so you think I'm good looking?"

She rolled her eyes with an exaggerated sigh. "Please. You do not need encouragement."

He slapped her ass. "Be nice."

Sam jumped and spun around. "Gage, oh my God." She turned back to his family and heat rose in her face. "I am so sorry."

His sister stepped forward. "I think we're the ones who should apologize."

"Nice to meet you."

Gage's father stepped up and grasped the ends of Sam's fingers. With a slight bow, he pressed his lips to her knuckles, and her heart skipped a beat. Wow. This man could give Prince Charming a run for his money. She could see Gage in him, but it was more than just his looks. It was the way he held his shoulders, the tilt of his head, and the intensity in his gaze.

He stepped back and smiled. "It's a pleasure."

Gage stepped up. "Nice way to show me up, Dad."

"Only you can help what you're not doing, son." Cutler Senior dipped his chin toward Sam. "I never miss an opportunity to enchant a beautiful woman."

Gage and Bel laughed as they filed inside the house. Gage leaned close and whispered in Sam's ear. "He's not kidding."

She giggled.

Gage, a natural host, plied everyone with food and drink, and then eased the crew into the living room in front of the fire. He left the sliding glass doors cracked so they could enjoy the rhythmic crash of the Pacific waves combined with the snap and crackle of the glowing embers.

Sam bit into crispy bread infused with chipotle oil and layered with sundried tomatoes and goat cheese. "This is good."

"I'm glad you like it. It's one of my favorites to make."

Sam's eyes snapped open at Gage. "You made this?"

His dad, sitting to his right on the long sofa, slapped Gage on the back. "Our boy here's been cooking before his voice dropped."

"Nice, Dad."

Bel piped in with a laugh. "Seriously, he has. We thought for a while he might pursue a career as a chef, but then he took off to the New York Film Academy."

Sam tilted her head. "I'm impressed." And she was. Every moment she spent with the man revealed something new she couldn't quite shake.

Chewing on another bite and content to listen to their banter, she looked from one Cutler to the next with a grin. Bel shared stories of the two siblings growing up, and Mr. Cutler nodded his head in rapt attention, the memories pulling smiles from each face.

Sam took the first lull in the conversation to ask, "So, why *did* you pursue acting?"

The question silenced the room, and Gage shifted in his seat. He pulled a long draw from his IPA and stared into the flames. "Different reasons."

His dad and sister settled back in their seats. Sam had touched on something serious. She could feel the tension thicken. Curious, she scooted forward. The fact Gage went after a career so different from his dad's and sister's, not to mention it mirrored his mother's, intrigued her.

"I had." He laughed. "*Have* my issues. As a teen, I didn't trust anyone, was lonely and frustrated, always trying to figure myself out. Acting made me feel whole for the first time. It gave me something to do with all of my energy."

"That's an understatement," Bel mumbled.

Sam's heart beat faster in her chest. He shared family stories, secrets, and the fact he shared them with her made her chest swell and her lungs ache.

"In the end, acting gives me a chance to be someone else. Gives me a break. Freedom."

So many more questions demanded answers. But now wasn't the time. She wanted to wrap him in her arms. Shield him from Cecilia Lombardi.

She froze.

Protect him? Her mouth went dry. She shifted in her chair, searching for something to say and picked up her glass of wine. "In my opinion, you made the right choice. You're brilliant in front of the camera." She winked and picked up another hors d'oeuvre. "This is excellent. I know where I'm coming when I'm hungry."

Gage narrowed his eyes and pulled the corners of his mouth up in a sly smile.

Her statement caused a chorus of agreements followed by favorite movie moments from his family. Gage's shoulders relaxed, and he held her gaze. He leaned back in the couch, and the tense light in his eyes faded to a content gleam as he took in the praise.

Bel and Cutler Senior fell into a debate about which was his best movie, and Gage leaned his head toward Sam. "See how great this is?"

Sam nodded. It really was, sitting with his family without having to judge every move, poker face every emotion. She wished for a different time and place where it could be real. She stood. "I'm going to get more wine. Can I get you anything?"

Gage stood. "I'll help you."

Stepping into the kitchen, he leaned against the counter as she looked over his choices of wine. "Let me take you out, on a real date."

She shook her head, the past warping to the present, leaving her motion sick.

Turning toward her, Gage took her hands. "Sam, you keep telling me we can't be together because of what happened with Ethan, because of how intrusive Hollywood is, and how you're afraid your past will hurt my future. Let me show you it doesn't have to be that way." He held her gaze with such eagerness she couldn't look away. He had strength, he was different now, steady and strong, but would he be able to sustain that?

"Yes, there will be paparazzi, yes, there will be fans, but there will also be *us*…you and me. We're different from you and Ethan, Sam. Let me show you."

Fear snaked up Sam's spine, but no faster than complete and utter joy. She wanted to say yes, hell, she wanted to shout yes, but the fear still had a muzzling effect.

He squeezed her hand, pleading with his eyes.

"Can we talk about this later? I can't think. I—"

Gage stilled and pressed his lips together with a curt nod. "We'll talk more once they leave." Pressing a kiss to her forehead, he grabbed a bottle and headed back into the living room. "Grab the other bottle."

She joined Gage and his family, pasting on a game face worthy of an Oscar. They laughed and teased until Bel yawned and Mr. Cutler called it a night. Sam stood and wrapped her arms around Bel. "It was so nice meeting you. Enjoy your students."

Bel laughed. "You say that like you won't be hearing all about it, but I assure you, you will. I need someone else to complain to besides these two."

Sam cleared her throat and then nodded. "Of course."

More hugs and goodbyes found Mr. Cutler and Bel on their way, and Gage closed the door. He stood a moment and then turned to Sam.

She refused to look away but couldn't help stepping back as he approached from down the hall. He strode right past her, and she released a huge breath and hung her head. Following the sounds of dishes clinking, she made her way back into the kitchen. Gage couldn't stand the thought of dishes in the sink overnight, so regardless of the hour, if he entertained, he washed every one. Sam swore he was the only celebrity she knew who even knew how to wash dishes. The corners of her lips turned up. His back was to her, broad and strong, capable of carrying a lot, but there were times he shouldn't have to.

"Need any help?"

He turned from the sink and tossed her a towel. "You can dry." Turning back, he picked up a plate and scrubbed it until it was covered in a sudsy froth. "I love you, Sam. I know that'll scare you, but I do."

She placed her hand to her chest, and she felt as though she couldn't breathe. Everything she ever wanted and always feared lay at her feet. "You love me."

"I. Love. You." He set the plate down and angled toward her, leaning his hip against the counter.

The truth of his words swelled in her chest. She wanted to run from him and to him at the same time. "Gage, I..." She stepped toward him, but he put his hand up.

She slid her fingers through his. "You know I have strong feelings for you, too."

He pressed her hand to his chest. "We can make this whatever we want. It's one of the things you've worked so hard for, *you* making choices for your life. *You*."

"I know, you're right."

"We need to at least try, Sam."

"We are trying."

Shaking his head, he glanced down at the floor. "No, we've been dancing around the idea. It's beginning to look like the woman I love doesn't think I'm worth the hassle of Hollywood."

A gasp spilled past her lips. "I never, I—"

"Then prove it. We can do things to lessen how intrusive Hollywood can be, my attorney can handle anything that comes up with Ethan's family, and like I've said before, we can minimize the effects of any paparazzi. There are ways, Sam. We're not helpless. You're not helpless. Hell, you're hands down one of the strongest women I know."

A small light warmed her chest and grew, spreading over her shoulders and down her back. She was strong, and this was her life.

"I'm not asking you to marry me. I'm asking for us to try. I can't show you how it really could be between us if you don't let me."

She looked into eyes that saw her so much more clearly than she saw herself. Maybe the only way was to let him try. "It might work, but I'm afraid it will eventually fail, and I hate to think what that might do to us."

"One day at a time." He stepped to her, this strong man with deep emotions, and as he slid his warm hands up her arms to her shoulders, her body naturally melted into him, his words rumbling against her chest. "But what we have? We're worth the try."

Her heart turned over, as if waking for the first time. As happiness welled, her grin stretched so wide her cheeks hurt. She didn't nod meekly or whisper, but rather looked him straight in the eye. "Okay."

He leaned back, holding her gaze. "Okay?"

She smiled and nodded again.

Yanking her to him, Gage wrapped her in a hug so tight she could barely breathe, but she needed more. Pushing her hands up between their bodies, she slid her fingers into his hair and pulled his mouth down to hers. Tears she hadn't even known were falling mixed with dinner's wine, and she pushed into him tighter still. These tears were different than all the others, almost sweet.

There was so much more of him she wanted to feel, to taste, but his words whispered in her mind, reminding her of something she kept forgetting.

One day at a time.

Chapter Eighteen

Sam laughed as Gage pulled her along behind him. Wednesday nights at Café Habana were one of his favorite things to do. It was time Sam had some fun, and he was just the man to show her. The spot was located in the Country Mart's paparazzi-free zone, the perfect way to ease her into being out with him.

"Karaoke? Are you serious?" The panic in her voice was adorable.

A palm leaf caught on his shoulder and smacked her right in the face. "Ow!"

Concerned, he spun around to check her face and distractedly placed a kiss to her forehead as she giggled. "I'm sorry. Come on."

A camera flashed here and there, and a slew of fans stopped them for autographs and cell pics. Gage took care of as many as he could and then with a "thank you" moved Sam farther into the restaurant. He skirted around tables until he found his favorite. Karaoke was a long-time love of his and one he loved to share—with the right person. It was a mix of theater and music, entertaining the performer as much as the audience.

Pulling out a chair for Sam, he waited until she settled in her seat and then took the space across the table from her. "They have the best Cuban-Mexican food on the planet. Do you want a drink?" He signaled to the waitress.

Sam blew out a breath but laughed and slowly lowered her hand to her lap. "Cuban Mexican?"

Gage acknowledged with a raised brow. "You'll see."

They ordered their drinks and an appetizer, some sort of Sangria special and shrimp ceviche to start. The drinks were dangerous, and Gage couldn't wait to see Sam let her guard down a bit. She'd held it tightly in place since they started work on the film, and it was way past time for her to let it go.

He'd loved seeing her with his dad and sister, knowing they'd see in her what he saw. The people he loved most in the world together laughing, sharing stories, making memories.

She closed her lips around her straw and his gut tightened. Images messed with his brain, none of which were appropriate at the moment, but when she was around he couldn't quite help his baser instincts.

"Wow. That is good."

Gage grinned. The energy of the restaurant raised his own to the occasion. He tapped his fingers to the rhythm beating over the speakers. They'd filmed late, which accommodated his plans perfectly. The fun here really started at ten.

Sam bit into a fresh shrimp and closed her eyes.

He shifted in his seat. "Told ya."

"You're right. It's different, really good."

She studied him with deep brown eyes. Always so serious, he loved to see them lit in amusement or passion. He wanted to remove all of her fears. He wanted to protect her; since the night they'd met, he'd never stopped wanting. It sucked ass. But tonight held the promise of something more.

Reaching out, she tapped the top of his hand with her fingertips, lingering a moment before she wrapped them around her glass. "So, karaoke. What else do you like?"

A ghost of the sensation remained, and Gage missed the contact. He chewed, lost in thought. They talked about a lot of things the night they'd met, but not everything. He knew she loved peanut butter and had an athlete's passion for swimming. She knew he enjoyed volunteering at Pepperdine's Smothers Theatre and worked to move his career behind the camera instead of in front of it.

He jabbed his fork in the direction of the Pacific. "I love the water. Anything in the water, surfing, knee boarding, floating on a raft. The heat of the sun, the cold lapping of the ocean against my skin. The solitude."

They ignored the periodic flashes of cell phone cameras, the whispers, and turning heads. Most were subtle, a few overt, but nothing aggressive or rude. After a while, they became a sort of white noise, like a fan buffering the silence when trying to sleep.

Sam leaned toward him while he spoke, really listened. One of the things he loved about her—damn, there was that word again. Full eye contact, leaning in, as if there wasn't anything more important in the world than hearing his next word.

He couldn't remember the last time anyone had made

him feel that way. Usually people were happy to humor him. They laughed at all the right times, nodded their heads appropriately, and answered with agreeable smiles. It drove him nuts. No one cared what *he* said. They just wanted to get on *Gage Cutler's* good side.

"I can see you out there. Surfing is so you, Mr. 'I like to live on the edge.'"

Gage couldn't deny her claim, but there was more, always more. "Partly, but it's also the idea that being me has nothing to do with it. The waves aren't going to be gentle just because of the movies I'm in. The sun isn't going to not burn me just because I'm good publicity. It's real. Just me and physics. Mother Nature. A challenge and freedom."

Sam nodded. "I can see that. I feel like that when I'm swimming, but come on. You can't tell me you don't like the adoration." Her tone was light, teasing.

He shifted in his seat. "It's hard to explain. If the adoration were honest, then I'd love it. But none of it is. Or rarely. Most of the time it's pure bullshit, people only using me to gain something for themselves. I have a hard time knowing if I'm even any good anymore, because no one will tell me when I do suck. The public as a whole will, hell yeah, even when I don't. But my associates? They're on the hunt for the next buck." He took a long swallow from his glass, the frost on the sides melting under his fingertips. "It's exhausting. I'm constantly judging my performance while I'm performing. I'd love to just let go, get lost in each scene, but I fear losing sight of what I'm doing and not being told that I need to fix it."

He pushed back in his seat. "I can't afford to in this movie. Especially with my name attached as director as well.

I'm a serious artist and want to be seen as one."

Sam smiled. "You're incredibly talented."

His chest squeezed. He couldn't help the goodness that spread through him with her words. She had no desire to fill him with shallow praise, on the contrary. She enjoyed putting him in his place. He lifted his glass in a toast. "Thank you."

Looking around the restaurant, she turned back to him with a smile. "This is nice, being with you here, I mean. I knew you were a big deal, but even the starring actor from *Stranded* is watching you from the corner of his eye."

He squeezed his hand into a fist under the table to keep from grabbing her and pulling her to him. "Thank you for coming with me."

"I thought a lot about what you said, about how strong I really am."

He stilled.

She pulled her shoulders back. "I'm building the life I want, and spending time with you is one of the things I want. It might not work out, but I want to try."

The heat in his chest was too much, and he drew a long swallow from his glass. It was everything he could do to keep from dragging her the hell outta there and making her his over and over again. That's all he could ask for, for now, her to try. They clinked glasses, and the sound lent a cheerful note to the buzzing melody in the room.

"So, why directing?"

Gage leaned forward onto his forearms. "I want to have more options. More control." He looked about the room. "Hollywood isn't sweet. It's bitter and jealous, and eventually I'm not going to measure up. Hell, as it is, my past misdeeds seem to color opinions everywhere I go, though I'm slowly working on that. When the masses decide I'm not handsome enough, hot enough, or *it* enough, I want something else to fall back on that still enables me to create."

She nodded. "I get that, the need to create."

He smiled. "Of course. You would. There's something amazing about connecting with people on such a visceral level, isn't there? We make them feel. That's powerful."

"The most powerful. Isn't that what people look for or avoid every second of every day? Experience, emotion. We take them there. Sometimes we yank them, and sometimes we tiptoe in, and they never even know what hit them."

She got him in ways no one ever had before. Creating was as much part of him as his next breath, and he didn't want to limit it to paper or the screen. Having a family was another form of creation, the purest form.

He emptied his glass, the cool liquid warming his head and loosening his tongue. "I want to create a stable environment for my kids—tuck them in at night, and see their smiling faces each morning. Like my dad did for Bel and me."

Sam squeezed his hand, and he held her gaze.

"I think it's really sweet, but do you think it's realistic?"

Her tone tightened his shoulders. "I'm not asking you to think it's sweet. It just is."

Sam sipped from her glass, holding his gaze over the rim, and then set it down, reaching out for his hand. "I'm sorry. I don't mean to offend you. It's just that we see it all the time. Hollywood couples have children and then the poor kids are left in the care of a nanny or shipped off to school, under the guise of offering the best education, so the parents don't have to give up their Hollywood lifestyle. Or else, only one of the parents is in the game. I feel bad for the kids. I certainly don't want that for my own children. You only have to look as far as your own mother to see what I'm saying."

He felt like a sledgehammer hit him in the face, and he released her hand.

Sam threw her hands out. "No, I'm not saying you're like her in any way. I'm not."

Gage pulled air in through his nose. "No? Because that's exactly what it sounded like."

"I was wrong to even bring her up, I'm sorry. You are nothing, nothing like her. I only meant, that we see it everywhere, even in our own lives."

His shoulders relaxed. "Like with Ethan."

She nodded and twisted her hands together at her waist. "I'm sorry, I didn't mean to bring her up that way, but what I'm saying is true. The celebrity lifestyle has commitments that don't allow much quality time."

Not for him. Not for his kids. "It doesn't have to be that way, Sam."

Her gaze darted around the room, then returned to him. She leaned back as the waiter removed their plates. "Let's have some fun. What songs are you singing?"

He raised a brow in challenge. "You mean *we*."

"What?" she squeaked, and her eyes widened.

Their names boomed over the speakers, and he stood. Immediate applause roared from the crowd with catcalls and whistles.

Sam shook her head from side to side. "No, no, no. Gage! I can't sing," she finished in a furious whisper.

"Well, lucky for you, I can. I've loved karaoke since college." Before she could decide to leave, he wrapped his hand around her small wrist and helped her to her feet.

"I'm going to kill you. Seriously. Murder you."

A full-bellied laugh erupted from his throat. It felt good.

She narrowed her eyes at him. "I am not going up there."

Their names were announced again, and cameras flashed. Cell phones lifted with the red recording button on. Gage didn't care if there were videos of him singing all over YouTube, but she would.

He turned her toward him. "It'll be fine, fun. This is a paparazzi-free area. Relax." Turning her toward the stage he added, "You have to. At this point, resisting will make a bigger scene." He enjoyed this too much. Why, he should even be ashamed. But he wasn't. Shit. Sam needed to loosen up and quit taking herself, and everybody else, so seriously. It was impossible to get in front of a group of strangers and sing without letting go a little. He counted on it.

Sam drew back her shoulders and narrowed her gaze at him. "I'll do it, but not because I have to, but because I like a challenge. Got it? But you owe me."

"What's that?"

"Ice cream."

He raised a brow, but she simply nodded. "My favorite place is down at the Country Mart."

Adrenaline surged through him, and he grinned, followed by a fist pump. "Deal. Ha ha! Let's do this!"

A look of horror crossed her face but determination soon took its place. Gage had no idea what ran through that head of hers. He bet in about five minutes she'd be having too much fun to care.

• • •

The flashes, hoots, and hollers sucked the air from her lungs as Sam and Gage stepped onto the stage. How was she supposed to sing with no breath? Her fingers tingled with the pins and needles of shock. Holy hell, the last thing she needed was to pass out on stage.

Pull it together, Dekker. She shook out her hands and pulled in a breath.

She watched as Gage said a few words to the D.J. and then joined her front and center.

"Ya ready?" The look of excitement on his face did something to her insides.

She was over being so afraid of everything. This was a chance to be bold and brave, and damn it, she *was* ready. "Yes."

He stared at her a minute. "Sam...I..."

"You what?"

The familiar heavy chords of "Enter Sandman" keyed up.

Sam squealed. "Oh my God."

She closed her eyes, focusing on the intro music, willing herself to absorb the dark strength of the song and chase the butterflies from her stomach. She glanced out over the expectant faces of the crowd and then over to find Gage rocking his air guitar, and she laughed.

Adrenaline built within her, and with one last breath in, she belted out the first line of the song in unison with Gage.

His eyes shot to hers, wide with surprise as they continued on singing, he with a huge grin stretching his mouth wide. After the first two lines, Sam's heart found its way back to a gentler cadence, and her lungs filled with air. She felt like she was flying, so light, carefree. How long had it been?

Maybe the song was right, maybe the beast *was* inside her head, and all this time she'd blamed Hollywood.

A warmth of love infused her as she sang, staring into Gage's eyes. The man opened her up, helped her face her fears, the world. She grinned at him, and he yanked her close, smacking a kiss to her lips in the exhilaration of it all, lights flashed like a disco ball and the crowd roared, but before she could even think, the next song's guitar blend blasted from the speakers.

They sang Oasis' "Wonderwall," both angled at forty-five into one speaker. The feeling of having so much attention focused on her could be dangerous. The crowd screamed their approval, and Sam warmed to her toes.

She watched Gage soak in the applause, and the smile on his face was as if he smiled with his whole body. That was how he did everything, how he would do everything—with all of himself. He put all he was into showing her how strong she was; he was a guide. The song had spoken of winding roads and blinding lights, but she wasn't blinded. She could see Gage hadn't let Hollywood change him. He enjoyed singing, so he did it regardless of who he was. He wasn't like all the rest, which meant maybe they actually had a chance at making this work.

Minutes later, Sam and Gage took care of their bill and took the back door out to their car. Sam's heart beat at a furious speed in her chest, and she gasped for breath. Gage bundled her into his car, and she all but gushed, "That was the scariest thing I've ever done."

Gage's deep bark of laughter filled the car as he accelerated north on Pacific Coast Highway. "You nailed it! Who would have thought you could even sing, but Metallica and

Oasis? Nice."

Sam screamed, "Woo-hoo!" She'd never known such a rush. He'd given her a tiny peek into what he experienced every day on set, and wasn't that like him? She wasn't sure if she'd ever met a more a more generous man.

They couldn't get to his house fast enough. Seeing him on stage living the life he wanted, not letting Hollywood force his path, shifted something inside of her. She hadn't felt this alive in years, and her body was on fire. With blatant approval, she ran her gaze along the length of his body, anticipation drumming to the tips of her nerve endings. Long and thick with muscle, he was nothing but hard planes and sharp angles—just the way she liked him.

Security stopped them at the gate and did a quick sweep of his car. Sam twisted in her seat to see and then turned back around, fisting her hands in her lap. "Are you kidding me?"

Gage chuckled. "Almost there."

Sam threw her hands out. "Wait. We forgot. You owe me ice cream."

He threw her a look that said she was crazy without opening his mouth. "Tomorrow. All you want. Right now, I want you."

I want you. And just like that, she couldn't argue if she wanted to. And she did not want to argue.

He pulled into the garage, and they bolted from the car as the door closed. He flew through the entryway, yanking Sam in behind him. As soon as the door was locked, she pushed him up against it, sliding her tongue into his mouth, demanding a response.

All of the adrenaline and excitement of the night pushed

them higher, not just the singing, but the conversation, and something else — the time to learn about each other. He understood her, really understood, her need for independence, her need to create. No other man ever worked so hard to *know* her before.

With fast, jerky movements, they tore off each other's clothing, throwing the pieces across the hall. "Fuck, I want you so bad." Sam tugged at his lower lip, grabbing the condom from his hand. Ripping it open, she dropped before him and wrapped her hand around his length. His skin seared her skin, hard and smooth as she rolled the latex down to the very end with a firm squeeze.

"God, Sam." The ragged tone of his voice empowered her in a way karaoke never could.

Standing, she pulled him in for a kiss and then in one smooth motion, using her arms behind his neck for leverage, hopped up, and wrapped her legs about his waist.

Without waiting for him to catch up, she maneuvered over his length, suspended with him pressed thick and hot against her core. Her body screamed for release, and waves of anticipatory flutters spread out to the ends of her limbs.

It was always this way with him, hot and urgent, like trying to get to the surface of the water in order to breathe. She wanted to be around him and in him all at the same time. Holding his gaze, she slid down in one, long, satisfying motion, her body stretching to accommodate him and then gripping him to keep him there. With him pressed tightly to her, she closed her eyes, reveling in the wholeness of it all. She could get used to this, and for the first time she wasn't scared.

"Holy fucking shit." Gage's words groaned out through

gritted teeth and set Sam off hotter than before.

She smiled, lifting her body and then lowering back down to the hilt over and over again. Gage lashed his tongue against her breast, and she tugged at his earlobes, sliding her tongue along the ridge of his ear, down his neck, then back over his hot, wet mouth.

Every time he stroked her tongue with his, she timed her body to slide down his shaft, and white-hot heat washed over her, cresting, building a fire.

Squeezing her thighs tight about him, she rose one last time, her body pulsing, begging for one more deep thrust to take her over the edge and shatter every inhibition she ever dreamed of having.

Gage squeezed her ass, the pressure increasing the throbbing pulse low in her core, and drove her down his length, with a shout of pure animal release.

Wave after wave of blinding pleasure poured over her, and he held on with a death grip, as if determined not to fall.

But she'd already fallen. Hard.

Chapter Nineteen

As promised *tomorrow* came and Gage delivered. After a full day filming on set, they strolled in companionable gluttony as they made their way leisurely through the Country Mart. Sam licked the ice cream sliding down her cone and onto her thumb. One thing she loved about California was ice cream in March. The evening sun still warmed the concrete, and barely a breeze ruffled her hair. Café Habana had been an amazing experience. She'd never had so much fun in her life, and to her surprise, no photo-ops covered the tabloids that morning when she got up.

A few camera flashes went off here and there, but nothing too bad. The Country Mart was known for not welcoming paparazzi. She took a bite from her cone with purpose.

Gage chatted on about the complexity of his character in the film as they wound through the meandering crowds of the Country Mart, ignoring muffled whispers. A few brave and starry-eyed souls approached for autographs, and Gage delivered with a grace and sweetness that surprised Sam, and then they'd continued walking as if it was all so very normal. For him, it was. For her, she wished people would quit interrupting, which left her feeling selfish and petty. She shoved the feeling down with great effort, determined to enjoy her ice cream and their walk.

When the last pair of fans walked away, Gage hesitated. "Wait a second."

Puzzled, Sam turned. She wiped at her chin and lips. "What?"

Smiling, he stepped close and molded his warm lips to hers. His heat was a delightful contrast to the chill of her ice cream. He tasted her with his tongue. "I wanted a bite."

"Well, well, if it isn't our Hollywood wannabe clinging to the shirttails of the playboy actor."

Sam reeled around, wishing she could shove her ice cream into Mrs. Evans' face. But she'd never treat ice cream so poorly. "Playboy? That's funny coming from Ethan's mother."

Mrs. Evans stood next to Brigitte, both chins tipped up so far, Sam could see up their nostrils. Not a flattering view. "No class, but you won't think it's so funny after this," Ethan's mother said. She shoved a glossy magazine into Sam's chest.

Once the sharp sting of her brain freeze subsided, Sam pulled her shoulders back. These little run-ins were getting old. "Really? You stopped my afternoon for mean-girl jabs? Talk about no class." She turned to Gage. "I'm sorry." Flashing him a brilliant smile, she looped her arm through his as they stepped away from the two spiteful women.

Determined to show the women she didn't care, Sam flipped the magazine over but not without a little dread. She glanced at the cover and froze.

Gage leaned in for a closer look. "Son of a bitch," he ground out.

A picture of him kissing her on stage stared back at her, which she could deal with, but the article heading threatened to empty her stomach, and she really hated to waste ice cream.

Tensing against the words, Sam read the heading again. BEHIND THE LOSS OF ETHAN EVANS: AN INTIMATE INTERVIEW DETAILING THE DAUGHTER-IN-LAW'S TRYST WITH THE ENEMY.

"We want the pictures." Brigitte stepped forward. Her pitchy voice grated against Sam's ears.

A crowd had gathered, and camera flashes started anew. Sam wanted to disappear.

Gage's bicep tensed under her hand.

"Relax. They aren't worth a scene." She ran her hand down his arm, attempting to get his focus on her instead of them. Sadness filled her heart. The last thing she needed was a rescue, especially against something she knew would happen.

She could handle a couple of gnats on her own. She turned, keeping her voice low and pleasant. "Well, that doesn't really matter, does it?" She turned her back to the two women, as if the pictures didn't matter, as if the magazine didn't matter—as if. But dismissing the harpies gave her a measured amount of joy.

"We want the pictures of Ethan with those women. What kind of pervert would want to keep them?"

Sam turned back on her heel. "That is a very good question." Ethan's photos turned out to be more than casual nudes. She'd been mortified, horrified, and humiliated beyond comprehension. His mother and sister knew about them? What the hell? But more, they wanted them. The whole family was sick.

Sam tilted her head and whispered low to Ethan's mother. "You want to see your son entering a young woman, Mrs. Evans? Taking her from behind? That's what you want so badly you won't leave me alone? Crossing the line, even for you, don't you think?"

The woman sucked in a breath.

Gage stepped forward. "Sam."

She held her palm out to him, halting his approach. "No, just a minute. These women started this, and it's about time I finish it."

"You filthy, little —"

"I'm filthy?" Sam directed a look at Brigitte, who pressed her lips together, cheeks burning a deep red. More cameras flashed. Sam's heart slammed in her chest. Disgust was acid in her mouth as she directed her question to Mrs. Evans. "You knew. And you let it happen anyway, and now, *now* you want the pornographic evidence of your son's infidelity?" Her voice shook. She heaved in a breath, but her lungs constricted.

Gage stood by her side, her embarrassment acute. Now he knew her dirty secret. The one she'd hoped no one would ever know.

Mrs. Evans grabbed Brigitte's hand. Her voice trembled in apparent rage. "He *deserved* some happiness. He'd never gotten any from *you.*" The older woman all but spit the words. Brigitte stood silent, with an odd light in her eye. Sam couldn't, didn't want to, imagine what the woman was thinking. This family had problems. Problems she never saw, or never let herself see.

Brigitte spoke up as she smoothed her blond hair back over her shoulder. "The pictures belong to us. We want them, Sam. Enough of this." She reached a hand out. "Besides, they only bring you pain."

Sam laughed. "You worry about me, Brigitte? How touching. The two of you will burn in hell before you lay a hand on those photos." She turned to Gage. "I'm done here."

"Sam," Brigitte screeched and more heads than just Sam's turned at the sound.

Oh, this was just great. The damned paparazzi would have a field day.

Swinging around, Sam marched back to the women until she stood nose to nose. "I'm filing a restraining order."

Ethan's mother seized in a breath and then grabbed her daughter's hand, taking off the way they'd come. A few of the paparazzi yelled out a few questions, which only spurred Mrs. Evans along faster.

She stilled. He pulled her resisting form into his warm embrace, and the pressure of his hug calmed her.

She gave in for a count of three, then with gentle pressure, stepped back. Holding his gaze, she shook her head and swallowed against the lump in her throat. Tears burned behind her lips.

His face fell. "Sam, this picture must have been someone in the club. A cell phone, nothing more. This is different. It wasn't about us, not really."

The solid wall of his chest had shielded her; his strong arms had protected her. Fearless and loyal, he demonstrated the characteristics of a good man at every turn. They were tested and they handled it. Maybe it wasn't so much protecting herself from his life as it was protecting him from her life. He was right. It wasn't about them, and she didn't want him to find out what it had really been about.

Sam followed Gage into her condo. She needed a few more things, and the threat still hadn't been resolved. What she wanted to do was be alone, go for a swim, lose herself in the relentless rhythm of the ocean.

Walking through the kitchen, she dropped her bag to the floor next to the end of the counter and then walked over to the sliding glass doors.

Gage wrapped his arms around her waist, strong and sure. She leaned back into his warm chest and released a sigh of relief. He made her feel safe, whether she liked it, wanted it, or not. A feeling she hadn't experienced in a long time.

He nuzzled the side of her neck, and the fine hairs rose along her skin and down her arms. "You know we need to talk," he said.

Sam closed her eyes. Talking about the Evanses, especially Ethan, was the last thing she wanted to do. She'd rather get her teeth pulled, but like a cavity, if she didn't do something, it would fester and cause more pain.

Turning in his arms, she buried her face in his neck and breathed him in. The smell of his skin, the aromatic essence of *him* mingled with his cologne. Her favorite scent. She pressed her lips into his warm skin, sighed against the pulse in his neck. "Can't we just pretend that the Evanses never existed?"

His chest rumbled. "No. If that were true, I wouldn't have had to wait so damn long to have you in my life. You can't dismiss or pretend this away, Sam."

She leaned back and looked into his eyes. He was serious. No doubt remembering the night she'd walked away from him, hurting him in a way she'd never imagined. But what could she have done?

Been honest.

She blew out a breath.

Excelling remained somewhat of an obsession for her. The failing of her marriage had chipped away at her, insidious and persistent. She'd fought to polish and revise the relationship into a beautiful love story.

But there had never been anything to edit. She couldn't fix a story that never existed.

Whether she liked it or not. "I'm sorry."

He kissed her, rough, fast. "I don't want your apology. You don't have anything to apologize for. What I want—" He broke away and strode to the bar. He poured scotch into two tumblers and then pressed a glass into her hand.

She looked at the amber liquid then back to Gage with a raised brow. "Good call."

Anything to smooth the edge of anger that still simmered. She threw her head back and downed the scotch. The spirits burned her throat, and her breath seized. She grabbed onto the shelving unit and coughed.

Gage rubbed her back with a firm touch, removing the tumbler from her trembling fingers as she struggled for air. "Well, that's not exactly what I had in mind, but okay." He raised his glass in salute and then pulled a swallow.

Warm fingers linked with hers, and he led her to the chaise lounge. He settled back, pulling her down between his legs, her back against this chest. They watched the ocean in silence, while he ran his fingertips up and down her arm.

"Do you want to talk about it?"

"It's humiliating."

Gage squeezed. "There is nothing humiliating about fighting for what you believe. You believed in your relationship. People saw that and didn't have the heart to tell you any different."

"I wanted my marriage to be what it should have been. I didn't want to see what it really was." She turned sideways in his lap. "Deep down, I knew something was going on. That's when I'd decided to leave. But I never imagined the truth. That's for sure."

Resting her ear against his chest, Sam breathed in time with his even heartbeat. They stayed silent, listened to the ocean sounds, blanketed by the dark velvet of the night sky. Her throat tightened. "Why didn't he love me?" She whispered so low she hardly heard her own voice.

Gage tilted her chin and caught her gaze. "It wasn't you."

She dropped her forehead back to his muscled warmth.

He nudged until she sat up and faced him. Running his hand along the length of her back, he spoke, his voice low but succinct. "The man didn't love himself. So he hunted. The women gave him power. Made him feel like he mattered. In a way, I can relate."

"You are nothing like him." The vehemence in her voice a telling sign of how far she'd fallen.

Gage chuckled. "I appreciate the vote of confidence, and you're right. Ethan Evans and I are nothing alike. But I understand searching for ways to feel relevant. It never works. It's gotta come from within"—he tapped over the area of his heart—"or it's never enough."

Sam rested back, once again losing herself in the steady

rhythm of his heart. So calm, steady—like him.

He was right, but was he talking about Ethan or her? *Did* she love herself?

She was certainly trying, damn it.

But she was fighting an uphill battle. After everything Ethan had done, she was terrified, and the idea she considered putting her heart in the hands of a celebrity seemed ludicrous.

Gage was supportive and warm, challenging and fun, and most of all, nothing like Ethan, but if she did love herself, would she really risk that kind of position?

He brushed her hair away from her forehead. "What are you thinking about?"

"I'm going to file a restraining order tomorrow."

"Good. You need to, but what are you really thinking about?"

"How wonderful you are, and how scared I am."

He squeezed her shoulders, and she sat up.

Dropping his feet to the floor, he held her with his gaze. "Not all celebrities are alike. Being with one is not like being with another."

She hesitated. "I'm sorry, but—"

"Sam." He lifted her chin with a finger. "I'm not searching for anything to make me whole. I've already found it."

She tensed.

"And as much as I love you, it isn't you, so you can wipe the terrified look off your face. It's me, my acting, the chance to give back. I won't be constantly searching for something else. Which leaves me to love *you*."

Something unfurled in her chest. She opened her mouth to speak, but he placed his hand over hers.

"I know this is hard for you, and it's hard for me, too. I'm sure you expect me to trust you, too, but it isn't easy when I know you don't trust me. I want a partnership, Sam. I don't want this relationship to be all about whether or not you can trust me, but about trusting each other. Working together."

And then it happened: an opening, like a rush of fresh air, or sudden clarity, and her heart turned over in her chest with a firm thub-dub. She loved him. Plain and simple and beautiful.

Unable to say the words, she studied how his brows drew together over the intense light of his eyes, and turned her hand to link her fingers with his.

Ethan had never wanted a partnership; he'd wanted an assistant, a house keeper, or a convenient plus one.

But Gage wanted her and everything she had to give.

It was time to turn light and easy into bold and brave.

• • •

Gage watched his sister approach with hot coffee and a bag of Blinkie's donuts. Bless the woman. Coffee and donuts on the beach became their standard meeting place since he'd moved into his waterfront property. Already hitting the gym an hour each afternoon, these little visits required him to either cut down on dinner or add an extra thirty minutes to his cardio.

He helped her with the loot and then pulled her in for a hug. "Thank you. You're a life saver."

Bel stepped back and looked him over. "You look like hell."

"I haven't had any coffee yet." He took a sip. The liquid

scalded his tongue, and he jerked the cup back with a curse.

"Yeah, it's coffee. Supposed to be hot." She put her arm around his shoulders. "Are you okay?"

He glanced down at her with derision. "Like you care."

She laughed as they settled in the sand. Gage ate his donut in two bites.

"Slow down."

He sipped his coffee, with more care this time. Shoving his hand in the bag, he pulled out another and took a bite. "I don't know what I'm doing, Bel. I love Sam. The life I want is only possible with her in it. But I'm asking her to deal with it and live with all of the stress my job brings with it."

Bel lowered her coffee to her lap. "Well, considering her past, she's probably scared. Don't push her."

"She's scared?" He demanded, his mouth full of donut. "Any second she's going to leave. I'm the one who's fucking scared."

Bel glanced out over the rippling waves. "You left."

Gage stilled. "What?"

His sister took a dainty bite of her glazed donut and chewed. Washing it down with her coffee, she turned toward him. "You left. For school. I was crushed and felt abandoned, again, but I loved you so much. You aren't Mom; I knew that."

Gage sat in stunned silence. He'd never known his leaving affected her like that, or he would never have gone.

"You seemed half the world away. But I waited and you came back. Because you love *me* so much."

Guilt clogged his throat, and he dropped his donut back in the bag. "Bel, come on. I was at film school."

She nodded. "I know. And I was fourteen and had no big

brother to help me navigate high school. I didn't think about what you were doing, but what you weren't."

"Shit, I'm sorry."

Bel smiled and took another bite of her donut. "I know, and I survived. I think, in a way, it was good. Gave me and Dad some time to bond. I think how close he and I got is why I set my sights on Pepperdine."

Gage stood. "So what you're saying is that you owe me for your great success."

"Spoken like a true Hollywood elitist. No, what I'm saying is give her space, time. Things'll work out. If you push her, she *will* bolt, and you *will* be left alone."

He reached out and helped her up.

"She's afraid and with good reason. Being married to you means possibly months of being apart, keeping crazy hours. If you have a family, most of the burden will fall on her even though she has a job, too."

He opened his mouth to argue.

Shaking her head, Bel put her hand up. "You film on different continents all the time. She won't be able to just drop everything and go with you. Not if she is trying to build her career back."

They walked shoulder to shoulder, and Gage stared out over the surf. He and Sam would have their challenges, but they'd be able to face each one as a team. The how and the what could be figured out, but there would be no reason to without Sam.

Pulling in a breath, he settled his arm around Bel's shoulders. "I like the idea of being responsible for your success better. I'm going to stick with that."

Bel shook her head and punched him in the shoulder.

"Of course you would."

Gage squeezed her hand. "I'm really sorry. I had no idea."

"I know. If you had, you wouldn't have gone. Why do you think I never said anything? You'd always put me first. Before school, your friends, even Dad. I was young, but not stupid. I wanted you to be happy. You'd have never gone, and you needed to. It just sucked, that's all. I missed you."

The more he worked on changing and growing, the more mistakes he discovered he'd made along the way. Maybe he'd been kidding himself from the beginning. He thought he'd changed, but deep down, was he the same selfish guy he'd always been? He wanted a life with Sam, but if their relationship only brought her constant reminders of Ethan, fans intruding into their lives, and an absentee husband, was it fair to ask her to want him back?

Chapter Twenty

Gage needed the director and the producer to come to a decision yesterday and release the cast. It had been almost twenty-four hours since he'd last had any time with Sam. The end of their conversation had kept him on edge, and every time he went to go find her to check in, he got called into something else.

Last night, she'd grabbed a bottle of wine and knocked on his office door, but he'd been on a string of interviews, and by the time he'd finished, she was sound asleep. He'd thrown himself into a full-blown work out and then dragged himself to bed around two in the morning, only to find a message from his agent calling him into an eight a.m. meeting. There was nothing to be done but have security come and stay until Sam was up and ready to go to the set, which wouldn't be until closer to ten. A frustrating schedule, and it wasn't the first time it happened, but today was the worst time for it to happen.

Finally they'd wrapped up shooting for the day, and he rounded the corner of shelves to find Sam bent over her desk. He loved the curve of her back and the way the little hairs at the nape of her neck escaped the confines of her pencil-secured bun, as if they too were shouting their independence.

"I can't believe filming is almost over." Gage stood behind her as she poured intently over her copy of the screenplay.

She spared him a quick glance and nodded. "It's gone fast. You guys have been brilliant." Flipping a few pages, she settled on one. She pulled her pencil from her hair and tapped it against the edge of the manuscript. "If I can just get this last scene right. Something's missing."

Her hair fell in a cascade of alternating shades of chocolate, her scent wafting past his nose as the mass settled below her shoulders. Vanilla and citrus made him want to pull her in to ease the pressure in his chest like a pastry might do for an emotional eater. Gage searched the area she worked in, through shelves of equipment, props, lights, and microphones, until he finally discovered a stool under an oversized tarp. Dragging one over, he dropped down next to her. "Thank you for checking in with Martin."

She focused her attention on his face. "No-brainer. I don't want you calling my dad or brother to the set as my bodyguards."

Gage chuckled and dipped his head in acknowledgement and then tilted his head, studying her face. "I feel like it's been ages since I've seen you. I had to go in early this morning."

She set her pencil down and turned toward him, her

gaze roaming over his face and then down to his hands. He released his grip on the table, dropping his hands to his lap, and she lifted them gently into hers. "I know, but at least I finally got to those manuscripts I'd been putting off." She rubbed her thumb along the top of his hand. "We need to talk."

His gut twisted. "Yeah, I figured as much." He glanced down at where her knees rested against the side of his thigh, always so surprised by how much such a simple sharing of space affected him, and then back to her face.

She blew out a breath. "I'm terrified," she whispered. "And pissed."

Standing, she paced the small area. "You were right, you know. About me holding on to being a victim. I've been hiding, hoping no one would notice me." She stopped and faced him, her hands clenched in front of her. "All of this has been weighing on me, but I found some clarity when we talked. I just needed some time to process it. I'm done hiding."

Gage's heart dropped in his chest. He turned in his seat, leaning toward her. "What are you saying?"

She smiled, her lower lip trembling, and stepped between his legs. His arms wrapped around her waist, and he looked up at her, uncertainty snaking up his spine.

Running her fingers through the fine hairs at the back of his neck, she pulled in a breath. "Like I said, I'm terrified."

He stood, keeping her in his arms and sighed, dropping his forehead to hers. "You're not the only one."

"You're shaking."

Raising his head, he stared down into her eyes. "What are you telling me, Sam?" Blood rushed to his head, and he feared he wouldn't hear her response. His fingers flexed at her waist.

She tilted her head to the side, her gaze direct. "I think you know."

Gage shook his head. "No, I don't. Say the words." And please let them be the ones he wanted to hear. He closed his eyes.

She pressed her mouth to his, a soft caress. "I love you, Gage. I want to try to be with you for the long haul."

The air left his lungs, both fear and elation stealing his breath. "You love me?"

"I love you."

"There're no guarantees." That was an understatement, but he was so afraid she didn't know what she was saying. Could they really have a chance to make something real?

He dropped his face to her shoulder and held on tight. The possibilities raced through his mind on fast forward. He pulled back and looked into her face, her eyes wide and smiling up at him. She was worth it, and it seemed she thought he was worth it, too. A tentative staccato of acceptance beat in his chest. With a "whoop," he picked her up and spun her around.

Sam laughed and hugged him in return.

He wanted the chance to see that smile every morning, to watch her bite her lip when she was concentrating, and tuck her toes up under her when she wanted to relax, and he never wanted to let her go. Now more than ever, he needed to show her the life they could have together, regardless of his work in Hollywood.

She stepped back to her desk, arms folded across her chest, still smiling but her brows furrowed as well.

"I know you're scared, I am too, but we can handle

anything they want to throw at us, Sam. Look how far we've come already."

She nodded. If there was ever a time for her to show her strength, it was now. He hoped she could reach deep and tap into what made her survive the past few years.

"I'll let you get back to work. Don't make any plans for tonight, okay?"

She nodded. "Okay."

· · ·

The rest of the day had flown on set. They were making great progress on the film and even projected an earlier wrap-up time than expected. Sam and Gage had gone back to his place, and now she stood in his kitchen, wine in hand, watching him add the final touches to dinner.

She loved that he cooked, and having someone cook dinner for her was a treat she hadn't experienced often.

He added two large portions of lasagna to each plate with a drizzle of an olive oil and marinara sauce over the top. Pulling garlic bread from the oven, he looked over his shoulder and sent her a wink. He set the tray on the counter and then cut off thick chunks, adding them to the plates as well. "If you grab our wine, I'll take these to the table."

His phone rang, and they both froze. With his brow furrowed, he checked the number and with a sigh answered it. "Hey, Martin."

He lifted a finger asking her to wait a second and spoke quietly into the phone. "Not tonight, Martin. I can't." Nodding, he paced the small space in front of the area in front the counter. "And I understand, but I'm not in the scene.

You can show me tomorrow. I gotta go."

Martin's annoyance rang out over the phone as Gage disconnected the call.

"What did you do? He didn't sound happy."

Gage lifted their plates and made his way to the table. "He wanted me to come down and watch a last minute scene change they decided to shoot."

"Don't you think you should go?"

He shook his head. "No. I'm not in it. Nothing will be lost if he shows me tomorrow."

His gesture warmed her but worried her, too. He might get away with it because he and Martin were close, but another director might have been pissed. "Gage, I don't think—"

Narrowing his eyes, he nailed her with a look. "And I want to spend time with you, and only you." She decided to drop it and settled into the wonderful feeling, her mouth watering at the savory aromas, as Gage set their plates on the table and took the chair across from her. The garlic bread was stuffed with whole roasted garlic cloves, and she pulled one out and tossed it into her mouth. "We are going to be fresh tonight."

He grinned and tossed one of his own in his mouth. "As long as we both eat it, we won't even notice."

She watched him take his first bite of lasagna. Everything he did was always so big and all in. There was no half-assing anything where he was concerned. "Thank you for making me dinner; this is a nice surprise."

He held her gaze. "You're welcome. I wanted to do more, and now I can."

"You've already done more." She rushed on before he

could comment. "Have you always cooked?"

Shaking his head, he then sipped from his wine. "Since I was a kid, but it was Raquel that got me hooked. Every time I'd go over to their place for dinner, she'd have me help her in the kitchen."

"You're really good."

He dipped his head. "I want big family dinners, the kind where everyone helps, where we talk about our day. I know how you feel about the kids of celebrities, but I'm doing things differently. I want to be around, and that's one reason I'm making the shift with my career."

The idea warmed her. She could imagine herself chopping vegetables while drinking a glass of wine, him firing up a grill, the kids setting the table and teasing each other as they went. The vision no longer sent a shot of fear down her spine.

She tilted her head to the side. "If that's what you really plan on doing, then you'll do it."

Reaching his hand across the table, he slid his fingers through hers. "Can you see yourself in a situation like that?"

A month ago, she'd have closed down or run away, but now she could see it clearly, and she loved it—loved him. Nodding, she said, "Yes."

He squeezed her fingers gently, then released her hand.

"How many kids do you want?"

"At least two. I love Bel. She's one of my best friends. I want that for my kids, too. But no matter how many I have, they will have the support they need."

She loved that he saw that. As crazy as Luca and Addi might make her, she was so thankful to have them. "I think two is a good number. It'll make supporting them that much easier because you won't be out numbered."

The corners of his lips lifted, and he ran his gaze over her face. "I'm glad you're here."

"I'm scared, but I'm more mad right now that I was making decisions based on Ethan. So stupid."

"It's not, it's normal. Changing the way we think is nearly impossible."

She put her hands out, and he touched the tips of his fingers to hers, then let their fingers twine together. "One day at a time?"

Polishing off the last of his lasagna, Gage pushed back from the table. "Finish your wine and relax. I'll be back in a minute."

Sam leaned back in her seat and sipped her wine. She loved the vision he'd painted about his dreams for his family. Solid connections and healthy relationships. She had both with her family, and she wouldn't be who she was without them.

A short time later, Gage stepped back into the kitchen. "Come on, I have a little surprise."

She followed him into the steaming bathroom, the lights dimmed to a soft glow. He turned to her, and she looped her arms around his neck. "What in the world are you doing?" She swept her hand out to indicate the full over-sized tub and the steamed mirrors.

"A little TLC." Pulling the tie at her waist, he opened the front of her shirtdress and pushed it from her shoulders. He slid his fingers back down her arm and along the sensitive skin on the underside of her wrist and whispered, "Sam, trust me."

Sam watched as he pulled his shirt up and over his head,

leaving his chest bare, and a pair of cotton lounge pants low on his hips. Her fingers itched to touch him there.

She was left standing in a pair of low-hipped briefs and a bra, both just a blush darker than her skin. Taking his hand, she stepped over the edge of the tub, the heat enveloping her legs, radiating to the point between her thighs. With a shaky laugh, she asked. "What are you up to?"

He stood before her, just outside the tub, and with a pitcher, trickled water at the hollow of her throat, then trailed it to the right and then to the left. Heat licked along her collarbone and down over her breasts and puckered nipples. Her bra became transparent and, as the water trailed down her breasts and abdomen in lazy trails, so did her panties. She felt more exposed than if she'd been fully naked, while he remained clothed.

The moonlight shining through the sky light, along with Gage's hungry gaze, caressed her skin.

A boldness, still new to her, kicked up her chin. It wasn't fair for her to be a blazing inferno, yet him be so cool and collected. She eyed the well-built man in front of her and slid her foot forward, lifting it to just below the surface of the water and sending a spray of water over his body. Laughing at his slack-jawed expression, she held her sides. He narrowed his gaze and tilted his head, a mischievous grin pulled up the corners of his mouth.

Alarm shot to her limbs and she turned to run, but where she had no idea. He caught her in a step and swung her up in his arms. Water ran down her limbs.

"Put me down." Her words were a laugh.

She screamed as he plunged them both into the tub. The shock of heat against the areas of skin that were still dry made her suck in a breath. Gage turned her in his arms, leaving her kneeling before him, and with his hand around the back of her neck, pulled her in for a kiss. Heat ignited within her, and she all but climbed over his head to get a tighter grasp. She poured every ounce of herself into kissing him back.

One of his hands roamed about her slick skin while the other held her in an iron grip against his warm body. "Oh my God, that feels so good. I've missed you."

"We've been busy, but I'm always right here."

She shook her head. "It's different when there's tension."

She wrapped her legs about him, and she rubbed against his erection. She could see the condom-covered tip of him over the band of his sweats, wondering when he'd rolled it on, and a wanting pulsed through her so strong she dragged her body against his. Need swirling and swelling in her middle.

Reaching between their bodies, she released him from his heavy soaked sweats. Pulling her briefs to the side, she slid onto him slowly, enjoying the sensation of being filled one inch at a time until her pelvis pressed flat against his, moaning into the sensation of sweet pressure and hot water.

"Sweet Jesus." Her words came out of his mouth in a drawn out breath.

Sam leaned backward, forcing him to support her lower back. Clenching her muscles, she pulled up and then relaxed to slide back down his shaft. Each slippery glide increasing her building pressure, the hot water, his hotter flesh, sensations close to spiraling out of control, she wished to die in that moment if she had to go at all.

He sucked on her lower lip and swept his tongue into her mouth, salty sweet, and she moved faster. Harder.

She slammed down his length again and again, water sloshing over the rim of the tub and hitting the floor in a trickling waterfall. Her heart raced, pounding in her ears. The water lapped up her naked sides, drenching her covered breasts with heated water, only to have the air leaving the fabric cool and her nipples tightening to an almost painful peak. His body providing a seductive friction against her every nerve ending.

In one final drop, with him fully inside her, Sam threw her head back as an intense contraction pulled from her core and then burst out in pulsing waves.

Gage followed, holding her in an iron grip, bending over her as his body bucked deeper into her hot, wet, body. "Fuck." The expletive came out in a throaty masculine groan.

Sam wiped water from her face and buried her nose in his neck, hiding her smug smile. Her breath came out in short gasps, and her heart continued to thunder against her chest. She leaned back and looked into his dazed expression, and then she pressed a wet kiss against his mouth.

His lips kicked up into a smile.

She returned with a grin. "Exactly."

Looking about the tub and floor, she wiggled her brows. "We've got to clean this mess up before Anita comes back tomorrow."

Gage smacked her ass with a playful swat, and standing, set her on her feet. Reaching for the band of his pants, hanging about mid-thigh, he pushed them the rest of the way down. He picked them up, wrung them out, and then sent them flying toward her sink. Turning back to her, he challenged her with his gaze, crooking his finger at her.

She looked at him out of the side of her eyes, a giddy

excitement humming through her and barely able to stand. "What are you doing?" She loved this playful side of him, so comfortable with his body, with her. If she'd been holding anything back, he'd obliterated any chance of her keeping it that way.

"I think I hear your shower calling." He grabbed her hand, stepping out of the tub.

And she followed him.

She could see things so differently now. They'd do more than create a life together; they'd live one.

• • •

Gage and Sam tripped over their feet, laughing, as they stumbled through the front door of the film set house. The front foyer remained clear of equipment and movie fodder, leaving an open space with stone tiled flooring, a front table crowned with an impressive iron mirror. Two plush cream chairs and a low bench warmed the space, an invitation for visitors to sit. So they did.

Sam clapped her hand over her heart. "Oh, my God, that was too funny."

Gage leaned back against the light gray wall and blew out a breath. "Whew. At the time it wasn't."

She laughed. "The girl's locker room? How could you make that mistake?"

He chuckled and threw his hands up in defense. "I was fourteen and in a school I didn't know. I'm innocent."

"I'm sure *they* didn't believe you, either."

Gage opened his mouth to speak, but Martin walked in and stood before them with a knowing gleam in his eye and a slow nod.

Gage and Sam looked at one another with a grin and then back to Martin.

A smile spread across Martin's tanned face, chiseling his lines into deeper grooves. His black brows rose toward his hairline in stark contrast to the thick white thatch on his head and his salt-and-pepper beard. "Finally."

Sam grinned, she imagined like an idiot. Leaning into Gage's warmth, she waited for Martin to continue.

"It's like the two of you have known each other for years."

Sam tensed. She couldn't help it.

Gage nodded. "We have actually. I met Sam a few years back, both out of town on business." He glanced at her. "Haven't been able to get her out of my mind since."

Martin sunk into a chair to their right, leaning forward, his interest unmistakable.

Gage shrugged. "But Sam was married, and I was heartbroken."

She elbowed him in the side. Tension rolled from her shoulders with his deep chuckle, and she smiled at Martin. No censure showed in the depth of her mentor's eyes and relief washed over her. The fact remained Martin's opinion mattered.

He waved away Gage's words. "I know, your timing was just off, boy. Good thing you don't have that problem with acting."

"Seriously off."

Martin studied Gage and shook a finger. "You are brilliant. This movie, well, you've exceeded my expectations."

Gage dropped his chin, a hint of pink flushing up his

neck, and Sam's heart warmed. Humble was not the word that normally came to mind when Gage Cutler's name came up in conversation, but she witnessed it now. Another layer. Another way he was different from other celebrities.

He continued to surprise her.

With a half smile, he extended his hand toward the director. "Thank you for the opportunity. I've been wanting to dive into the directing side for a while. A couple years back I would have without worrying about whether or not I could actually pull it off. Studying under you has shown me sides of it I'd never have seen on my own, and I'm better for it. You can imagine what would be said if I'd have flopped."

"Gross rumors. Fodder of Hollywood's entitled, covetous, and bored," Martin interjected. The older man stood, elegant in his dark hounds tooth blazer. He scanned the open space of the house they'd used for the past weeks. He glanced back at the two of them. "Raquel and Dani booked a weekend for the two of you at the Sunset Marquis in West Hollywood."

Sam blinked. She got to her feet. "Martin. We can't accept that."

"Girl, Raquel and I love the both of you like one of our own children. I wanted to do something to say thank you for saving me by agreeing to work on the film."

Warmth suffused her heart. "Martin."

"Get that wide-eyed look like you're about to bolt off your face. This is a gift. The choice is yours, but if you give it back, I'm not the one telling Raquel." Martin winked.

"Ahhhh, here she is." The director gestured to the arched doorway, dismissing Sam.

Dani stepped into the circle and handed Sam a travel

envelope. "Your reservations and the information for the weekend are inside." She grinned, and Sam's own lips quirked up at the corners, but the young girl wasn't looking at her, she was eyeing Gage from head to toe and back again. Well, she couldn't blame the girl. Who wouldn't look at Gage that way. She caught herself doing it all the time.

She took the envelope with a chuckle. "Thank you. I hate for you to have gone through so much trouble."

Dani waved the words away. "Are you kidding? It's like shopping with someone else's credit card. All the glory and none of the consequence." She smiled and headed back toward the main set with a small wave.

Sam turned the envelope over in her hand, studying the intricate design on the back flap. Glancing up, she held Martin's gaze, gratitude clogging her throat. "Thank you."

He pulled his dark brows together. "You've been like a daughter to me. Raquel and I both. With a house full of boys, you've been a refreshing addition."

Martin leaned in with an avuncular hug. "Have fun. Quit thinking."

"I try to tell her—"

Sam cut her gaze to Gage. "Really? You've been quiet all this time, and that's what you want to add?"

The director laughed, a loud boisterous bark. "Smart man."

Affection shone from his eyes as he looked from one to the other. "Don't forget the party." With that he gave a salute and disappeared into the great room of the film set.

Gage shook his head. "I'll never be as wise as he is, but it's a good aspiration."

Sam let her gaze run the length of Gage from the dark hair of his head, to the distressed leather of his dark square-toe loafers. Such a big man, full of power, and an energy that pulled with inexplicable force. Combined with observations like that, and she was a goner.

Martin had always communicated with her in a way that left no room for argument, and in those moments she couldn't resist. He drove every point home as to why he was right. Same way he handled his films, his manuscripts, his actors. He wielded a special kind of enchantment otherwise absent in Hollywood these days. Gage saw that.

And that said something. He had what it took to follow in Martin's footsteps, and Sam wanted to be around to watch it happen.

Chapter Twenty-One

The thump and swell of music followed Gage and Sam as they made their way to the car, arms wrapped around one another's waist, heads close.

"I'm glad we're going. I think this is going to be really good for us," she said.

"Me, too. A little time away, just you and me." He took her hand. "Martin really knows how to celebrate." Gage's low rumble sent shivers down Sam's spine.

"You mean Raquel."

The party had been a collaboration of music and beauty — Hollywood style. Flowing silks and alcohol. Art for the ears and eyes alike. A spread of delectable dishes decadent enough to tempt the most dedicated super model.

"You can never give a man the credit, can you?"

Sam laughed. "No. I can't."

Gage chuckled as he closed her door and made his way around to the driver's side. He shook his head, still smiling, as he lowered into the car.

Giving into impulse, she leaned over and pressed her lips to his warmth. He tasted of spice with the promise of lingering heat. This weekend belonged to them. Starting now.

She pulled away, and Gage's lips slowly widened into a grin. "What was that for?"

"That was for me." Sam settled into her seat and cast him a sideways glance. "I'm ready for some time away, alone. How about you?"

"I've been ready for years."

She returned his grin. Her fears and hesitations were on holiday. "Let's go."

Gage followed the winding road out of the hills and turned south to follow the Pacific Highway to I 10 east into Hollywood. Clear skies boasted a glowing moon and clusters of little diamond nightlights.

The air cooled since the setting of the sun, Sam rolled up her window and snuggled into the warm leather of the seat. She turned, angling her body toward Gage. "What do you want to do first?"

His focused gaze made her stomach roll, low and slow.

She bit her lip. "I like the way you think, but in addition to our lurid affair with the hotel bed—"

"You mean *on* the hotel bed and in the shower, the pool, the—"

"Ha! I get your point." She squeezed her hands together in her lap, anticipation stretching the fifty-minute drive into a lifetime. Wanting to be close, she slid her arm through his and settled with resting her hand on his thigh. His muscles clenched under her touch. She giggled.

Gage cut a look her way, a look of surprise on his face. "Did you just giggle?"

"Shut up." She slid her hand higher on his muscled thigh and squeezed.

His leg jerked and the car surged forward. "If you don't knock it off, we won't make it to Hollywood."

Sam relaxed her hand, enjoying the heat radiating through his slacks. The freedom of the moment released her tension, calmed her nerves, and joy spread from tip to toe. She'd almost forgotten what an existence free of ridicule and loneliness and guilt felt like. If she could only hold onto it for a little while.

Gage pulled up to the front entrance, and a valet jogged to open his door. With little hassle and loads of courtesy, they stepped into their villa and waved good night to the staff.

Sam turned in circles. "Wow. Martin gets brownie points."

The villa flowed from a richly ornate living space and dining area out to a terrace overlooking a tree-lit garden. She could forget time and responsibility in a place like this.

Rich warm wood, deep burgundy, and pumpkin lent a heat to the space that frankly, she didn't think they'd need. She turned to find Gage and bumped into his chest. He steadied her without thinking. It was his way, taking care of people as natural to him as breathing. She studied her hands.

"Hey." He placed his fingers under her chin and applied a gentle pressure.

She met his serious gaze, wishing with all her heart she could be his forever, but she knew the chances of that were slim. "What if we can't do this? We both have so many issues we're still trying to work through." She shook her head, the truth of it all clogging her throat.

"Sam, don't you see? You and I are a great team, and that is why we'll come out of this not only okay, but stronger than we ever imagined." He picked her hand up and placed it over his heart. "I promise to always protect you, to always consider your needs and your wants. This won't be a relationship about me, Sam, but about us. I will choose you, every time."

She tilted her head, wanting to believe every dream his words evoked. Her chest burned with emotion and she smiled. To be chosen—every time? What an amazing way to be loved.

He pulled her to him, keeping her hand under his. "I'm a better man with you. Don't you get that? I'd never risk losing you."

She slid her hands up and around his neck, dragging her nails lightly against his skin. The tension building inside her had everything to do with the man in front of her and nothing else. "Show me."

A strong hand touched her stomach, then slid to the buttons on her slacks. Deft fingers made quick work of the clasp, and he pushed her pants and panties to the floor. He bent forward and gathered her up into his arms. She wrapped her legs around his waist as their tongues tangled with and tasted each other. His hands were everywhere, and the night air cooled her skin before she saw her shirt on the floor. Gage turned and pressed her back against the smooth surface of the closest wall.

Sam gasped for breath.

Gage leveraged her weight against the wall and thrust his hands into her hair. He ravaged her mouth, leaving her ability to think nonexistent.

Frantic to touch him, Sam tore at his shirt and sank deeper into the kiss. Her stomach fluttered, and pressure grew between her legs. The buckle of his belt pressed into her sensitive flesh, and she pressed into him, trying to increase the sensation.

Gage pulled away just enough to slide his hand between their bodies. She moaned, "Don't stop."

"Never."

Sam pushed his hands away; he gave a low growl. She released his belt, shoving his pants past his hips, and then closing any distance between them. The length of him, hard and hot, pulsed against her folds. She was ready and in control, the feeling heady, giving her a new kind of power and strength. She flexed her fingers in his hair, tugging at him. "Gage, now."

He held her, leveraging the weight of her with his hips and bracing her against the wall as he rolled on a condom. She ran her fingers up and down his arms as he finished.

"Look at me." His fingers flexed into her skin, his arms trembling.

She obeyed his husky demand, holding his gaze with a lift of her chin and got lost in the intensity of his green eyes, as he pushed in. "It's you and me, Sam." The intimacy of eye contact as he entered her body sent her senses spiraling. Stars exploded, and her periphery went black, but she held his gaze.

Gage thrust into her hot and fast, his body surrounding her in a way that claimed an open invitation. Clinging to his shoulders, she pressed down against his pubic bone. She rubbed, desperate to relieve the pressure building deep inside. She held on tight, running her lips along his jaw and down his neck.

Without pause, he pulled from her heat and then thrust back. Again. And again. Gage slid a hand between their bodies and pressed his thumb against her most sensitive part in slow rhythmic circles. He chose her; he'd choose her. She knew the truth of his words as he loved her with his body.

Sam went blind with need, nothing but the bright sparks of pleasure and crashing, convulsing, waves penetrated the pleasure focused center of her mind. Sensation rolled through her. Over her.

She pressed. He pulled. She squeezed. He thrust. Wet skin smacked with purpose. A deliberate sharing of hard pleasure and sweet pain. Once again flowing into a partnership, they moved as a team, effortless, seamless. Giving all of themselves so the other might rise higher, and the effort was returned tenfold. Sam was in awe. The sensation of being one so great, tears burned the back of her lids. Oh, how she loved this man.

His own groan of release joined hers, and he gripped her hips, digging his fingers deep. Their frenzied movements slowed until he sagged into her, and they slid down the wall, limp and sated.

Gage's low rumble barely audible over their gasping breaths. "I love you."

Sam melted into the floor, welcoming his weight, and keeping her arms wrapped around him. "I love you, too."

She always thought she knew what love was, but she hadn't, not really. There was an extraordinary sense of wonder to be chosen by someone, a recognition, an acceptance, of being forever changed from inside the heart out.

• • •

Gage stretched, muscles aching, and a satisfied smile curving his lips. Totally worth it.

Sam lay on her side with her back to him. Carefully, so he didn't wake her, he slid closer to her warmth — her radiating, musky warmth of sleep. His chest met her silky skin, and she rolled back into him with a sigh. Waking to this would never get old. Every time they were together surprised him with its intensity, the depth to which she grabbed him. It was the difference of having sex and making love, and he never wanted to go back.

The first golden glow of morning tiptoed through the window sheers and cast the room in a sheen of copper. The hum of the fan the only break of silence. Ferns fell in a waterfall of green from the corners of the room, lending a feel of paradise even if they weren't already in the lap of luxury. He owed Martin for this one.

Sam peered over her shoulder through her lashes.

"Good morning." His whisper was barely audible.

She sighed again and turned to face him. Snuggling in, she mumbled against his chest, "Good morning. I'm so hungry."

He chuckled, and joy allowed room for nothing else in his heart. "You should be." Sam had surprised him, taking charge, telling him what she wanted. He couldn't help but feel they were headed in the right direction. She needed time, and he wanted to give it to her.

"Yep, so feed me."

"But you're so warm." He wrapped his arms around her

and pulled her in closer.

"You are, too." She released a contented hum. "But I'm starving."

Rolling onto his back and pulling Sam onto his chest, Gage reached out toward the bedside table, grappling around until he closed his hand over the hotel phone.

A short time later a knock sounded from the main door. Gage grabbed a thick robe, then shoved his arms into it and tied it at the waist. Minutes later, he returned to find Sam propped up in bed. He wheeled a cart laden with fresh fruit, sweet cream, an assortment of pastries, scrambled eggs, avocado and tomato slices, and smoked salmon. Coffee and orange juice topped it off.

Sam clapped her hands together and rubbed, practically salivating. "Perfect."

He pushed the cart against the side of the bed with a grin, and Sam scooted closer. She pulled the sheet over her breasts and tucked it under her arms, sitting with her legs crisscrossed in front of the cart. Gage joined her and looked around. "This kind of place is perfect for us. There's no paparazzi, on the inside at least, since they cater mostly to celebrities. We all have our starry-eyed moments, I mean come on, Al Pacino is Al Pacino, but we're less rude."

Sam mumbled her agreement through a pastry.

"This is just one of the things we can do to protect what we have, Sam."

Swallowing, Sam studied him. "This place is great, but we can't do this all the time. We have to be able to live, Gage."

"And we will."

She drank half of her orange juice and then set her glass down. "I've been thinking a lot about what I need for this to work, and I think one of the things that makes me nervous is the time apart." Her phone buzzed. She glanced at it and then set it aside.

"I can understand that. I know my next film will be on location in Australia for two months, but you can go with me."

Her smile froze on her face. "I can't do that."

"Why not?"

"I have my work. This film is my jump back into the arena. I can't just disappear for two months."

He lifted his hands in the air and then dropped them back to his sides. "When I transition more to director, I'll be able to stay close to home more if I choose, but I need some time to make that happen. You asked me once to give you time. I'm asking you to do the same."

She pulled in a deep breath and released it with a smile. "Time."

"Look, it won't be perfect at first. But give us time to figure things out, and then later we can make the rules. Agree to never travel without each other, and if there's an international location, we'll go together. We make a good team on set, Sam. Our relationship will be no exception. We just need to build up to that within our careers."

She tilted her head. "My career, which is why I can't go with you. You career is pretty much there. You get to pick the roles you're in."

He pressed a firm kiss to her mouth. "I can't pass this one up. It is a leading role, and I'm hoping it will allow me to start transitioning while at my peak."

"I'm not asking you to give it up."

He breathed her in, flexing his fingers with the hope he'd

never have to stop. One more kiss on her mouth, and he looked her in the eye. He might not have all the answers right now, but he'd find them. "We can do this."

She nodded, but the look on her face wasn't very convincing. Tension clamped down on his shoulders with each tick tock of the clock.

They ate their fill, drank the coffee, everything casual and light-hearted, until Sam's phone buzzed. She glanced at it and then tossed it back to the bed. With a nonchalance to her voice that immediately set him on edge, she brought up Cecilia Lombardi. "Why do you still care so much?"

Gage studied her, the familiar knot heavy in his gut, competing with his breakfast for room. Pushing away from the almost empty cart, he settled back against his pillows.

Sam cradled a cup of coffee and shifted to face him, her head tilted, quiet, and waiting. Her phone buzzed again. She hesitated and then picked it up. With a sigh, she tossed it back down to her bed.

"What's going on?"

She bit her lip. "I didn't want to bother you with it, but Cecilia keeps texting me."

"What? Let me see that."

She tossed him her phone. He gritted his teeth as he read text after text for Sam to call, for them to meet again, followed by more bullshit. "Son of a bitch."

His mouth dry, he reached for a glass of orange juice and with two long swallows, he emptied the glass and returned it to the tray. "This is why I care. I've made my mistakes." He tilted his head. "I want to make sure I learn from them, make sure I don't repeat them with my own kids."

"You'd never let that happen."

Her vote of confidence made him grin. "You're right, I won't. And I won't make the same mistakes with you, either, but I need you to trust me. You need to tell me things like this." He pointed to her cell. "Team, remember?"

She nodded. "I should have told you right away." She watched him. "Thank you for caring so much."

He gave the cart a slight shove aside and dropped his feet over the edge of the bed to the floor. Turning back to her, he grabbed her hand. "Come on. Enough of Ms. Lombardi. Let's go have some fun." He'd take care of his mother later.

He made quick work of the window shades, flooding the room with light. "What should we do first?"

Sam studied him for a second longer and then pressed her lips together, looking toward the ceiling. "I'm dying to meet a celebrity."

Gage stared at her a beat, then lunged. He grabbed her about the waist, swung her up and around with a growl before lowering her to her feet, her body sliding along his length. Her squeal echoed in the room. He bit her earlobe. "I'll show you a celebrity, you brat."

She laughed and it soothed him.

He wanted more of this Sam. Sitting on the edge of the bed, he grabbed her hand. "We're going to need to trust each other, Sam. One of the things I can do is make sure you know the actors I'm working with, let you know where I'll be, and when shooting runs late."

She stood in front of him. "And me, what do you need from me?"

"Promise to always hear me out. Don't run."

Nodding, she bent over and pressed a kiss to his mouth. "I can do that."

He pushed up from the bed and then pushed her dark hair back over her shoulder. "It's simple really. We just need to choose each other."

His phone rang, breaking the moment. "Get ready, we'll go see what's going on down in the lobby."

Moments later, she breezed into the room. Tan, glistening—youthful. She was healing and it warmed him. A cobalt blue sundress hugged her delicious form in all the right places. His mouth watered. Nude, strappy wedges brought her almost up to his height. He stood and found her at the perfect level to lean in for a taste of her lips. So he did. "Ready?"

She spoke against his mouth. "I was, but now—"

Her lips slid against his own, and the length of him immediately hardened. "We better get out of here before I change my mind."

"Maybe I'll change mine."

He smiled and slapped her ass. "Let's go find my girlfriend a celebrity to meet."

Sam stilled, and Gage shoved his hands in his pockets, watching her. She tilted her head to the side. "Girlfriend." She said the word as if tasting it for the first time. A smile pulled up the corners of her mouth. "Do you know how long it's been since I've been someone's girlfriend?"

His shoulders relaxed, and he put out his hand. She slid hers in his without hesitation, and he swore if even one idiot hit on her, he'd hit him.

They made their way down to the main lobby and mingled with the other guests, stopping for a chat here, an exchange of information there. Having taken their time, it was now past noon, and many guests trickled out to the pools and the bar.

A string of well wishes followed them as they wound their way out to the patio.

"Gage Cutler."

"Man, how's it going?"

"I love you in *When the Tide Turns*." A beautiful blonde wrapped herself around Gage's waist. He slid his hand between them and brought it out with hers firmly in his grasp. "Thank you." Smiling, he released her hand and kept moving.

"Nicely done." Sam slid her arm through his, and he couldn't help the little flicker of hope that it had something to do with marking him as hers, even if it was somewhere deep down.

Some were fellow actors he knew and others new friends. He pulled his shoulders back, at least an inch taller. Interested stares roved over Sam, dying to know the name of his latest paramour. He pulled her close. Let them talk. This one he'd keep.

If he had anything to say about it, he'd continue to show her. One step at a time, one day at a time until they found a lifetime.

Sam leaned close and whispered in his ear. "No matter what you do, Hollywood loves you."

A light sensation ran across his shoulders and down his arms. Relief? Anticipation?

"Maybe." But Hollywood was a fickle mistress, no telling how long her good mood would last, and in the end hers wasn't the love he was fighting to keep.

Chapter Twenty-Two

The rest of their weekend away had delivered exactly what they'd needed. Time spent together without all of Hollywood's bullshit, allowing Sam to open up and relax, and allowing Gage to show her a side that wasn't all about work. Once they got back, she filled her schedule with meetings to set up her next project, and he'd had a meeting with his agent. For so long his schedule kept him going at all hours, day or night, but he found that momentum a little too spontaneous now. He wanted to be able to make plans with Sam, evenings in, evenings out, it didn't matter, but it would never happen with his current schedule. His agent would tighten the reins on Gage's availability.

The producer of the film he'd just finished also produced his buddy's latest flick and his after-party was in full swing. Sam had a few new scripts to go over and another she wanted to work on, so Gage let her off the hook. He imagined her back at his place, lying on the sofa with her feet propped up on the arm, computer in her lap, and a glass of wine in her hand. Maybe the fireplace was on, maybe she played a little jazz on the stereo. Either way, now he wished he was home with her.

He pulled in a deep breath and squared his shoulders. He hated these events, but he'd promised to show. Thirty minutes and then he was out.

He ignored the multitude of camera flashes as he walked in, his gut tight, and made a beeline for the bar. Sliding a finger under his collar, he pulled at the fabric. His throat constricted against the tailored fit of his shirt and tie.

With a tumbler of scotch in hand, he scanned the room. A sea of Hollywood's most beautiful mingled in a cacophony of conversations and laughter.

Fake. Overdone. Every one of them acting.

Tonight's goal was simple: set up a few meetings, take a few pictures, and throw one back with his buddy. Quick and painless. Most after-parties were a lot of fun, but not when he had a better after-party option waiting for him at home. Tension strained his neck, and it was all he could do not to start pushing people out of the way every time he wanted to move. In the end, he kept his promise, made his rounds, and reconnected with a few old acquaintances. He mentally patted himself on the back for a job well done.

The harsh glare of a bleached blond coif caught his eye, immediately followed by a waft of heavy, overly sweet perfume. His stomach rolled. Of course she was here. After-parties of movie premiers were a great venue for networking, and his mother would be selling her wares like a streetwalker.

The music suddenly grated, and the crowds closed in.

Gage shook out his free hand and threw back the rest of his scotch. He set the empty glass down on a tray and picked up another, draining half the glass a bit fast. It wasn't called liquid courage for nothing. He took another deep swallow. The alcohol slid down his throat with a burn, and he coughed on the fumes. No reason to waste the opportunity to persuade Cecilia to direct her efforts in another direction and leave Sam alone. He wouldn't get into anything with her tonight. Not here with eyes and ears hunting for gossip and heartache.

Pasting a neutral but friendly expression on his face, he moved in and out of groups of celebrities. Many stopped him for a quick word or to congratulate him on his finished film. As he approached the small group, his producer glanced up and broke into a smile. "Gage. I bragged on you all night. The film is going to be a classic."

Gage shook the producer's hand. "I agree, but not because of me. It's a great script." He dropped his hand to his side and resisted the urge to wipe it on his slacks.

Cecilia's face pinched into a thinly veiled glare, her narrow lips pressed so tightly together they all but disappeared, leaving her over-lined lipstick like a halo of clown make-up. He nodded in her direction. "Ms. Lombardi."

She turned away and placed a hand on a bony hip pushed out so far he thought she might fall over. His heart drummed in his ears, drowning out all the other conversations. Both hate and hurt burned deep in his chest. "Can I have a quick word in private, Ms. Lombardi?"

The producer spoke up. "I'll go get us another drink."

Gage shook his head. "None for me, thanks." Regret for what he already consumed muddied the alcohol in his gut.

She spun to face him. "A private meeting? How perverse, why you're young enough to be my son." She tilted her head to the side, a smirk played at her mouth. "At least isn't that the tired old rumor?"

Gage tamped down the pain of his younger self as he looked at his mother. Ignoring her he said, "Sam isn't interested in any collaborations, and she'd like you to quit contacting her."

"Sam isn't interested in any collaborations? What a joke. Next you'll tell me I have a daughter, too, and a broken-hearted husband who loved too hard and demanded too little." She laughed at her own humor and shot him a look, as if daring him to stay and finish the conversation.

A waiter walked by with a tray of shots. He grabbed one and threw it back, the burn barely registering. On impulse, he reached for another but stopped, dropping his hand to his side and pulling back his shoulders.

He ran his hand down his chest. "A rumor, Mother?"

The producer stepped forward, shock on his face. "Mother?"

Cecilia let out a screech, her face turning the exact shade of her lipstick.

Heads turned. Conversations quieted.

"Mother?" She stepped toward him, speaking through gritted teeth. "I'm no more your mother now then I was back then. You were nothing but a disobedient brat and your sister a simpering waif. Don't get me started on your spineless father."

He clamped his teeth together.

She quickly looked around to assess the damage her admission may have caused. The woman was Satan's spawn, or worse, his mistress—wanting it all but entitled to nothing. Being powerless to be anything more left her bitter and cruel. Why did she ever have children in the first place?

He forced himself to speak beyond the boulder lodged in his throat. "We were better off without you."

"All worthless. Every one of you," she hissed.

The producer put a restraining hand on her shoulder, and she wrenched away. "Worthless. You did nothing but hold me back. I could have been great. But sticking around. It was too late. You"—her red tipped finger shook in his face—"ruined my life." Great black trails of mascara ran down her cheeks, and her breaths came out in great heaves, almost exposing her man-made bosom.

Gage clenched his teeth together. His head spun. *Fucking bitch.* He tried to breathe but couldn't get any air. He needed to get out of the overwhelming crowd, the music, the noise, the stench of desperation. Stumbling, he pushed past the masses.

The doorman snapped to attention and flung open Gage's only exit just in time.

Martin Gallagher appeared and ushered him to his limo.

Gage folded into the back seat, his head pounding.

Martin slid in behind him and instructed the driver to go. He turned to Gage. "What the hell were you thinking, boy? Were you, for that matter? The woman isn't worth it; when are you going to see that?" Martin drew his brows together. "I saw the look on your face once you'd seen her, but couldn't get to you in time. Why would you confront your mother here?"

That got Gage's attention. He snapped his head around to look at Martin, then quickly pressed his hands against his temples. "Ohhh." When the spinning slowed, he peered over at the director. "You knew?"

Martin settled back against the dark leather. "Anyone with half a brain does. Don't worry, that leaves out ninety percent of Hollywood. The remaining ten have too much class to speak of it."

"I didn't mean to."

Martin sighed. "Didn't mean to what?"

His movements slow and measured, he shifted in his seat. "I only meant to tell her to leave Sam alone. She's been blowing up Sam's phone since they had lunch."

"Why wouldn't you just call her?" Martin demanded.

Gage peeked at the old man. "She'd never answer."

Martin scoffed. "Sam can take care of herself. You executed a fool's mission, boy." He rubbed his hand over his face and studied Gage. "Cecilia walked out on you when you were what, ten?" He didn't wait for confirmation. "The woman was able to walk out on a crying boy, a begging child. Something most people can't comprehend. Now that boy is a man, a very successful man who has usurped her dreams and made them his reality. What on God's green earth made you think she'd ever be compassionate toward you?"

Gage's head hurt, and his stomach ached. His heart heavy and empty in his chest. He didn't know, couldn't find an answer.

And finally realized, there might not be one.

Chapter Twenty-Three

Martin pulled into his garage and Gage moaned. He wanted to be by himself. "Martin, take me home."

"No can do. If Raquel found out I left you to your own devices in this condition, she'd kill me, and I'm more afraid of her than I am of you."

They walked into the kitchen, and Gage passed into the living room and dropped onto the buttercream leather couch.

Martin piped up. "Throw up on that couch and Raquel will kill you."

Sam ran over to Gage and dropped to her knees at his feet. "What happened? Raquel called me. I came right over." She touched his forehead, then slid her hand to his cheek, her cool skin soothing.

He pulled away. He could hear Raquel question Martin, their conversation muffled. Who cared? Muddled with an alcohol-laden brain, Gage leaned back and closed his eyes.

Raquel walked over and wrapped her arms around his shoulders. Helping him up from the couch, she patted his back and then directed him to the kitchen table. "Let's get some coffee into you."

For a moment Gage leaned into her embrace and then lowered to a chair. A steaming cup of black coffee was placed before him. His stomach rebelled at the thought, but if he didn't get it down, they'd never let him leave.

Sam sat to his right and placed her hand over his. "Do you want to talk about it?"

"No."

"I never wanted you to say anything to that woman. I just didn't want to not tell you, like last time."

Gage pulled his hand away and used it to pick up his mug. "I don't want to talk about it."

A pained expression crossed her face, and Sam slid her hand back under the table. Taking a deep, pained breath, he closed his eyes. Her hurt expression was the exact reason he wanted to go home. In this state he was just as destructive as he used to be, racing around Malibu in his Ferrari. He couldn't count how many front yards, mailboxes, or rear bumpers he'd torn up or how many close calls he'd had. He dropped his pounding head to his hands.

"Don't be an ass." Martin joined them at the table.

Raquel raised a brow at her husband and then winked at Sam in a conspiratorial manner. "Martin, leave him be, and Sam, don't take it personally. Men don't handle, well, anything with poise or grace. All they know how to do is beat their chests, and when that doesn't work they hide behind arrogance." She carried a tray of starchy foods to the table, her flowing skirt swirling around her legs. The movement made his head spin.

Gage didn't look at Sam and ignored Raquel. He couldn't care less about what any of them had to say.

He forced a dinner roll down his throat and finished his coffee. The spinning in his head settled. Sam watched him, her eyes concerned. He didn't mean to hurt her, but he needed space to figure out why the hell he was so angry, why he'd let Cecilia of all people push him to drink like that.

With a sigh, he rubbed his face. "I need to go." He pushed back from the table. "Raquel, thank you. Martin." A nod of thanks to each of them. "Can you keep an eye on Sam for me tonight?"

Sam shot up. "I'm not the one who needs to be babysat." She grabbed his arm as he stepped from the table. "Gage, let me take you home."

He shook his head. "I need to be alone. Just— "

Her dark eyes filled, but she nodded, slipping her hand to her side.

Gage turned toward Martin. "I'm fine. Really. Thank you."

"We really wish you'd stay. We have plenty of room, guest beds aplenty." Raquel appealed to him with a smile.

He forced a slight smile. "Thank you, but— "

Martin stood. "Fine. Stubborn ass. But I'm driving you. Don't argue."

The drive to his house was made in complete silence, but Gage slid from the passenger side and sent Martin a wave. Once inside, he grabbed his twenty-five-year Macallan and flipped on his fireplace. What he really wanted to do was hop in his car and race the Pacific Highway until his head cleared. Turning off the fireplace, he grabbed his keys. An hour or two on the road, and then maybe go down to the local bar and hide in the back corner, drinking and watching the crowd.

He tossed back his drink. Anger burned him more than any whiskey could. Twenty-eight years he'd avoided the woman. Kept his mouth shut. In two minutes, he'd handed the harpy all the power, and she'd snatched it, with relish—just as she had his trust when he was a boy.

It was no different than the night of the accident with the paparazzi. He'd spent years taking his anger, his anxiety, out on the road. The speed and adrenaline pumping through him as he raced down the highway calmed him like nothing else. The salty ocean air filling his lungs, and the vibration of the road through the steering wheel filling his palms made him feel alive—human. He'd traveled speeds that pushed any car's engine and his luck. After years of being an irresponsible ass behind the wheel, he'd grown up, slowed down. Miracle of all miracles, he'd started following traffic laws and became a law-abiding citizen. Then one night the paparazzi caused an accident while chasing him, splashing the tabloids with his past transgressions, calling him "murderer" and accusing him of manslaughter, making him un-hirable for a time. There was an official investigation—more invasive than the paparazzi ever dreamed of being.

Gage scowled and tossed his keys back on the coffee table. He poured himself another drink and then sank into his couch.

It would be the last one for the night. He'd told Sam he wanted to learn from his mistakes, and as much as the road and the crowds and the rest of the damn bottle of scotch called to him, they wouldn't fix a damn thing.

• • •

Sam rolled onto her side and blinked her eyes until they accepted the morning light. She sighed and flopped to her back, the guest bed large and lonely without him in it. A world away, he slept in his room. Present but not. Quiet and somber, he'd spent the last forty-eight hours in his head. She'd thought they'd gotten closer during their getaway, but now she felt like she couldn't even reach him.

When he'd pulled away at Raquel's, her heart broke, and it scared her. For all of her digging in her heels, the idea of Gage walking away terrified her in a way that caught her completely off-guard.

Shit.

Muffled voices floated through her bedroom door. She scooted to the edge of her bed and sat with her feet dangling just above the floor. A high-pitched laugh tightened her shoulder blades. Who the hell was there at seven in the morning?

Sam grabbed her robe, slid her arms into it, then belted it at the waist. She pulled the door open and then padded silently to the kitchen. As she rounded the corner she found a bright-eyed Dani stepping back from a sleep-mussed Gage. *What the hell?*

Dani clapped her hands together and smiled. "Good morning."

Sam nodded, then tilted her head at Gage.

"Morning." He stepped past Martin's assistant and poured a cup of coffee. "Want one?" he asked without turning around.

"No, thank you," said Dani.

"Yes," said Sam. The two women responding in unison.

Gage turned around, and raised an eyebrow.

Sam stepped forward. "I'd like one, please."

Dani laughed. "I'm sorry, I didn't know who you were talking to."

Gage filled Sam's cup and handed it to her.

She studied him. "Thank you." His face remained blank. Sam turned back to Dani. "How can we help you this morning?"

Dani shook her head. "Done. Mr. Gallagher needed to get a script to Gage, so I offered to drop it off on my way to the beach for a run. I called ahead and security let me in."

Sam nodded. "That was nice of you. Do you get a few days' breather in between Martin's, I mean Mr. Gallagher's, meetings?"

The assistant's laugh jingled like a wind chime. "As if. He never seems to slow down."

"That's Martin," Gage agreed. He leaned a hip against the counter, and his robe loosened, exposing his broad, molded chest. He wore pajama bottoms low on his hips and a light sprinkling of dark hair shot down from his navel, disappearing beneath the band of his pants.

She flicked a glance toward Dani. The young girl stood mesmerized. Sam wished Gage would belt back up. A surge of jealousy turned her stomach.

Gage pushed from the counter with an outstretched hand and engulfed Dani's in a shake. "Thanks again. Let Mr. Gallagher know I'll call him soon."

The girl dipped her chin and pulled open the front door. "Have a good day, guys."

Sam usually enjoyed Dani's sunny presence. But this morning her muscles tightened, and her hands wrapped around her coffee mug in a tight grip. She followed Gage into the living room. "Well, that was chummy." She regretted the words as soon as they were uttered. *Crap*.

"Was it?" He settled onto the chaise lounge, sipping his coffee as he stared out over the Pacific.

Giving her shoulders a shake, she walked over to him and lowered to the chaise next to his knees. She ran her hand along his thigh and looked up at him through her lashes. "Are you going to talk to me today?"

He briefly met her gaze, then turned his attention back out to the water, but turned his hand over as an invitation. "I didn't realize I hadn't been."

She slid her hand into his, running her fingertips along his calluses as she went. "Are you kidding? You've barely spoken to me in two days, and I've been sleeping in the guest room."

On a long exhale, he nudged her so he could spread his legs and then invited her to sit.

She stared out the window and then back to him. Stepping closer, she lowered to the edge of the seat. He pulled her back toward his chest. She resisted and then relaxed against him as he rested his chin on top of her head. They sipped their coffee in silence as the sun made its way higher into the sky. His voice rumbled against her back. "I'm just in my head right now, processing. Give me a few days."

"Did I do something?" *Did I do something? What the hell? He isn't Ethan.*

"No."

Relief lightened the heavy weight that found its way

into her chest. This was why she didn't want to get close. This need for acceptance, for love. The desire to remain close. It opened doors to pain. Doors she'd never meant to open, at least not until the odds ran in her favor. Dating an actor did not increase her odds.

Gage's phone vibrated, and he glanced at it, then set it back down.

"You need to get that?"

He shook his head. "No, just Dani sending a message from Martin."

Sam settled back against his chest, both comforted and on edge. *Ugh.* She hated this feeling. Insecure, jealous. Gage was a super star, and women fell at his feet every day. She tried to act as if it didn't bother her, but she had yet to pull it off. This was an area she'd need to trust him in, whether she felt like they were connected or not.

Fuck.

This whole love thing left her twisted in knots as often as it sent her soaring.

It had torn her up to see him so broken the other night, and worse, to be pushed away. Now all of a sudden Dani turned out to be his right hand girl, and he continued to linger just out of Sam's reach.

She shook off her worry. No matter. He'd said she could trust him, that she needed to trust him, and she would. They were together, and they'd work things out. Everything was going to be just fine.

• • •

Gage stepped into Martin Gallagher's reception area fifteen

minutes early.

Dani greeted him from behind the front desk. "Good morning, Mr. Cutler." Her smile stretched from ear to ear.

How was anyone that happy all the time? He returned her smile. "I'm here to see Mr. Gallagher."

She directed him to follow her. "Of course, you can wait in his office."

Gage walked a step behind Dani and noticed for the first time a significant swing in her hips. She pushed open the door and held it for him. He stepped past her and could have sworn she leaned toward him ever so slightly as he walked into the office. He glanced at her, confused, but she merely stepped in behind him and closed the door.

Gage looked around the familiar space. Dark woods and darker leathers graced the room with warmth and elegance. Just like Martin. Two tufted chairs sat across from a large desk with a maroon blotter. He made his way to a chair and turned to ask Dani a question.

She stood right at his side, which brought him up short. He stepped back. "Sorry, I just wanted to ask—"

Dani drew her messenger cap off and followed his retreat. "Anything." Long blond curls cascaded down and over her shoulders. Her fingers worked at the buttons of her shirt, opening one, two—

"Whoa, wait a minute. Dani, what are you doing?" What the hell was going on? His eyes darted to the right, then to the left.

She bit her lip and looked up at him through thick black lashes. "Oh, come on, Gage. You know what I'm doing."

The desk behind him stopped him cold. "Why? I'm with Sam. You know that."

Dani pouted, then licked her lips. She trailed a finger from his buckle up and over his chest, then tapped his chin. "Don't play with me, Gage. I know a come-on when I see one, and when you let your robe fall open, that was for me. I know it was." She splayed her hands, fingers down, on his abdomen.

Leaning away, as far as the desk would allow, he grabbed her hands and pushed them back to her side. "Knock it off."

What the fuck was she talking about? His robe? He shook his head. "Dani, I don't know what you're talking about, but I assure you I did nothing to purposely send you any kind of message."

Dani narrowed her eyes into glittering slits and cupped his crotch. "A tease then?"

Shock shot from his balls to his toes. Panic froze him where he stood. His mouth dry, he demanded, "Stop."

He pushed her hand away, but she crowded closer and pressed her breasts to his chest. "Say you want me."

Gage widened his eyes. "Dani." Who the hell was she? For the first time, he saw the age around her eyes, the calculated gleam and hardened line of her mouth.

A cough at the door startled Gage, and he shot a look up to find Martin standing in the threshold. "Martin."

Just then, Sam walked in beside him and froze. Her hand flew to her throat, and she pressed her lips together, an incredulous stare nailing Gage where he stood.

He shoved Dani away.

She laughed. "Oh, come on now, people. This is Gage Cutler." She turned and ran her fingers across his jaw. "He was just showing me the ropes, weren't you, Gage?"

Gage grabbed her fingers and flung them away. He

searched Sam's eyes. She looked at Martin and then the floor. *No, no, no. Goddamn it.* "This is not what it looks like." He skirted the office chair. "Sam."

Sam stepped back. "No? You promised me, Gage." Before he could say a word, she turned and ran from the room.

He stepped to go after her. "Sam!"

Dani moved in front of him. "Let her go. We have some unfinished business." She grabbed his crotch again.

Fury surged through him and joined his utter confusion. Who was this woman? "What the fuck?" He shoved the woman out of his way. "Martin?" A glance at Martin showed nothing but disapproval, his lips turned down and pressed in a tight line.

Gage shot him a look. "I can explain this later. I've got to go talk to Sam."

He didn't wait for an answer and ran out of the office.

He'd promised to always choose her, and now he had to convince her he had.

Chapter Twenty-Four

Sam brought her car to a screeching halt in front of Raquel's house. Sobs wracked her. Pain radiated from her chest, her head ached, her fingers numb. Damn it. She knew this would happen.

She pushed the door open and made her way to the front entrance. Within seconds Raquel answered and ushered her inside. "Martin called. Come on in, honey."

Sam followed her friend to the kitchen and sat at the breakfast bar. Tears streamed down her face, and she couldn't catch her breath. "Why? Why would he do this?"

Raquel filled a glass with water and a tumbler with scotch. She handed both to Sam. She indicated the tumbler. "Drink this, then wash it back with this," she said, pushing the water in front of Sam.

"It's not even noon."

"It'll settle you. Do it, darling."

Sam did as she was told, thankful for once for her bossy

friend, and her breath seized as the liquor burned down her throat. After a fit of coughing, she downed the water. Her insides warmed, and she pulled in a deep breath.

"Now." Raquel took a seat next to her and folded her hands in her lap. "Tell me what happened."

Sam filled her in, as well as she could. She hated crying. *But it's Gage.*

Raquel smiled in the understanding way that mothers did. "What did Gage say?"

Sam rolled her watery eyes and blew her nose with an offered tissue. "What could he say? I left." She shook her head. "I'm not going to let anyone do this to me again, living or dead."

"Darling, I doubt Gage is as guilty as you think."

"What?" Sam tilted her head, desperate to know how Raquel could come to that conclusion. "Since he had that debacle with his mother, he's pulled away from me. Dani's been stopping by, sending him messages. Along with all the crap on the set, he's Gage Cutler."

"And you're Samantha Dekker."

Sam sniffed. "What's that supposed to mean?"

Raquel sighed and studied Sam. "Ethan hurt you—"

"This has nothing to do with—"

"Darling." Raquel sent Sam a look that both questioned the interruption and warned of arguing. "As I was saying. Ethan hurt you, in many ways, while living and after he killed himself."

Sam's stomach turned. Moments of disbelief still caught her off-guard at times.

Raquel continued. "You are primed to distrust, to believe the worst, to run instead of facing your fight."

Her head hurt, and she rubbed the space between her brows.

"Darling, it isn't meant in one way or another, and you know it, just simply is. Gage will always be chased by women, but to my knowledge *he's* only been chasing one."

Sam dropped her chin to her chest. The image of Dani pressed up against Gage, a black and white glossy in her mind. Then, too, Dani all but jumping away from him the morning at the condo. She'd reeked of guilt.

Sam shook her head.

Gage pushing her away, caught twice with Martin's assistant, along with the drinking the other night—was that what she was in store for? The tension between her shoulder blades twisted painfully. A heavy weight settled in her chest.

His world was impossible. It wore on him in the past, and she couldn't help but worry.

Which meant she needed to find out what had really happened. One thing he'd always been was honest; it wasn't fair to act like he hadn't been. He'd said he'd chosen her, that he'd always choose her.

She pulled her shoulders back and squeezed Raquel's hand. "Thank you."

A genuine smile shone from her friends face. "Whatever for?"

"For helping me see clearly."

Raquel leaned in and wrapped Sam in her arms. "We're not just friends, we're family."

She returned the hug with a nod. Gage was part of that family, too. They needed to have a conversation.

Loving Gage meant she owed him that much.

Sam thanked Raquel and headed toward Gage's. She let

herself into his place, thanks to his instructions to security. Even when she'd run from him he took care of her; that said a lot that words never could. The house was quiet. "Gage?"

The silence triggered memories and her heart pounded in her chest, but she pulled in a deep breath and tamped down her panic. *Gage isn't Ethan. Let it go.*

She walked through the house, looking for signs Gage was there as she went. "Hello?" Rounding the corner into his room, a breeze blew the sheers hanging from the ceiling in front of his sliding doors, and she saw the shadow of his form through the gauzy fabric.

Stepping through the doors, she stood and looked at him. He sat with his wetsuit unzipped and hanging at his waist, water dripping from his hair, off his chin, down his chest, and his board leaning against the railing.

She cleared her throat. "You went surfing?"

He looked at her—pain shone from his eyes, and she felt ten times a fool—and then back out to the waves, his lips pressed into a grim twist. Fatigue left his expression bare. "I didn't expect to see you here."

"Then why'd you tell security to let me in?"

He made a sound low in his throat, a mix between a grunt and a laugh and full of derision. "Because for some reason, when it comes to you, Sam...I keep hoping." He leaned back in his chair and stretched his legs out in front of him. "You can't keep running every time something happens."

Denial sprang to her lips. "I don't...I—"

His look silenced her. She did, every time, but what was she supposed to do, stay and be humiliated—again? Find out in front of everyone that she wasn't enough—again?

She moved in front of him, sliding her hand along his

shoulder, keeping it there though he'd flinched. "It looked bad, Gage."

He continued to stare out at the ocean, stubborn and defensive. "Looked bad. We've talked about this." His eyes locked on hers. "You, I want you, have been waiting for *you*. Do you really think I'd toss it all aside for that woman…any woman?"

She'd been a fool, but she was scared. Her future was processed by her past, and her past overflowed with betrayal and infidelity. "I'm sorry…I…" Tears welled in her eyes, and she pulled in a breath to keep them in check.

Gage slid his hands to her waist and dropped his forehead to her belly. "Seeing you run was torture. I can't keep chasing you, Sam. Someday you're going to run too far for me to reach."

Sam ran her fingers through his hair, down to his neck, and then over his shoulders. She nudged him back and slid onto his lap. Staring into his eyes, she lowered her mouth to his, hovering a breath away. "I have to get used to women throwing themselves at you all the time. I knew it happened, but I wasn't prepared to see it."

With a firm rub of both hands up her arms, Gage slid his calloused fingers under her hair and gripped the back of her head, holding her tight while he kissed her, gently exploring her mouth.

There was so much to lose with her love holding onto him so tight.

Gage stood, still kissing her, and she gave a yelp into his mouth, wrapping her legs about his waist. He smiled against her lips and it warmed her heart. He'd forgiven her. Walking to the edge of his porch, he slid her to the ground and grabbed his board.

She rained kisses over his face. "What are you doing?"

"I'm going to show you how much I love you, so there is no room left in that over-thinking brain of yours to ever doubt it again."

Sam tilted her head.

He looked out to the water and tucked his board under his arm. "I'm going to share something with you I've never shared with anyone."

Glancing at his board, she turned back to find a determined glint in his eye. "Really?" Her heart picked up its beat. He wanted to take her surfing? Her lips trembled into a smile.

He gave one tip of his chin and held out his hand. After making quick work of a wetsuit, she took his hand for a second time and followed him down to the beach and into the water. Gage floated his board between them. "Slide on."

Darting glances between him and the waves washing into shore, she hesitated. He held her gaze, steady and sure. Sam slid on the board and then sat up, her legs straddling each side. Gage went to the back of the board and found his way behind her, wrapping his arms about her waist. They floated in silence for a bit, the sun's rays still warm as they reached from the horizon. He settled his chin on her shoulder, and they rode the waves in lazy rolls. His voice rumbled close to her ear, sending shivers down her spine. "So beautiful."

She glanced at the sunset, but when she looked back at him, he was looking at her, and her heart squeezed. "Thank you for bringing me out here."

He looked out over the ocean. "Solitude and freedom are amazing gifts, Sam, but you have to fight for them as much as accept them when they come. The waves are a challenge, but the reward is worth it."

"Are you talking about the ocean or us?"

Gage turned her chin toward him with the slightest pressure at her jaw. "Let's ride, Sam."

He slipped back into the water and steadied the board. "Lie on your stomach and then slide your knees under you."

She rubbed the smooth surface of the board.

He placed a strong hand on her knee. "Do you trust me?"

She looked down at him. Water droplets clung to his lashes, his eyes intense. She nodded. "I trust you."

• • •

A few days later, Sam hummed while she slicked gloss along her lower lip, picturing Gage's naked ass as he'd walked to the shower earlier that morning. They'd woken early and gone out to the water with Gage's board. She sighed, remembering the peace of floating on the ocean waves together in silence.

She didn't feel like going out, but obligations held her to it. Another party promoting the new film, and Martin required her attendance. Of course.

What she really wanted to do was curl up on the couch with Gage—and his ass—and watch an old movie, tucked safe and warm in his house away from the world. She wanted to laugh and talk and have a hot, steamy evening away from the potential of something ruining it.

Especially with the latest tabloids hitting the markets. Headlines like, CUTLER STRIKES AGAIN and CUTLER'S PARTY

Trick. The paparazzi splashed old photos of his hot-rodding and photos from the accident between him, the paparazzi, and Ethan, alongside photos of Cecilia's screaming face from the night of the premiere party. Gage was an easy target. He was an A-list actor who lived large. The guy couldn't seem to stay out of trouble years back, and now the trouble was simply dangled in front of his face like day-old meat. This time, though, she was ready for it. Gage's publicist let them know before the magazines hit the market and did quick damage control. Sam had a feeling he had his work cut out for him.

Smoothing her hands down the front of her dress, she studied her image in the mirror. She looked a bit tired, but the pink flush to her cheeks at the thought of why she was so tired helped, and the side-sweep of her flowing curls lent more of an appearance of mystery than weary, thank God. The ivory pencil-skirt dress glowed against her tanned skin. A few days passed out on her balcony had brought a glow to her skin at least.

Martin sent a town car to pick her up. She relaxed back against the seat but had to force her fingers out of their tight grip. Her stomach performed somersaults as she imagined Gage in his tux. He had a slew of interviews scheduled right before the premier, so he needed to get there early. She worried about how he'd been dealing with all the drama lately, his own with his mom and hers with the Evanses. Apparently dating her came with a lot of baggage, too. She winced. The film was a big deal for him as a debut director, not to mention as the star of the movie, and it needed to be a box office hit. The last thing he'd needed was Ethan's name splashed in the headlines again.

The driver pulled up to the front door of the event. A mini red carpet stretched before her as the car door opened. Sam made her way along the red pathway, heart pounding in her chest, the atmosphere thick with excitement and anticipation. Cameras flashed and strangers called her name. Something was definitely in the air tonight. She thought of Gage, and head held high, grinned into the cameras. He needed some good energy.

One brave individual stepped in front of her and shoved a magazine under her nose, all but shouting in her face. "Do you have a comment? What do you have to say about dating your husband's killer?"

Shock numbed Sam for a heartbeat. *Wait. What?*

Just then, Brigitte Evans marched forward. So much for a restraining order. "You're sleeping with the man who killed my brother? Was it planned all along?" Brigitte slapped at the magazine shoved in Sam's hand. Sam's first assailant stepped back, his camera flashing, capturing the verbal attack on film.

Sam turned the magazine over in her hand. Her stomach sunk. Pictures of her and Gage from the night they met, dates included, splashed across the front page with inset pictures of Ethan's dead body. A wave of nausea rolled over her. "Oh, God." The world around her faded gray with each beat of her heart.

This couldn't be happening, not again. Sam turned, trying to make her way back to the car, but Brigitte stepped in front of her. The woman's eyes glittered. "Tell me now, you bitch. Were you fucking Gage Cutler all along? Did the two of you plan this?"

Security grabbed Ethan's sister by the shoulders, but she

screamed and struggled against their grip.

Sam snapped. "Your brother killed himself." Tears burned behind her eyes, and she blinked rapidly in an attempt to hold them at bay. *I have to get out of here.*

"So you say," Brigitte sneered, her breath rapid and her cheeks pink with adrenaline. "I want those photos, Sam. Get them for me, or I will ruin you."

The paparazzi swarmed, tossing out questions over the noise of the crowd. "Some people are saying this will end Cutler's career. What's your take on such statements?"

"If you were with Cutler when you were married, when did your relationship with your husband end? When did things go bad? Was it because of the accident?"

Sam turned, and another stopped her from moving away. "Miss Dekker, Miss Dekker, If you were sleeping with Cutler for this long, did the two of you plan his death, or was it just a welcomed accident?"

Her stomach rolled. Nothing made sense. Sam blinked rapidly and took a step backward. If she didn't know better herself, the pictures would make her question the truth. *Oh my God, is that really what people think? That she and Gage had been having an affair, poor Ethan?* Sam shook her head "No." It couldn't be.

Brigitte screeched as the officers dragged her back from the ropes. "Give me the photos, you whore."

The paparazzi stepped back, forced behind the ropes. Finally, a path cleared for Sam. She made her way back toward the road as Gage's car pulled up. The crowd burst into an uproar as he exited and stepped onto the red carpet. She gulped for air as she held her hand to her stomach.

He looked at her with concern. "What's going on?"

She looked at Gage and saw a beautiful man who couldn't breathe without it being caught on tape, and then she glanced down at her shaking hands and the ugly, heavy load she carried. Anything they tried to do would be tainted by an ugly past. She closed her eyes against the pain. They'd never make it out alive, and the man she loved needed the chance to try.

Gage looked at the magazine she held, his brows drew together, and he shook his head. "What is this?"

Martin stepped up with Raquel just then. "Sam."

She looked into Gage's eyes, a vivid, intense blue in his confusion and concern. Sadness weighed heavy in her heart and sobs clawed up her throat. She had to let him go, or he'd never have a chance at the career he wanted, the life he dreamed about—the life she didn't want. For his own good, and hers.

Stepping to him, she spoke close to his ear, the cacophony of the crowd around them making it almost impossible to hear. Panic left her fingers numb, and she clenched them together. She needed to get out of there before she broke down in front of everyone. The kindest thing she could do was make it fast and give him his life back. "I love you. This just isn't the life I want. It will only ruin us. Goodbye, Gage." She stepped back, and her eyes filled with tears that escaped down her cheeks.

He put out a hand to stop her. "Sam, wait. I can't...I don't understand."

The crowd grew louder with every word, and her world threatened to turn black. She gazed into his eyes for a fleeting second, and then brushed past him. She hurt, physically hurt.

Gage grabbed her arm, desperation in his voice. "Sam,

you don't need to do this."

Her chest squeezed, and she couldn't breathe. "Yes, I do. You don't see it right now, but you will." Cameras flashed, blinding her, a multitude of heads bent furiously, writing the event down on notepads or punching them into smart phones. Recording it for prosperity.

She shook her head, exhausted. "It's too much, please… Let me go."

The chauffeur shifted back and forth on his feet. He grabbed onto the handle, but hesitated, waiting for Gage to direct him.

Sam settled back in her seat. Her lungs burned, and she pulled in huge gulps of air. Gage stood facing the opened door for a beat. With a flick of his wrist, he gestured to the chauffeur and closed the door with a *thunk*.

Chapter Twenty-Five

Raquel and Mrs. Dekker spoke softly in the kitchen of the Dekkers' apartment. The muffled cadence of their voices washed over Sam in a steady hum. She lay on the couch, curled up in a ball, a tissue fisted in her hand. She swiped at her nose as more tears fell, then threw the overused tissue into a pile on the floor. A box of Kleenex sat beside the white, soggy corpses. Sam grabbed another from the top and blew her nose.

She curled tighter, pulling her knees up against the sharp pains in her stomach.

The local news had covered every agonizing moment of the debacle. They'd titled it the Carpet Massacre: Talk about Running Red. Her mother had unplugged the T.V. "Don't watch this garbage, honey. They're parasites capitalizing on someone else's pain."

Sam agreed. *People* were cruel. She might be one of them. But that fact didn't change a thing. She and Gage would have never worked, and she'd known that. But damned if she hadn't fallen in love with him anyway.

Her mother approached the couch with a hot cup of tea. "Here, honey, sit up. Drink this."

"I don't want anything."

Raquel stepped beside Sam's mother. "Darling, don't argue." She then stepped over to the sliding glass doors and opened the blinds.

Sam shielded her eyes. "Shut those. I just want to sleep."

Raquel shook her head and then went one step further and opened the doors, letting a warm breeze into the living room. "Absolutely not. It's been two days. You've turned your parents' home into a morgue. You've run your father off. Enough is enough."

Sam turned to her mother. "Mom," she pleaded.

Dee smiled. "I'm sorry, Sam, but Raquel's right. I should have done the same thing already. Sit up." Her mother tapped her hip until she did as she was told.

Raquel walked through to the kitchen and rummaged a moment in the pantry. She returned with a garbage bag, filling it with Sam's litter of tears. "There. That's a start."

In seconds, the two women had the room aired out, Diana Krall singing low on the stereo, and each of them settled in chairs, facing Sam with their own tea.

Sam wrapped her hands weakly around her teacup. She tucked her head, breathing the spicy aroma in through her sore nose, then gingerly took a sip. The brew cleansed her mouth and warmed her aching throat. She raised her head and settled back into the corner of the couch.

Raquel and Dee exchanged glances.

Sam narrowed her eyes, which didn't take much. They

were so puffy from crying they were half shut already. "What?" Her voice was raw and strained.

Her mother nodded at Raquel.

Raquel sipped her tea, her silver and blue-jeweled bangle bracelets jingling with the movement. A flowing summer dress in turquoise spread over her legs, the hem brushing her strappy silver sandals.

Sam brushed her hair out of her face and tucked it behind her ears. She glanced down at her wrinkled and worn T-shirt. Nothing could help that.

Raquel cupped her tea. "Darling, we need to talk."

Sam lifted her brows.

"The incident has created a bit of a buzz, you could say." Raquel fingered the turquoise earring dangling from her ear.

Dee continued, "Honey, Gage is holding a press conference with his official comments about the accusations in the magazines."

Sam stared.

"It's been hard on him, and he's had to face it all alone." Her mother sipped her tea and glanced at Raquel.

Why the two women tiptoed around the subject, Sam didn't understand. She'd been a snotty, sobbing mess for the past couple of days. Everyone knew what had happened. The urge to just yell at them to spit it out pushed at her. She wanted to yell, because anything would be better than crying anymore. "I told you, he's better without me. His career won't survive the suspicion of attempted murder. I won't hurt him anymore." Her eyes filled, and she wiped at them for the umpteenth time.

Raquel narrowed her eyes. "That's the easy way out, Samantha. You get to hide in your mommy's house, shielded, protected from the paparazzi. You aren't in the public eye with obligations to answer personal, intimate questions."

Resentment settled in Sam's chest. One of the reasons she couldn't be with Gage was because if she were, there would be no hiding. Being an actor was his choice, so unfortunately he had to pay the piper. It was harsh but true. He was a strong man and would get through it.

Fresh tears filled her eyes, and she blew her sore nose. She wasn't made of the same stuff, and the other night proved that. She couldn't do it. "Gage has a lot riding on this film, changing careers, repairing his reputation. Being with me is damaging his chances to finally step clear of his past by keeping him tied there. With the whole Dani situation, and his mom…" She spoke through her tears. "He doesn't need any more crap holding him down. Besides, he's a different kind of person than I am. He can handle it."

Dee expelled an exasperated sigh. "Really, Sam? He's exactly who you thought he was. Human, first of all, prone to mistakes, failing due to pride, pushing people he loves away when he's hurting. You're just like him."

Sam's jaw dropped. "I am not."

Her mother raised a brow and pressed her lips together.

Sam drained her teacup, then set it aside. "It doesn't matter. I need to find my own way. I need to be independent, learn how to count on myself. I can't do any of that by letting someone else take care of me, and I certainly can't do that knowing my past could hurt his future."

Raquel rolled her eyes. "Oh, piss."

"Raquel!"

Raquel scooted forward to the edge of her seat, draping her arms, one over the other, on top of her knees. "You think you're so independent—or that you need to be. You're proving that how? By throwing Gage under the bus? Pushing him out of your life? You're not independent if you're allowing Ethan Evans' family—of all people—to control the direction of your life. Or allowing anyone else to, for that matter. You're just using Gage to avoid facing your own misguided sense of responsibility when neither of you are to blame."

"Honey, why in the hell are you letting Ethan control you from the grave? Your father and I never understood it before, but now?" Dee asked.

She stretched her hand out to her daughter. "Being with Gage wouldn't be about him taking care of you, but you taking care of each other."

Just then, her father walked into the room. Sam had no idea he'd even returned or been home in the first place. He stepped in front of her and looked down his nose at the crumpled heap she made on the sofa. "You need to get your beautiful head out of your ass."

"Dad." Sam gasped.

"I've had my say." Mr. Dekker walked into the kitchen.

Her mother nodded. "He's right." She tilted her head and offered Sam a kind smile. "We love you, honey, but you're making a mistake. I don't believe Gage should face the masses on his own. Don't think I'm not aware of what had been happening on set, and how hard he worked to keep you safe." She placed her other hand against her chest. "I owe him for helping my baby. No offense, but neither dating a writer, or the ex-wife of Ethan Evans helps his reputation in any way, nor will it ruin his reputation. It will all blow over, but he shouldn't have to weather the storm alone."

Could they be right? Would it all pass? The idea of being hurt or hurting Gage any further made her heart ache, but not risking it, not being with him, wasn't living. She'd made a rule not to date celebrities and then broke it for Ethan, but she could finally see that so much of it had to do with how sick he was and nothing else. The lifestyle still scared her, but now that she faced her future free of it, free of Gage, her terror knew no bounds. She would learn to live one day at a time, handle challenges one day at a time. If she pictured Gage by her side, she could see her shoulders back and her chin lifted, and she liked the view.

An image of Gage facing all the parasites that attended press conferences searching for fresh blood settled in her mind, and the uncomfortably familiar weight of guilt pressed down on her shoulders.

She'd put him in the spotlight by not standing with him. Sam stretched her tight muscles. The conversation with her mother and Raquel repeated ad nauseam in her mind as if they continued to speak right in front of her; nothing shut them up. She stood, and three tissues fell to the floor. Scooping them up, she then shoved them in the trash and pulled in a breath. Time for her pity-party to end.

"Where are you going?" her mother asked in a soft voice.

Sam glanced over her shoulder. "I'm going to run home and shower."

"Wait, I'll go with you."

"Mom, the movie's wrapped up; nothing else has happened. I'm fine. I'll call you as soon as I get home."

The two women stood, and Raquel smiled. "What are you going to do?"

"I don't know, but I have to start somewhere."

A short time later, she stood under the spray of her shower, rinsing the suds from her skin. It felt good to be back in her home, though she missed the sounds of Gage cooking in the kitchen or running lines in the living room. His place or hers, it didn't matter. His presence made it warmer, safer—home.

She'd been terrified and so determined to show her independence. But at what cost? Did she really feel the hassles of Hollywood and their individual baggage—great as they may be—were worth losing the man she loved over? Losing the one person who really loved her? Was the time she'd spent without him since the premiere happier than the time she spent with him?

In shorts and a tee, she stepped barefoot onto her balcony. The usually calming rhythm of the waves failed to soothe her, and the sun shone with less light, the sky a murky blue. Anyone else would sing the praises of a beautiful day—funny how losing the love of your life took the color of the world right along with them.

Gage.

At every turn, he'd tried to help her. Take care of her. Love her. She fought his every attempt, striking out, running away—making it worse.

Yet he remained strong and determined. She straightened. All that strength, and she knew what was best for him? She placed her palm on her forehead. His career, his life. Whether or not she was part of it should have been partially his decision.

She sighed and shook her head, dropping her chin to her chest. She'd been the greatest fool. The waves called to her, and she looked down the length of the beach. Pushing away from the railing, she stepped down the few steps off her porch. The summer sun warmed her face as the soft particles of sand warmed her feet. She wiggled her toes until her pink polish disappeared underneath the grains.

"I thought you'd never come out of your hole."

Sam jumped and spun around, her heart in her throat.

Dani strode toward her, but Sam blinked twice. This woman didn't look like Dani at all. A tight dress hugged her curves, all but pushing her breasts from the neckline. Her blond hair, usually shoved inside her messengers cap, fell past her shoulders in molded waves. Her makeup, perfect and bold.

Dani nodded. "Believe your eyes, Sam. *This* is the real me. The simpering, smiling fool you knew was just an act. However, you have simpering fool down to an art." She stopped an arm's length from Sam.

"Dani?"

Hatred glittered in her black-lined eyes.

A slow smile formed on the woman's face. "Oh, I've been *here* for a while. Waiting. I'm very patient. Each morning I've come. I knew you'd eventually emerge from your pathetic self-imposed hermitage." Dani circled Sam, running her hand along Sam's shoulder.

Sam stepped aside. "What do you want? Gage isn't here." She shook her head and backed up. She looked down the beach in both directions, but no one was around.

Dani scowled. "Gage?" She laughed, a sharp maniacal sound. "It was so easy, what with your insecurities and all. A few well-placed magazines and his boxers. The briefs were a brilliant touch. Easy enough to figure out what he wears when he uses a laundry service. I just picked up a matching pair." She winked. "Didn't want him to notice anything missing. But I never wanted Gage. Why do you think I defended you over lunch with Ms. Lombardi?"

Sam shook her head.

"Oh, you didn't know?" She chuckled softly and then pinned Sam with a look. "I didn't want him to end anything. I wanted *you* to walk away from the best thing in your life. All. By. Yourself. Screwing with the script was just for fun."

Sam dug her nails into the palms of her hands, trying to keep her voice from shaking. "Never wanted Gage? You all but painted yourself all over him in Martin's office." She scanned the ground for a stick or a rock. Anything to arm herself. She forced a swallow past the fear in her throat.

The young woman smirked. "He resisted my affections like a good boy. But you didn't see that, did you? I knew you wouldn't." She shook her head. "So predictable."

Dani ran her hand down her hip. "I'd have enjoyed taking him for a ride, but he merely served as a means to an end." Glancing out across the water, she appeared lost in thought for a moment.

Sam's mind reeled. Gage had resisted, just as he'd said. All she'd seen was a woman wrapped around his willing form. His immediate look of panic and denial should have given her pause. But she'd been too prideful, blinded by the possibility, and what the situation meant. Repeat performance. Relief she'd gone to him swamped her. She'd have thrown away the best thing that had ever happened to her. She froze. "Oh my God."

Prone to mistakes, failing due to pride. Her mother's voice was loud and clear.

Dani turned from the ocean and locked eyes with Sam. "You see, you've always gotten your way. So spoiled and weak," she spat out. "Ethan was an artist, a master, so masterful." She seemed to get lost in a memory as she caressed the side of her neck with fingertips tipped in blood red polish.

Sam's mouth dropped, even as her heart sped in her chest. "Ethan? What does Ethan have to do —" An image of a beautiful blond bent over a trunk, exposed in a very intimate way, and Ethan standing behind her, his hand on her ass while he looked straight into the camera lens, flashed in her mind. "Oh my God."

Nausea turned her stomach, and she spun away.

Dani laughed and clapped her hands together. "Did a flash go off? Perfect. You must have seen his photographs. Like I said, he's an artist, and those hands. So demanding, so strong." The woman shivered.

Sam bent over. "Stop." Her throat filled with bile.

"Oh, poor baby. Does this hurt you? Are you jealous? Good," she spat. "Because I had to go home each night knowing he returned to you. You didn't deserve him, but he wouldn't leave you. Not out of some undying love, of course. I wouldn't want you to misunderstand. He had a reputation built around his perfection."

Sam straightened, her eyes watery from her efforts to control her roiling stomach.

Dani paced, her hands fisted at her sides, knuckles white. "We would have been fine. Our time together filled with pleasure, oh, such pleasure. But you had to ruin that, too. He became so focused on having a child. A child you refused him."

Sam walked backward, trying to put some space between

her and Dani, but the woman just followed. "It would have been perfect, too. You could swell with his baby, while I took care of swelling his…" She leered. "Well, you get the picture. Literally. Oh, I'm brilliant." Stopping in her tracks, her hilarity flipped to rage. She pointed a shaking finger at Sam and gritted her words out through clenched teeth. "You killed him."

A small wave rushed ashore, covering Sam's feet to her ankles. With shaking fingers, she slid her phone from her pocket and around her back, trying to dial 911. She refused to be a victim any longer, though her heart hammered in her chest. The conversation was over. "You weren't the only one."

That pulled the woman up short. A look of shock and disbelief contorted her face.

"There were others. Many, many others. Believe me, the stunts he pulled with you were tame compared to the other photographs." Sam stood her ground, though what she wanted to do was run. "Seems you may have gotten the short end of the stick, so to speak."

Dani shrieked. "You bitch."

A resounding smack across her face made Sam gasp for air, and with her hand to her cheek, she stared at the woman. Dani lunged at her, propelling them both into the water. Sam threw her phone to the sand as they submerged under the surface. She struggled to get up and catch her breath, but Dani pushed her back down by the shoulders, screaming obscenities.

Her lungs burned, and her muscles ached trying to break free. Leveraging her foot up and under her hip, Sam shoved with all of her might, rolling the two of them in the water. As soon as she broke free, she rushed back to the sand, slipping away when Dani tried to grab her ankle. She spun to face her. "Are you fucking crazy?"

Coughing, Sam dragged herself to the sand. Grabbing her phone, she pressed send before collapsing to her side.

Dani pulled herself from the water, sputtering.

Sam dialed 911 and threw her hand up at Dani. "Stop."

Pulling her lip up at one corner, Dani's eyes darted about, calculating her chances. "Once again someone's running to your rescue. They won't always reach you in time, Samantha." Then yanking away, she took off down the beach.

Sam spoke into the phone, giving her location and a quick rundown of the situation as she watched Dani.

This time Sam let herself sink to the sand, her heart pounding in her chest. The rush in her head noisier than any surf. The police would have questions, but all she could think about was Gage. She needed to go see him and apologize for running, for making decisions that affected both of them by herself.

Now the decision about them would be his, and her chest tightened. She looked like a poor investment, high risk with poor returns. Her baggage and distrust, not to mention running away, but if she could explain to him how her perspective had changed. Maybe…

She'd rather face fifty more Danis than have her future lie in the hands of the man she loved.

Chapter Twenty-Six

Gage poured two fingers of scotch into his glass. A numbness already set into his limbs, a heaviness in his chest. He pulled in a breath and brought the drink to his lips, but stopped before taking a sip. "Fuck." Setting the scotch next to the bottle, he turned from the wet bar and dropped onto his couch.

The impending press conference weighed heavily, like a multi-million-dollar production doomed to fail. Sam's goodbye was an unrelenting loop in his head, increasing the pressure behind his eyes.

They were done. Had to be.

She didn't trust him. Oh, she said she did, she would, but her actions said something different. She'd finally run farther than he could reach. It was time to stop. He dropped his chin to his chest.

He'd spent the last couple days avoiding phone calls and skirting the paparazzi. His home became a shelter and a prison. His dad, Bel, and the Gallaghers all called on him, ducking in with food or a consoling word. The surprise came with a call from Mr. and Mrs. Dekker. They'd felt awful, but Gage assured them he was fine. It was a good thing he excelled in acting. The last thing he wanted was another reason for Sam to hate him. Her parents taking his side would only validate her fears about his celebrity status.

He'd attempted to go surfing, but for the first time, he came out of the water feeling washed up. Stubborn, he'd stayed out in the waves, repeatedly beat down by the big surf time and again. Instead of the water lifting him up, carrying him home, it punished and mocked him for thinking he could change the way people saw him. The way Sam saw him. Finally, he'd limped to the shore and fallen, exhausted and bruised to the sand.

He and Sam were finished, but his pain was just starting. Love wasn't the half of it. His life had been built up by her, filled with her, from the first night they'd met. He'd never been able to shake her smile, soft voice, or pensive stare. Patience blew into his life at the perfect moment, allowing him to wait for Ethan to move on. The man's activities were notorious, his split from Sam inevitable.

But Gage hadn't counted on or been prepared for the baggage Ethan had dumped in his wake. Sam carried his suicide around as an excuse to keep from moving forward, as a reminder to stay away from the celebrity lifestyle, and worst of all, from allowing love to enter her life. Gage was certain he'd done it on purpose.

Stretching his arms over his head, all his muscles tight and tired, he stared at the empty fireplace. California summers weren't exactly the best time for the heat of the flickering flames, but he needed something to focus his eyes on, but when they rested on a picture of him and Sam, he closed them.

He filled his mind with the project Martin promised, another opportunity to direct—once the scandal fell behind him. Directing tempted him each time he acted; he wanted his hands in the creative process, and his vision played out on screen. Martin agreed to give him the chance.

A knock at the door pulled him from his plans. With a sigh, he pushed up from the sofa, stepped over to the mantel, and lowered the photo onto its face. He made his way to the front door and then peered through the window. His gut twisted, and he lowered his head to the cool wood, closing his eyes.

Sam.

Not sure what more she could say, he opened the door.

She glanced at him, shifting from one foot to the other. Her lower lip caught between her teeth.

Gage straightened and pulled his shoulders back. He needed her to leave.

He remained silent, waiting for her to speak.

She glanced down at the ground, then back to his face, twisting her fingers together at her waist. "Can we talk? For a minute? I know I don't deserve your time after running away, but I need to apologize."

Gage hesitated. There really wasn't anything for her to say that hadn't already been said. He shook his head slowly. "I'm done chasing you, Sam."

She dipped her chin. "I know. Just a second?"

He stepped onto the patio and pulled the door closed behind him.

Sam glanced at the closed door, then pulled in a shaky breath.

Gage gestured to the dark wicker chairs surrounding a stone fire pit, not much in use with California's ever present fire bans.

She wiped her palms on her shorts and made her way to a chair.

He had to brace himself against the subtle scent of her hair lifted by the breeze, and the wary look in her eyes as she looked at him. He settled across from her instead of beside her, needing the distance. "Why are you here?"

"I'm so sorry." Her voice trembled on her whisper and broke.

So was he, but it didn't change anything. "Sam, nothing can fix this now. We could plan all we want. We can avoid going to industry events. We could refuse to hire a nanny and promise to raise our children together."

Sam watched him, pulling in a breath.

"Hell, I could buy an island so the paparazzi couldn't ever find us." He shook his head. "But it would never work. You'd still run at the slightest hitch in the plan."

She leaned forward. "But I wouldn't."

He steeled against the tears trailing down her cheeks, and whispered, "But you would, and I can't do it anymore."

She lowered her head with a small shake, brown curls cascading over her shoulders, and hid her face.

He waited. Making this easy for her served no one.

Sitting back into the chair, she blinked rapidly and blew out a breath. "I had a visitor today. Dani. I came here straight from the police station."

Gage straightened. "Are you okay? Did she hurt you?"

She studied his face. "I'm okay, just shaken up. She's responsible for the pranks. All of them. She informed me of what happened in the office. She was never really after you, just using you to hurt me. She'd been one of Ethan's toys, thought she was the only one, and went pretty crazy when I told her there had been many more."

Gage reached out a hand, then let it fall back to his lap. "Why were you alone?"

A raw laugh escaped through Sam's lips. "I've been staying with my parents, but since the film wrapped up and nothing's happened, I wouldn't let my mom go with me. I wanted some time to myself." She fiddled with the hem of her shorts.

The afternoon sun warmed the dry air, even under the shade of his triangle awning. The urge to invite her inside pushed at him, but he pushed back. "Sam, I'm glad you figured some things out, got the harasser solved. I'm surprised it wasn't Ethan's family—"

"Me, too. I've figured out why Brigitte and her mother are so desperate to get those photos back."

Gage frowned. "Why?"

"Let's just say, Brigitte is very photogenic when her brother is, ahhh, working the camera."

Gage choked on a cross between a bark of laughter and a dry heave. "Wow."

"Yeah. I think the issues run deep in that family." Sam smiled, a small sad curve of her lips.

They remained silent for a few seconds. Gage shifted in his seat. Seeing her but not touching her hurt him—everywhere. He missed her, but they had real issues. She'd never be able to handle the constant intrusion of Hollywood, and he couldn't live fearing any second she'd leave again.

The reflection of the sun glinting off the glass-tiled vases along the edge of his patio fatigued his eyes. He squinted against the glare. "Sam, why are you here? I'm sorry for all of it, but really."

She stared off into the neighbor's palm trees. "Your career brings a lot of hard things to deal with, but my past does, too. I left because I'm tired of hurting you, tired of my baggage hurting your career." Scooting to the edge of her seat, she looked at him. "I shouldn't have made a decision that was yours, but I was trying to protect you. Do you understand?"

He looked off above her head and then back to her. "Of course I do, but you've always been worth any shit I'd have to deal with, any bumps it might cause me. *I'm* not worth it to you."

She looked at him, her eyes welling. Shaking her head with a tilt, she whispered, "That's not true. I was horrified that they'd do that to you, to us, the night of your premiere, and sick of feeling like it was all my fault."

"And you took it out on me by turning your back? Pretending like you weren't part of something…part of me?"

"Yes," she rasped.

That was it? "You ran. Again," he yelled, but then jerked his chin to the side and pulled in a breath. "You left me standing there alone."

She flinched. "I was so angry and exhausted. I thought you'd be better off without me. I'd convinced myself you deserved better than your past constantly thrown in your face, and if I stayed with you, that's exactly what would happen." She reached for him with an outstretched hand. "But you didn't deserve to be abandoned."

"No, I didn't, and it's taken me a long time to figure that out…to *believe* it." He dipped his chin and then looked out to the lazy street. Beautiful homes dotted with palm trees and tropical flowers stood in paradise—his personal hell. The woman he loved with every breath sat before him, and he had to make her leave. She didn't trust him to take care of her or to protect his own career. And she didn't trust they could handle what Hollywood threw at them. It was too much, and now he no longer trusted her.

He held her gaze. "You can let go of any guilt about hurting my career. It isn't something I worried about because I can handle it. I know what I'm doing. You made my decision for me, and you ran. But that doesn't explain why you're here. What's changed, Sam?"

Folding her hands in her lap, she swallowed. "Not being with you didn't make it better. You're still dealing with crap, and I'm miserable without you. I love you, Gage, and I just didn't understand exactly what that meant before."

His chest burned, and he clenched his jaw, pulling air in through his nose. He wanted to believe her, but he couldn't.

He pushed from the chair.

Sam hastily stood and then stepped around the fire pit.

Gage put his hand out to stop her from stepping closer. He shook his head.

She stilled, her eyes wide and filling with tears. Stepping toward him, she reached out her hand. "I'm sorry."

"Me, too."

"Gage."

He sucked in a breath and closed his ears to the plea in her voice, focusing over her head at nothing, at everything. "I need you to go, Sam."

She wrapped her arms about her waist and nodded. "Okay." Her word barely a whisper. She hesitated, then stepped toward him once more.

He stiffened. *Please, God, don't let her touch me. If she touches me, I'll cave.* "No."

She stopped.

Gage couldn't take anymore. Her sobs squeezed his chest in a painful grip. He turned, opened his door, and then stepped through. Turning back, he sent her a nod. "I hope you find what you're looking for."

She tilted her head. "Gage."

The pain and pleading in her eyes tugged at him. He closed the door slow, but with a solid *thunk*. Once again, he leaned his forehead against the wood and then turned and sank to the floor.

He hung his head, shoulders heavy. "Fuck."

Gage sipped his chili pepper hot chocolate, watching the families and couples walking through the courtyard outside of the Chocolate Box.

Sliding into her seat across from him, Bel eyed his drink and pointed at his choice. "It's nearly one hundred degrees outside."

"Yeah, but it's cold and empty in here."

She frowned. "Oh, Gage. I'm sorry."

He felt like a candy ass. *Shit.* He was a man, damn it. Bellyaching and pity-parties never sat well with him. He raked a hand through his hair.

"So what happened?" Bel watched him as she tossed a

small piece of dark chocolate into her mouth.

"I envy you."

"If you mention the fact I can eat anything and never gain weight, I'll kick you under the table."

"No, no." He chuckled. Bel's waif-like figure challenged her every day. She ate and ate, but never gained an ounce. Most would thank God for that phenomenon. Hollywood would pay millions to bottle the ability. But not Bel. She prayed for fuller hips and thicker thighs. The grass was always greener. "No, I envy you for being single."

She did kick him. Hard.

"Ouch. Come on." He reached down and rubbed his shin, throwing her an angry glance.

"You're an ass." She shook her head, brows drawn together.

"I'm not kidding."

She wound up to kick him again.

"Stop." He moved his legs out of range. "Look, right now, you're traveling, working, and enjoying each day with no obligations, no need to prove yourself, no need to fit within someone else's agenda. I'm just saying I envy your carefree days. Pain-free days."

Bel studied him. "That's bullshit. I'm lonely. My nights? I fill them with movies and books and music. Anything to keep the awareness that my house is quiet and not another soul is breathing the air I breathe." She bit into another piece of chocolate. "I'd risk the pain. At least then I'd be feeling something."

"It's not worth it." Gage raised his glass in a toast.

"Really? Knowing that someone wants only you, to create a life with *you*. That they count the hours, the minutes, until they see you again. Dream your dreams, love your loves. Yeah. Sounds horrible."

"The worst pain you can imagine is when something you love goes away and nothing you can do will ever bring it back."

Bel studied him, silent.

He broke her gaze and looked back out to the interior courtyard. A man snapped photos of him and his sister from behind a potted ficus. He rolled his eyes. Didn't they see the no paparazzi sign? They weren't fooling anybody. The urge to flip them off was strong. So he did.

"Gage."

He turned his gaze back to his sister. "What?" Pressing his lips together, he looked away, then back. "They're all parasites."

"I agree, but you don't need any help looking like an ass."

He smirked. "Nice."

His sister reached across the tabletop and rubbed the top of his hand. "You have to forgive her. Understand, she is who she is. The pain you go through? She's not worth it."

Gage drew his brows together. Sam may have verbally severed an artery, but listening to anyone, even Bel, speak of her in such a way pissed him off. "Look, you're my sister. Be mad. But don't talk about Sam like that."

Bel's brows rose, her eyes wide. She smiled. "I wasn't talking about Sam. But it's nice to know you haven't given up. Not completely."

Gage narrowed his eyes, confused. "I'm losing my patience."

"Mom, you idiot. You need to forgive Mom." Bel squeezed his hand. "She's broken. I heard about the other night. You never should have approached her. She's lied to herself so much and for so long, she believes, to the bone, that we held her back."

He shifted in his seat. His mother's words were an incessant poison.

"Pity her, feel sorry for her, and then forgive her." Bel tilted her head to the side. "Don't you see? She isn't happy. She threw away the best things that ever happened to her."

Gage turned his hand over and held his sister's. "When did you get so smart?"

"Let her go and hold on to me, to Dad, to Sam."

He put up a hand asking her to stop. She smiled but said no more.

They sat in mutual silence, finishing off their treats. Bel glanced at her watch and pushed back her chair. Gage smiled. "I love you, Bel."

She punched him in the shoulder, then pressed a kiss to his cheek. "I love you, too." When she reached the door, she turned back. "Gage, forgive Mom and then let her go. Forgive Sam and then hold on tight." She waved, stepped through the door, and disappeared down the sidewalk.

Doubts swirled in his head. He'd pushed Sam away because he was so terrified she'd leave. In the end, she was still gone. Did the pain really hurt any less because it had been his decision? It would take a lot of work, but he'd rather risk it. If she left, she left, but there was also the chance that she'd stay.

He flexed his fingers. Besides, hard work had never bothered him before, so why the hell should he let it now?

Chapter Twenty-Seven

Gage walked through the outdoor arena where the press conference would take place. Chairs, tables, and microphones in position with the typical back drop. Thank God he arrived before the press and spectators. The whole thing reminded him of the staged local hangings back in the day.

The sun still hung low in the east sky but already radiated its midday heat. He pulled in a deep breath, but the dry stifling air irritated his lungs and made him cough. He tipped his water bottle back for a long swallow to ease his parched throat. Tomorrow couldn't come too soon.

Weary, his eyes heavy, he ran a hand over his face and gave his cheeks a couple of slaps. Another cup of coffee called to him, but he'd already downed three, leaving him with a jittery, all-consuming exhaustion.

Sam's visit the other day haunted him day and night. He dreamed of her. Woke frustrated and alone. He'd wanted nothing more than to drag her inside and lose himself in her softness. But he had to stop fooling himself.

He walked up the steps to the stage and looked out over the groomed lawns. The tops of palms trees waved off in the distance. The Pacific rushed ashore, calling to him, from the other side of the man-made wall of homes and buildings. Maybe some time out on the water would center his energies. Just him, his board, and liquid nature.

A few yards off to his left, a car pulled into the designated parking area. His agent, Adam Nicks, emerged from his car accompanied by Martin. The two men met Gage behind the backdrop of the stage.

Martin sent him a salute. "Hanging in there, boy?"

"About as well as anyone can be when publicly accused of the attempted murder of their girlfriend's ex-husband, and then being abandoned on the spot." His lips twisted in wry humor.

"Not as bad as all that. The police aren't trying to re-open the case." Adam clapped him on the shoulder. "Thank God, or I'd have to murder *you*."

Gage shot him a narrow-eyed look, then lifted a brow back at Martin. "No, but people do think I'd been shagging his wife under his nose. Which, regardless of the man's reputation, creates sympathetic support for the asshole."

From behind the privacy screen, Gage heard the rumbling of cars and the chatter of conversations as people arrived and took their places. "I can't wait to put this behind me."

Martin nodded, sympathy in his eyes. "You'll be fine. Just a formality."

Adam spoke up. "Look at this as an opportunity to say hello to your public, your fans. Take this on as a PR opportunity and from a place of communication, not guilt. Be forthright and positive. Wish everyone a good morning, and thank them for sharing the beautiful sunrise and all that."

Gage nodded. "Got it." He appreciated the support. His friends, family, and fans. He never took any of it for granted. Well, maybe he used to back when he thought he hung the moon and the stars. Maturity helped him drop back to earth and opened his eyes. He understood why celebrities fell victim to over inflated egos. The phenomenon had been hard to avoid when every person in his life jumped to do his bidding, bent over backward to please him, and fulfilled his every whim. The more movies he'd made, the more money he'd pulled in, the more ridiculous his demands. Everyone had answered.

It wasn't until the right combination came along before he pulled his head out of his ass. Age and a video of him ranting about some stupid thing—he didn't want to remember what exactly. Watching the evidence filled him with shame because he hadn't recognized himself. The idea of his dad or Bel seeing it made his stomach turn. His behavior had been way too much like Ms. Lombardi when the person he'd wanted to emulate was Dean Cutler.

But that kind of behavior was a distant memory. He'd started to take the steps to repair his reputation shortly before he'd met Sam.

Sam. Gage exhaled. *Fuck.*

The two men stepped out from the screen to check in with the tech people. Security milled about, assuring order. Gage peered through the space between screens and finished his water while watching the masses collect. Spectators and reporters filled the space.

He caught a glimpse of his mother. *Why is she here?* A

sharp pain stabbed him between his brows. She smoothed her hair and adjusted her over-exposed bosom, then peered into a hand-held mirror and applied more lipstick. Tossing her makeup into a clutch, she looked around at all the people and then smoothed her hair again. Again with her top and then pulled out her lipstick. Her restless movements cried desperation and insecurity.

Gage narrowed his eyes and studied his mother further. He saw her. Really saw her. For the first time in his thirty-eight years. She looked old and tired. So self-conscious that every move was an attempt to make sure she looked her best. There was no mistaking the fact that no matter how many adjustments she made, she never settled into her skin. Misery and hate shone in her face. For herself? For everyone else? Probably both.

The sick rolling in his gut that usually showed up when he saw his mom never arrived. Gage straightened on a revelation. In a way, he had his mother to thank for the life he enjoyed, the closeness he shared with Bel and his dad. His pursuit of his dream, regardless of his initial motivation. All he'd learned *not* to do.

A lightness released the tight grip in his shoulders.

He was okay.

He'd survived just fine. Gage shook his head. Why had it taken him so long to see it?

He'd never had a mother to lose.

Martin stuck his head around the corner of the screen. "Five minutes." His friend studied him. "You okay?"

"Yeah, I am." Gage smiled.

"I hate to bring her up, but is Sam coming?"

"Doubt it."

Martin sent him a nod. "I'll be two rows back if you need a focal point."

Gage acknowledged the comment with a dip of his chin. "I'll be right out."

Martin took off toward the front of the stage.

Gage took a few deep breaths. Surfing. Definitely. As soon as the press conference concluded.

The announcer opened the proceedings. Gage stepped around the screen and took the steps at a leisurely pace to his seat. The crowd quieted to a few whispers and rustling of papers and clinks of equipment.

A cup of water waited for him next to his microphone, and he took a sip. He scanned the crowd of onlookers. Some faces he recognized, others were new. People stared back, expectant, predatory, worried. The mix of emotions was somewhat amusing. This was Hollywood, not the U.N., and a career in acting was not brain surgery. The almighty dollar held the only motivation here. Who had the most to gain, the most to lose. Who did his actions—the accusations—impact, and could he successfully manage damage control? The parasitic nature of the masses was painfully on display.

Gage cleared his throat and pulled the corners of his mouth into a wide smile. A few in the crowd returned one in kind. "Good morning. I want to thank you all for joining me for such a spectacular sunrise." He raised his hand to indicate the colorful sky off to the east. Seagulls called just at that moment, and a few in the crowd giggled.

"As you know, I'm here today to clarify a statement all of us already know to be not only false, but insulting. Samantha Dekker and I never dated while she and Ethan Evans were married. Ethan's accident was just that. An accident. Unfortunate, yes. Premeditated, no." He glanced at his agent who nodded discretely.

A hand shot up in the crowd. "How do you explain the pictures then?"

Gage nodded. "We met years ago while both on business."

"We know all about the business trips of the Hollywood elite, Mr. Cutler." The snarky comment came from somewhere in the left side of the crowd.

Gage scanned the faces, amused that the speaker refused to identify themselves. Cowards. Every one. "From experience, no doubt."

A murmur rose amongst the onlookers.

Adam shook his head, so subtle Gage almost missed it. He pressed his lips into a tight line. That's right. Cater to the people. They could mock, but not be mocked. Fuck that. "As I was saying, Samantha and I had met. We shared conversation and a drink, nothing more. Period." He paused. "Samantha Dekker is a talented writer. Without her, Hollywood would be less. She doesn't deserve your censure or judgments."

Another hand rose. "You've had a reputation for fast cars and faster women. Why should we believe you now? Why should we care?"

The frequency of his misdeeds being pushed in his face was a constant reminder of the life he'd chosen. Made him question if it was all worth it. He clenched his hands under the table, his leg bouncing. He kept his face neutral, refusing to show even a glimpse of emotion or reaction. These people were like circling sharks. One hint of blood and it would be a feeding frenzy.

"That's a good question. Yet you're all here, so it is obvious you do care. Lessons of our youth. We all grow, mature, see the world in new ways. My past isn't perfect, I'm well aware. But my past isn't relevant to today."

The hammering continued in the same vein. Accusations, indiscretions, no longer about Samantha Dekker or Ethan Evans, but rather the early Hollywood youth of Gage Cutler. Let them. As long as they weren't focused on Sam. The last thing he'd ever wanted was for her to get harassed because she'd chosen him. He wouldn't have to worry going forward, because she hadn't chosen him. The Hollywood scene too large of a concern for her from the get-go. He understood why, but had hoped she'd ignore the hungry, desperate media as he had. However, he'd had a lot of experience. Experience she'd never needed—until him.

He volleyed more questions. Some he refused to answer on principle, others so ridiculous he only laughed.

"How did it feel to be publicly accused of murder by Ethan Evans' sister and then left on the spot by the one woman who could clear you?"

A hush fell over the crowd. Martin and his agent stood.

Gage blinked and gripped his hands under the table.

• • •

Enough was enough. Sam's heart twisted in reaction to the heartless questions and barrage of judgment thrown Gage's way. *Aren't you as guilty?* Regret rushed over her.

She stood in the back of the crowd. A crowd so intent on hanging Gage—at least until his next movie—they never noticed her. But why would they? Her face was only recognizable from a few tabloid magazines. The focus was on Gage. The actor. No one really cared about the writer in the first place, unless she provided them access to Gage. Well, she had. *Good job, Sam.*

It hit her then. She'd never been in any real danger from Hollywood. There might be a story or two—some that might even start with her—but the focus would always be on Gage. He would be the one to face the pointing fingers and accusing stares. The judgments and the ridicule. He was the main dish. Sam was nothing more than an accompanying side. She just wished she'd realized it sooner, but now she knew what to do about it.

She studied Gage. She didn't know if he could ever forgive her, but she had to try. She wanted Gage, she wanted a life and family with him, Hollywood be damned, and now was the ultimate chance to show just that.

She dreamed of a certain kind of life. No one but herself could make that happen. It started here. With Gage.

Pulling in a breath, she straightened and lifted her chin. Making as much noise as possible, she shoved her way through the crowd toward the stage. She didn't want to tip-toe in.

Let them all look. In fact, *make* them all look.

Gage's eyes swept the crowd. He couldn't see her yet. Determination propelled her forward. He would.

Finally, Sam broke through the throng of people. She veered right and then up the stairs to the stage.

Surprise shone on his face, and he pushed his chair back and stood up.

Sam's heart pounded in her chest. Love for this man gave her strength. He looked beautiful. A word he'd most likely abhor, but it was true.

His eyes, an endless blue, studied her with a questioning

look.

She threw him a tentative smile as she approached. Two security personnel rushed forward.

Gage stopped them with an upraised hand.

When she reached where he stood beside the table and the microphone, she stopped. The crowd settled, waiting—expectant.

He leaned over and covered the microphone with his palm. "What are you doing here?" His whispered words for her ears only.

"We're in this together." She pulled back her shoulders.

"Sam?" He gave a slight shake of his head.

She strengthened her smile and turned toward the crowd. Leaning forward, she removed his hand and then lifted the microphone. Blank faces stared back at her. People shifted from one foot to the other in the silence. The ocean breeze rustled the palm leaves overhead, loud now that each person held their breath, waiting to see what would happen next.

"Good morning." Her voice trembled. She cleared her throat and tilted her face to the sun for a beat. The rays warmed her, and Gage stood by her side. Stronger, she continued, "My name is Samantha Dekker. I came to relieve Mr. Cutler from this unnecessary, unreasonable barrage of questions."

Whispers rose as the onlookers glanced around, pointing fingers with a look, as if not a single one had a part in the morning's progress.

"Mr. Cutler and I met years ago, that is true. But he never once acted in any way but honorably. Mr. Cutler was not responsible for Ethan Evans' accident or his death." She straightened and looked at Gage, stepping over just enough for him to reach the microphone, and he stepped next to her, shoulder to shoulder.

His face remained blank, almost shell-shocked. His blue eyes met hers, but told her nothing. Would he ever forgive her? Was it even fair to ask?

She broke his gaze and turned back to the crowd. "Ethan Evans was responsible for his own decisions, just as I'm responsible for mine." She turned her head and caught his gaze once again. "I love Gage Cutler. I would be proud to stand beside him, because we are better together. And I am deeply sorry for leaving him to face all of the ugly accusations alone."

A wave of conversation rose from the crowd, and more hands shot up. She remained by Gage's side as he addressed each question one by one. The topic soon turned to his upcoming projects, and she felt the tension ease from his body beside her.

He answered the last question and thanked the crowd for coming.

Sam smiled at him and then pulled his head down to hers. In front of all of Malibu, she kissed him.

Desperate to flee before the dam broke, and she embarrassed herself even more, Sam tore herself from the kiss and pressed her forehead to his. "I'm so sorry. I love you, more than I thought I had in me." She released him and skirted the chairs on the stage, down the stairs, and then off to her car, thankful for security holding everyone at bay.

"Sam."

Gage's call reached her ears, but she didn't pause.

Approaching her car, she hit her remote which unlocked the car and started the engine.

Martin appeared and opened her door. "Go. I'll take care of him. I knew you two would work things out."

She wished she shared his confidence. "I don't know, Martin."

He laughed. "Oh, I do. I do."

After ducking into her car, she backed out of the lot and sped toward Pacific Highway, reporters and cameras filling the space her car had just occupied, Martin waving them all away, his figure receding in her rear-view mirror.

She focused on the road ahead, pulled in a deep breath, and held it. Her lungs burned, but the pain came as a relief. She felt truly alive for the first time, in a long time. Courage was a new piece of her reality. Dreams long held were now within reach. All simply because she took steps in the right direction. No longer would she wait for life to happen in order for her to live, but rather, she'd take each step with purpose and passion.

No one had held her back but herself. A lightness replaced the tightness in her chest. She drove toward the ocean. Whether Gage ever spoke to her again, she couldn't be certain. But she'd finally taken true steps toward the life she wanted.

• • •

Gage couldn't get out of there fast enough. The atmosphere switched in a blink from lynch mob to well-wishers. Not a soul apologized. Of course not. This *was* Hollywood, after all. Every single one of them were actors. Switching characters to fit each scene, to most successfully complete each sequence. He shook his head. The tension in his shoulders dissolved, and the pressure in his chest increased with his pulse. At this rate, a heart attack was imminent.

Adam Nicks, his agent, pulled up with Gage's car. Martin held the reporters at bay while Gage made his escape. Again, appreciation for those close in his life overwhelmed him.

The door slammed closed, and the sudden quiet was utter bliss. Air actually flowed into his lungs instead of choking him. He blew out the breath. Pulling onto the highway, he wracked his brain. Where would she go?

He'd been stunned by her public declaration. Putting their relationship on display opened them up to an immediate barrage of paparazzi intrusions, one of the things she'd always feared. He shook his head. She'd said it in front of the world today, put herself in the spotlight. For him.

He broke into a huge grin that made his face ache, in the very best possible way.

When she'd escaped, he got caught up answering a few questions. His agent kept the time to a minimum, but obligations to the public had to be met. Adam had refused to let him off the hook.

The sun, now high in the sky, beat through his sunroof. A tentative happiness settled in a comfortable position in his chest. He rolled down his window, enjoying the wind whipping through the car.

Shock. That was the sensation that had slapped him as he found Sam in the crowd. His reputation with the public be damned. Sam had chosen him.

Gage followed his gut and turned in the direction of the beach. Sam sought out security and solitude in times of need. This might be one of those times.

Finally, Gage approached the path leading to the

ocean side of Sam's condo. The rhythmic hum of the waves beckoning him.

Sam came into view, lying on her side facing the water. Her hair cascaded in various shades of chocolate and gold over the sand. His fingers itched to dive in.

Heart pounding, Gage slipped off his shoes, then his socks, finally sinking his toes deep in the warm grains. He removed his jacket and dropped it to the ground and then unbuttoned the top few buttons of his shirt.

She still didn't budge.

He lowered onto the sand next to her, separated by nothing but pain and confusion—and love.

Her eyes were closed, a tear running down her cheek. His chest squeezed. No more. For either of them.

"I'm hoping those are tears of joy."

Sam started. She blinked and wiped her face with a small shudder. Turning her head to face him, she smiled—a small, tentative curving of her lips. "What are you doing here?"

"You're here."

She studied him. Dark, luminous eyes. Was that even possible? Luminous and dark at the same time? Gage moved to sit closer. He had to touch her, but not yet. Too many questions, too much at stake for a casual caress. He rested his elbows on his knees and clasped his hands between his thighs. "Did you mean what you said?"

"Every word."

Gage gazed out to the Pacific. The waters calm, smooth. He wished he mirrored the ocean on the inside, but too many emotions left him wired, anxious. "Sam."

She slid her long legs in front of her to sit up facing him. The hem of her cream linen slacks gathered at her ankles.

Gage reached out and followed the gentle curve of her neck over the smooth cap of her shoulder with his finger. The white silk of her camisole was bright against her tanned skin.

She shivered. "I am so sorry."

The words meant more knowing she loved him. It remained a mystery, even to him, but the apology washed away years of pain. Memories and yearnings for his mother, visions of Sam's retreating back, accusing glare—all flowed out to sea with five syllables.

However, relationships took two. "Me, too."

Her eyes widened. "Why?"

Gage moved directly in front of her and then took one of her hands in his. He looked over her swollen, red rimmed, eyes, and plump lips. They begged to be kissed. So he did. With a gentle touch he kissed one eye, then the other, finally pressing his mouth to hers.

She sighed against him.

"Sam, I'm sorry for measuring you with the same stick I used for my mother. You're nothing alike. But losing you would hurt even worse, so I pushed you away and condemned you for running."

She turned his hand over in hers and ran her fingertips over his calluses. "I'm sorry for not trusting you."

"I'm sorry for not trusting you. It's something we need to work on."

Gage pulled her to him. She straddled his lap and wrapped her hands around his neck. He kissed her, a soft caress. "We're stronger together."

She smiled and her eyes filled with tears. "Together?"

He kept his mouth against her as he spoke. "Don't you think?"

Nodding, she placed kisses all over his face. He held on tight. No turning back. If she ever tried to leave, he'd go with her. Wrapping his hands around her rump, he pulled her closer onto his lap. Sam belonged to him now. "You're mine. Don't ever walk away from me like you did when we first met, like you did on the red carpet, like you did today. Stay. Fight with me. Challenge me. I promise to do the same."

Sam laughed, tears streaming now. But full of joy this time. "I promise."

He'd have to trust her and ask her to do the same. "If we really mean it, then let's prove it. I know you are what I want. I've waited for you, Sam. Dreamed of you. Marry me. Make all the pain worth it." His heart thundered in his ears. His whole life held in her hands.

In her hands.

"You can trust me to protect you, to take care of you without changing you. Together we will be strong enough to handle anything Hollywood has to throw at us, and then some. We can limit how visible we are, increase security, and I'll shift from acting to directing."

She shook her head, eyes wide. He placed a finger over her lips. "It's what I've been wanting to do. I want a family, Sam, and I feel like directing can give me that. Give us that."

Pulling back, she cupped his cheek. "Are you sure?"

"More than anything in my life."

She nodded, her eyes bright, a blush rose to her cheeks. "Yes, Gage Cutler. Yes, I'll marry you."

His lungs locked down. "You will?"

She threw her arms around his neck, holding on tight.

He prayed she never let go.

Chapter Twenty-Eight

The wedding decorations shone like chocolate diamonds coupled with the most brilliant aquamarine, and the crystal shine of citrine. Silky brown, bright blue, and lush green sheers draped the stucco walls. Cascading ivy and potted palms created intimate bubbles of escape. White orchids bloomed on every surface and called to the luminescent china that graced each round table scattered throughout the backyard paradise.

Sam tempered the giddy burst of affection that threatened to spill out onto each and every guest. She tightened her hold on her husband's hand.

They'd promised to always walk toward one another, never away. To nurture the strength of individuality and cherish the unbreakable link of their unity. To trust and never condemn.

Gage glanced down into her face with his brilliant blue-green eyes, reminding her of what was coming later that night. She giggled.

"You're happy," he whispered next to her ear, sending a shiver down her spine.

"Even better, I finally feel alive."

He pulled her in front of him, her back to his chest, and wrapped his hands around her hips. The heat of his body a silent promise for later. They admired their colorful mosaic of guests, family and friends, dancing, mingling. Enjoying the celebration and each other. Laughter floated above the music, silverware pinged, and corks popped. Sam had never heard a more beautiful melody.

She nudged Gage in the ribs with a giggle. "Oh, he's in trouble."

Across the way, her sister, Addi, hands on her hips, shook her head at Martin and Raquel's nephew, Roque.

She tried to go around the hottie—Sam would have to feel her forehead later. She must be sick to walk away from that—but he stepped in front of her once more, blocking her path. Addi shoved her finger into Roque's chest, vehemence in her expression, making him back up with each pronounced jab. Before he opened his mouth to respond, she spun on her heel and walked away.

Gage laughed and whispered in Sam's ear. "He's a crazy man. I never want to get on Addi's bad side. She scares me."

Sam nodded. "Smart man."

They watched Roque stare at her as she stalked off, a half smirk on his face. His cousin, Liam, elbowed him in the side, and Martin Jr. shook his head with a devilish grin.

They glanced from Roque to Addi, who darted angry glances in his direction from her spot next to Bel.

"Ooooh…*that* is interesting," Sam said, pulling Gage's

arms around her tighter. He kissed the side of her neck.

"We're not the only ones who saw it." Gage jerked his chin in the direction of Raquel and Martin. The two stood with their heads close, whispering, and a look of determination playing across Raquel's beautiful face.

Gage pulled in a breath. "Should I warn Roque?"

Sam shook her head. "Hell, no…no one warned us."

He laughed. "Thank God." Turning her toward him, he brushed his lips across hers once, twice, then repeated the action against her forehead. She was loved and the knowledge warmed her.

The event was more than she'd ever dreamed. Their families had connected instantly, to the delight of both Gage and Sam. Bel and Addison conspired in a corner, Luca and Cutler Senior laughed at something Mr. Dekker had said, and Sam's mother walked arm in arm with Raquel through the crowd.

The two women approached, and Martin stepped up alongside his wife.

Raquel kissed Sam and Gage each on the cheek. "Do you love it?"

They nodded. "This is amazing, thank you." Gage's deep voice held a catch, and they all studied his face. He threw his hands up. "What?"

"Leave the sentimentality to the ladies, boy," Martin said, turning to blow his nose.

They all laughed, and Martin pulled Raquel closer to his side.

Martin nodded at Sam with a smirk. "You had me worried, girl. But Raquel assured me we'd succeed."

Sam shook her head with a confused chuckle, but deep

down she knew, and she was thankful. "What are you talking about?"

"Whatever happened to the bro-code? You should be warning your fellow man, not conspiring against them." Gage nailed Martin with a look.

Raquel, who seemed deep in conversation with Dee, placed a hand on her husband's arm and looked at Gage. "Bro-code? Don't be silly. I'm his wife." The tone in her voice warned against denying it.

Martin tossed a wary glance her way and then shrugged back at Gage. "What can I say?"

Gage put his hands up as if in surrender and chuckled. "Not a damn thing. Smart man."

In a flourish, Raquel selected two champagne flutes from a passing waiter and presented one to Sam's mother as she sipped from the other. "It's simple, darling." She spoke with her hands, her dress of layered sheers catching on the slight breeze with a dramatic flair. "I know what's best for my babies. Or more to the point, *who,* is best for my babies."

Sam narrowed her eyes, hoping for clarity. "What—"

Raquel slid her free hand back through the crook of Dee's arm and then repeated the action with the other, careful not to spill her bubbly while ensnaring her husband. "Come, it's time to cut the cake." She led her companions to the triple-tiered confection, leaving Sam and Gage in their wake.

Sam looked at Gage, and he raised a brow. Her lips pulled up at the corners. "I have no idea how she thinks she knows."

Gage returned the grin. "Maybe it's better that way. Martin and Raquel terrify me sometimes. Somehow I feel like the less we know, the better off we are."

A rush of emotion threatened to spill over as Sam's eyes filled. Her chest squeezed with the power of it. "I am better off with you. It's a wonderful feeling to have someone believe in me, and to have someone to believe in."

He pressed a kiss to her forehead. "I do, and it is." Pulling her close, he rested his cheek against her temple.

"Thank you for waiting for me, for reaching me." She wrapped her arms around his waist.

Gage cupped Sam's face in his hands. He held her gaze with an intensity she'd never witnessed before. "Sam." He kissed her forehead, then each cheek, finally pressing his lips to hers.

He released her from the kiss but continued to hold her gaze. "I *have* waited a long time for you." Brushing his thumb over the curve of her lower lip, he smiled. "And you are worth every second."

Sam got lost in the intensity of his gaze, feeling at once whole and part of something greater. Not because she found a man, but because she found herself, and she was someone to love. Staring into his eyes with growing excitement, she slipped her fingers through his, delighted in the sensation of his skin and the promise in his eyes.

A promise of a life filled with love and friendship and passion.

Green, his eyes were green.

Acknowledgments

To my children and husband, otherwise known as my hearts and soul, thank you for believing in me, and always knowing I could do this even when I didn't. To my big brothers Tommy, Todd, and Billy, as goofy as I am, you've always held me up. Todd, having you read my book, and like it, was an experience of a lifetime, and Billy you're the best cheerleader a girl could have. To Paula, my sister of the heart, I'm forever in awe of you. And to my mom who's continued to mother me from the other side, I hope I have a fraction of your grace. Thank you.

Thank you to my editor Kate Brauning who somehow knew exactly how to lift me up and push me forward without letting me fall. To my editorial director, Candace Havens, for giving this story a chance and pushing for it to be better and better, to Liz Pelletier for being so all-around generous, and giving this writer a home, and to Robin Haseltine for loving my story first. You've all made my dreams come true. Thank you to the marketing team—you know you hold a special place in my heart—to the production team and everyone in between. You're my very own super heroes, and Entangled Publishing is a family I adore.

Thank you to Cherry Adair, a champion of new writers, for seeing something in me that allowed your generosity to flow onto the cover of my book in such wonderful words.

Thank you, Gina L. Maxwell, for looking at my words when I needed you and seeing what I couldn't. Marni Bates and Cecily White, there are no words…and you both know why. I love you all.

Thank you to Romance Authors of the Heartland, with special love to one of my very dear mentors, Cheryl St. John, who told me to never stop learning, and also: Sherri Shackelford for always keeping me in stitches, Eve Savage for your sassy energy, Queen *lizzie Starr for your sparkles, Barb Hunt for your caring ways, Debra Hines for understanding me, and Donna Kaye for your sweet affection. Thank you, Terri Oswald, for sending me to the best RWA conference I've ever experienced all because you saw promise in me back in 2012, and I promised not to let you down. And never last nor least, Victoria Alexander for helping me plot, plan, and becoming a beloved friend, even though upon introduction I asked for twenty seconds of fan-girl time before acting normal, though I'm not sure the normal was ever there to begin with. Without all of you, my story would have no beginning.

Thank you to Kameron Claire for your friendship and for believing in me enough to help create my street team, MK & Co. I love everyone in this family, from the very first to the still to come.

Thank you to Colorado Spring's Pikes Peak Writers for continuing my growth and entrusting me with your conference for a year. Writer's Night was one of my favorite meetings with my inspirational heart, Rebecca Davis, my literary chops, Deb Courtney, my example of perseverance, Karen Emanuelson, and my first critique buddy, Deidre Greenly for learning with me. For the push and encouragement from M.B. Partlow, Donnell Bell, and Susan Mitchell. There are too many of you to name here, but you know my heart is overflowing with your faith and support. Thank you to all of my lovely friends in Writer's Write for keeping me motivated and dreaming the dream.

I want to send a special shout out to Shannon Smithwick who beta read this book for me before anyone else. Her first comments, 'Loving your book…and can't put it down…' gave me the first real feeling that I might just be able to do this. I'll forever love her. Thank you to L T Kelly who, through threatening me with a punch in the face if I didn't stop making certain mistakes, ensured I quit making said mistakes. Our mutual love of red wine and the word 'aluuuminum' has grown our acquaintance into a lovely friendship. To Julie Fairfield, and all my other beta readers and friends, your feedback, your time, and your support helped me get through the scary process of getting my work out there. To Kenny Golde for your time answering my questions and your suggestions on resources while I researched this book. One more exuberant thank you to the readers of this book. Experiencing life with you in this way is magical. I hope that at least one scene, one line, or simply one word resonates with each of you.

And to my sisters and brothers in the fight against breast

and all types of cancer. I know both sides, having lost my mom to breast cancer at a young age, and surviving myself. I got hit during the last edits of this story. My writing was one of the things that carried me through. I have many more books to write. And I'll get to.

To my Facebook family, you held me up with such overwhelming love I'll never be able to express what it meant to me to have so many people sending out healing light, praying, pushing positive thoughts, and checking in to make sure I'd win in both my health and publishing, many of you've I've never met in person. I'm still spinning from it all. Thank you.

Hugs and loves and peanut butter. MK

About the Author

MK Meredith writes single title contemporary romance promising an emotional ride on heated sheets. She believes the best route to success is to never stop learning. Her lifelong love affair with peanut butter continues and only two things come close in the battle for her affections: gorgeous heels and maybe Gerard Butler...or was it David Gandy? Who is she kidding? Her true loves are her husband and two children who have survived her SEA's (spontaneous explosions of affection) and live to tell the tale. The Merediths live in the D.C. area with their three large fur babies...until the next adventure calls.